I0585288

Ernest William White

Cameos from the Silver-Land

The experiences of a young naturalist in the Argentine Republic

Ernest William White

Cameos from the Silver-Land
The experiences of a young naturalist in the Argentine Republic

ISBN/EAN: 9783337378493

Printed in Europe, USA, Canada, Australia, Japan

Cover: Foto ©Andreas Hilbeck / pixelio.de

More available books at **www.hansebooks.com**

CAMEOS FROM THE SILVER-LAND;

OR THE

EXPERIENCES OF A YOUNG NATURALIST

IN THE

ARGENTINE REPUBLIC,

BY

ERNEST WILLIAM WHITE, F. Z. S.

IN TWO VOLUMES

V O L . I .

WITH MAP

FAMAM EXTENDERE FACTIS

LONDON: JOHN VAN VOORST, 1 PATERNOSTER ROW

MDCCCLXXXI.

(All rights reserved)

PREFACE

I have been induced to project and publish the
following work in order to place before my countrymen at home a true sketch of the Argentine Republic
as it is. The notions about this vast and progressive
country current in England, are at times absurd, at
others biassed, and if my efforts serve to enlighten the
one and correct the other, they will not have been in
vain. My deepest acknowledgements are due to my
father for his valuable assistance and advice in preparing the present volume for the press; and to other
friends throughout the confederation, who have lightened the labours and lessened the perils of my journeys, I return my sincerest thanks.

E. W. White, F. Z. S.

Buenos Aires, May 1881.

TABLE OF CONTENTS

CHAPTER I.

CHAPTER II.

CHAPTER III.

CHAPTER VII.

CHAPTER VIII.

CHAPTER IX.

CHAPTER X.

CHAPTER XIII.

CHAPTER XIV.

CHAPTER XV.

CHAPTER XVIII.

Colophon.

ERRATA et CORRIGENDA

The reader's indulgence is claimed for the numerous typic errors that have crept obstinately into the work.

PAGE	LINE	ERROR	CORRECTION
6	15	divica	dioica
9	19	Palma	Palms
21	24	dry	wet
21	25	March to November	November to March
22	1	wet	dry
22	1	November to March	March to November
28	20	Terebintaceæ	Zygophylleæ
46	3	dry	wet
50	27	Island of Tierra del Fuego	Brunswick Peninsula
53	15	Verbenas	Daisies
54	17	Canicularia	Cunicularia
74	3	is	it
109	19	puffing	fuffing
110	18	Æcodoma	Œcodoma
110	25	indigenons	indigenous
113	24	Rynchœa	Rhynchœa
128	1	fundation	foundation
163	16		*dele* and
176	28	of	so
179	13	ramifications	ramifications
211	4	Argentine	Argentines
221	16	healte	health
221	22	cowd	crowd
228	29	years	years'
242	1	Culicides	Culicidæ
265	3	steem	esteem
273	1	torquatus	tajaçu
275	30		*dele* to
277	5	a	an
286	6	embracing	embracing
293	19	scence	scene
299	11	endevoured	endeavoured
331	19	is	its
344	4	deliquesenct	deliquescent
352	8	prefering	preferring
359	9	journies	journeys
366	9	Chinchillidæ	Chinchillidæ
370	14	soou	soon
370	15	swaddled	swaddled
374	4	asingle	a single
378	24	succeded	succeeded
384	1	Dasypodidæ	Dasypodidæ
391	6	Zygophylleæ	Zygophylleæ
411	22	crystalized	crystalline

ARGENTINE REPUBLIC

CHAPTER I.

LIMITS — PHYSICAL APPEARANCES — CLIMATE — HEALTH and SALUBRITY.

THE ARGENTINE OR PLATINE REPUBLIC, occupying the south-eastern portion of South America, forms an irregular triangle, twenty-five times the size of England and Wales together, whose apex, pointing to the Austral Pole and deeply indenting the Southern Ocean, chronicles a remote period when the mighty rock-mass of the Andes, far higher and bolder then than now, was able to resist that overwhelming hurricane from the south-west, which denuded the nether hemisphere of its land and left, surrounding this gigantic breakwater, merely the debris of its fury. Cradled in the hurricane, the winds have never ceased to hover over this territory, as if still eager to claim their prey.

The Republic derives its name from the river La Plata, a mighty stream forming one of the principal physical characteristics of the region and which was so baptized by Sebastian Cabot, a countryman of ours, as laving in its course the territories whence the Indians derived their copious supplies of silver. Nor was he far wrong! The glistening metal is there

in rich abundance, and no long time will now elapse
ere that swelling tide shall bear on its bosom argosies
far more precious than was ever Spanish galleon, to
render appropriate that title of Silver Land which, in
the mouth of the man of Bristol, was scarcely other
than a prophetic utterance.

Lying in south latitude between the 22nd and
56th parallels, and in west longitude between the
meridians 50° 30′ and 73° 30′ from Greenwich, this
vast country possesses an area of 1,500,000 square
miles, with a population slightly exceeding 2.000.000.
Bounded on the north by Bolivia, Paraguay, and
Brazil; on the east by Brazil, Uruguay, and the
Atlantic; on the west by Chili and Bolivia, she bares
her giant plains, her rivers, mountains and valleys,
nay, her deserts even, to the gaze of over-peopled
Europe, and ready to pour into the lap of industry
her manifold treasures, bids the crowded denizens of
the Old World seek a haven of rest in her bosom,
where want is unknown and the new gospel of labour
sheds her beneficent rays to bless, dignify and enrich
all such as lay offerings upon her altar.

On inspecting a map of this Republic, the eye is
arrested by the wonderful variety, no less than the
vastness of its physical features; as within its limits
are perceived, mighty mountain ranges distilling their
precious dews into smiling valleys beneath, immense
rivers, lakes, lagunas, extensive treeless plains, formidable deserts, swamps, grassy plateaus and dense
forests; in comparison with which the corresponding

features of English landscape are dwarfed to mere points.

The mountain systems, which have all a meridional direction, divide themselves naturally into four groups:

(a) The Cordillera of the Andes with its innumerable spurs shooting up summits to an elevation of 25,000 feet.

(b) The network of ranges in the Northern Provinces yielding elevations up to 18,000 feet.

(c) The central system containing the ranges of Córdoba and San Luis reaching a height of 8,000 feet.

(d) The Southern Sierras of Volcan, Tandil, Tapalquen and Ventana, no peak of which exceeds 4,000 feet.

One very remarkable feature connected with the first of these groups is, that although forming a section of a sublime mountain chain extending 4,000 miles, which is the father of grand river systems, in fact giving birth to two of the largest streams in the world, yet within the limits of the Argentine Republic it sheds none of any magnitude, and such as it does originate do not reach the sea but are lost in the plains or debouch into lakes, except in the case of three in the far south, the Colorado, Negro and Chubut, which do manage to disembogue into the Atlantic; so that the eastern slope of the Andes may be said to form but a sterile watershed for the country. Nor is this difficult to understand, as the peaks being so lofty and eternally covered with snow, the the moisture-laden breezes from the Pacific are condensed, ere they reach them and precipitated thither again by the western slope.

Further, the northern and central ranges, although of lesser dimensions, form another wall towards the east which, for a similar reason, prevent much of the rain-distilling clouds from the Atlantic reaching the interior and thus maintaining it in a continuously barren condition, whilst the provinces east of this barrier, viz., Tucuman and the northern part of Santiago del Estero, are preserved humid. The northern ranges, moreover, give rise to no rivers of any size, with the exception of the Bermejo and Salado, which go to swell the mighty Paraná, and the Dulce which is lost in Lake Porongos and never reaches the ocean; and yet, during the rainy season, extending from November to March, the upper part of the Republic is reticulated by an immense number of mountain streams which, although fertilizing the immediate valleys, are considered by the Argentines who, unlike their forefathers, dislike water, boats and ships, as obstacles to their freedom, and not as highways contributing to wealth; and to cross which, the native, after divesting himself of clothing, proceeds to cling to the tail of his swimming horse. So the central system of Córdoba and San Luis although giving birth to five streams, is unable to bestow upon any one of them the dignity of an affluent, but submits to see them either buried alive in the Pampas or engulfed in lagunas.

The great rivers of the Republic, the Paraná and Uruguay (*guay*, Guaraní termination meaning "river"), are the gifts of Bolivia and Brazil, and receive no considerable affluents but the Salado directly from Argentine territory, the Pilcomayo being altogether, and the Vermejo very greatly, Bolivian streams, tumbling their muddy contributions into the bosom of the clear Paraguay: so that, on the whole, the Republic is poorly watered, a fault that is partly redeemed by the possession of those two noble highways, the Paraná and Uruguay which, uniting their volumes, swell into that majestic estuary of the La Plata that pours into the Atlantic a greater mass than all the rivers of Europe combined.

The Southern system of Sierras, consisting chiefly of isolated peaks, merits little notice as a watershed.

The lakes throughout the Republic are exceedingly numerous; many of the more considerable lie at the base of the Andine range, the chief of which, the Nahuelhuapi, is one of the sources of the Rio Negro; but the largest is that of Porongos in the Province of Santiago del Estero, which certainly covers 4,000 square miles and, as before mentioned, is fed by the Rio Dulce; although in the Northern part of Corrientes there exists an immense number of extensive lagunas of excellent, clear water, one of which, the "Ibera," cannot have an area of less than 6,000 square miles. Many of the lacustrine waters are either bitter or salt, or both.

The next physical feature of interest is the Pam-

pas, slightly undulating treeless plains, which form
so remarkable a characteristic of the landscape. Starting from the coast of Buenos Aires and extending
westwards to the Andes and southwards to the Rio
Negro, the greater part of this vast silent tract of
perhaps 300,000 square miles is still uninhabited,
save by scattered Indian tribes; and yet this silence
which to-day is so oppressive, was not always so observed, if we may believe the prodigious fossil record
beneath its surface, where lie the magnificent remains
of those antediluvian monsters, the Mastodon, Toxodon, Glyptodon, Mylodon, Megatherium, &c.

Nor do space and time pass by quite unheeded
even here; for scored on the rugged bark of the hoary
sentinel of the Pampas, the Ombú (*Pircunia divica*),
are the centuries and the leagues. This, the chief
solitary indigenous tree, rising with its dome-shaped
outline to break the monotony of the scene, emerges
like a beacon from a sea of rank verdure, at once to
guide the traveller across this trackless ocean, and
afford him a dense and grateful shade from the scorching sun. With the poetry of its existence however,
naught else is linked, for although rivalling the oak in
longevity, sturdiness and nobility of appearance, and
although before entering the ground, its stem throws
out knotty protuberances giving at times a circumfer-
ence of ninety feet, it is worthless for timber as the
interior is simply herbaceous growth. From what has
just been said, it must not be supposed that the Pampas are carpeted always and throughout as a meadow,

far from it ! Large districts are covered with thistles, others with low thorny brushwood or with Jume (*Sali-cornia*), others again with sand dotted here and there with pajanales or coverts of the Giant Pampa-grass (*Gyncrium Argenteum*), others with cañados (swamps) mantled with a dense sward of aquatic plants, others with saline deposits as white as snow, and which at times, in seasons of drought are as brown as a berry or altogether bare as a highroad; in the former state, dry as tinder, the herbage is apt to catch fire and give rise to those dreadful prairie conflagrations, which raging for leagues and sweeping onwards with irresistible force, now and then overwhelm whole caravans.

The absence of arboreal existence on this silent and extensive territory may be accounted for by the presence in excess of saline matters in the soil, by the frequent alternation of the extremes of moisture and drought, as well as by the prevalence of high winds which, in the absence of any protection, sweep over it often with the force of the hurricane.

The Sandy Deserts of the Argentine Republic occupy a considerable portion of its surface and con-tribute, in some of the Upper Interior Provinces such as Rioja and Catamarca, to stamp an Oriental phase both on landscape and people. These deserts, of which Eastern Patagonia and a considerable part of the "Gran Chaco" are notable examples, are such by virtue of the absence of water and could be rendered exceedingly fertile by its quickening presence, as the soil consists chiefly of the detritus from the metamorphic mountains

in their neighbourhood. Here and there where streams
cross these tracts and afford means for irrigation, or
water is collected in represas, there an oasis starts up
as if by magic.

Other Sandy Deserts, the Travesias, the dread of
travellers, and which are completely uninhabitable
and even pestilential, by reason of their scorching
blasts, finely comminuted dust and complete deprivation of even a drop of water to mitigate the fierceness
of their climate, exceed even the Salinas in inhospitality.

The Salinas, in their turn, which form large barren
tracts, some of them as extensive as an English county,
and whose argillaceous soil is impregnated with various
salts from which, even by means of wells, water
cannot be obtained, are likewise unfitted for the residence of man. In many districts are found depres-
sions covering immense areas, one especially lying
westward of the Sierras of Catamarca and Córdova
occupies 1,000 square miles, containing water saturated
chiefly with the Chloride of Sodium and the sulphates
of Magnesia and Lime which, on evaporation by the
sun's rays, deposits its salts in separate crystalline
forms; the processes of solution and crystallization
continually alternating. In others now unprovided
with moisture, the salts remain as a permanent snow-
white incrustation, or in case of alteration of the land
level, these tracts becoming either plain or slightly
elevated, the salts are merely moistened by showers
sufficiently to convert what before was a hard crunchy

soil into a mephitic slimy morass, ready in places to
engulf horse and rider, if the hard beaten track be not
religiously held to. Such are the Salitrales, the chief
sources of the salt supply for the interior.

The characteristic indigenous arboreal vegetation
of the Republic, especially in the Upper Provinces,
belongs to the class of the Leguminosæ, represented
principally by the families, Mimoseæ, Papilionaceæ,
Cesalpineæ and Terebrinaceæ, species of which the
Tala (*Celtis*), Chañar (*Gurliaca decorticans*), Brea
(*Cesalpina precox*), Algarrobo (*Prosopis alba*), Quebracho (*Aspidosperma quebracho*), Virarú (*Ruprechtia
excelsa*), Ñandubay (*Acacia caveniá*), Queñoa (*Polylepis
racemosa*) and many others, though of dwarfed and
scattered growth in the dry regions, become bosquetish
in the quebradas (ravines) and other damp localities
generally throughout the country; yet, although in
addition the Mesopotamia is endowed with her noble
groves of Palma (*Yataï* and *Coronday*), whilst her
woods at Montiel are densely crowded with Ñandubay,
Quebracho, &c., which claim notice the one for beauty,
the other for commercial value; and although South
West Patagonia is thickly studded with the more
sturdy Fagi, whilst many other parts of the Republic
abound in extensive woods; it is to the North and East
alone we must turn to view forests so magnificent,
as for luxuriance and grandeur have few equals, and
which those acquainted only as yet with the other districts of the Republic are quite unprepared to expect.
It is in Oran, the Gran Chaco, Misiones and Tucuman

that the beauty and magnificence of tropical forests
culminate and present those inexhaustible stores of
lofty, bulky, hard and durable stems, so admirably
fitted for the engineer, builder, cabinet-maker, ship-
wright, dyer and tanner. It is a question however,
should the present rate of destruction continue or
increase, although hundreds of years may elapse before
the supply is totally extinguished, whether in the
meanwhile the climate of these regions will not
undergo serious declension ; nay, whilst the government is offering premiums for planting in one part, as
a sovereign remedy for ameliorating climate, abolish-
ing drought and protecting against hurricanes, in the
other a wholesale and ruthless destruction of the very
elements of climatic excellence is permitted.

On entering one of these wonderful forests and
beholding patriarchal trunks which saw the light,
ere the foot of Spaniard trod the soil, the traveller
must be regardless, as he certainly will be, of torn
raiment and scratched hands and features, for the
grandeur of the scene, like that of mountain masses, is
such as to take man out of himself, nay almost to
annihilate him for a time. The Cedro (*Cedrela Brasiliensis*), Nogal (*Fuglans nigra*), Laurel (*Nectandra
porphyria*), Cebil (*Acacia Cebil*), Urunday, a species of
Bignoniaceæ, Quina-Quina (*Myroxilon peruanum*), Quebracho colorado (*Loxopterygium Lorentzii*) Mistol
(*Zizyphus mistol*), Tipa (*Machærium fertile*), Lapacho
(*Tecoma stans*), Pacara (*Paulinia*), *Araucaria brasiliensis*, and multitudes of others arboreal giants, the

intervals between whose lichen-and-moss-covered stems are filled with the thick bushy undergrowth of the *Urera boerifera* and such like shrubs, very difficult to penetrate, have shut out sunlight for ages from the earth for leagues upon leagues.

As for the stems themselves, they are almost hidden under the loving embrace of ambitious climbers, the clasp of multitudinous *Tillandsias* and Orchidaceous Epiphytes, *Epidendrium*, *Serapias*, *Ophrys*, &c., and the closer hug of gigantic Lianas, *Canavalia gladiata*, *Sycios montanus*, &c., whose descending ropes made fast to the soil almost invite one to ascend to the aerial abode of their magnificent bouquets of white, blue and scarlet. Beneath the feet is spread a carpet of moss and everywhere around the thick tangled thorny masses of Talpa (*Celtis acuminata*), Garabato (*Acacia Tucumanensis*), &c., rendering movement almost impossible; and in the moister parts Ferns in abundance, some of which, as the *Pteris deflexa*, reach the height of five or six feet.

No noiseless scene is this however! the air is deafened with the shrill chorus of the screaming Parrot, myriads of which of all shades of green and gold confound the view; of the clamorous Uraca (*Corvus picá*) which would hardly be recognized by his more sombre-coloured European brother, in his gay suit of azure, yellow and green; and of the clattering top-heavy orange-coloured Tucan (*Ramphastos*); besides a host of smaller fry looking on, whose dulcet notes are drowned in the general gabble. To add to the brilliancy of the spectacle, the gaudy Humming Birds, *Sparganura, Chlorostilbon*, &c., dart and poise, whilst the gorgeous-hued Butterflies, *Heliconia, Papilio*, &c., threading their silent and mazy way, come floating along to aid in chastening the display.

Besides the indigenous arboreal vegetation, the forest and fruit trees and shrubs of other countries have been introduced and succeed admirably: the various species of Eucalyptus, Poplar and Willow, the elegant Paraiso (*Melia Azedarach*), the *Robinia pseudacacia*, &c., all of quick growth, are in great favour and have been planted extensively, although people are beginning to complain that they impoverish the land.

The physical features of this vast country being so variable, we are naturally led to infer a corresponding diversity of climate and such is the fact. Situated in the Southern Hemisphere, the seasons are the very reverse of those in England, but not so marked: the distinction is rather into wet and dry than hot and cold and their gradations. The Christmas numbers of the English illustrated papers are much esteemed for their emblematical Cartoons which act as refrigerators at the time of our greatest heat: Christmas itself as understood in England is here a myth; the Holly and Mistletoe are not to be found in the country, the waits are dumb and Plum-pudding with the thermometer at 95° in the shade becomes an impossibility.

The Littoral Provinces are very moist in winter, drier in summer, and in general subject to inundation

on account of the inferior lay of the land; in them it
is impossible to preserve iron from getting rusty or
boots mouldy.

The Great Plains swept at times by violent hurricanes, are unceasingly the residence of the winds,
and no matter how hot the day, enjoy a delicious freshness of morn and evening, accompanied by a heavy
dew, which frequently assumes the shape of hoar frost
or thick fog; but these regions are likewise subject
to very sudden changes of temperature, a scorching
day being sometimes succeeded by chilling blasts.
During the summer months, Mirage is a common
incident and so deceptive that a stranger seeing it for
the first time can hardly be convinced that the semblance of water is only an optical delusion.

The Central Provinces, though hot and subject to
drought, enjoy an equable climate, with but little
rainfall; the sky by day the bluest of the blue and at
night so clear as to render the brilliant constellations
of the Southern Hemisphere a wonderfully beautiful
heavenly landscape.

The attempt to reduce the whole of the Andine
Provinces under one general climatic level is vain;
this much however may be said that dryness is their
general characteristic; and to such a degree, in some
parts, than even domestic vermin find but a precarious
subsistence; whilst Cache, in the province of Salta,
is desiccated so completely, that it is difficult to roll
up a cigarette without first moistening the paper:
there, decay is almost unknown, a fact familiar to

the Aboriginal Indian Race, who made it the centre
of their sepulchral catacombs. As they required
not caves for the living, they dug them for the dead,
closing them with a flat stone, on raising which the
mummies are discovered in a perfect state of preservation, as to hair, teeth, skin and nails, and in a
sitting posture, with the chin close to the raised knees
and copper instruments resembling cornucopiæ in their
hands : in one instance the shrivelled temples of one
of their caciques was found adorned with a crown of
pure gold, but the cupidity of the finder lost it to
science.

Of the Andean Provinces, Mendoza and San
Juan lie as it were upon the outskirts of that region
which is subject to sudden extreme atmospherical
vicissitude and in consequence enjoy one of the purest
and most genial airs under the sun ; whilst Rioja and
Catamarca, mountain-locked and forming a funnel for
the fiery Northern blasts, sigh in vain for a drop of
that water which periodically pours on either side of
them in profusion, and are doomed, like Tantalus, to
perpetual thirst. If however we extend northwards
our travels in this same Andean district, we shall
find Tucuman, Salta and Jujuy, like tropical countries
generally, subject to two distinct seasons, the wet and
the dry. During the six hot months of the year, November to March, the clouds distil their daily torrents
regularly at the same hours, the remainder of the
year being dry. The day, commencing with a morning of supreme clearness and burning heat, gives no

promise of what is to follow: but about two or three
o'clock in the afternoon, the storm suddenly brews,
the lightning flashes, the deluge descends for a couple
of hours, and all is again serene till the morrow. In
these mountain regions, every climate is represented
from the coldest to the hottest, from the wettest to
the driest.

Two remarkable winds are prevalent in this
country, the Pampero and the Zonda.

The Pampero, peculiar to the Pampas, blowing
from the S. W. is caused by the super-heating of
those immense plains and the consequent rarefaction
and ascension of their atmosphere. The cold blasts
from the Andes sweeping down to fill the void, gather
in their train the loose dust of the Pampas and meet-
ting with no obstacle on the face of the denuded surface, acquire both force and dust at each step of
their mad and quickening career, until on reaching
Buenos Aires, after an impetuous race of 1000 miles,
the frantic hurricane, in company with the others torm
fiends of lightning, thunder and rain, whose services he has enlisted on the way, bursts on the devoted
city with overwhelming energy.

A close, suffocating, heavy day, here as elsewhere, denotes electrical disturbance and portends
meteorologic change. As the day wears on, the wind
becoming gusty, fitful and inconstant, raises the finely
powdered soil, and in never ending maze sends it
whirling over the thirsty roads. Then dead calm
ensues and an indefinable dread seems to seize upon

man and beast.   A cloud arises in the West and forcing its way up against the wind, rapidly spreads its
lurid glare over the western sky.   The Pampero!
The Pampero! is the scream heard on all sides as
footsteps hasten to close the doors and windows.
Dense clouds of dust appear high up in the air, travelling in a straight line with incredible velocity, apparently keeping pace with similar advancing ones below:
the River leaves its banks: the birds seek shelter:
lightning of the severest flashes and the heavens roar;
in a few minutes a mighty rushing sound, and the
fierce fury of the blast, driving before it columns of
suffocating dust which penetrating every crevice fills
the houses with its impalpable mantle and suddenly
envelops nature in darkness thicker than night.   The
buildings tremble as in an earthquake, roofs are
untiled, chimneys levelled, trees struck down as with
a blow; some, lashed by the storm and bending to the
very earth, creaking and crashing bemoan their torn-
off limbs. Heaven and earth are confounded. Intense
cold accompanies the din of the elements, the thermometer falling 20° in five minutes.

Then comes the Deluge, the direct product of the
continuous electric discharge in the celestial laboratory,
which washing out the dust from the atmosphere, descends in inky sheets, and sweeping along the earth,
tears out Stygian-laden gulleys in every direction.
The darkness lasts perhaps a quarter of an hour, but
for twice that period the tempest accompanied by
more or less penumbra, usually rages with such ex-

treme violence that nothing living can face it. Flocks
of sheep and herds of cattle are driven before it and
perish in thousands.

The suddenness, confusion and uncontrollable
energy of the tornado, almost preclude calm reflection,
especially in those unaccustomed to the scene; and it
so affects the nervous system of ladies, as to cause
them to scream and faint, and in some cases to lose
their reason permanently. Before the storm drains
were built in the city of Buenos Ayres, some of the
streets, on such occasions, became torrents, down
which coaches and carts with their drivers were
swept to swift destruction.

The Pampero lasts three days, sometimes as a
tempest, but more frequently in a mitigated form, and
as a scavenger of earth and sky is invaluable: but if
this heaven-born visitor be a blessing in disguise, what
shall be said of the Zonda?

The Zonda is a wind that takes its name from a
beautiful valley in the province of San Juan, which
will be described hereafter; and as this valley, fringed
with deserts, is very subject to its pernicious influence,
it has been erroneously debited with its birth. We
must proceed farther north to ascertain its source,
which lies in that enormous flat sandy saline desert,
Atacama, that skirting the sea coast and indenting
deeply the land, belongs pretty equally to Chili and
Bolivia. There, under the scorching rays of a tropical
sun, arises this Argentine Sirocco which, laden with
hot salted dust, traverses as a North Wind the nume-

rous meridional funnels offered by the mountain defiles,
desolating the upper country and producing many
sudden deaths. As in the case of the Pampero, on its
approach, the inhabitants shut themselves up closely
within doors, the temperature rising 20° in five minutes
instead of falling as with the Pampero.

Finding no obstacle to its progress, this death-dealing Boreas, passing over the dry Northern plains
becomes robbed of every particle of moisture, if it
ever had any, and sweeping onwards reaches Buenos
Aires as a dry, scorching, furnace blast, which though
deprived of much of its spleen, is sufficiently deleterious to produce general lassitude, headache, irritability
and in some nervous subjects a manifest disposition to
suicidal mania or homicide.

Although the changes of temperature, especially
on the plains, are sudden and at times extreme, snow
but rarely if ever falls, except in the Andine provinces, but hail, sometimes of fabulous size, is more
frequent.

On two occasions however, one in 1864 and the
other in 1880, the Argentine plains where whitened
with veritable snow to the depth of a foot, and on the
latter date, the fall being accompanied by a strong and
bitter South Easter, proved disastrous to the flocks
and herds, who were in poor condition from the previous drought; no less than half a million cattle and
several millions of sheep perished in the course of two
or three days.

The very great irregularity of the rains on the
littoral produces at one time Drought and at another

Inundation, both so eminently prejudicial to cattle
farming as well as agriculture : but no surprise can
be felt at such results when we reflect upon the physical conditions of the problem. An almost dead level,
without trees, badly watered, shut out from the Pacific and relying upon the Atlantic alone for its rain
supply, immense mountain-masses on the west and
vast deserts on the north acting like magnets to determine the wind in directions contrary to those from
which it can be recruited with moisture, are some of
the inducing causes to this want of uniformity.

On the whole the Meteorology of the Argentine
Republic involves questions of considerable difficulty,
depending upon the extraordinary variety and com-
plexity of physical phenomena, so that to become
weatherwise is an exceedingly rare accomplishment
and forecasts are of little value : but it may be stated
broadly that here, par excellence, the winds are the
determinants of the climate. The North wind is dry,
hot and very malignant : that from the East brings
rain; the South wind, coming straight from the icebergs
is cold and moist ; those from the West and South
West cold, dry, bracing and salubrious.

According to the definition of James I, " the best
climate is that in which it is possible to be out in the
open air the greatest number of days in the year and
the greatest number of hours in the day." Estimated
by this standard, the Argentine climate will bear comparison with any other, nay will have but few equals,
The natives indeed, especially those of the Upper

Provinces, must think so, as they may be said to live perpetually in the open air night and day; their lofty rooms, whose doors and windows are always open, enclose internal patios (courtyards) exposed to the bright blue vault above, which indicates a pure and provides an elastic joyous atmosphere untainted with any of the corrupt emanations of manufacturing industry and contributes to a longevity which is especially observable amongst the Blacks and Indian races, who live in a simple, frugal and regular manner. The climate of the Republic, taken as a whole, includes all the good sanitory qualities and but few of the bad of the most favoured countries; what one part needs, the other supplements; the deleterious in the one, is altogether absent in the other—but a few qualifications are undoubtedly necessary. That of the great plains, apart from its general dampness to which the habit of building in river mud and other soil impregnated with salts contributes, is indubitably trying to persons of weak lungs from the sudden changes of temperature from one extreme to the other to which it is exposed, and which renders the mortality amongst this class of patients considerable and increasing; but on the other hand, the dry, equable and bracing mountain air of the interior is a panacea for all such ailments, even to healing cavities in the lungs. Again acute chronic Rheumatism is very prevalent on the littoral, but comparatively unknown on the desiccated Highlands, which contain besides many springs very beneficial for its permanent cure.

The common diseases of Europe are rife here,

but usually in a mitigated form; small-pox and typhoid commit their fearful ravages, but chiefly amongst the coloured population, the former simply because there is no compulsory law of vaccination, the latter on account of their filthy habits. On the littoral too infants are exposed to a malignant form of indigestion, unknown in Europe, and for which the native doctors prescribe raw meat; due to this ailment and the general neglect amongst mothers of the lower orders, tender life is sacrificed to an alarming extent. Diseases of the digestive organs amongst adults, the result of irregular living; tetanus arising from wounds, which should never be exposed to the air; apoplexy from over-feeding and want of exercise; Heart-disease caused by riding bucking horses; and Goitre in the mountainous districts, pretty well complete the list of disorders at all characteristic of this country, with the exception of Chuchu, about which a few words must be added.

Chuchu (Intermittent fever) is the curse of the Upper Andine Provinces, but is unknown elsewhere. It arises from the malarious evaporation from stagnant water and will disappear, as soon as proper drainage works are undertaken. At present during the dry season, from March to November, it is almost impossible for a stranger to visit those parts and expect immunity from attack : even the natives themselves are not exempt, as in almost every house, at that period of the year, one or more patients are found laid low with it: but curiously enough during the wet and hot season, from November to March, it either altogether vanishes or presents a milder type.

Europeans, especially from the North, who visit this country, are apt to bring with them the robust style of living to which they have been accustomed at home, but such is not found suitable here. Some subtle atmospheric influence (probable ozone) imparts to the nervous system a higher degree of tension in America than in Europe and indulgence in eating or drinking is quickly followed by retribution : but by moderation in both, daily ablution and regular exercise, the natural salubrity of the climate will have fair play and be found to conduce to a pleasurable and lengthened existence.

It is indeed true that two severe epidemics of Cholera and one of Yellow Fever have visited the Republic during the last decade or so, but their possibility was entirely the fault of the authorities who, relying too much upon past immunity, upon the virtues of a fair name (Buenos Aires, good airs), neglected to take suitable precautions.

CHAPTER II.

PROVINCES—TERRITORIES—CITIES

The fourteen provinces into which this Republic is divided may be classified as follows:

Four littoral, that is lying on the great rivers: Buenos Ayres, Santa Fé, Entre-Rios, and Corrientes.

Three central: Córdova, San Luis, and Santiago del Estero.

Seven Andine: Mendoza, San Juan, La Rioja, Catamarca, Tucuman, Salta and Jujuy.

Besides these, four immense Territories await population in order to be become enrolled on the Argentine banner, viz., Patagonia, the Pampas, the Gran Chaco, and Misiones.

The littoral provinces are well situated for commerce, and generally well watered, and not only contain the most wealth and population, but being in direct contact with European civilization, are more advanced than the rest. They present an arena not alone for the display of the capacity and intellect of the nation, but also for the organization of the resources and commercial operations of the foreigner, and stand in relation to the body of the Republic both as

mouth and head. Of these, Buenos Aires leads the
van with an area of 73,836 square miles or very nearly
equal to Great Britain, and a population of 800,000,
or 10.8 per square mile. Its plains are dotted, in parts
thickly, with sheep, cattle and horses which have to a
great degree obliterated the indigenous vegetation;
the thistle (*Cynara cardunculus*) and rank trefoil,
although probably both originally imported, being
alone left to dispute the territory as a survival of the
strongest if not fittest. The soil consists for the most
part of a rich argillaceous loam, covered usually with
a considerable thickness of humus and is equally fit
either for agriculture or pasture. Water can be had
at the depth of a few feet. Its superficies is nude of
trees, even the Tuna (*Opuntia*) and Ombú (*Pircunia
divica*) are, under the invading plough, rapidly becoming things of the past; nay so bare is it of anything
in the shape of fuel that the Cardo (thistle) and the
droppings of animals have to serve for that purpose.

Santa-Fé lying to the North of Buenos Aires has
an area of about 40.223 square miles, that is as large
as England, and a population of 100,000 or 2,5 to
the mile, and is the centre of the great foreign coloni-
zation schemes. Upwards of 30 colonies nestle
within its borders, in which agriculture and cattle
and sheep farming are prosecuted with success.

The soil and gramineous vegetation, as they
belong equally to the Pampa formation, are similar
to those of Buenos Aires, but its plains are neither so
absolute, nor so devoid of arboreal growth, inasmuch

as their determination on the one side by the Paraná
gives rise to Barrancas (cliffs), which at Rosario ascend
to 60 feet above river level, and in the northern part
of the Province forests of Algarrobo (*Prosopis alba*),
Ñandubay (*Acacia cavenia*), Tala (*Celtis tala*), Viraró
(*Ruprechtia excelsa*), &c. are met with. Although
agriculture is very risky from drought and locust, the
colonists succeeded, in one of their late seasons, in
raising 30,000 tons of wheat of the finest quality.
Fish are exceedingly abundant and of many species
in the Paraná and its numerous canals, the fine Dorado (*Salminus maxillosus*) the River Plate Salmon,
reaches the extraordinary weight of 100 lbs. and if laid
on the Haymarket slabs, would rival its European
brother in the eyes of London epicures. In that ini-
mitable satire "Gulliver's Travels" the academy of
Lagado included amongst its philosophers one who
utilised spiders' webs to the detriment of silk, inasmuch as one was woven, the other simply spun: what
existed only in Swift's imagination, is a fact in Santa
Fé. A remarkable spider (*Epeira socialis*) is here
found, which forms a beautiful cocoon of orange-
coloured silk suitable for working, and already manufacturing industry has been busy with it.

This province of Santa-Fé is the highway from
the interior of the country, through which all its products must flow and from which in turn its stores
must be recruited, and possessing a fine and commodious port, Rosario, and an industrious and enterprising people, cannot but have a great future before it.

Entre Rios, the garden of the littoral, the Mesopotamia, or rather forming with Corrientes and Misiones the great Mesopotamia, of the Republic, would
be very rich and prosperous, were it not the hotbed
of political strife, which has retarded both population
and industry. Its soil is beautifully varied by hill
and dale, stream and forest. The cuchillas (ridges)
which rise to a height of one or two hundred feet, and
its well-watered vales are clothed with a coarse grass
suitable for herd-grazing and the forests composed
principally of Ñandubay, Quebracho, Tala, Vivaró,
Chañar (*Gurliaca decorticans*) etc. cover at least a
fifth part of the province, the largest being that of
Montiel in the North West.

Every point of this favoured Province enjoys
easy access to one of the two magnificent rivers which
lave its sides, the coasts of which are fringed with
innumerable islands. Those on the Paraná, loamy,
rich and soft from the detritus which, by frequent
inundation, enriches them to an extraordinary degree,
are covered with aquatic and orchidaceous plants and
produce fuel and all kinds of fruits : those on the Uru-
guayan shore however, differ in their vegetation and
inclining to sterility, do not present the frondose luxuriance of the other side. On the islands, the Carpincho (*Hydrochœrus capybara*), the Nutria (*Myopotamus
coypus*) the *Hesperomys squamipes*, &c. are numerous,
whilst the dales or forests are still frequented by the
Jaguar (*Felis onça*), Gama (*Cervus campestris*), the
Rhea &c. and abundance of smaller game. The area of

Entre-Rios is 39,030 square miles, that is considerably larger than either Scotland or Ireland, with a population of 150,000 or 3,8 to the square mile.

The last littoral province, Corrientes (the seven currents), forming the central part of the Argentine Mesopotamia, is one vast swampy plain of almost tropical luxuriance, studded with lagunas and rich in forests, although not of lofty growth. Two species of Palm, the Caranday (*Palma Copernicia*) in the humid districts, and the Yataï (*Cocos Yutaï*) in the dry, adorn the landscape, whilst that magnificent Water-Lily the *Victoria regia* floats its huge prickly leaves and gaudy flowers on the waters of some of the esteros. Numberless are the rare wild fruits and medicinal herbs of this fine region: numberless the orange groves whose fruit is exported to a large extent. Its forests are tenanted by the Jaguar, the Puma (*Felis concolor*), the Tapir (*Tapirus americanus*) the Peccary (*Dicotyles tajaçu*), &c.; its plains by the Anteater (*Myrmecophaga jubata*), and various species of Armadillos, in particular the *Dasypus gigas*, although it is now rare; whilst Aquatic birds of all kinds, the Cayman and the Ampalagua (*Boa*) haunt its swamps.

The inhabitants, mainly of Guaraní descent, still speak that language and are devoted to cattle-breeding, the lumber trade, especially the indestructible Quebracho colorado (*Loxopterygium Lorentzii*), and the export of fruit: agriculture does not tempt them to any extent, although the soil and climate are capable of producing anything. Its population of 160,000 is spread over an area of 42,966 square miles, that is about the size of England, giving an average of 3,8 to the square mile.

We now pass to the three Andino-Pampa, or Central Provinces, where the Sierras first meet with the plains and introduce a different set of physical conditions which, to a certain extent, influence both the character of the population and the productions of the soil. Agriculture, the artificial feeding of cattle, the breeding of mules and goats, which latter here supplant the sheep, the culture of the vine and drying of fruits, divide the attention with mining.

Córdova, the most central of the three, lying in fact midway between the two oceans, presents a vast plain, in the centre of which rises a chain of beautiful granitic Sierras occupying a fourth part of its territory, whose slopes dotted with forests of Ñandubay, Algarrobo, Tala, Quebracho, Brea (*Cæsalpinia præcox*), Jarilla (one of the *Terebinthaceæ*), &c., in addition to shedding four rivers named respectively the first, second, third and fourth, give rise to numerous streams, the product of summer rains, which might be rendered available for irrigation and increase of wealth. The climate of the province enjoys a reputation for salubrity second only to that of Mendoza, especially for consumptive patients, hundreds of whom have sacrificed a cock to Æsculapius on their return thence. Its valleys are exceedingly productive and devoted principally to agriculture, whilst on the plains graze

multitudes of sheep and oxen. The mineral wealth of
Córdova is considerable, although but little worked as
yet; besides a magnificent display of marbles, extensive veins of argentiferous galena exist, as well as
copper principally in the form of pyrites, and now and
then both horn and native silver are discovered in the
quartz. The fauna of this province is characteristic
in one or two particulars : the two species of Condor
make it their headquarters: several species of Lizards
one of which the Chelke (*Enyalus letirepo*) has a very
bad reputation : and an infinity of Parrots chiefly of
the genus *Conurus*. Córdova, with its 74,438 square
miles, equal to England and Scotland together, and
250,000 inhabitants, sighs like the rest of the Republic
for population.

The aspect of the droughty province of San Luis,
like Cordova, is in general that of a plain, broken on
the North East by a solitary group of mountains,
which give rise to the Rio Quinto (fifth river) and are
especially rich in native gold in a quartz matrix, whilst
the plains on the river banks are exceedingly fertile.
On the South West lies the vast Salt lake the Bebedero as salt as the very Ocean, most probably the
remains of a great inland sea which at one time
covered the whole of the interior provinces and from
this lake the Province is supplied with salt. The
Sierras and Mountain plateaux are poorly watered and
covered only with coarse, scanty pasture : the thickly
wooded districts between the mountain ranges are
crowded with Tala, Algarrobo, Calden (a species of

Ceraionia) and Quebracho blanco, and are suitable for sheep: but the Pampa lands, more or less dotted with stunted mimoscæ, are the plains on which the Puntanos raise elephantine cattle, goats, asses, mules, and horses, for which purpose artificial grass, Alfalfa (Lucerne) is employed. Without irrigation works however the Province would be a desert, as although in common with the other central provinces it has a wet season from November to March, in which copious rains fall, it suffers very much from drought. The enormous meat-bearing beeves are exported to Chili, but sometimes in seasons of scarcity find their way down to Buenos Aires, where they astonish the natives by their extraordinary size. Great attention is likewise paid to horticulture and the drying of fruit : the orange, pomegranate, fig, peach, vine, pear, apple, almond, apricot, &c. reach perfection in this "hortus siccus."

San Luis possesses a fine dry climate of especial benefit to consumptives, but suffers not alone from drought but oft-recurring revolutions and Indian invasions, which retard its progress, and maintain it in a state bordering on poverty ; it ought to occupy a much better position amongst the fraternity of provinces, considering its agricultural and mining wealth and pastoral interests : it remains for the railway now in course of construction to raise its status. The condor and numerous other vultures and kites, as well as the puma and guanaco, haunt the plains and mountains of San Luis, whose area contains 43,523 square miles,

about the size of England; its population, which is
less intermingled with the indigenous races than in
any other province, and consequently increases but
slowly, only amounts to 60,000, giving an average of
1,6 per square mile.

The remaining central province of Santiago del
Estero, consists of a low plain adjoining the Gran
Chaco, not more than 600 feet above sea level, characterized by swamps, dunes and salinas in which no
amount of digging will realise water and in which in
seasons of drought, the dust is sometimes so overwhelming as to suffocate the traveller.

This plain is traversed by the river Salado which,
after passing by the Capital, of which the Santigueños
are very proud as the oldest internal city in the Republic, and rendering it an oasis surrounded by a dense
forest, ultimately terminates its career in the immense
inland lake of Porongos. The surface of the province
is here and there besprinkled with low hills sometimes
rising to Sierras and containing exquisite marbles. By
drainage and canalization much might be done to
render its soil as fruitful as its sky is blue and climate
salubrious : in the neighbourhood of the hills it is
formed of granite debris, but in general, although
sandy and saline, a thin crust of humus is mostly
present and northwards towards Tucuman becomes
firmer, richer and argillaceous. The prevalent vegetation is Ñandubay and a class of saline bushy plants,
of which Jume (*Salicornia*) is so wonderfully abundant and so impregnated with soda-salts, to the extent

of 50 per cent of its ashes, that the inhabitants use
them for the manufacture of soap: in fact the whole
ground is saturated with nitrate of soda. Here is a
wonderfully lucrative business in store for future
enterprise: the soda is present in inexhaustible profusion and merely demands the labour of gathering
and incinerating the Jume; there is a plethora of
animal oils and fats, from the mare to the sheep, and
which is at present exported; the soil and climate are
eminently fitted for the growth of the castor-oil plant;
numberless species of sweet-scented herbs grow in the
immediate neighbourhood, whose fragrance could be
easily extracted; and lastly, when the railway in
course of construction is finished, the province will
have easy access to all parts: so the days of "Old
Brown Windsor" and "Price's Patent" are numbered!
Santiago should be of rights soap and candle maker to
the universe. The Sugar cane here first comes into
notice, and its cultivation is being pushed rapidly forward, as it is a very safe and highly remunerative industry; in that and the culture of fruit consists almost
all the agriculture of the province; and as the only
grass is artificial and that not to any great extent,
cattle rearing is insignificant and the price of land
nominal; nevertheless cattle are frequently met with
in a superb condition, although on pastures as bare of
grass as a turnpike: they must feed on the prickly
mimoseæ or on sand.

The Santigueños however, who speak the Quichua,
the classic language of the ancient Incas of Perú, if
not agriculturists, are very industrious in manufacture.

especially in weaving different textile fabrics; but
their province is little known as yet, as it has the misfortune of lying on the highroad to nowhere. The
two remarkable species of the Chuña, together with
innumerable parrots and parrakeets, make Santiago
their home. The area of this province is 37.364
square miles, or considerably larger than Ireland, with
a population of 160.000 or 4,3 to the square mile.

The seven Andine Provinces comprehend the
beauty and salubrity of the Argentine Republic, and
whilst enclosing within their bosom illimitable stores
of undeveloped wealth are doomed themselves to present poverty, and yet an extension of various industries indicates in their midst a laborious and enterprising population. The cultivation of the Sugar Cane
and Vine, Cotton, Indigo and Tobacco, the drying of
Fruits, the manufacture of Dulces (preserves), the
breeding of Mules and Horses and fattening of Cattle,
the extensive irrigation of the land in some, and the
general working of Mines, are reduced to something
like system; but as yet everything is in its infancy
and a general sigh escapes from the Andine summits
for capital and labour to develop their resources.

The agricultural province of Mendoza, which
Europeans persist in assigning to Chili, a pardonable
mistake as it was first peopled from the other side of
the Cordilleras, lies upon the Andes proper, which it
rises gently to meet, and consists on the North and
East of normally arid, sabulous plains, only relieved

by Medanos (Sand Dunes), but on the West becomes mountainous, although nowhere very bold. These Medanos, formed of exquisitely fine sand, are liable to continual alteration of shape and mass by the action of the winds and were if not for the saline plants that fix their roots in them, would be blown away altogether.

The naturally sterile plains however are rendered exceedingly fertile, in fact blooming, and fit not only to fatten immense herds of cattle for the Chilian market, upon its alfalfares (enclosed lucerne fields), but to produce large crops of cereals, fruits and vegetables, by utilising the numerous streams shed from the Cordilleras, which on the melting of the snows become destructive torrents. Its one solitary river, a twin brother of the Rio San Juan, nursed both from the slopes of the same noble peak Aconcagua, after very devious and independent courses, arrive at one goal and disembogue at opposite extremities of the same reservoir, the remarkable chain of the Guanacache lakes.

The vine is here cultivated to a greater extent and more successfully than in any other part of the Republic: the Mendoza Burgundy is a very close imitation of that magnificent French wine, slightly inferior in bouquet, but decidedly superior in body. Mining is still almost dormant, although silicate and carbonate of copper and argentiferous galena lie awaiting the pick in profusion in the Paramilla del Uspallata, and oozing from its Stygian bed, almost unnoticed, an inexhaustible supply of Rock Oil which on analysis is found to yield 54 per cent of volatile combustible material. The climate of Mendoza requires no comment, it is simply superb! in its dry and invigorating air consumptive and asthmatic patients rapidly improve, and when the railway, now in course of construction, is finished, a sanatorium on its slopes would soon be inundated with the European victims of confined and overcrowded dwellings and impure air.

Notwithstanding its general aridity, animal life is pretty well represented in Mendoza by the Jaguar, Puma, Guanaco, several species of Deer, three species of the Armadillo, the *Chlamydophorus truncatus*, the mountain Biscacha, etc. and a multitude of small game; whilst the Guanacache lakes abound in Fish, including a species of Trout, which seems supremely indifferent either to salt or fresh water. The hardy Laguneros (dwellers on the lakes), the pure or nearly pure descendants of the Guarpe Indians, supply the market of the capital with fish. Mendoza, the gem of the three gardens of the Republic, has an area of 53,420 square miles, or pretty nearly the size of England and Wales, with a very industrious population of 80,000 or 1,7 per square mile.

San Juan is a very mountainous territory, abounding in mines which yield native gold, silver principally extracted from galena, carbonates of lead and silver, beautiful marbles, lime, sulphur, petroleum, Chloride of Sodium and Carbonate of Soda, interspersed with lovely valleys forming oases amid the

deserts and salitrales, one of which the desert of the
Salinas has a breadth of 50 miles. It boasts but of one
river of any size, the Rio San Juan, which has been
before mentioned as rising on Aconcagua, falling into
the Guanacache lakes and containing trout in its waters;
it is a curious fact however that waters formed from
melted snow and pure as they may be are found to be
unfit for human consumption, and such is generally the
case with Andine streams fresh from the summits. The
extensive chain of the Guanacache lakes lies between
this province and Mendoza and consists of salt water,
but not so intense as that of the Bebedero in San Luis.
Its climate is exceedingly dry, as it rarely rains even
on the mountains and scarcely ever on the plains, and
its salubrity perfect, if we except the season of the
Zonda wind (Argentine Sorocco). Deprived of natural grass and woods, but endowed with barren sierras,
and plains which form little else but one vast travesia
(waterless desert), occupying together one fourth of
the province, the Sanjuaninos, besides devoting themselves to mining, make the most of their fertile valleys,
and succeed in producing cattle unrivalled for size,
and raising large crops of cereals and dried fruits; but
viticulture they don't seem to understand as yet,
although both climate and soil are highly favourable.

San Juan contains an area of 35,671 square miles,
or considerably larger than Scotland, and a population
very much intermingled with the original Guarpe
Indians, and amounting to 75,000 or 2,1 per square
mile.

The Province of La Rioja may be styled one vast desert, traversed by a single river the Zanjon, and even that is only considerable on the melting of the mountain snows in summer. As the sandy soil is formed of the debris from the sierras, it is naturally fertile, so wherever there is water, there is prosperity ; wherever absent, complete sterility. If nature, with one hand, has denied the province her cornucopia, with the other, she holds out a casket full to the brim of mineral treasures, sufficient to attract to its borders those miners par excellence the Chilians and Peruvians. The ranges of Rioja, especially that of Famatina 19,000 ft., offer, as none others, gold, silver, copper, iron, nickel, tin, lead, cobalt, marble, &c. besides all the material necessary for the construction of reducing furnaces and infusible crucibles. In spite of all obstacles however, the sandy saline soil and dreadful dust which, on the slightest provocation, or indeed without, is ever ready to mount in dense clouds, the Riojanos do manage to raise agricultural crops, fruits and wines, and fatten cattle on artificial grass, in the numerous and splendid valleys threading in and out of their lofty sierras. Some of the Mimoseæ, that in scattered bushes cover its salted plains, produce a gum equal to Senegal and everywhere is to be seen the Jume, both the sources of ulterior wealth.

The climate of Rioja is remarkably dry and healthy : not a cloud is ever visible in its azure dome, except perhaps for the two summer months when it rains slightly.

In the North of the Province are still found the pure descendants of the native Calchaqui Indians.

La Rioja has an area of 38,000 square miles, or considerably in excess of Scotland, with a population of 60,000 or 1,6 per square mile.

The large but sparsely populated province of Catamarca consists of an immense plain, surrounded on all sides by high mountain ranges, which in the North-East throw up one eminence, Aconquija, that rears its lofty head 17,000 feet. In the North lie extensive deserts, and the centre is a hot, sandy, arid and dusty plain, but its fine well-watered valleys, producing a vegetation similar to that of Tucuman, are peopled by an exceedingly industrious agricultural race, where tobacco, cotton, sugar, rice, fruits and wine are cultivated to perfection, and herds of cattle fattened for exportation to Chili; the last being an enterprise in which all the Andine provinces are more or less engaged.

This province is very rich in mineral wealth; gold, silver, copper, nickel, lead, &c. are abundant, but copper is principally worked, the mines of Atajo being the richest; but the transport of everything on muleback is a great hindrance to progress.

The climate of Catamarca is dry in the mountainous districts, moist in the valleys, and in spite of the heat and dust of the interior, taken as a whole, is very salubrious. With respect to the Fauna, it is neither rich in amount nor variety; the two Chuñas and the magnificent *Spurganura Sappho* are met with, whilst

the Vicuña and Guanaco are not rare in the North
West mountains, where they are periodically hunted
for their skins, although the habitat of all four species
of the genus Lama, the Guanaco, Alpaca, Vicuña and
Llama, is not in the Argentine Republic.

The Catamarqueñas, like the men, are very industrious and excel in all the textorial arts, especially in
the manipulation of the Vicuña wool; a poncho made
by these fair and lithe fingers costs £20 and a shawl
£40. Very few English people are aware of the existence of a London in this province; it was founded
in honor of Queen Mary by her husband, but hitherto
has not done much honor either to its royal lineage or
its name.

The area of Catamarca, being 83,112 square miles,
is very nearly equal to that of Great Britain, but its
population reaches only 90,000 or 1,1 per square mile.

Tucuman, the song of poets, the theme of travellers, is one vast garden; here are concentrated
every agreeable, useful and ornamental vegetable production of which the Argentine Republic can boast.
The deserts are left behind, everything blooms as in
a paradise, and yet this paradise is almost hermeti-
cally sealed to strangers, at least six months in the
year, on account of the Chucho or intermittent fever
which here rises at times to an almost epidemic form.
Here are mountains, plains, forests of gigantic growth
and very numerous foaming torrents the gift of the
noble Aconquija range, which forms the Western
boundary of the Province, but through which it pene-

trates to enclose the fruitful valley of Tafi, where
some Swiss colonies produce a cheese rivalling the
Roquefort. On the whole, Tucuman is a plain with
an extremely fine and varied sub-tropical landscape,
and with no necessity for irrigation works, as the Rio
Dulce with its numerous tributaries flows directly
through its centre, whilst very many affluents course
eastward through its territory to meet the Salado,
which forms its eastern limit.

The climate is deliciously soft and balmy though
hot, and the year is divided into two seasons, the wet
and the dry; the wet is identical with the hot, from
November to March and almost every afternoon then
witnesses an impromptu storm of lightning and rain,
lasting an hour or two, after which the sky clears
and the same is repeated day by day.

Although mineral treasures exist in Tucuman,
they are not sought after, as the population is almost
purely agricultural or pastoral, the distinction between
which two classes seems to be more accentuated here
than elsewhere; the former enterprising and laborious, the latter spending a somewhat dreamy existence on horseback, like their brethren of the South.

Since the opening of the railway connecting the
capital with Córdova and thence with the littoral, the
various industries of the province have received immense impetus: Sugar, Rice, Tobacco, Woods, Hides,
Tans, Caña (White Rum), Cheese, Oranges, &c. flow
down in continuous streams, inaugurating a very remunerative internal commerce, capable of vast expansion.

The useful arts are likewise not neglected, especially tanning and all kinds of leatherwork, weaving, dyeing and embroidery: altogether Tucuman, which is the smallest yet most densely populated of the Provinces, is certainly the most industrious and progressive. Although however the least, her area of 22,384 square miles, which is all in the hands of private persons, is still twice the size of Belgium, and her population amounting to 150,000 gives 6,7 to the square mile.

Lying on the north of Tucuman is the province of Salta, one of the most extensive in the Republic, a purely Highland region, built up with meridional ranges whose peaks vary in altitude from 10,000 to 18,000 feet and these interspersed with valleys which, watered by multitudinous mountain streams, almost rival Tucuman in fertility, producing excellent coffee, bananas, sugar and wines of which those of Cafayaté are especially celebrated. In the rainy season, these streams become irresistible torrents, and then render travelling, which is solely by muletrack, difficult, dangerous and in fact scarcely possible. Although this province is situated almost within the tropics, it enjoys every variety of climate from the hottest and moistest in the valleys, to the coldest and driest on the sierras, and like Tucuman, and exactly under similar conditions, has its year divided into two seasons, the wet and the dry.

Its metamorphic mountain masses abound in precious metals and marbles, its valleys in Kaolin and

valuable woods, the former of which results from the
decay of the felspar of the plutonic rocks above;
resources which, with others, are almost untouched as
yet; but if the upper part of the River Bermejo,
which borders the province, and which is only navigable as far as the colony of Rivadavia in the Gran
Chaco, five days' journey on muleback from Oran,
were rendered accessible to commerce, immense im-
pulse would be given to the various industries which
now languish from isolated position, want of roads,
great distances, and default of capital and labour.
This river, which forms the Northern boundary of
Salta, is one of the most tortuous, as well as the most
difficult of navigation, on the face of the globe : in its
higher parts, it bars further progress on account of
its rapids and the velocity of its stream, which especially in the rainy season hurls down boulders and
trunks of trees, threatening instant destruction to any
frail adventurous bark ; it abounds in fish, and at
some future time by canalization and blasting, will no
doubt form, not alone a source of wealth, but the chief
highway for the produce of the extreme north of
the Republic.

Numerous herds graze in the splendid valleys,
destined as usual for the Chilian market and as the
Salteños cannot export the hides resulting from home
consumption, they are driven to find means to tan
them, for which purpose abundant material is at hand.
The Cebil (*Acacia cebil*) is a tree whose bark contains an
excess of tannic acid, 20 per cent, and grows in wonder-

ful profusion throughout these northern districts, but there is such a wanton destruction of it, as is lamentable to behold. The usual practice is to strip the bark off all round the stem only as high as a man can reach, when of course the tree dies. Stringent forest laws are sadly wanted in this country and will be applied when too late. The chase of the Vicuña, Guanaco and Chinchilla, and the breeding of mules, give further employment to the inhabitants, but the Vicuña and Chinchilla, from the wholesale destruction practised, will certainly soon be extinct on Cis-Andine territory.

Salta, including the wonderfully rich inter-tropical district of Oran lying on the banks of the Bermejo and which is under its jurisdiction, includes an area of 53,456 square miles, nearly the size of England and Wales, and has a very orderly, but in the country parts nearly pure Calchaqui Indian, population of 100,000, or 1,9 to the square mile.

The last of the Andine Provinces is Jujuy which, walled up by snow-clad Sierras, sundered both from the Atlantic and Pacific by extreme remoteness at the north of the Republic, entire absence of roads with the exception of dangerous muletracks over the precipitous and rugged mountains, almost if not altogether impassable for six months in the year, relies for internal communication solely upon the mule, and for external chiefly upon postal and telegraphic facilities, which with wise prevision the Argentine Government strives to push to the utmost limits of its vast territory.

The surface of the province is covered by lofty masses, dotted to the limits of perpetual snow with the "*ichú*" or coarse grass, the favourite food of the Vicuña, which at the height of 12,000 or 13,000 feet stocks these inaccessible regions with its marvellous hordes : here too are immense forests of Cactus (*Candelabrum*) which raise aloft their fantastic spiny arms defying, with grotesque attitude, alike the blast and snow, the frost and rain, and whose woody stems, though porous, are much used for roofs and very durable : and lower down, mantling the slopes are other still denser forests, where the Pacara (*Enterolobium timbavica*), Lapacho (*Tecoma stans*), Quina-Quina (*Myroxilon peruanum*), Urunday(allied to the Lapacho) Queñoa (*Rosacea Polylepis racemosa*), Cascaron (one of the lofty *Leguminosæ*), Espinillo (a thornless *Leguminosa*), Tipa (*Machærium fertile*), Pine (*Podocarpus angustifolia*), and numerous other of the *Mimosæ*, *Leguminosæ* and *Bignoniaceæ*, anchor their tenacious roots.

One very remarkable physical characteristic of Jujuy is the Puna, a lofty, rocky, sterile, salt plateau, sown with ravines, fully 10,500 feet above sea level, occupying a third of the province and only inhabitated here and there by the pure descendants of the Quichua Indians, who graze flocks of sheep and goats wherever a little coarse grass presents itself.

Puna in Quichua signifies " *difficulty in respira-*

tion caused by rarefied air" and is a term applied throughout the Andine provinces to the regions in which such an effect is produced.

From the surface of the Puna rise snow-clad peaks and within its bosom are two very extensive salt lakes : salt, in fact, is so abundant that it can be cut into blocks of any dimensions and transported on mule-back to the interior and Bolivia, forming a not unimportant article of commerce.

Jujuy has but one river, but that one of the most precipitous and picturesque ever beheld, especially in its upper course : rising in the lofty Abra de Cortaderas, one of the borders of the Puna, and flowing southward through rent, twisted, broken and scarped ravines of inexpressible beauty, its course thickly edged with forest growth, it reaches the capital and making an abrupt bend eastwards at right angles, scuds along to join the Bermejo, a day's journey below Oran. Here it is, in the region of the Puna, and in the northern districts of the province, that Nature has played some of her most tremendous freaks : such deep gorges, frightful chasms, precipitous cliffs, inverted caverns, split rocks, heaped tilted broken and jagged fragments and strata, and burst mountain sides, could scarcely be imagined, and a feeling of awe creeps over one in beholding such evidences of terrific convulsion, both by plutonic and aqueous agency.

The landscape of Jujuy is immeasurably superior to that of Salta, but its climate, similarly determined by two annual seasons, the wet and dry, is equally salubrious in the mountains and elevated valleys, although in the lower, owing to the accumulation of stagnant water, Chucho is prevalent in the dry months; and goitre, a common ailment throughout the Andine region, is here, at times, accompanied by Cretinism.

The ranges of Jujuy are rich in minerals and mineral oils: in gold, silver, copper, tin, nickel, lead, antimony, iron, marble, jaspers, rock-crystal, &c., which lie still in their virgin beds, awaiting the summons of capital and labour. Jujuy indeed may be called the Ophir of the Republic; the dream of the Alchemists is here realized; gold dust glitters, and after rain, which partakes of the nature of a deluge, gold nuggets literally grow in the alluvial deposits rendering the "*Virgula Divinatoria*" unnecessary; a golden age is about to dawn upon the province and witness a rush of gasping diggers, to whom the Puna shall be as nectar.

Having no fertile plains, agriculture is very carefully fostered in the valleys, where every drop of available water is used for irrigation and crops of sugar, cereals, rice, cotton, coffee, tobacco and all kinds of fruits are raised. Herds of horned cattle are very rare, but the Jujeños breed mules, asses and a few horses and feed sheep and goats on the mountains, by means of which they have established an extensive trade with Bolivia, whence in return almost all their wants are supplied.

Various tribes of Indians, especially the Matacos, come periodically from the Gran Chaco to hire them-

selves out as labourers; they are invaluable in all kinds
of crushing toil such as mining and clearing of forests
where, in comparison, the European or even Negro
would be almost useless.

In Jujuy, the usual Andine battue is organised
for the destruction of those useful animals the Vicuña,
Guanaco and Chinchilla; and a very laborious chase
it is, at an altitude of 12,000 or 13,000 feet amidst
snow and very broken and precipitous ground; but to
annihilate the noble vicuñas for the sake of their wool
alone, as is done, is simply a piece of barbarism, that
would not be tolerated in any other country and which
calls aloud for repressive game, as similar arboreal
destruction does for forest, laws. Condors and various
species of eagles abound and the *Lama peruana*, the
American camel, is here put to its proper use as a beast
of burden.

Jujuy has an area of 32,210 square miles, about
the size of Scotland, with a scanty population of 50,000
or 1.6 per square mile, whose ordinary language is the
Quichua, Spanish being but little spoken in the province.

Of the four vast Territories belonging to the Republic and not yet incorporated into its body politic,
Patagonia claims the first notice, as being better known,
by name at least, to Europeans, and having somewhat
of a history of its own, although the greater part of it
is still a "*terra incognita*" even to Argentines themselves and has never yet been trodden by Christian
foot.

"Patagon" is a Spanish word, augmentative of *"Pata"* a paw, and therefore signifies *"large-pawed,"* a term applied by the early Spaniards to the Indians of that region when they first beheld them with feet swathed in Guanaco-skins : Patagonia then is the land of the large-pawed. Starting from the Rio Negro, its northern limit, to the Straits of Magellan : from the Andes to the Atlantic, this triangle has an area of 372,815 square miles, into which Great Britain and Ireland, France, Denmark, Holland and Belgium could be packed ; inhabited by numerous tribes of Indians numbering perhaps 25,000, of which the chief is that of the Tehuelches ; but it is very probable that all these various families have a common descent from the Araucanians of Southern Chili, whom the Spaniards were never able to subdue, and whose language bears the relation of mother-tongue to all their manifold dialects.

The story books relate that the Patagonians are of extraordinary stature and some of the tribes are so ; but they are chiefly remarkable for enormous busts, and fleshy features which laid over projecting maxillaries and square mandibles, give immense breadth and solidity to the face. The upper limbs are of great power and size, but the lower do not correspond to the bulk of the trunk. Thus, seen on horseback, they appear veritable Titans, an impression which, inspection a-foot, although it subdues, yet cannot altogether dispel, as they are undoubtedly very large men who strike the beholder rather for their extreme breadth and fleshiness than exalted stature, which however not uncommonly does reach six feet and upwards. These huge Macropods, with hair long, dank, straight and jet-black ; eyes so dark that they shed even over the sclerotic a rufous tint ; teeth superlatively white, probably the result of drinking saline waters ; complexion a dark ruddy brown; and features the reverse of ferocious; impress one, on the whole, more as good-natured giants than savage Indians.

The sandy saline and stony surface of Patagonia, formed chiefly of mountain detritus, rises gently in barren plateaux from the Atlantic towards the Andes; when, on nearing the Cordilleras, the traveller catches sight of some of the most fertile grass-lands in the Republic, interspersed with numerous lakes ; and not alone gramineous verdure but vast forested districts consisting in great part of the Coniferæ, Araucaria (*Araucaria Dombeyi*). Cypress (*Cupressus sempervirens*) and the' Robles (*Fagus Dombeyi*), &c., and which, nestling under the shadow of the Sierras, are sheltered from the blasts on the plain ; whilst as the Straits of Magellan are approached, extensive woods of the *Fagus antarctica, Fagus betuloides, Fagus Dombeyi, Pinus chilena, Lomatia obliqua*, &c., adorn this sub-antarctic zone. As from the Rio Negro to the Straits of Magellan, scarce one river of any size is found, with the exception of the Rio Chubut, where our daring Welsh cousins have succeeded in establishing themselves, after encountering great hardships ; and as the rain-fall is but slight, inhospitality and bleakness accompanied with furious winds characterize generally the Patagonian plains, unrelieved except by low, scanty, thorny Mimosean shrubs, cacteæ with thorns as hard and sharp as nails, and saline plants, especially the June. It seems problematical indeed whether such a desert region, only comparatively lately abandoned by the sea, and possessing no probable means of irrigation, will not remain so permanently; and yet, on the other hand, if the rain-fall could be increased in any way, it would be impossible to assign a limit to its fertility, and under this condition, with a coast-line of 1000 miles on the Atlantic sea-board indented by numerous bays and gulfs, although at present it may be a territory which Indians in common with animals shun; dangerous, from the complete absence of potable water and food, alike to the traveller who attempts to cross and the immigrant who seeks to colonize it, its future would be secured and hordes from the North of Europe, finding here a climate similar to their own, would soon clothe its area with cereals and forest trees and fill its harbours with shipping.

The possession of the southern part of this immense tract is disputed by Chili who, contrary to all right, has made good her footing at Punta Arenas (Sandy Point), a harbour lying just without the Straits on the island of Tierra del Fuego which, with all the surrounding archipelago, is claimed by this country : the reputed mineral and maritime wealth of Patagonia in diamonds, nitrate of soda, guano and seal-fisheries, have tempted our neighbours to transgress their natural limits, and this act seems likely to lead to war between the two countries at no distant period.

The zoology of Patagonia is characterized distinctively, principally by maritime birds, the Auks, Penguins, Cormorants, &c. and the numerous ganoid Fish, many new to science, which with seals and whales render the surrounding seas alive. The Rhea, Guanaco, Condor, and several species of Deer, make it their haunt and the land avi-fauna generally is pretty nearly identical with that of the Pampas.

Let us cast our eyes for a moment oceanwards over the intervening strip of Atlantic, and view a microscopic archipelago, consisting of upwards of 100 islands, containing in the aggregate 8,000 square miles scarce 300 miles from Sandy Point, and over every inch of which the Union jack floats. Britons call them the Falklands. Argentines the Malvinas. The capital, Port Stanley, in East Falkland, is the residence of the Governor. Military, and Anglican Bishop, and one of the islands. Keppel, is the station of the South American Missionary Society, directed by the energetic Bishop Stirling. A little bit of British exclusiveness envelops this sea-swaddling of less than 1500 souls, inasmuch as the territory is limited and no spot under the English flag offers greater inducements to the man of small means to acquire a fortune either by sheep or cattle-farming or in the valuable sea-fisheries.

The climate, soil, and vegetation resemble those of North Britain, but the grass is infinitely more fatten-

ing. Although only 14 years have elapsed since the
first settlers arrived, much of the land is already in the
hands of capitalists, and farms of 100,000 acres and
upwards are numerous ; but one island Georgia, lying
800 miles to the East, in the same latitude as Yorkshire, is still completely uninhabitated and invites
British colonists. Whilst the region is treeless, fuel
is abundant in the shape of peat and brushwood; and
as drought is unknown, and excellent vegetables and
fruits are raised, and the climate is exceedingly
healthy in spite of the strong winds ; to men who can
afford to disregard for a few years the advantages of
society in the certain prospect of bettering their for-
tunes, and who have hitherto perhaps been content to
vegetate upon such interest as the English funds provide, here is a plan by which the three-per-cents can
be converted into thirty-per-cents, consolidated in the
one case equally with the other.

The Pampa, a Quichua term meaning *"level"*, is
another unexplored territory of 170,000 square miles,
or three times the size of England and Wales, and of
which less is known in fact than of Patagonia. It lies
between the frontiers of Buenos Aires, Mendoza, Córdova, San Luis and Santa-Fé and is inhabitated by
four or five nomadic tribes of Indians, amongst whom
the Puelches occupy the first rank and which altogether cannot number more than 20,000 individuals.
The soil of the Pampas is a tertiary compound of
either arenaceous or calcareous marl, covered generally with a thick coating of turf and for the most

part abounding in marshes or lagunas, which receive
and bury the streams from the Cordilleras or are fed
by internal springs, and in some places saline deserts
which are valuable as salt-licks : or if dry on the
surface, water is always to be found at the depth of a
few feet.

In climate, soil and vegetation, the territory of
the Pampa differs in toto from Patagonia : the former
is a vast, usually moist, level, grazing district, in
which it would puzzle the most inveterate petrologist
to find a stone the size of a walnut, sown with numerous and generous *Gramineæ*, the *Poa, Lolium, Fes-
tuca, Holcus, Panicum,* &c.; and others harsher, such
as *Stipa* and *Melica,* interspersed with Trefoil, and
Margaritas (Verbenas); the Cardo-asnal (Thistle) whose
leaves serve to nourish sheep and cattle in time of
drought and whose oily seeds form the principal support of the birds; and Hemlock ; and in whose damp
and swampy parts are multitudes of aquatic grasses
and sedges, the *Phalaris, Dypha, Cyperus,* &c. with
here and there thickets of the giant (*Gynerium argenteum.*) Although the fauna of Patagonia is much
more restricted that the Pampean, less distinction
occurs between them than between the flora of the two
territories : some of the most ordinary forms of animal
life common in a great measure to both are : The Puma (*Felis concolor*): Guanaco (*Lama huanacos*); Gama
or Deer (*Cariacus campestris*): Zorro or Fox (*Canis
Azaræ*); Comadreja or Opossum (*Didelphys azaræ*);
Biscacha (*Lagostomus trichodactylus*) ; Patagonian

Cavy (*Dolichotis patachonica*); Rhea americana; Perdiz grande or Rufous Tinamou (*Rhynchotus rufescens*); Perdiz comun or Spotted Tinamou (*Nothura maculosa*); Aguila or Eagle (*Geranoaëtus melanoleucus*); Chajá or Crested Screamer (*Chauna chavaria*); Teru-tero or Cayenne Lapwing (*Vanellus cayennensis*); Chimango (*Milvago Chimango*); Carancho (*Polyborus brasiliensis*); Lechuza or Burrowing Owl (*Speotyto cunicularia*); Espátula or Rosy Spoonbill (*Platalea ajaja*); Black-faced Ibis (*Theristicus caudatus*); White Ibis (*Eudocimus albus*); Cigüeña or Stork (*Ciconia maguari*); Black-necked Swan (*Cygnus nigricollis*) Ganzo or Goose (*Cygnus coscoroba*); Flamenco or Flamingo (*Phœnicopterus ignipalliatus*); an innumerable variety of Ducks and Pigeons; Silky Cow-bird (*Molothrus bonariensis*); the Horneros or Oven-birds *Furnarius rufus*) and *Geositta cunicularia* : Tuco-tuco (*Ctenomys brasiliensis*); Iguaná (*Podinema teguixin*); Tatú or Armadillo (*Dasypus villosus*); Escuerzo (*Ceratophrys cornuta*); and many serpents, some very venomous as the Víbora de la Cruz (*Trigonocephalus alternatus*) : whilst gad-flies and mosquitos torment man and beast.

The whole of this vast plain is sprinkled thick with fossils ; and the remains of enormous Antediluvian animals, which the Indians assert belonged to a race of giants formerly inhabiting the country, are usually met with close to the surface.

Although snow never falls in this region, except in proximity to the Sierras, on a winter's morning the ground is covered with hoar frost and frequently the

thermometer indicates a temperature below freezing
point ; the winds, meeting with neither hills nor trees
to deviate or modify their force, blow with extreme
violence ; winter is the season of rain-fall, whilst the
summer is usually dry : droughts are frequent and this
is the main cause that prescribes a nomadic life to the
Indian. The air of the Pampas strikes the dweller in
cities as very fresh and pure, the result of the never-
ceasing play of the breezes which continually restore
its vitality : in fact, the indigenous inhabitants are
subject to few diseases ; but when the small-pox, one
of the two great curses inflicted upon them by civilization, breaks out amongst the Indians, its issues are
very fatal ; they apprehend it with such terror that if
any individual of a tribe is attacked, the rest leave
him mercilessly to his fate in a tolda (skins stretched
over canes) with a little food and water by his side.

The Pampa Indians are strict Hippophagists, not
alone do they devour mares' flesh all hot and quivering, but quaff the very blood, asserting that it is
sweeter then beef, which I believe ; so that, when
they make incursions and drive off herds of cattle, it
is not for the sake of food but barter. These children
of the wilderness love strong liquor too and know
how to brew it from the algarrobo pods, thereby
drunkenness, the second curse, is universal, including
at times the whole tolderia (encampment) in one general savage symposium.

Although having probably the same origin as the
Patagonians, the Pampeans differ from them widely

in physique and character, being of medium size inclining to low stature and of a more cunning and ferocious disposition. Their weapons consist chiefly of a bamboo spear 15 to 20 feet long, large knife, bolas and lasso, in the use of all of which they are proficients, and when attacking on horseback, nothing is seen of these Longobardi Centaurs, who, lance in hand, lie along the outer flank of their steeds remote from the adversary.

On account of the frequent murderous inroads of late years made by the Pampa Indians upon the adjacent provinces, General Roca, then Minister of War, determined to organise an expedition in the year 1878 in order to drive them back and establish a secure south western frontier to prevent further incursions ; and for this purpose 4,000 men were told off. The enterprise, in which I was invited to join, was completely successful and reclaimed 15,000 square leagues of very fine territory from the Red Skins, and great was the surprise universally expressed at the beauty and fertility of the lands in the neighbourhood of the Rio Negro, which now forms the southernmost protected boundary of the Argentine Republic. The natural result was an attempt to colonise the district and Government by offering the lands at 2d. an acre, succeeded in disposing of the greater part, but on the elevation of General Roca to the Presidency towards the close of 1880 he, being friendly to the English, further offered to establish a small British colony there as a nucleus, giving the first twenty families land, and supplying them with seed, implements, cattle and food, to be repaid in five years: and as the National frontier is marked out by a deep and broad fosse, guarded by forts, those who settle within this line are comparatively safe, being either defended or avenged by the National troops; but such as are adventurous enough to pitch their tents in advance, do so at their own risk: very lately an explorer, to his extreme surprise, came upon some hardy Englishmen in the very heart of the Indian territory enjoying complete tranquillity on some of the finest lands of the Republic, by merely paying the "braves" an annual tribute.

Thus then slowly creeps on the inevitable destruction of the indigenous races in this Republic; their stakes are loosening, their cords tightening, leaving no testimony that they were, save in the Upper Provinces a few inscriptions on bare rock surfaces, some mighty conduits or the sadder memento of their tombs: and it is to be regretted, as their tongues are unwritten, that no competent philologist has as yet undertaken the classification, whilst still living, of their numerous polysynthetic idioms, especially the Araucanian, Quichua, Guaraní, Puelche and Tehuelche, and the assignment of their relative positions on the tablet of universal language.

The National sub-tropical territory of the Gran Chaco consists of two well-defined districts: the Northern a parallelogramic dead plane about 500 feet above sea level, lying between the rivers Pilcomayo,

Paraguay and Bermejo, a Tripotamia which contains some of the finest land in the world either for agriculture or grazing, a rich thick humus on an argillaceous subsoil, and has perfect means of communication in its magnificent rivers : and a Southern, an irregular quadrilateral with an area four times as great, and pretty nearly equally level, which bounded by the Bermejo, Paraná and Salado forms another Tripotamia of even superior merits.

The Chaco is often styled a desert, a term liable to misconception, as it is so only because it is as yet abandoned to an indigenous population numbering from thirty to forty thousand, and hitherto it has been found impossible to traverse it centrally on account of the complete absence of water. The riparian fringes and for some distance inland, are subject to inundation from sudden freshets, converting the hollows into lagunas and covering the earth with a thick rich alluvial deposit, as in Egypt, at which time forests of Palms may be viewed standing in water and the banks of the Paraná are thus rendered pretty well uninhabitable : but if we glance at the gently rising interior we find it, in general, covered with dense forests descending in some parts to the coast line, interspersed with luxuriant meadow land, rich to riot and easily worked, and entirely free from stones, and covered with grass five or six feet high : the picture however is not without its chiaro-oscuro in the shape of sterile sandy deserts.

In common with the whole of the north of the

Republic, the climate of the Gran Chaco is subject to
two seasons, the wet from November to March corresponds to the hot; the winter is excessively dry and
then especially, as it is impossible to obtain water in
the interior, the very Indians are driven coastwards
and exploration becomes excessively dangerous. At
Salta I met a gentleman, Dr. Fontana who, with forty
attendants well-armed, provisioned and mounted, attempted to cross the territory in a direct line from the
city of Corrientes to that of Salta. He was unable to
accomplish it, for after floundering for days through
muddy swamps, his animals died off and then attacked
by Indians in the possession of firearms, some of his
party were slain and he himself severely wounded in
the shoulder. The Expedition however plodded on
a-foot day after day under a scorching sun, unable to
find a drop of water, until at last to save their lives,
they were obliged to change their route and heading
northwards for the colony of Rivadavia, reached it in
safety after 42 days of intense suffering from hunger
and thirst. Although the olive-brown Indians, especially those of the interior, are as a rule very hostile
to Christian occupation of their territory, those dwelling in the vicinity of the rivers are quite sensible of
the advantages which civilization offers in the shape
of remunerative employment and willingly hire themselves out both on the Correntino and Salta sides, when
in the one case the orange harvest and in the other
the sugar, is ripe for gathering; as also in the numerous colonies that sprinkle the extreme south and north
of the Chaco. These children of the wilderness are

chiefly nomadic and yet completely different in their
habits from those of Patagonia or the Pampa, although
allied in race with the latter; they are not such terrible horsemen as the Macropods nor such inveterate
cattle-lifters as the Pampeans, for which two reasons
exist, the difficulty of keeping horses in the Chaco on
account of the Hippoboscidæ which actually bleed them
to death, and the immense number of impenetrable
forests. The best-known tribes are those of the Chi-
riguanos a noble-looking race of men, the dirty nude
Matacos of the coast, and the warlike Tobas of the
interior who put a bullet in Fontana's shoulder. These
and other tribes of the Guaraní race are merely left
in possession of the territory until immigration forces
the National Government to undertake an expedition
either for their incorporation or extermination : in the
meanwhile much expense is incurred by the necessity
of maintaining a large military force for the protection of the frontiers and colonies from their attacks.

Numerous streams for the most part completely
unnavigable fall into the large rivers surrounding the
Gran Chaco : these and the coastwise lagunas abound
in the Carpincho (*Hydrochœrus capybara*), Nutria
(*Myopotamus coypus*), Cayman (*Alligator latirostris*),
Yacaré (*Alligator sclerops*), &c.: the lowlands are the
rendezvous of the Boa (*Boa constrictor*), the Rattle-
Snake (*Crotalus horridus*), &c.: and throughout the
territory generally, the Jaguar (*Felis onça*), Ocelot
(*Felis pardalis*), Coati (*Nasua rufa*), the Argentine
Wolf (*Canis jubatus*), the Saki (*Pithecia*), Giant Tatú

(*Dasypus gigas*), and the Great Anteater (*Myrmeco-phaga jubata*), &c., are found. The insect and reptile plagues which at present are so numerous will disappear with the forests and as cultivation increases; one of the former the Mosca Brava (*Stomoxys calcitrans*) will scarcely allow the nobler domestic animals, the horse and the cow, to exist in the Gran Chaco: it settles on them in millions, allowing them no rest even to feed and actually sucks them to the last drop of their blood.

The present great source of wealth in this fertile district lies undoubtedly in the variety and abundance of its excellent woods, yielded by forests which, although not of so noble a growth as those of Tucuman and Oran, are yet sufficient to stand the strain of the present or even an increased rate of destruction for 200 years to come. Urged by repeated warning however the Government has at last ordered a slight tax to be laid on the lumber-men in the hope of staying in part the wholesale slaughter, but in vain.

The Quebracho colorado (*Loxopterygium Lorent-zii*) is a wonderful wood for sleepers, hydraulic construction or ship repairs, lasting twice as long as oak and which, if completely immersed in water, may be considered indestructible. Some few years ago, one of H. M's gunboats was repaired with it to the astonishment of the carpenters on board, who declared they had never seen such hard wood.

The Gran Chaco with its deep loamy soil, beneficent climate and its 213,000 square miles, or nearly

four times the area of England and Wales, will not
long rest content with yielding woods alone ; already
it gasps for population to open its teeming womb and
empty therefrom into the lap of industry inexhaustible
offerings of cotton, sugar, indigo, rice and coffee.

The last as well as the smallest of the Argentine
Territories is that of Misiones, which forms the extreme north-east of the great Mesopotamia and snugly
enbosomed in the arms of Brazil and Paraguay possesses an area 21,500 square miles, that is, a little
larger than Holland : and as there is no natural boundary between it and the province of Corrientes, the
latter for a long period claimed jurisdiction over it,
until at last Misiones has been formally declared National territory.

Of this splendid region it is impossible to speak
otherwise than in terms of the greatest enthusiasm.
No spot perhaps on the earth's surface could be selected
where the gifts of Nature are more bounteously be-
stowed. The sensual delights which arise from hills
and mountains, dales, plains and valleys, forests and
meadows, a fruitful soil and deliciously balmy climate,
are here presented with a liberal hand : no sandy desert nor Salina, no Salitral to engulf the wayfarer, no
Travesia to make the traveller gasp for breath, no
death-laden Zonda nor fierce Pampero, but instead
thereof, a soil of rich thick humus, luxuriant vegetation, a parterre where the Storm-fiend gives place to a
continuous zephyr.

In these Elysian fields it was that the Jesuits held

the centre of their famous missions, hence the name
of the Territory ; and whatever view may be held of
the labours and objects of those zealous pioneers, it
cannot be doubted, that to them is chiefly due the fact
that to-day the inhabitants of the interior provinces of
the Argentine Republic profess and practise Christianity and are characterized in the main by habits of
industry, sobriety, order and obedience. Under the
administration of the Society the population of Misiones numbered at least 30,000, but at present no more
than 3,000 or 4,000 remain, a heterogeneous resi-
due of the Guaraní Indian with the Sub-European.

The red ferruginous clay which forms the subsoil
of this favoured region maintains the upper crust permanently moist, so that besides gramineous profusion,
its area is clothed with numberless indigenous and rare
medicinal, tinctorial, or scented herbs, wild fruits,
Indigo (*Indigofera añil*). Castor oil plant (*Ricinus
communis*), Wild Cotton (*Gossypium peruvianum*).
Chaguar (one of the *Bromeliaceæ*) a fibre superior to
Manilla hemp, bosquets of the Yerba Maté (*Ilex paraguayensis*), with an endless succession of trees whose
saps yield gums, resins and balsams, or barks tannin,
and lastly magnificent forests of Urunday, Lapacho,
Cedar, Pino de Brasil, *Jacarandá chelonia*, &c. in whose
recesses the Tapir, Peccary, Carpincho, the Howling
Monkey (*Mycetes fuscus*), the Capuchin (*Cebus faluel-
lus*), the Marmoset (*Hapale pencillata*), the Curassow
(*Crax alector*), one of the Iguanidæ (*Anolis puncta-
la*), and an infinity of the Psittacidæ dispoet them-

selves. The Mulita (*Tatusia hybrida*) and the Peludo (*Dasypus villosus*) are very common, likewise
the Vampire (*Vampyrus spectrum*), but as for the Parrots they are in such incredible numbers that interminable war must be waged against them to secure a
crop.

As the soil and climate of Misiones are alike
favourable for agriculture or pasturage, and everything
grown under the sun here comes to perfection, and as
no point of the territory is more than 30 miles distant
from one or other of the two fine rivers, the Paraná
and Uruguay which clasp it on either side and abound
in affluents, thus rendering it the best watered district
in the Republic with ample means of outlet for produce, its claims to population cannot much longer be
deferred and the time is doubtless nigh when a million
at least of industrious settlers will render it a paradise
of plenty, as assuredly it now is a paradise of beauty.

The capitals of the various provinces have the
same names as the provinces themselves and are in general fine cities, invariably built in square blocks of
150 yards by 150 and with streets at right angles to
one another in the usual Spanish chequered fashion.
Here exist most of the elements of civilization to
render a residence in their midst agreeable though
somewhat monotonous: Government and Courts of
Justice, Police, Churches, Theatres, Schools, Libraries, Hotels, Markets, Hack-coaches and Saddle-horses,
Clubs, Baths and Newspapers; but the Lighting and
Paving bad in all, are simply execrable in some. An

Englishman travelling through these capitals may not always be sure of meeting a countryman, but scarcely ever fails to encounter a pair of spectacles indicating one of his first cousins the Germans, who invariably speak his tongue and from whom I have at all times received the utmost courtesy.

But if we descend a grade lower, to the rural towns, the case is somewhat altered. These generally consist of a central Plaza (square) containing the Church, School and Police-court, from the four corners of which radiate at right angles unpaved streets whose roadways are delivered over alternately to the twin fiends mud and dust, a chemical analysis of which is unnecessary as their composition may be inferred from the fact that the streets form the general receptacle for the basura (house rubbish) ; so that pantanos (holes filled with slush) abound, in which it is not uncommon to see a cart almost engulfed and abandoned for days, whilst every passing horseman or laden waggon either bespatters the footpassenger with filth or suffocates him with comminuted tosca, and at night the darkness is relieved only by a few wretched glimmering kerosene lamps hung at long distances.

A great similarity prevails in all; the same bleak desolate appearance, devoid as they are of any environs which give such a charm to European towns ; nay, sometimes the very desert reaches to the doors and is only kept from invading them by the feeble remonstrance (mañana, tomorrow) of the natives. The houses, which here and there dispute the territory with the mud cabin, are limited to the ground-floor, but spacious internally, with an azotea (flat) roof, and are built of a soft porous brick, which soon loses its colour, cemented in mud, and not even plastered, much less pointed. To the meanness, dirt and untidiness of the exterior, the interior corresponds : the woodwork of the roughest and never made to fit, the floors of uncovered brick or pressed earth, the unhewn trunks as rafters viewed in all their nakedness without the intervention of ceiling, the plain and scanty deal furniture, the mudformed uneven dust-laden walls, the windows which once perhaps may have been glazed with transparency but to-day powerless to transmit light or altogether socketless, are some of the internal factors of general discomfort.

The patios (courtyards) and gardens, which are generally attached to the houses, would, if kept in order, add somewhat of a charm to the otherwise general sombreness of the dwellings, but alas ! they too partake of the general character which distinguishes these rural centres ; and where one would expect to find cultivated flowers and fruits, rank weeds usurp ; hemlock, wild parsley and camomile contend successfully with the rose, peach and grape. Nor does the appearance of the inhabitants themselves relieve but rather intensify the monotonous prospect, as they, clad in garments all dabbled with mud, unkempt and unshorn, their children unwashed from the day of their birth and running about with naked feet, and the women in tattered dresses much in need of good honest soapsuds, cross the view; their very horses un-groomed as themselves and plastered over with the results of the night's revel in patanos look disreput-able; whilst the odours of strong cookery assail the nostrils at all hours, smelling overpoweringly of grease, onions and garlic, the trinne lar that sways all purely native kitchens.

An Argentine rural town in fine, never looks picturesque or blooming, the freshness of youth seldom accompanies even its earlier years, despondency sits from birth on habitations and inhabitants who fail to make either their dwellings or persons inviting, and this very frequently not the result of poverty, the affectation of which is so general throughout the Re-public, but of choice: all the ornamental seems re-served for the capitals and these rustic spots are incap-able of enticing the beholder, as does an English village, to cast in his lot among them.

CHAPTER III.

Anthropologists very properly assert that races, in their external and internal characteristics, reflect the regions they inhabit and this, which is so evident when a comparison is instituted between peoples who live under very widely divergent natural conditions, as the mountaineer and the dweller on the plain, is not the less true, although less patent, when the differentiæ of their existences are convergent ; so that we must be prepared for very various race phases in a country whose Physical Geography embraces not only such colossal phenomena but distinctions so numerous and significant.

With the exception of Corrientes, which is still Guaraní in race and language, the coast provinces are very much imbued with European blood, at a rate ever increasing, and although the people are dark, they resemble Europeans in feature and form ; the populations of the Interior however still retain a great preponderance of Indian blood and character and are perhaps the most independent set of fellows on the face of the earth, a peculiar people with whom money is not a motive power and whose only talisman is the

"hágame el favor" (do me the favour); the Eastern
slopes of the Andes have attracted a large Chilian
immigration in pursuit of mining, fully a third of the
inhabitants of Mendoza are thus of trans-Andine descent; and the Territories are occupied as yet by semi-
savage races. Of the indigenes existing at the time
of the Spanish conquest, the Quichuas, Guaranis and
Calchaquis still survive, but do not increase, and being
servile and obedient are everywhere employed in the
most laborious offices, with which they are quite content, and it is a remarkable fact that a mixture of
Spanish and Quichua produces degeneration, but the
contrary with Spanish and Guaraní.

Against the Pampa Indians the Argentine Government has begun a war of extermination and it is
not an uncommon sight to behold cartloads of these
abject-looking creatures passing through the streets of
the littoral en route to different parts of the country
for enforced menial service.

In vain is it therefore to seek as yet a welded
homogeneous race in the Argentine Republic, an "e
pluribus unum"; it is too early in its history, they
are a noble work in embryo ; and if the race be only
in process of formation, the character must lie still
undeveloped and the attempt to solve the large and
complex problem of its estimation, based upon un-
settled conditions, be either unfair or flattering : nevertheless, taking the Argentines generally to mean the
descendants of the ancient mixed race of Spaniards
and Indians throughout the Republic who, unblended

with modern European admixture, possess features in
common and form the general body of the people, they
partake together of the virtues and failings of the Latin race, accentuated on the one hand by race proclivities and on the other by that idiosyncrasy that external
Nature tends to stamp upon them.

Endowed with a vigorous imagination, the Argentine is ever ready to lend ear to Utopian political
schemes and forgets, in his pursuit of idealistic perfection, the more practical life of societies and is thus
easily made the dupe of anarchy; and although capable of managing his own concerns with a rare degree
of tact and intelligence, is a child in concert and wanting in that enterprise and sustained energy necessary
to educe great results from combined action: although
well aware of the boundless resources of his country,
he makes but feeble efforts to promote them and in
his aversion to everything new, rests satisfied with
pinning his faith to the bovine tail, as his fathers did,
and seeing the foreigner gradually filch from his grasp
the rich interests daily arising on all hands.   Personally dignified and cultivating self-respect, he demands
what he readily concedes, courtesy; well-bred, polite
and hospitable, to the gentler emotions a slave, but to
most of the Spartan virtues a stranger, he excels as a
companion and acquaintance, but is too fickle to
endure the chains of abiding friendship.

But in addition to those broad lines of race demar-
cation, of which we have spoken, the result of migra-
tion, conquest and subsequent intermingling, others

due to the necessities imposed by physical configura-
tion are scarcely less important, involving as they do,
even in the same absolute family, a difference of idea,
manner, dress, custom, form and feature : for instance,
there will always be a perceptible difference between
the dweller on small restricted plots, hemmed in by
arbitrary stipulations, the offspring of a crowded civilization, and him who roams free as the wind over
endless plains, climbs the mountain, or breasts the torrent, in contempt alike of indulgence and comfort :
between the refinement of the larger town on the littoral and the coarser development of the lesser in the
interior ; nay even between the countryman and towns-
man inhabiting the same district : the former of
whom, contrary to European experience, never copies
the latter but affects to despise him and ridicule his
dress.

Thus in passing through this extensive region,
the traveller will meet with the Arriero (Muleteer),
the Vaqueano (Guide), the Rastreador (Tracker) the
Lagunero (Dweller on the lakes), and the Gaucho
termed Campeano in some parts, in others Paisano ;
classes as distinct as the circumstances which give
rise to them.

The normal Gaucho (Araucanian word signifying
companion) of the plains merits more than passing
notice as forming one of the chief salient features
conjured up to the mind when the Republic is spoken
of. To those who devote themselves to a camp life,
especially the management of horned cattle, the Gau-

cho is an absolute necessity, although near the coast,
in what may be styled the Home Counties, as the Estancias become wired in, the Basque and Italian are
rapidly supplanting him. A half-wild, self-reliant,
courageous man, abandoned to his own instincts, with
but little notion of civilized life, a serf and yet rioting
in freedom, having to face the elements by day and
night, to curb the horse, subdue wild cattle, living in
a domain of brute force and with his few advantages,
it is a miracle he is so good as he is. Polite, attentive,
skilful, a firm friend as long as he is treated with consideration, but when slighted, a fatal and relentless
enemy whose facon (long knife) is ever ready to
avenge contempt : in dealing with such, an employer
fresh from Europe is likely to arouse immediate and
dangerous hostility by attempting to maintain here
any such caste as is dominant there ; in fact one of
the greatest difficulties, a stranger, who is anxious to
embark capital under his own superintendence, has to
contend with, is the management of the lower classes,
who in the Upper Provinces are hyper-independent
and in the Lower hopelessly dignified : to ask as a
favour is the stereotyped formula for the master in
both.

As far below the European labourer in physical
comfort and the outward marks of civilization, as
superior to him in urbanity and manly bearing, the
Gaucho, possessing few wants and poor in the midst
of inexhaustible riches, is the child of unconcern; with
food or without, with shelter or not, a paper cigar, a

little maté (Paraguayan tea), one meal a day of meat
cooked in the open air without bread or vegetables,
and his guitar at night, and he rests content : but if
you add a Sunday suit of clothes with silver-mounted
trappings for his horse, his pride and delight are un-
bounded, and as he curvets over the plain, having
attained the summit of his ambition, no more vivid
picture of human self-satisfaction could be presented.
In vain do we search for a country lout in the Argentine Republic, her peasant is one of Nature's gentlemen, a simple, superstitious yet withal chivalrous
child of Nature in whom the love of song is inherent
and who is readily amenable to its influence; even
yet there exists amongst them a race of minstrels
who are universally welcomed as guests, and who
celebrate, in melancholy strain accompanied by the
guitar, deeds as epic to them as those of Homer's
heroes to the bards of old.

By increase of population and consequent enclosure of land, the Bashi-Bazouk propensities of the
Gaucho will gradually be represed, and influenced by
example, law and education, casting aside the chiripá (*) and poncho as marks of his present serfdom,
may either become an enlightened citizen, or as the
increase of sheep is already working his destruction,
descend into the mere shearer, or as he is thought to
be incapable of improvement and incompatible with

(*) A square piece of cloth which folded round the loins and brought
up between the legs has its corners secured by a gaudy girdle and serves for
loose trowsers.

progress, more probably will be well nigh extermi-
nated in the process.

This son of Ishmael thinks is quite a matter of
course to get half-seas-over on Sundays and holidays
(Saints' days), for which the number of pulperias
(dram shops) spread over the camp and which retail
nothing but flavoured spirits of wine for gin, afford
ready assistance, and at which cock-fighting, cards,
billiards and horse-racing are preeminent. These
orgies are seldom closed without disputes, often by
appeal to the formidable facon which is universally
worn in a plated sheath in the belt behind and in the
use of which they are dexterous to a degree : yet even
in extreme cases life is seldom taken, but ugly gashes
on the face are given and received and few Gauchos
reach the grave without carrying thither long seams
on their features : but if by chance death occurs from
the use of the knife, an accident not surprising considering that the general insecurity of life in which
he has been bred from infancy produces in the Gaucho indifference to death especially a violent one, then
the sympathy of the public is invariably with the criminal : the all-powerful Dictator Rosas it was who,
nothing but a sleeved Gaucho, set the fashion of pet-
ting the assassin at the same time that he was unmer-
ciful to thieves, whose throats he cut without benefit
of clergy.

There frequents the plains however and lives in
the thickets and other places of concealment, another
type of Gaucho, the refuse of the former, styled the

Gaucho malo (the bad Gaucho), the brawler and bully of the camp, a man whose knife thirsts for blood and is never satiate, whose mission is to kill, destroy and rob, who thinks no more of slaying his fellow than a sheep; this wretch it is who generally leads the Indian forays, who is the great horse-stealer of the country districts and will kill a cow merely for the sake of its tongue, a morsel, of which the Argentines, like the Condor, are immoderately fond. Strange to say, the Gaucho malo, a criminal of the deepest dye, whose hand is against every man but unfortunately every man's hand is not against him, is everywhere received with respect, a respect based on fear, which even the authorities share, as they seldom dare to prosecute him ; but what justice dares not, and society is too feeble to attempt, the whistle of the locomotive and the flash of the electric wire are by degrees accomplishing, and the days of the red-skin and his treacherous ally are assuredly numbered.

As may be imagined the Gaucho dwelling all his life on the Pampas is gifted with an astonishing faculty for finding his own way or directing others; even if a spot be fifty leagues off, he goes direct to it like a pigeon, although here are no fingerposts nor milestones, but in common with all the country-people he always understates distances : another very important quality, amounting almost to an additional sense, is his consciousness, even on the darkest nights, of the proximity of water, distinguishing the sweet from the salt. Amongst his special powers however must

be early enumerated, skill with the knife, by the aid
of which he is more than a match for an Englishman
with his revolver: of course the latter is unaware of
the mode of attack, and this is the great source of
danger. Formerly the Gaucho was afraid of the
revolver, but not so now: perhaps the knife is up his
sleeve and whilst addressing his victim with great
politeness, it is allowed to run down into the hand
and, before a revolver can be levelled, is plunged with
lightning stroke into the heart of his adversary, no
mistake is made, the aim is always deadly; sometimes
the knife reposes in his long riding boot, and stooping
down apparently to arrange that, is suddenly withdrawn and launched on its fatal mission; at others
resting with the hilt on the curved middle finger and
the blade along the forearm ready to be darted point
first, and at a distance of ten yards it is winged with
certain death. In fact it would take a good swords-
man with his favourite weapon to obtain an advantage
over a Gaucho with his facon; when they fight, they
cover the left arm with two or three folds of the poncho, allowing the ends to hang down and form a
shield which, kept in perpetual motion, effectually
screens them and dazzles the eyes of their adversary,
and so it is very difficult to see or get near them; they
are stupendously quick with the arm and wrist but
clumsy on the lower limbs: yet take his knife from
him and the gaucho is helpless for business, pleasure
or attack. With equal facility the Gaucho manages
the bolas and the lasso and at the distance of thirty
yards blunders are seldom committed; these instru-

ments in his hands are really formidable, so that a
European, whether on horseback or on foot, and
engaged in a deadly struggle with him, is to a great
degree helpless : if again in treachery a Gaucho hides
behind a rock or tree for the passing traveller, his
doom is pretty well sealed ; his horse entangled with
the bolas or himself with the lasso, there is no escape
except perhaps by the instant severing of the latter
with a very sharp knife, which many keep for the
purpose. But besides his address with knife, bolas
and lasso, our hero prides himself upon his strength,
his horse and trappings, and above all on his equestrian skill ; like a cat he will always alight on his feet,
whatever happens to his horse. A number of gauchos on foot, each armed with the bolas, will form a
line, one on horseback rides by at full gallop, the bolas are launched and bring down the horse all of a
heap with thundering thud, amid a cloud of dust
which momentarily hides from view both horse and
rider, but on clearing away, the Gaucho instead of
lying extended with broken neck or at least senseless,
is seen tripping along with the momentum in front of
his prostrate steed, a feat no other horseman in the
world could accomplish.

Utmost submissiveness combined with tremendous
endurance are the chief characteristics of the Gaucho's
horse ; he never forgets the lasso, by whose dread
fibres his ardour first quailed before man ; the Do-
mador (Tamer) succeeds in breaking him in by destroying all spirit within him ; although small however,

this wiry unshod mustang, if allowed to proceed at his
own pace the canter, now and then varied by the Pampa shuffle, is able to traverse forty leagues in one day
without fatigue to himself or rider; the sinewy ginete
(horseman) who, centaur-like, seems of one piece with
his steed and never appears under any circumstances
to exert muscular force, laughs at the English trot
and the English method of riding to it, and let him
but once get his right leg over the saddle, nothing
that a horse can do will unseat this splendid jockey.

In the public races to which the Gaucho is passionately attached, the native rider has another opportunity of displaying his equestrian skill, but such
contests are without interest to Europeans, who never
compete in their lists, as they are limited to the very
short distance of a few squares and consist mainly of
a series of false starts (paradas), sometimes to the
number of thirty or forty, until one succeeds in obtaining a manifest advantage. The race itself likewise is
conducted throughout with great unfairness according
to English rules and hampering an antagonist in every
possible way even to violence is common; on these
occasions gambling is fast and furious, the bets not
always in money, which is scarce among the fraternity,
but horses, sheep, cattle, recado (native saddle), bridles
and silver ornaments, change hands.

The Sortija is a universal game at which skill of
a different kind is exhibited. A gold ring, generally
of slight value is suspended from a cross post supported by two uprights, sufficiently high to allow a

horseman to pass beneath and reach it with a short
wand. The object is to disengage the ring by running the stick through it whilst the horse is at full
gallop, the starting post being about fifty yards
distant.

A group of gauchos with their swarthy but
comely visages and graceful dress of calzoncillos
(white linen drawers fringed with lace), chiripá, poncho, gay silk handkerchief, gaudy girdle, slouched hat
and long boots, either sitting Oriental fashion or
squatting on their haunches beneath an Ombú, sipping
mate or something stronger, awaiting the spluttering
asado (roast), regaling themselves with a mite of hard
blue-milk cheese which they divide very neatly with
their long knives, or intent on card-playing, whilst
the blue smoke from the paper cigarette is blown in
clouds from their nostrils, their hoppled horses quietly
browsing in the neigbourhood, forms altogether a
picturesque scene. These hardy vagabonds, if purely
Creoles are generally well-formed, handsome in feature and with refined extremities, but if negro-blood
has intervened, the impress of that degraded race at
once spoils the picture. When the asado is ready, the
instinct of the wild beast seems to seize them, for
dividing and clutching a long piece of meat between
the teeth and the left hand and with the right bringing down the huge facon with a quick stroke close to
the nose, they sever and swallow junk after junk, so
close a shave is it that a stranger momentarily expects
the nasal organ to be included in the sacrifice. The

card playing is invariably accompanied with gambling, for the Gaucho, from the day when the soldiers of Pizarro staked the golden ornaments of the ill-fated Atahualpa till now, always has been and ever will be an inveterate gamester; and notwithstanding he spends his whole life in the pure fresh air and is invigorated with abundance of exercise, he is not a long liver.

The language recognized throughout the Republic as the national tongue is Spanish, not Castilian, but a language which bears about the same relation to it, as the American does to the English ; indeed the one is the analogue of the other; and it is spoken with much energy accompanied with considerable gesture, by the men, and by the ladies, in such shrill loud tones as to make the stranger imagine they are quarrelling. A European language transported to America, amid different physical aspects and modes of life, of necessity undergoes change, but these changes, which are very limited and incapable of affecting its organism, are chiefly phonetic, as are also the dialectic peculiarities which exist in the different provinces of the Republic itself. From the very first moment of the introduction of Spanish into South America, began that struggle for existence which has already resulted in the premature death without issue of several of the indigenous polysynthetic languages, about ten of whose groups have existed within the limits of the Argentine Republic, offering a fine field for linguistic study : but if the struggle for existence has hitherto been severe what may we not expect in the future from polyglot immigration? in the conflict of idioms, there is no quarter, not even a truce, under which some possible arrangement or amalgamation might ensue, a mixed language is an impossibility, each has inscribed on its banner "conquest or death", and which shall remain with the laurels?

In the large towns throughout the Confederation, Spanish is spoken, but outside these, in the country districts of some of the central and all the Andine provinces, various Indian tongues still maintain their supremacy.

CHAPTER IV.

EDUCATION — RELIGION — CONSTITUTION — GOVERN-

MENT—ARMY—NAVY.

In those days when even kings could neither read nor write, it might be no stigma to a nation to possess a population ignorant of alphabetical mysteries, or unable to master the difficulties of pothooks and hangers, but towards the close of the nineteenth century it is an anachronism, a severe reflection upon any government to include within its borders a single individual destitute of those necessary keys to knowledge. This stigma the Argentine Government has been making strenuous efforts of late years to remove, but the immense distances in the interior have hitherto formed an insurmountable barrier to the complete accomplishment of its designs ; yet it is rare even now to find a man, however ill-dressed, who cannot both read and write. The great fault of preexistent educational arrangements has lain in the desire of providing the higher classes with gratuitous instruction and neglecting the lower : the former well able to pay for their education may be safely left to their own resources to secure the advantages which competent instruction affords.

As there is no country in South-America which spends more money on education than this, it has attained in consequence the front rank in respect of it, in spite of local obstacles. Two great educational centres, Buenos Aires and Córdoba, radiate their beams in all directions from their Universities, Literary and Scientific Societies and National Colleges, and degrees in the various faculties are to be obtained from both. Each capital of a province has its National College, besides local institutions; several Normal Colleges and 200 public Libraries are dotted throughout the Republic; and at least two thousand primary schools, one for each hamlet of this vast territory, and at which, as far as possible, attendance is obligatory, are engaged in disseminating elementary instruction; and as a supplement, the whole of this extensive machinery is put in operation to afford a more or less gratuitous, and up to a certain point successful, education for the masses. The exertions of the provinces are still further stimulated by a premium of $10,000 gold (£2000) to such as have 10 per cent. of their children at school, a bonus as yet claimed only by one, San Luis. Yet notwithstanding all this commendable scholastic provision, with its turgid programmes, and abundance of professors and inspectors, it may be safely affirmed that the higher instruction throughout the Republic is deficient in one main element, the moral; Conscientiousness which makes the pursuit of truth for its own sake a life devotion and leads to the diligent study of fundamentals, eschewing all scamping of work, is not so much divorced from the intellect.

as its very existence is quietly ignored; the deep-sea
line that fathoms the reasons of things lies rusting,
teacher and scholar are alike impatient of continuous
plodding toil, the flower is sought 'ere the seed is sown,
the memory and apprehension, both of which need no
stimulus here, are alone quickened by a nimble send
over extensive courses merely for the purpose of examination, and after the stream of knowledge has
passed over the mind at too impetuous a pace to precipitate its fertilizing sediment, the intellectual soil
remains for ever barren. To babble of lean philosophy without understanding one of its elements, and
chatter foreign idioms without comprehending gram-
matical structure, such, as yet, are the unsatisfactory
results of modern Argentine education. As of con-
scientiousness, so of the old-fashioned virtue of Obedience, the total neglect of which may be traced to the
false notions of Freedom current in society, coupled
with the absence of all home training. Neither to
parents nor to tutors is that respect rendered which is
their due, the decalogistic first law with promise is a
dead letter, and the Argentine youth have yet to be
taught that man must be subject to regulation, the
more so the higher his social position, that even the
Pope glories in the title of *"Servus servorum"*, and
that Livy in describing the character of that foremost
warrior Hannibal speaks in the following eulogistic
terms of a virtue so shamefully neglected in this Republic, *"Nunquam ingenium idem ad res diversissimas,
parendum atque imperandum habilius fuit."* If however, deaf to the voice of friendly remonstrance, the

youth of this country continue to worship Freedom under false pretences, there is a danger lest the Goddess, doffing her Phrygian cap and throwing it into their midst, exclaim with stentorian voice, *"Take hence your offerings, 'tis not to me but to Licentiousness they belong."*

The Public Press, excluding the technical periodicals, which elsewhere is a mighty educational engine, here reflects the same general want of serious purpose and being altogether of a partisan nature is useless for the instruction or improvement of the community and possesses but little influence; and although at times its writing is characterised by a Platonic style full of classical beauty and adornment, its power evaporates in rhetoric, it is but the lifeless grace of the statue, lacking the vital essence of earnest conviction.

The Roman Catholic Religion is established by law throughout the Argentine Republic, but perfect toleration is accorded to all to meet for the worship of God in any way they may think proper, to build and hold churches, and support clergymen whose functions in marriages, baptisms, &c are respected, and this not alone without hindrance, but even with liberality; the Anglican Church in Buenos Aires was built on a site furnished gratuitously by the Government. The personnel of the established Church consists of one Archbishop and four Bishops, besides a multitude of inferior clergy mainly drawn from Italy and who do not impress as a class; but native theological seminaries

are springing up and will no doubt effect an improvement in this respect: whilst many Irish priests,
some of great eminence, minister to their numerous
countrymen. The Protestant churches throughout the
country are few: one English clergyman in Buenos
Aires, another in Rosario and both supported by their
congregations; a travelling Missionary who visits the
various estancias in the home province, and a medical
missionary in Patagonia, both dependent upon the
South American Missionary Society; four Scotch
ministers, one German, and one American Methodist,
all in like manner deriving support from their respec-
tive congregations; Religion however sits lightly upon
the male portion of the natives as well as foreigners,
but the ladies are very assiduous in the practice of
spiritual duties.

The Argentine Constitution, thanks to the labours
of the two eminent native juriconsults Alberdi and Velez Sarsfield, especially the latter, is one which, culled
from all the best sources of lofty jurisprudence, merits
to be considered, in the letter, one of the most perfect
on earth. On perusing its 110 articles detailing rights
and privileges, attributes and functions, prohibitions
and restrictions, so equitable, liberal, complete, advanced and paradisiac, the conviction gains ground
that the shade either of Plato or Sir Thomas More
must have presided over its birth; and if the Government can only succeed in developing the people, even
after a lengthened apprenticeship, up to this high

standard, then without doubt the Argentine Republic
will be a model for all future time; at present however,
the body politic is by no means in a fit state for self-
government, from lack of moral education, want of
convictions, and from utter apathy. To possess a noble
constitution, filled to the brim with just laws, is one
thing, to apprehend it in a proper spirit and seek to
coincide with it. is another; the Argentines are
assuredly a law-making people, they cannot yet be
styled, without exaggerate euphemism, a law-abiding
people.

According to the Constitution, the National Government consists of an executive, the President and
his ministers, the former of whom is elected for six
years ; a duplex legislature, the House of Representatives with 86 deputies, chosen directly by the people
on the basis of manhood suffage, and Congress with
28 senators who, selected by the provincial legisla-
tures, must posses a property qualification ; and its
jurisdiction is paramount throughout the Republic in
matters relating to the levying of taxes, the construction of railway and telegraphic lines, postal communication, coining money, the raising of armaments, internal peace, the negotiation of loans, foreign relations,
&c., but extends not to the domestic administration of
the provinces, only so far as is necessary to guarantee
the republican form of government, to reinstate con-
stituted authorities when its aid is invoked by them,
or to repel invasion ; and its revenue is secured main-

ly by the proceeds of the various Custom-Houses
scattered along the coast, which are all national property.

Each province is free to make a Constitution for
itself, provided it be in accordance with the republican representative system, and secure Municipal government, primary education and the due administration of justice, and hence with all the paraphernalia
of independent sovereignty the Governor, ministers
and legislature conduct their uncontrolled financial
operations, distinct from the National Treasury, borrow
and impose taxes, very arbitrarily at times : have full
power to foster or extinguish any interest, such as
colonies, banks, &c.; and thus with influence and patronage so extensive, it is scarcely strange that frequent
revolutions occur, which however are seldom attended
with bloodshed.

This dual form of government which is very
costly, onerous and frictional, but whose several rôles
are mathematically balanced by the code, requires
frequent adjustment by reason of the perpetual strife
that agitates its individual components in matters
financial, jurisdictional or political. The National
authorities whilst straining their utmost to follow in
the wake of the United States and to form "*e pluribus
unum*" have hitherto found their path strewn with
difficulties tending to reverse the motto, from the oft-
recurring insurrections of various provinces against
their sway, two of which Buenos Aires and Entre-Rios,
never fully acknowledging the National jurisdiction,

after enjoying for a long series of years a quasi semi-independence, received their quietus in 1880 and were both reduced to a loyal subserviency to national interests.

The funds of the National exchequer are derived chiefly from import and export duties, and, as has been already remarked, the Custom Houses throughout the Republic are the property of the nation ; of these, that at Buenos Aires is beyond compare the richest and as the public revenue is continually burdened by subsidies granted to the poorer provinces, to foster education, construct works of utility or make their budgets and expenses balance, the Porteños (inhabitants of Buenos Aires) have long grumbled that whilst they had to support and make good the deficiencies of, the other provinces, they in return received no *"quid pro quo"*, and considered themselves entitled to an influence in the direction of the councils of the nation commensurate with their monetary sacrifices ; but in the national elections, the rich metropolis found herself swamped and as the last three Presidents, all Provincianos, were carried over her head, in spite of her utmost endeavours to the contrary, the long-indulged dream of withdrawal from the Confederation was attempted to be fulfilled, and in June 1880 the city was fortified, an army of several thousand badly-equipped men raised, and one or two bloody battles fought in the immediate vicinity; but as the conspiracy, though bravely and vigorously conducted, was unsuccessful, was quenched in the blood of the nation, it served only to

rivet her fetters, and thus the last remnant of anta-
gonism to strict federation was swept away, and the
Republic, under her new President General Roca,
looped up another hole, and is now in a fair way to
obtain the object of her deferred ambition, a strong
National Executive. To aid in the accomplishment of
this, nothing further was wanting than the cession of
the city for the capital of the Nation, and this was
loyally granted by the legislature of Buenos Aires
towards the close of the year 1880 : hitherto the National Government had never had a fair chance, not
even a local habitation, but was obliged to live on
sufferance amongst the Porteños, subject at times to
much indignity at the hands of the provincial authorities; but now the long-suffering guests of yore were
transmuted into hosts, and from the 8th of December
1880, the date of the federalization of the city, the
National Government became strongly entrenched, the
days for insurrection against its sovereign authority
vanished never to return, the rising sun of Argentine
prosperity witnessed a stronger grip of the fraternal
hands, and under the brightest auspices the career of
the Republic as a veritable nation commenced, and the
dream of Rivadavia was fulfilled.

As a trained engine to carry out the behests of
the National executive, the standing army merits
notice. It consists of about 20,000 troops including
line and artillery, a considerable portion of which is
constantly employed in guarding the various frontiers
against Indian encroachments. The line regiments

composed chiefly of blacks, creoles or Indians, many of
whom are gaol-birds, are all armed with the Remington rifle and are well-disciplined, hardy troops, full of
martial ardour; the artillery are supplied with Krupp
guns and know how to use them: but officers enjoy
little or none of that social position here which is so
readily accorded to them in England, and yet although
drawn generally from an inferior grade, they are a
chivalrous and brave body of men, amongst whom
may be found many Europeans who have seen considerable service and who give a tone to the profession.
The old palace of Rosas, situated at Palermo, on the
outskirts of the city, serves as a Sandhurst and
Woolwich combined, for the aspirants to military
honours. But in addition to the regulars, every Argentine between 17 and 45 is liable to serve in the
National Guard, so that there are but few of the
natives who have not undergone drill and been taught
the use of the rifle, at some period or other of their
lives; of such, it would not be very difficult to place
in the field 200,000 in ordinary, or even 300,000 in
hyper-critical times: and in order to tempt foreigners
to assume citizenship, any naturalized subject can
claim exemption from military service for a period of
ten years after the barter of his fealty.

Since the commencement of the war between
Chili and Perú, the Argentine navy has claimed more
attention, as the conviction is universally held that
sooner or later a trial of strength must ensue both by
land and sea, between this country and her trans-An-

dine, if not imperial, neighbour, and the manifest
strength of both on the ocean has led to a nervous
increase in the number of Argentine war-vessels,
which now, including half-a-dozen ironclads, a torpedo
boat of the most modern construction, and many
smaller craft, present a formidable flotilla of about 30
ships. That fine old Irishman, Admiral Brown, a
veritable chip of the old-block from which Nelson was
carved, has left an imperishable halo of prestige
around the Argentine marine, which his successors
are determined to maintain. A naval school for the
instruction of officers has been formed on board a training ship, and the President of the Republic holds the
reins with a watchful eye, as commander-in-chief of
all land and sea forces.

CHAPTER V.

RESOURCES—ESTANCIAS—IMMIGRATION

The resources of the Argentine Republic are practically boundless ; whether in gifts or products, above or below the soil, in the air or water, it contains within its own borders everything to minister to the necessities, comfort, convenience and even luxury of man's existence. It is to be regretted however that owing to the embryonic state of statistical science amongst us, clear, definite and concise abstracts of industries and enterprises are not yet within reach of the economist: these to be valuable should be apart from or include Custom-House returns, which do not reflect interior development and are themselves susceptible here of great reform, but which are generally appealed to, rather erroneously, as the barometer by means of which the progress of the country may be gauged; for Customs' revenue is not in direct but rather inverse proportion to internal prosperity. Precis-writing is not practised in this country, for although on the launch of any undertaking, it is customary to witness the speedy inflorescence of a full-blown board of administration with an office full of clerks, and voluminous reports ere the seed is well sown, the whole partakes too much of the nature of the windbag.

This year's forthcoming Exhibition will however
furnish a bird's-eye view of the vast field open to
investment in—precious and useful metals, especially
the rich and universal argentiferous galena, coal, mineral oils, salt, marble, lime, animal vegetable and
mineral dyes, cochineal, ochrous earths, brick and delft
clays, sulphur, kaolin, soda, woods, tanning-barks,
mineral waters ; and in—hair, wool, furs, animal and
vegetable oils, glue, soap, boneash, artificial guano,
hides, tallow, meat-extracts, tobacco, cotton, coffee,
sugar, flax, silk, corn, fruits, wines and spirits.

The above list is susceptible of great increase
both in amount and variety ; for Mining is as yet undeveloped, although the mountain sides are bursting
with hid treasure ; and Agriculture, albeit fostered by
a Department which does good service, in giving sound
advice, distributing unadulterated seed and urging to
fresh experiment, it still a weakling, in spite of the
possession of a virgin soil requiring no manure, no
works of irrigation where deep-ploughing is used, and
which both in chemical constitution and facility of
working resembles that of Lower Egypt, the synonym
of fertility, and in spite too of the manifest success of
the already existing colonies, thanks to the immigrant
farmers. The fact is that the lag of agriculture is
due in a great measure to the disinclination of the
large landholders to split up their property into settle-
ments, as cattle they say pay better; no doubt if the
whole country were cut up into allotments and entirely
devoted to agriculture, in case of general failure of

crops from drought, inundation, locusts (*), storms or
sudden atmospheric changes, universal famine would
threaten, but so fascinating an appearance does Ceres
here present with her level fruitful bosom swept clean
of every pebble, no clearing of land, no laborious
grubbing of forest roots, that although most probably
the plains of the Republic will never be either purely
agricultural or purely pastoral, the epoch is merely
deferred when they shall become a vast cerealic
and frugiferous as well as lanigerous and pellife-
rous region. The same may be said of Manufacture, it is still in its infancy, the profusion of raw
material is powerless in presence of a high rate
of wages, and absence of skilled labour and fuel, so that
it is in the Upper Provinces alone, where immense
distance from the centres of commerce, difficulty
and expense of transit, more moderate remuneration
for labour, and exuberance of wood, determine the
inhabitants to supply their own wants, and not rely
on Europe, as do the littorals, for every simple article,
that the first serious attempt at manufacture is displayed and where, amongst other productions, the
beautiful textures of the fine Vicuña and useful Alpaca, from the rough-made country looms, excite
admiration.

But the great and overwhelming resources of this

(*) So overwhelmingly numerous and voracious are locusts at times that
they not only devour crops, but, enter houses, destroy clothes and boots and
even the woodwork of farming implements and poison the wells; in Santa
Fé the authorities offer 3d. a lb. for their eggs and it is the common employment of women and children to hunt for them.

country lie at present in its cattle and sheep farms, on
which are grazing 15 millions of beeves, 5 millions of
horses, 80 millions of sheep, 200,000 mules, besides
asses, goats and pigs innumerable ; so that every man,
woman and child in the Argentine Republic may be
said to own 6 cows, 2 horses and 32 sheep, in addition
to a proportionate interest in ovnine, capric and por-
cine flesh. It is somewhat surprising, considering the
extraordinary abundance of the thistle, that the ass,
in spite of Squire Hazeldeane and his pound, has not
strayed over these plains in ceaseless numbers ; as
however no Humane Society exists, a report of the
barbarous treatment to which all the Equidæ are here
subject may have deterred him : so common is the
horse, that not even his increased utility saves his
patent of nobility and he is literally beaten and driven
to death, and as for the mare which is never saddled
nor put into harness, she is reserved alone for breeding, treading corn, puddling clay in the brick fields,
as food for the Indians or the manufacture of potro
oil.

But in order to bring these various resources into
play, foster their production and transmute them into
available wealth, the immense opposing distances must
be spanned by other means than the lumbering diligence, the tardy creaking bullock-cart, or even the
nimbler foot of the horse or mule ; and moreover the
different Bolivian, Chilian and Argentine moneys now
current in various parts of the republic must be assi-
milated, as those of weights and measures have already

been, and one currency established, and these are
the problems which the present administration has set
itself to compass, by establishing a Mint, laying out
extensive lines of railway, and uniting all parts of
the territory by means of telegraphic communication;
however, with everything arranged for speed, and the
distance half bridged by rail and steamboat, it still
takes eighteen days for a letter to reach the capital
from Oran, the extreme northern point of the Republic,
that is, nearly the same time as from Europe.

The ordinary method of land-carriage in the camp
is the towering narrow-gauge covered, bullock-cart
with three yoke of oxen, built up on a pair of broad
wheels of eight feet diameter, unstable structures
which are not unfrequently toppled over, or if not
well loaded hoist the wheelers on their own petard;
the driver sits on the shaft-yoke and directs the
leaders by means of a goad of extraordinary length
made of Paraguayan bamboo. As many as 20 or 30
of these sometimes follow in line, forming a caravan
over which a capataz (head-man) reigns with despotic
authority, and creaking and creeping along day and
night at a pace of about three miles an hour, occupy
months to reach Buenos Aires from the far interior.
Near the frontiers these trains are liable to be attacked
by Indians, and so great is the fear inspired by these
wily bloodthirsty savages, that even the soughing of
the wind amongst the Pampa grass is sufficient to
send a thrill of apprehension through the peaceful
procession.

At present the Republic possesses 1,600 miles of railway in full operation, besides two extensions, one of the Tucuman line northwards, and the other of the Andine westwards, in active progress, and for some reason, chiefly the apathy of the British ironmasters, who seem to be indifferently represented here, the two latter are being laid with Creusot French steel rails ; in this country the English appear to lag behind both French and Germans, and need reminding that *"sero venientibus ossa."*

The Electric Telegraph, after flapping its lightning wings along 7,000 miles of Argentine wire and materially assisting the locomotive in developing home industry by its remarkably moderate tariff of eighteen pence for ten words to any part of the Republic, then takes an ocean flight to Europe, messages from which frequently beat time by two hours; and the Post Office, another well-managed department, contributes its aid to the same end at the low charge of 3½d. for every half-ounce of interior correspondence and double this to such foreign parts as are within the postal league. The railways are profitable, but the telegraphic and postal services are still burdensome to the national exchequer, and probably will remain so until the doctrines of Sir Rowland Hill meet with more favour.

No country in the world offers such inducements, as the greater part of this, for the construction of railways, where there are absolutely no engineering difficulties to combat, except in the central and nor-

thern provinces which are mountainous and intersected by numerous torrents, and in the south which,
subject to inundation, is in general swampy : the lines
running usually on a dead level and flanked by ditches
are unenclosed and as animals are so numerous, the
sacrifice of bestial and even human life is very considerable. On all sides are seen the carcases and skeletons
of victims, which the owners, who have no claim
upon the company, take care to skin, but not remove.
A scene of slaughter I once witnessed will for ever
remain engraven on my retina : a train passing our
house down a declivity, at a rate of 30 miles an hour,
dashed into a herd of 150 mares as they were leisurely
crossing the line on their return to rest and fodder
after the labours of the brick-field : they supped with
Pluto ! the train spouting gore and mottled all over
with hair and carrion, was thrown off the metals,
and no battle-field could present so ghastly a sight of
mangled remains.

The Trans-Andine line passing through Mendoza to connect the two oceans, will vie in importance with the Great Pacific of the United States,
and all the railways, not constructed or owned by
Government, enjoy or have enjoyed a national guarantee of seven per cent., with the exception of the
recent extensions of the Great Southern, a remarkably well-managed English interest which, becoming
impatient of exoteric support, has learned to walk
alone.

That the trade of the Argentine Republic must

be such as to add to its wealth and stimulate its
resources is proved by the fact that the exports
exceed the imports by nearly one million sterling,
ten millions of the former to nine of the latter, which
for a young country with but little savings, is a
direct measure of its prosperity and shows that the
vaunt of the late President Avellaneda, was not without
significance, when he declared, that two millions of
Argentines would rather starve than leave their public
obligations unliquidated; in fact, with a revenue of
four millions derived chiefly from imports and the
sale of public lands, and a debt of only fifteen, light
taxation and all the elements of civilization based upon
illimitable means, with moreover a race of intelligent
and honorable statesmen at its head, the position of
the country is sound and need excite no uneasiness in
the minds of any of its bondholders.

In speaking of agriculture a comparison was instituted between much of the soil of this Republic and
that of Egypt, but there all resemblance ceases ; no
hostile irruption of the dreaded Hieso here stamps
contempt on a hated race and occupation ; pastoral
life is held in the highest honour, and to be styled an
estanciero, especially a rich one, is a title to such
nobility as the country aspires to and the loftiest object
of Argentine ambition.

The native estancia proper deals only in cattle ;
but within the last forty years the sheep, introduced
first by Scotchmen, has thriven so wonderfully, principally under the care of Irish shepherds, that now, as

the grasses in the home counties have been refined by
long bovine occupation, the timid bident has usurped
the place of the bellower and neigher, and driven them
thence, northwards, southwards and westwards to
pastures new ; some estancieros however still endeavour to combine both elements.

Different grasses are required in the two cases :
cattle demand the cortadera or pasto duro (hard Pampa grass), which being long and losing all succulence
after flowering is completely unfit for sheep, which
must have the pasto blando (soft grass), The former
becomes converted into the latter by stocking, so that
beef is the avant-courier of mutton : but of course by
ploughing and sowing the change is effected more
quickly ; the usual economical plan of refining coarse
gramineous vegetation is to sow mixed seed of either
barley or wheat with alfalfa (lucerne) and the grain
coming up first may be cut for fodder or reaped to
pay expenses, whilst the alfalfa remains to exterminate
the roots of all indigenous growth.

Some model estancias such as Urioste's in Arre-
cifes, Hale's at Tatay, Carril's in Mercedes or Dorre-
go's 200 miles westward of the capital, the last of
which takes hours to drive round and has accommodation for 250 puestos, yielding an income of 8,000.£
a year, would be considered very fine establishments
even for an English gentleman-farmer ; in such, a
high style of living is maintained, but on the whole,
comfort and elegance are sacrificed to profit, as it is a
camp maxim that "to appear well-off is dangerous."

Time was indeed when the rich estanciero, in default
of chairs, was found squatting on an ox-skull, in the
midst of an almost furnitureless mud cabin quench-
ing his thirst with maté and satisfying his hunger with
the out-door asado (roast), supremely indifferent to
appearances; but now, owing to the greater security
afforded by wiring-in properties and the general invasion of luxurious tendencies, the better-class modern
estancia-house is usually well-appointed. Although at
present by equal subdivision at death and a general
rise in value, especially in the province of Buenos
Aires, estancias are generally contracted to the moderate dimensions of a square league or two, in former
times much larger unenclosed tracts of twenty up to
one-hundred were not uncommonly massed together
under one owner, and even now such is the case at
very remote distances from the metropolis. A central
small village, containing the various dwellings for the
family who are usually absentees for six months of the
year, those for the peons (labourers) under the orders
of a capataz, corrales (cattle enclosures), galpones
(outhouses), with an adjoining monte (plantation),
yielding fruit and fuel, and a garden for vegetables
and flowers, the whole at times belted by the scraggy
eucalyptus or the towering poplar, forms at once a
landmark on the distant horizon and an hospitium at
which the traveller is sure of a welcome either to
refresh or pass the night; an " Ave-Maria" at the
gate is the magic watchword which gains instant ad-
mittance to a haven where, whatever else is wanting,
well-bred courtesy is not.

It is usual to plant a puesto (shepherd's hut) on every 120 squares (500 Acres), an allotment sufficient to maintain a flock of 2000 sheep; but as the land is becoming enclosed and each post acts as a constable, the services of the puesteros are gradually being dispensed with, whilst the land is found to carry more stock.

The price of estancia land has increased at least five-fold during the last few years and the time has gone by when every wax-match struck to light the cigarette was considered to represent a square yard. A league can now be bought at from £50 to £5000 according to grass, permanent water, and distance; nay in Oran on the banks of the Bermejo, in the extreme north of the Republic, 20£ will suffice to purchase that amount of extremely fertile territory; whilst in the far west 200 miles from Buenos Aires, land with permanent water may still be obtained for 600£ the square league, and in the Cuyo provinces for 280£ with, or 100£ without it. A square league, when stocked with sheep alone will carry from 5,000 to 50,000, or if of mixed grasses, 10,000 to 20,000 sheep and from 500 to 1.000 head of cattle, besides mares and saddle horses : and a profit of 25 to 50 per cent. may be expected from a really well-managed property. The camps of the province of Buenos Aires, especially not very distant from the capital, are subject to much competition and command a very high price; yet even here the profits must be considerable, as men are found to grow rich by working on

capital borrowed at 12 to 18 per cent., which numerous scriveners are ready to advance at those rates;
but in the interior, the estancias, which are much more
moderate in size as well as infinitely less expensive to
purchase and work, yield at the same time a much
higher return: here there is absolutely no competition and exceedingly small risk from drought, storm
or locust, so that 2,000 head of cattle to the league
and an insatiable market in Chili for which buyers
arrive to pay extremely high prices for fat beasts, a
man with £1,000 invested in the business may soon
retire with a fortune, or if preferred, half that sum
will conduce to a like result when laid out in sheep
nearer home.

One great reason of the growing difficulty in
obtaining camp near the capital arises from the fact
that agriculture, which can afford to pay an annual rent
of 7/- to 8/- an acre, is beginning to usurp the sites
formerly devoted to sheep and cattle farming, and
so the stock-raiser is banished westwards where the
lands, not being subject to inundation as are those of
the south, are yet endowed with permanent water and
hard and soft grasses of such prolific growth as almost
to prevent locomotion by twining around the horses'
feet and legs; still as the Western Railway will soon
be in possession of an extension from Bragado to Lin-
coln and Lavalle, with a branch to join the Andine at
Villa Mercedes, these western camps will then enjoy
direct communication with both the Atlantic and Pacific
and recompense estancieros for their exile. Where

there is complete security, pastoral life is the rule, but near the frontiers there is a tendency to agriculture, which diminishes the temptation to robbery and hence to murder.

A remark has been made that the profits on an estancia range from 25 to 50 per cent.; but the losses, at times severe, are occasionally overwhelming, due in the one case to the carelessness of shepherds at the lambing season, and in the other to drought, inundation or the complete absence of any protection for the animals on the open, bleak, treeless Pampas, in case of a storm. The fact is, estancieros prefer a " campo limpio " (a camp with no obstacle to break the view), so that they object to grow trees on their lands and are equally averse to them near their dwellings, as they shelter robbers and render their approach unseen; but as losses of late years have been so frequent, the demands of arboriculture meet with more favour, and extensive montes to serve as a refuge from the tempest are about to be planted. Should a hurricane of cold wind direct from the Antarctic regions arise, accompanied by rain or sleet, both sheep and cattle are invariably driven before it, and if in lean condition from previous drought, there is scarcely any limit to the loss, a case which actually occurred in August 1880, when half a million of cattle and several millions of sheep succumbed to a two or three days' storm and piled the camp with their carcases.

A few years ago no attention whatever was paid to the improvement of breed either by selection or the

importation of fresh blood ; the sheep with its short
coarse wool and scanty carcase, the ox with its flaccid
hide and osseous build, the horse with its narrow chest
and scraggy quarters, were all allowed to degenerate
by indiscriminate admixture, until all trace of their
parentage was lost. Who, on looking at the Pampa
mustang could credit his descent from the noble Au-
dalusian ? although to give him his due, with the loss
of form he has certainly gained endurance : what new
arrival straight from Cotswold, the Downs or the Fens,
has not mistaken the flock of miserable dirty sheep
for a drove of pigs ? or been amazed at the watery-
looking bovine structures all run to bone, horns and
hoofs ? Now however a new era is dawning, the first
streaks are already visible; almost every steamer
brings English, French or German blood-stock, which
meets with ready sale up to £200 for a stallion or bull,
and is now common on every good estancia ; stud-
farms of high repute have been for some time in
action, notably those of Kemmis for horses and Nazar
and Elia for horned cattle and sheep ; races with
heavy stakes for the encouragement of breeders, and
a Rural Society with its annual exhibitions and medals;
all are striving unitedly to transform the Aurora into a
meridional splendour, when even Albion herself will
be unable to compete with Argentine stock or wool,
when with sheep at 6 -, horses at 4£, and cattle at
£2, instead of devoting to the vats of the graserias
(tallow melting establishments) the surplus of mutton,
or to the Saladeros (meat salting places) the superabundance of beef to feed Brazilian and Cuban slaves,

a live cattle trade with Europe shall flow from these shores to demonstrate the unlimited producing power of the country and to enrich the lucky investors in so profitable an enterprise.

Life on an estancia is one of the freest and most enjoyable perhaps on the face of the earth. The European accustomed to strict limitations on all sides, perceives everything on such a grand scale ; the land bounded in every direction only by the bright blue vault of heaven, the immense herds and flocks, the wealth that grows unbidden, the abundance of saddle horses, the exhuberance of game, the free and hospitable welcome, the absence of formalities, of any trammel to action or control to motion, and the vast silence; and these so impress him that for the first time in his life he begins to experience what freedom is and drinks to the full of the delicious exhilarating draught; hereafter the compression of town-life becomes distasteful ! and it is astonishing that the English who are fond of bucolics do not avail themselves more extensively of the opportunities offered them here of not only indulging their propensities but at the same time making the most of a moderate income ; instead of the hundreds now scattered throughout the camp, including one baronet, many retired army-officers and the remains of that gigantic bubble the Henley Colony, hundreds of thousands might prosecute a pleasant and profitable existence. And yet the life of a working estanciero is not all smiles : to a certain degree of rough freedom are linked at times hardships, priva-

tions and losses; formerly it was very much the
custom to smoke, drink and play cards the livelong
day (and night), letting the sheep and cattle out of the
corral in the morning, bestowing no thought upon
them during the day and saddling up at sundown to
bring them back; but to-day, steady, intelligent industry is required here as elsewhere to command the
future.

To enjoy the camp, early rising is indispensable;
to sniff the deliciously fresh air, bound over the plain
and plunge into the laguna, arroyo (running stream),
or river, 'ere the bloated redfaced orb yet peeps over
the horizon or gathers strength for his maddening
midday career, is the great camp stimulant, although
there are many more not quite so salutary.

Riding over the estancia on a tour of inspection,
in which, although animals generally take little notice
of a man on horseback, but frequently (especially
cattle) pursue one on foot, the continuous roll of the
horses' hoofs disturbs the watchful Teru-tero (*Vanellus
cayennensis*); the majestic Stork (*Ciconia maguari*); the
lovely Ibis (*Ibis chalcoptera*); or the flame-plumaged
Flamingo (*Phœnicopterus ignipalliatus*); and crowds
of wild wood pigeons fast flying to their feeding
grounds match the whir of the small quail-like partridge (*Nothura maculosa*) (*) as she springs from

---

(*) The *Nothura maculosa* is a solitary bird and is never found in coveys,
whilst the large partridge (*Rhynchotus rufescens*) the size of a hen pheasant
is now only met with far out.

beneath our feet; whilst the bulky Chajá (*Chauna chavaria*), lightened by the immense size of its air cells, rises like a lark to heaven's gate, all the while screaming its ear-splitting calls to its mate ; and the Fly-catchers, the glowing Churinchi (*Pyrocephalus rubineus*), and the Scissor-bird (*Milvulus tyrannus*) with its aspen-like caudal forceps, after performing evolutionary antics in the air, descend with closed wings to settle on the nearest thistle-head to digest the tit-morsel and then off for another capture; whilst the *Progne chalybea*, which arrives at the latter end of August and departs again in March, darts hither and thither in numbers. As we proceed, the skulking Fox (*Canis azaræ*) shows its bushy tail and sneaks off on its prowling errand (*); almost every covert makes us unpleasantly aware of the presence of the Skunk (*Mephitis suffocans*); the shamming *Geositta cunicularia* strives to divert attention from its nest ; and the wise-looking little puffing Owl (*Pholcoptynx cunicularia*) turns its knowing head, but refuses to budge as the fast friend and faithful gatekeeper of the Biscacha (*Lagostomus trichodactylus*), but as its patron is doomed to rapid annihilation (**), the sage little Lechuza will no longer be lodged free of expense, but

---

(*) Here the vixen usually has a litter of eight and not of four as in Europe, which accounts for the great abundance and destructiveness of the fox family.

(**) A well-known gentleman after purchasing four square leagues of land for $300,000 was obliged to spend $315,000 more to get rid of these pests.

left to rely upon its own resources, as is the case up
the country. On reaching a puesto, we dismount to
accept the offered maté (*Ilex paraguayensis*) which is
sucked as a sweetened boiling infusion from a gourd
through a bombilla (silver tube) and scorches the lips
of the unwary, but is to the initiated a grateful morning draught. Nor are the insect and reptile worlds
less active! swarms of hungry house-flies, mosquitos,
bees, wasps and ichneumons cloud the air; of the
Lepidoptera the most common forms are the *Fritill-
aries, Colias lesbia, Callydrias, Danaus Archippus* and
the Peacock; but on the river banks *Papilio Thoan-
tides, P. Perrhæbus, P. Lycophron, P. Cleotas, Eury-
ades Corethrus, E. Duponchellii, Acrea mamita, Itula
Ilione, Heliconia Phyllis, Morpho epistrophys* and other
stray specimens from the north may be encountered;
ants innumerable, especially the large black one
(*Æcodoma*), whose clean-cut lanes, filled with hurrying
leaf-bearers, intersect the sward in every direction and
who seems indifferent to weather, whilst the roasting
sun excites beyond toleration the already fiery nature
of the small red one, so that any vessel is rapidly
cleared of them by mere exposure to its direct rays :
but the whole persistent tribe are a great curse to any
vegetation that is not indigenous, as well as to household stores. Here the hypocritical *Mantis religiosa*
pretending to a devotional attitude, is all the while on
the watch for its prey, there the Green Lizard (*Tcius
viridis*) scampers by to its hole to keep company with
the numerous beetles (*Scarabcidæ*) which beneath, as
the Caranchos above, are the great scavengers of the

camp. In the damp grass may perhaps be perceived the leering eyes and mottled black and green body of the huge Esquerzo (*Ceratophrys ornata*), whose gaping mouth crammed with the body of an unfortunate sapo (toad), surmounted by threatening horns inspires terror; this said Esquerzo bears an awfully spiteful character and is credited with the deaths of many children at least; his appearance is certainly against him (*), otherwise he is perfectly harmless: on the other side, scudding along the hedgerows to their burrows are the funny little wild guinea pigs, the Quisos (*Cavia aperea*), whose hair falls off on being handled; and if in the neighbourhood of a stream, a whole army of fresh water Chelonians may be observed standing erect and motionless but suddenly splashing into the water at our approach. Proceeding leisurely on our return homeward through the monte, the impenetrable hedge of Pitas (Flowering alues) attracts notice, some of which sending up stems crowned with flowers to the height of thirty feet would grace Kew Gardens; the pretty merry little wren (*Troglodytes furvus*), which carries its tail in a more reputable manner than his English relation, is chirpingly creeping up the stems in search of insects; the branch is visible covered with blood, whereon last night the Opossum (*Didelphys Azarœ*) was shot as she lay in wait for poultry or eggs wherewith to regale her

---

(*) When angry the Esquerzo swells to double his size; one in this condition irritated by boys with sticks was seated on the rails at Flores, when a locomotive passed over it and it exploded-like a cannon.

pouched young; the thievish formidable looking
Iguana (*Podinema Teguexin*) rushes along the ditch
to conceal itself amongst the knotty Ombú roots; or
perhaps a glimpse is had of the venomous Ophidian, a
true viper, the Vibora de la Cruz (*Trigonocephalus
alternatus*) which carries a black spot in the form of a
cross on its head, one of the few venomous snakes
found in this province; or the graceful Humming-
bird (*Trochilus flavifrons*) darting from flower to flower
in rivalry of the bee which is sometimes cultivated
extensively so as to yield an annual profit of £500 or
£600; the *Cicadæ* are very noisy and almost every
tree is covered with the Basket-worm (*Æceticus
Kirbii*), as well as every trunk bored through and
through by the destructive larvæ of a species of the
Lepturidæ (*Bicho taladro*), whilst the magnificent
green caterpillar of the *Ceratocampa imperialis* wends
its way over the poplar leaves, and the pretty little
tree-frog is by no means uncommon.   The soft melody
of the " *Columba picazuro* " reaches us from the tops
of the lofty talas, the smart crimson-crested carpintero
(*Chrysoptilus cristatus*) rests its weary body, supported by its tail, against the trunk, and the oven-like
mud nest of the fearless Hornero (*Furnarius rufus*) is
dotted here and there on the fencing posts or the
various forks, whilst the sweet whistle of the Cardinal
(*Paroaria cucullata*) greets our willing ears, and the
Pitangus bellicosus madly striving to dislocate its
neck, at the same time erecting its crest and crying
"Bien te veo," makes known to the other air-denizens
of the monte that "his eye is on them;" whilst the

harsh screaming Uracas (*Guira piririgua*) in flocks assail the intruder with their deafening cry; so then picking half a dozen apricots or peaches, as we near the house, the savour of the ten o'clock breakfast assails the nostrils and we behold those camp scavengers the knavish and pugnacious Chimango (*Milvago chimango*), the wary Carancho (*Polyborus brasiliensis*) and a cloud of timid gulls quarrelling over the offal of the newly-killed (*) sheep which with hard biscuit and French wine presently serves for the morning repast. Soon after breakfast a siesta is found to be necessary as the sun has gained such strength as to hush all nature to rest during his midday course; if then the sportsman feels inclined to take his gun, he need fear no game laws, and quarry is abundant: on the lagunas the Black-necked Swan (*Cygnus nigricollis*), the *Cygnus coscoroba*, and very numerous species of Duck, Grebes, and Waterhens: on the banks the Nutria (*Myopotamus coypus*); or in the open, by moonlight the Biscacha, which if not shot dead invariably jumps up into the air and falls into his hole again out of sight; Batatuz (*Limicola brevirostris*) the best bird in the country for the table, a real lump of exquisite fat; Chorlos (*Rynchœa hilaria*); large and small Doves; endless Pigeons; the large Tinamou (*Rhynchotus rufescens*) and the smaller *Nothura maculosa* both delicious eating when served with white sauce, the former equal to a pheasant, the latter to a

---

(*) For in the camp no such thing as high meat or game is ever eaten everything must be cooked almost immediately after being killed.

quail: and on the outer camps the *Rhea americana*
and *Cervus campestris.* In the autumn when the
thistle seed is down, the partridge and other birds get
so fat that they are unable to fly and fall an easy
prey : the natives ride round them in rapidly narrowing circles (*) until the birds becoming bewildered,
they quietly slip a noose from the end of a stick over
their necks, in fact lasso them. The water-fowl battue
is conducted in a similar unsportsmanlike manner : as
no game take notice of a horse, but a man on horseback, especially if he carry a gun, is observed, and if
on foot, such an unusual spectacle creates alarm and
wildness, the huntsman dismounts and walking on the
off side of the horse, quietly directs him to browse his
way within gunshot of the game, when any number
can be potted.

The whole plain of the Pampas has but one fauna
and therefore what is found on one estancia differs
but little from that encountered on any other in the
province of Buenos Aires : no climatic or other physical agents are at work to produce differentiæ, but the
avi-fauna is perhaps the least subject to variation. The
parting of flocks and herds, the washing, dipping and
shearing of sheep, the branding and castrating of cattle
and horses, are all very busy and at the same time

(*) Like the solitary Irishman in the American War of Independence
who took three Hessians prisoners and when asked by his commanding
officer how he accomplished such a feat replied, "By surrounding them your
Honour."

merry seasons in the camp and remind one in some way of the harvesting at home.

As only two meals a day are taken in the country, dinner is always welcomed with an appetite and takes place immediately after the cattle or sheep have been penned for the night in the corral, and sometimes the dishes served are rare to European taste: the Peludo (Armadillo) although an insect feeder is very much esteemed and justly, as when roasted whole in its shell and served up with seasoning and lemon, its flesh, which is very white, reminds one of fine veal, inclining to pork: the young of the Biscacha likewise, a grass feeder, very much resembles rabbit.

The lighting of the lamps is the signal to the sleeping insect world to arise, the tocsin for Mars and Venus and so well answered is the summons that without zinc-wire blinds to windows and doors it is almost impossible to sit at table. The air is literally alive with Beetles, Grasshoppers, Neuroptera, Moths, Mosquitos, many of the Hemiptera and Diptera, some of whom are armed with stings; the Common House fly is an equal pest by day; centipedes and spiders, cucurachas (cockroaches) and the insect-feeding bats (*Gymnorhini*) are common, the first act as a barometer, never appearing on the walls except in the case of approaching rain; one or two of the Arachnidæ are formidable in size, but otherwise harmless, yet whatever is repulsive looking is always venomous in the eyes of the natives; the cockroaches attain great bulk though by no means so disgusting in appearance and

habit as the English black-beetle ; Scorpions are
occasionally met with but not longer than an inch and
a half ; the field and house cricket chirp as in Europe :
the Luciernagas (Fire-flies) dance in myriads in the
air and the little familiar glow-worm lights her pale
lamp in the grass ; the Bicho colorado (Red Mite) a
species of *Tetranychus* buries under the skin and is
especially attentive to strangers, its attacks cause
intense itching which nothing will relieve but scratch-
ing until blood flows and then applying either ammonia or spirits of wine. As for mosquitos which are
bred in intense masses wherever there is water, especially in wells and algibes (underground cisterns) and
swarm all over the Republic, comprehending perhaps
thirty different species, some of which fly by day and
others by night, man has no rest from their ceaseless
persecution: it is common to see good housewives
patrolling the different sleeping apartments candle in
hand and applying the flame just beneath the quies-
cent culex as it rests on the wall, invite it to a "felo
de se" which it never refuses. The "*Pulex irritans*"
and the "*Acantha lectularia*" are here excited to the
utmost limit of their productive powers, and even
ladies can scarcely sit still on a chair without involun-
tarily pursuing the less noble of the two nasty para-
sites ; to enter a house that has been closed for a few
days ensures an instant cloud of them on the lower
part of the dress. But infinitely more disgusting than
either of the two former vermin, is the Vinchuca
(*Conorhinus infestans*), the Pampa Bug, found all
over the Republic, an oval chocolate-coloured flat

disked insect that poises itself directly over the bed
on a thatched or other roof and deliberately drops
upon you during sleep and may be found in the morning on the walls, no longer a flat disk but a globular
bloated mass, and many are the marks thereon to indi-
cate a succession of vindictive squashes from the
various victims' slippers.

It is the custom in the camp for the native puesteros (shepherds) to come up to the estancia house in
the evening and singing some plaintive ditty accompanied by the guitar, ask permission to enter; and the
family within remaining quiet listeners till the completion of the refrain, the door is then flung open wide
and they are ceremoniously welcomed. Then begins
the nightly ball, for dancing is universal throughout
the country, and as the Pampas have stamped the
Gaucho a native-born Poet, he seizes the intervals for
extemporizing and like the Trobadours, Bards and
Minnesingers of the Middle Ages, to the melancholy
strains of his lyre, sheds a halo over fact and fiction,
hits off the peculiarities of dress and feature, winding
up with compliments to the host and family; midnight usually arrives and not unfrequently cockcrow
ere the departure of the guests puts an end at once to
the dancing and drinking.

The Puestero life whether native or foreign destroys much of the romance of Virgil's picture; Meli-
bœus is here a myth, the enchanting old-world cartoons
of the love-sick swain, with his crook, lackadaisically
watching the pretty sheep or indulging in silly amours,

are out of place; contact with the reality rudely destroys any such hallucination. The camp gospel may
be said to consist of the triad, Horseracing, Gambling
and Drinking, the God that inspires it, the Argentine
Pan is indeed a mightly spirit, but his true name is
Gin and in the atmosphere of his "adelphic" inspiration, Europeans rapidly degenerate.

Although estancia-house life is generally safe on
account of the number of people moving about, it is
not always so; in fact far otherwise, with that of the
foreign puestero, at any rate in the province of Buenos Aires. Many of these are very respectable, simple-
minded men lately arrived from Europe and intent
solely upon an honest and industrious pursuit, and
this very simplicity it is that marks them as the quarry
of the gaucho malo; for such pigeons he lies in wait,
and on them he expends all his cunning treachery.
Sundown is especially a dangerous time, 'tis then the
wretch, after a day passed in slumber, rises like a
wild-beast to make war upon the industrious, knowing
that the shepherd will be absent from home penning
up the sheep or cattle for the night, and so both his
residence and person will be found without protection.
The three following instances, which are true to the
slightest particular, will illustrate at once the cunning
of the Gaucho and the want alike of justice and protection to life and property that still exist in the province of Buenos Aires.

An inoffensive Irishman and his wife living near
Mercedes were about to retire soon after sundown,

when up rode a gaucho accompanied by a woman who appeared to be in labour and by her moans attracted the pity of the good-natured pair, who readily assented to their dismounting and occupying the kitchen for the night. The apparent husband then anxiously enquired of his hosts whether they knew of any woman in the neighbourhood who could be of service and the willing Irishman volunteered to proceed in search of such ; of course directly his back was turned, the feminine disguise was thrown off, the Irishwoman was bound and the house sacked.

A worthy priest in Buenos Aires had a brother settled in the Western Camp, a remarkably steady, sober, intelligent man who had lately brought a young and beautiful wife from Ireland and begun life as a sheepfarmer.   Hearing an "Ave Maria" about sunset, he walked out of his house and found an old grey-headed Gaucho who enquired if he had seen two bullock carts pass that way, but not being able to speak Spanish well himself directed him for information to his assistant an able-bodied Irishman, who was then driving the sheep into the corral.   Unfortunately the husband preceded the gaucho and upon nearing the corral, the latter thinking he had now secured both victims, suddenly drove his knife through the heart of the one, and at the same moment rushed upon the other who, being unarmed, fell an easy prey.   The poor young wife who was an eye witness of the double murder fled for her life: the assassin turned plunderer and when subsequently confronted by the wife before the Juez de Paz (Justice of the Peace), although she swore the fellow was wearing her late husband's boots, the judge was afraid to convict the tiger, lest his own should swell the already long list of eighteen assassinations with which the monster was credited.

On another occasion the wily gaucho met his match. An acquaintance of mine residing in the camp was summoned one moonlight night in winter by "Ave Maria's" uttered from the tranquera (bar across a roadway) and proceeded to open the door to enquire what was wanted, when he beheld three muffled gauchos with their horses' heads over the tranquera and apparently a woman about fifteen yards lower down the road. They enquired the way to a neighbouring town, and put many frivolous questions, but when they found my friend would not be enticed from his door, where a loaded rifle stood ready, then the woman began to whine and complain of being ill and begged him to bring her a glass of water; if he had done so, the three in advance would have been off their horses and into his house, whilst he was fooling after a sham woman with a glass of water, but being an old hand remarked, that on such a cold night a glass of icy water was a very bad thing for one in her condition and winding up with a ¡ Vaya, no mas! (Begone), slammed the door and went to bed. It is such scenes as these that are bringing to a rapid close the era of the ancient hospitality of the camp. The rural police, as a body, are notoriously in alliance with the worst characters, so that however anxious a country judge may be to do his duty, until that force is purged of rogues, no hope of anything like justice, especially to foreigners, can be expected. The Gringo (foreigner) is considered fair game and the gaucho malo pretty well lives out of him: besides this he hesitates not to take his life, knowing well that if arrested, a short imprisonment is all that awaits him; but on the other hand, if a foreigner shoot a marauding native, with all the influence of powerful friends and the payment of a heavy fine, an incarceration for six months at least is his fate. However the present vigorous government is fully alive to the urgent necessity of reform in camp administration and the first step no doubt will be to ensure that those that wear the livery of the law shall not be the foremost breakers of it.

There are two principal means of developing a country of exhaustless area; one from within, by promoting internal communication and education, removing restrictions from commerce, and rendering life and property secure; of these we have spoken in the previous pages: the other from without, by fostering an immigration which shall add permanently to the producing power of the nation. Argentine statesmen have not been slow in an earnest appreciation of some of the internal factors of progress, but have hitherto failed in a great measure in surrounding life and property with that sacred inexpugnable rampart, without which no interior or exterior measures can be of much real avail.

The promiscuous immigration that has as yet flowed to these shores, although providing a useful class of industrious workers, is scarcely of such a nature as to add to the greatness or character of a nation ; nor has it afforded such material as in the present synthetic condition of the Republic, a wise master builder would put his hands to, in order to rear up the political structure of a great people. An influx however profuse of the Latin element, especially of an inferior class, even if permanent, can scarcely aid much in strengthening and elevating the existing nucleus, but as it is notoriously fleeting and unwelding, the advantages of its cooperation are but temporary and insignificant. To add stability and resource, to assist in raising the moral status and give a permanent increase and physical stamina to its population, this country requires to intercept some portion of that stream of hardy, home-loving, law-abiding, agricultural and pastoral races which throng the ports of Northern Europe to seek elbow-room and found new Lares in the United States or Canada. Hitherto diversity of race and religion, insecurity, distance and expense, as well as general ignorance of the advantages offered, have formed insuperable obstacles, which only need liberality on the part of the Argentine government to smooth or altogether remove.

Half a century ago, a pioneer Scotch colony was formed at Monte Grande near Buenos Aires ; it failed and the colonists were dispersed, but their descendants are now all prosperous : subsequently a spasmodic

influx of foreigners took place, until the last score
years when a steadily increasing, spontaneous stream,
principally of Italians, set in, which amounts at present to about 50,000 per annum. A central department of Immigration exists in Buenos Aires, with
branches in all provincials capitals, an Intelligence
office where the newly arrived may obtain every information, an Asylum where such as desire it may secure
food and lodging gratis for a few days, and moreover
the department is ready to forward immigrants free of
charge to their destination. Further than this the
authorities, although disposed, have not as yet determined to favour the immigrant, in spite of the numerous and generous schemes of settlement which have
been broached from time to time. The Italians finding here an identical religion, a race and climate
resembling, and competence easy of attainment, bring
with them habits of extreme industry and parsimony
and in a few years generally retire to their native land:
they form the chief labouring and artisan classes, prosecute market gardening and invade the lower branches
of commerce. Since the termination of the Franco-
German war, a very notable increase has been observed in French immigration which, though not generally of a high class, consisting principally of retailers,
hair dressers, cooks and waiters with a sprinkling of
mechanics, is more permanent than the Italian. The
number of arrivals from Spain is very fitful yet considerable, composed chiefly of Gallegos and Basques
who are absorbed in commercial and domestic service,
or in union with the Italians engage in ministering to

the food supply. From all other sources the influx of
population is insignificant in amount, although perhaps
of greater relative importance: the English, as merchants, stock or sheep farmers and clerks, hold a position second to no other foreign community, which
they maintain by their capital and intelligence; whilst
the growth of Irish influence and wealth in the home
Province is perfectly astonishing; to them is due almost
the very existence of sheep in the Republic and many
of them starting almost without means have become
millionaires; and scarce a steamer of Lamport and
Holt's line, but brings recruits from Erin to share the
general prosperity. The Teutonic immigration, though
of somewhat feeble dimensions, supplies by sagacity
and industry what it lacks in number; engaged purely
in commerce, for which they have such aptitude, the
Germans enjoy a reputation in this market which will
not culminate short of the zenith.

Speaking generally, the Argentine Republic offers
perhaps more advantages to immigrants than any other
region on the surface of the earth: but such a statement to be true will have to be very much modified
when applied to the case of any individual race or class.
To the Englishman of capital, there is no doubt the
general enunciation would be found to be absolutely
true in its entirety, provided he acted under sound
advice: to one possessed of very moderate means, from
£500 to 1000£, and willing to work, most probably
fortune would smile equally upon him, under the same
condition; but the English artisan, mechanic or la-

bourer without means, unless under a distinct engage-
ment to their own countrymen resident here, would
be, to say the least of it, very heavily handicapped
against the Italian or Frenchman. The only possible
way in which emigration hither could be advantageous
at present to the British industrial classes, is to form
colonies, as the Welsh and Russians have done;
splendid land in fee could be obtained gratis from the
present government and under experienced directors
success could then most undoubtedly be predicated.

CHAPTER VI.

BRAHMA—VISHNU—SIVA

To decipher the past, read the present and predict the future of the Argentine Republic fully, demands inspiration from the triune Vedic God; but as without the divine afflatus, the landmarks of its history are so visible, the tendencies of to-day so patent, and the shadows of the morrow so lengthened, to guage its existents or cast its horoscope, requires but little judgement in the one case or sagacity in the other. If the country has as yet but a brief past to boast of, that little has been stormy and dates from the 9th of July 1816, the day on which, in Tucuman, the thirteen united provinces declared their independence, when its political life was ushered in under sponsors of giant calibre. A long and heavy chain, of what are commonly called calamities, enveloped the Republic from its very birth and reached its climax, when the gaucho Rosas seized the reins of power and eclipsed the nascent sun of liberty for seventeen long years; and glancing backwards upon that gloomy period from 1835 to 1852, all else is dwarfed in the bloody glare

of the holocaust of victims, which rises as an obelisk
to mark the epoch, when this modern Attila was
let loose as a scourge, to prepare the people for en-
franchisement. Anarchy, revolution, tyranny, exile
and bloodshed, both before and after the time of Rosas, even up to the present : what is the writing on
the wall? what the rendering? the fact is when the
act of independence was signed the bulk of the people
were in a semi-barbarous state, utterly incapable of
comprehending their position, to say nothing of political fusion : each district had its caudillo (chief)
elected much as in the days of Saul, feudal lords perpetually at strife, and so the struggle after homogen-
eity, which is an inevitable law of nature, rendered
these violent means necessary : thus it has always been
in the world's history with nationalities in similar
stages of growth. By what means did any European
nation become conglomerate? by the very same as the
Argentine : the only difference is in the rate of fusion.
In America, and in modern times, nations as individuals arrive at maturity earlier, society seems focussed.
So of the monster Rosas, colossal antagonist as he
appears, he is but a means to the same end : do we
seek the details of his atrocities? they are paralleled in
the annals of the fourth, fifth and sixth centuries of
the Christian era.

Thus then for the last sixty-five years, through
an apprenticeship of much suffering, has the Argentine Republic struggled after its "ignis fatuus;" yet
all the while, as opportunity offered, laying, in the

midst of her throes, brick by brick on the fundation of
the temple of Unity, until at the latter end of the year
1880, the building suddenly rose into proportions, the
keystone was fixed and the bright-blue banner of a
nation unfurled to greet a consolidated homogeneous
people emerging like Venus from a sea of foam, "*clarior
e tenebris*", to assume its majority, whose fraternal
strife, buried on the battle-field of the Corrales, snapped
for ever the spirit of Anti-Nationalism, sounded the
knell of the Gaucho and rendered the shocks of this
political *gymnotus* harmless for the future. The social
horizon presents to view the rapid growth of a refined
and luxurious civilization, which serves to embellish
society, cultivate the taste and attract foreign sympathy, and which conspires with political manhood
and security to foster sound industrial development,
at the same time that it is the direct result of it; and
yet we do not behold that strange anomaly of Mammon allied to abject Poverty, the palace contrasted
with the hovel, fine linen with rags, which is so painful to observe in England : nor although wealth is one
of the chief distinctions between classes and therefore
a power, is Poverty esteemed, as in England, a crime ;
but the great bulk of the population, contented and
happy in the midst of plenty, is singularly free from
crime which is very generally the offspring of want.

The Argentine Republic is a vast field for unrea-
lized possibilities, as everything, except politics, is in
its infancy : it possesses all the elements physical and
moral destined to form a great state, ample field for

individual or collective speculation, at the same time
that it is, of all other South American countries, the
best adapted for European immigration; by accessi-
bility, richness of soil, absence of obstacles to cultivation, a climate more than benignant, easy acquirement
of land in fee either by purchase or gratis from the
government, an air of freedom from the tyranny of
many European customs, the welcome extended to old
and young alike, the charm of native manners, and an
abundance of the necessaries of life. There is a say-
ing that a foreigner who has learned to roll up the
paper cigarette never leaves these shores; indeed faith
in the country is the orthodox creed of every stranger
that treads them; certain it is, that those who do
return home with the determination of remaining,
generally belie their intentions and are found in a few
months cropping up again, the victims of an indefinable magnetism which this country exercises : and yet
there is, at the same time, an unaccountable ignorance
in England, as to the geography of this Republic, its
character and resources and the advantages it holds
out to those who seek a home within it : thus a York-
shireman long resident in this country told me, that
on his return home, a short while ago, his friends
crowded around him with the astonished exclamation
"Why! thou'rt not black then!" a remark, in spirit,
characteristic not alone of the manufacturing districts.
If the English had only kept this country when they
took possession of it, or had listened to the proposition
of Alvear, presented by Belgrano and Rivadavia in
1815 to become a British Colony, then without doubt,
it would be better known and appreciated.

The political future of this vast territory, at whose birth presided a race of patriots, need inspire no uneasiness; the herd of politicians who succeeded the conscript fathers, have just terminated their era of injury and obstruction ; and the Juggernaut of public opinion looms up in all its terrible massiveness, demanding self-abnegation in her public men and threatening mercilessly to crush the obdurate, wild and selfish ambition of party faction. As for the material advancement of the Republic, little sagacity, as has been before remarked, is required to apprehend that ; travel over her millions of fertile acres musical, as yet, only in part with the lowing of cattle, bleating of sheep or the creaking of the plough ; inspect her boundless wastes hereafter to become smiling gardens ; sail up her mighty rivers idly pouring their mobile waves into the insatiable ocean ; ascend her mighty mountains filled to the brim with precious treasure ; breathe to the full her magnificent climate ; then witness the thousands, ere long the hundreds of thousands, streaming into her lap ; the long lines of foreign shipping already jostling her harbours ; the activity of her ports ; the intelligent and busy races that throng her cities : the wealthy phalanx of alien merchants ; the increased credit of the nation ; the light taxation and heavy budget ; the bulky imports and yet bulkier exports ; and say whether on the Earth's surface there is a spot where Nature is more generous or Progress more assured.

Speculation may enter perhaps into the question

of the future race and language ; but although the
country is heavily weighted with an already heterogeneous population which, in descent, disposition, culture
and habits but not interests, is manifold ; yet it seems
tolerably certain that the whole discrepant human multitude destined to fill her bosom, will in course of time
become homogeneously welded ; in fact the process,
like geologic change, is slowly taking place before our
eyes, especially on the littoral, where we view, as in
a kaleidoscope, race inequalities and lines of demar-
cation becoming less pronounced, nay slowly evanesc-
ing, new forms gradually emerging. and what was a
bare anatomy progressively clothed with the complex
tissue of the living physiology. Of all families, the
Latin possesses, par excellence, the faculties of absorbing and moulding, whilst the influence of foreign per-
meation reacts in a lesser degree upon it, and climate,
food and physical characters are unostentatiously
lending their aid to digest and assimilate the crude
mass : Prometheus directs the transformation, preparing his plastic material and modeling a new type; taking the bone, sinew and muscle, the blood, energy,
character and vital force of the European ; the lively
sensibility of the Frank, the solidity of the Teuton,
the dogged perseverance of the Anglo-Saxon, and the
frolicsome humour of the Kelt and infusing them with
the polish and amiability of the Argentine, is slowly
precipitating a Godo-Pelasgic race, which with the
heaven-born fire of the philosophic, poetic and Platonic native, the more practical and sober yet subtler
intellectual flame of Europe, is destined to give birth,

in this Arcadia, to a galaxy of Statesmen, Orators, Juriconsults, Savans, Architects, Painters, Poets and Musicians, who shall nourish the souls and strengthen the minds, as will its acres the bodies, of the civilized world.

It is, in fine, as safe to predict a great and noble future for this country, materially, morally and intellectually, as it is, to announce that the sun will rise tomorrow.

CHAPTER VII

BUENOS AIRES

Most cities revere the memory of their founders,
but in vain do we scrutinise Buenos Aires for a monument to Juan Garay, who in the year of grace
1535 set forth from Asuncion with a handful of men
to plough her foundations and lay the memorial stone
which still exists at the Western angle of the Cathedral
façade. Mementos of Argentine heroes are not wanting, so far is military renown antecedent to civic
virtue, and yet Don Juan may well not grudge these ;
his claim to an apotheosis reposes on the simple "*cir-
cumspice*" which reveals amongst the delicious fragrance of a "¡Qué buenos aires !" (what a delicious
climate !) of the early Spanish settlers, a magnificent
city of palatial piles, thronged by 250,000 souls, the
offspring of his far-seeing faith. The city of Buenos
Aires rears its majestic head in Lat. 34° 30′ S. Long.
58° W. stretching for four miles along the right bank

of the mighty La Plata, and as the now acknowledged
capital of the Republic aspires to the title of the Athens
of South America.

Placed with its breast reclining on this broad
estuary of 30 miles, at a distance of 120 from its
mouth, and at an elevation of scarce 40 feet, with
exposed anchorage in two parallel roadsteads, and a
river on either side into which coasters can run for
protection in foul weather, it would be particularly
well situated for commerce, did not the water shoal
rapidly shorewards, so much so indeed, that a man
can walk for half a mile or more directly from the
beach at low water with the flood barely above his
knees ; and in consequence ocean steamers have to lie
from twelve to fifteen miles from the port exposed to
all the fury of gales, which although not very frequent are powerful and dangerous. Several years
since very excellent plans for a secure port, harbour
and docks were submitted by the famous hydraulic
engineer Frederick Bateman, which although shelved
for a period through impecuniosity and local jealousy,
must eventually be carried out.

After passing through a crowd of shipping from
all parts of the world, to a foreigner approaching
Buenos Aires from the river, the city looks very imposing and massive : its whitewashed buildings and
lofty church domes reflecting the sun-glare over a low
but extensive coast-line, stand out in bold relief against
an intensely blue sky and flanked and fronted by
bright-green foliage, the whole inspires a thrill of ad-

miration, which unlike the case of Eastern cities, subsequent experience does not altogether dispel ; yet if the tide be out, although strictly speaking there is no regular tide but, on account of shallowness, ebb and flow are at the beck of the winds, supposing the traveller to have reached the inner roads by a small tender to the ocean steamer, he will have his patience further exercised by being transferred to a boat and after rowing some distance, again to a cart in order to reach terra firma, and this in spite of three moles which jut out about a thousand yards each, two for the disembarcation of passengers and the other for custom-house merchandise.

On landing, the endurance of the stranger is apt to be taxed by the jargon of tongues and noisy insolence of the peons (porters) who seize his luggage; but it is pretty much the same in most large ports, although the officials here, with hangers by their side, keep the turbulent throng somewhat in awe.

As in all cities planned by Spaniards, the streets run at right angles to one another, one set parallel to the coast line, thus cutting up the site into so many squares like a chess board, each side of which measures 150 yards, and many of them bear the names of Argentine heroes, or record political events; and this topographical form produces such similarity at all the boca-calles (crossings), that a stranger has great difficulty in finding his way. Buenos Aires covers an area of six square miles which although the streets are usually no more than twelve yards broad is considerably more than the same number of inhabitants would occupy in Western Europe, due principally to the many houses which still retain the ancient style of ground floor only with azotea (flat) roof, the existence of patios (internal courtyards), and in the suburbs, to the gardens with which almost every house is provided.

Formerly the paving of the streets was execrable, both in the roadway and on the footpath, in fact ten or twelve years ago, a lady could scarcely traverse on foot even the central parts of the city; to-day however, the principal thoroughfares through which tramways pass are well laid with adoquines (cut granite blocks) brought from the island of Martin Garcia, which lies in the fork of the Rivers Paraná and Uruguay, and the pathways flagged; and although but lately, at a little distance from the centre, the paving was pretty much in a normal condition, so that the Persian maxim was reversed, and it became by far pleasanter to walk than ride in a coach over the jolting highways of the city, that is being remedied and soon the whole capital will be paved with cut stone; as for the outskirts pedestrianism being disagreeable, wet or dry, the English miss their daily constitutional, which at home contributes so greatly to their robustness.

As three companies vie with each other in illuminating the streets, the lighting of the centre of the town is admirable, almost equal to that of London; nor are the outskirts neglected; for six miles from the

Plaza Victoria in every direction the main roads are lined with gas lamps, and even the outlying streets are no longer subject to the glimmering of villainous kerosene.

With regard to the water supply and means of sewerage; no city in the world requires a more ample provision of both, inasmuch as it is built mainly on rotting, festering rubbish, honeycombed every few yards by cesspools and has no natural drainage, owing to the feeble lay of the land. Will it be believed that it was the custom until very lately, on laying out new streets or paving for the first time those already exist- ing, to seek, by the direct permission of our city Ædiles, a secure and wholesome foundation by spread- ing over the surface the basura (house refuse) to the depth of two or three feet? "Rubbish may be shot here!" was a very general invitation and freely ac- cepted. Frequent insecurity of buildings is one of the necessary consequences, and not long since the prin- cipal city railway terminus, erected on such a basis, was within an ace of tumbling about our ears. These facts, coupled with the insufficient artificial water sup- ply, are enough to inspire apprehension in the minds of the thoughtful; in fact nothing seems to save the city from becoming the habitat of scathing epidemics, but the fineness of the climate and the periodical heavy semi-tropical rains. Bateman's scheme before referred to, comprehended a plan for ample water- supply and perfect sewerage works, both of which were abandoned, some few years ago, in a half finished state, owing to a severe monetary crisis, but which will forthwith be resumed by the present administration. In a warm climate like this abundance of water is a prime necessity, and the present supply is obtained from the existing water-works, algibes, wells or direct from the river.

The present water-works, which were constructed several years since, were planned for a city of about half the present number of inhabitants and in consequence are found insufficient, although completely effective as far as they go. They consist of filtering basins and reservoirs, a pumping house and a huge cistern supported on iron pillars a hundred feet high, erected on the highest spot in the city. The pipe-water is found to be wholesome, but the office-charges are high.

In the algibe (underground cistern), which is dug in the centre of one of the patios, generally the first, of a capacity of 100 hhds. and rendered water-proof by Roman cement, is collected the rain-fall from the azoteas ; and if the roof is not swept before rain, or even if that precaution be taken, the liquid is generally very impure, but when allowed to settle becomes limpid and palatable (*) ; at rare intervals however it presents a black appearance indicating, on analysis, the presence of a substance much resembling volcanic scoriæ, accompanied by a smell of sulphuretted hydro-

---

(*) A live tortoise *(Platemis Hilarii)* is frequently kept in the algibe to purify the water.

gen. The pipes which lead from the roof to the algibe
are so arranged that the supply can be regulated and
any surplus turned on to scour the marble patio, a
precaution which omitted, sometimes results in the
bursting of the cistern by the intense pressure. Again,
the water obtained from wells scooped in ground such
as I have pictured, stands a great chance of being
infected with decaying organic matter filtering from
the cesspools, and is therefore used in the city only
for cooking purposes; and as the banks of the river
for miles are occupied principally by coloured lavan-
deras (washerwomen) vigorously plying their trade on
bended knee and empting their greasy ooze into it;
and plunging into its waves, all the horses of the city
take their matutinal bath therein (*), the supply,
hawked in butts on wheels throughout the city at a
penny a bucket, although cheap cannot be considered
salutary, especially when the wind is off shore; so
that for all these reasons the need of a pure water
supply for drinking purposes is evident.

The importance of keeping clean the surface of
the streets, especially in the centre where men and
horses most do congregate, is well recognised and a
corps of sweepers daily employed, so that that part of
the city, at any rate, may be considered free from the
imputation of neglect : moreover a basura service of
one hundred carts is daily engaged in traversing every

(*) It is a remarkable fact that cracked hoofs are unknown in the River
Plate, and this is due entirely to the regular morning bath.

locality, the drivers plying lustily the knockers and
shouting into each open doorway "Basura!" to warn
the cooks to bring thither the daily refuse, which is
carried outside the city and burnt: it serves also to
rid the town of many of the yelping mangy mongrel
curs which infest the streets, whose bodies, poisoned
by the police or thrown alive into the carts, form a
part of the daily sacrifice : and as amongst the canine
race Hydrophobia is not uncommon in the hot season,
a policeman may sometimes be seen with drawn sword
pursuing a hapless victim or mounted lassoing it and
then galloping up and down the street, the poor dog
meanwhile bounding at the horse's heels until its
brains are dashed out, a further contribution to the
basura Moloch ; and if this otherwise irreproachable
service were conducted in the early morning instead
of, as at present, at all hours, the ears and nostrils of
the citizens would be greatly relieved. Here too is
not unknown the ancient fraternity of rag and bone
pickers, for the rubbish being farmed out as in England, and well examined by them before being burnt,
much useful material is turned to such account, that
a young man who used to purchase from them merely
the rags alone, baled a sufficient quantity to yield him
300 £ a year profit ; nor is this surprising as the Porteños are perhaps the most wasteful people on the
face of the globe, both in food and dress ; the latter
when soiled or needing only a little repair is tossed
at once into the basura box.

London is generally admitted to excel in the variety of her street cries, and yet they are comparatively so musical and soft that the ear soon gets accustomed to them; but for genuine lung power and grating discordancy, nothing that I ever heard there, can compare with the hawkers' chorus in Buenos Aires; the howling of a thousand Mycetes in a Brazilian forest could alone approach it. From sunrise to sunset, and even onwards, vendors shout their wares in such appalling tones, tramway cars toot so excruciatingly on cows' horns, that with the paroxysmal clangor from the church steeples, the prolonged blast of the icecarts' fog-horns, the morning and evening lowing and bleating of cows and goats with their tinkling bells, the barking of dogs, the rattle of the fast-driving carriage, the rumbling thunder of the heavy cart, the explosion of the bombs and crackers from newspaper offices, the whistling of the police, and the nightly grinding of the wheezy barrel-organ "*never ending, still beginning;*" they produce an uproar, aggravated no doubt by there being no escape from it, as the doors and windows all open and the rooms generally on a level with the street, admit even to the very penetralia a clamor which maintains the nerves in a state of perpetual irritation.

CHAPTER VIII

BUENOS AIRES

BUILDINGS—QUINTAS—PLAZAS—MARKETS—PLACES OF AMUSEMENT

The public buildings of the city and suburbs, although not remarkable for architectural beauty, are at least lofty, spacious and imposing; but the best points of some of them are altogether lost by virtue of the narrowness of the streets. Owing to the lack of proper stone, they are all built of brick, plastered, and soon become covered with fungoid growth, which disfigures them and necessitates constant colour washing. Amongst the Catholic churches, of which there are twenty, the Cathedral, occupying with the Archbishop's palace almost one side of the Plaza Victoria, merits the first notice as the seventh in point of size in Christendom. It consists of a Byzantine dome rising 130 feet over a Latin cross, with a Greek façade adorned by twelve Corinthian columns and is a noble structure, although disfigured exteriorly by two blemishes, the bas-relief in the tympanum whose perspective resembles the Chinese, and the utter want of proportion in the steps. The interior however, with its twelve side chapels, especially when lit up on any gorgeous festival, presents a remarkably brilliant spectacle.

The remaining churches, with the exception of Santo Domingo, call for no special notice, except to remark that the majority are surmounted with a cupola and many have a monastery or nunnery attached. The temple of Santo Domingo, situated at the crossing of the streets Defensa and Belgrano, contains certain historical mementos, the sight of one of which brings a tinge of shame to the Englishman's cheek, when he views hung from the dome the tattered remains of four of his country's flags, the sombre pall of that ill-starred expedition which, in 1807 under the incompetent or traitorous Whitelocke, dragged England's honour in the dust: the other memorial however simply provokes a merry twinkle of humour in his eye, when the grave and reverend Dominicans attached to the church point upwards to the tower and show how signally Heaven intervened to stop those heretical balls, fired by the English ships on the same occasion, and which to the number of twenty four are now embossed on its faces.

The new Post Office, *"le petit Louvre,"* standing in the Plaza 25 de Mayo, which may be considered the finest building in the capital and the only one that has any pretensions to design, is very complete too in internal arrangement and decoration, and includes within it the grand terminus for all the National Telegraph lines: to this we may add as worthy of notice the Hypothecary and Provincial Banks and the Moorish Cabildo (Town Hall) just restored with a Greek face, and then some huge masses of plastered masonry, such as the rambling government House, the quaint looking pigeon-holed Custom House, the two Opera houses and five theatres, two fine English-built Customs' deposits, Hospitals, Lunatic Asylum, Monasteries, Orphanages, Mendicants' Home, Barracks and Arsenal : and just outside the city, a couple of miles or so northwards, the old palace of Rosas now converted into a Military School and the magnificent Penitentiary erected at the enormous cost of £350000 and which is a close copy of that at Pentonville.

But if the public buildings of the city disappoint, not so the private, on which are lavished a degree of taste and ornament to which Paris, Genoa or Venice may not be strangers, but which excite surprise and admiration in South America, where so short a period has sufficed to transmute the tolda of the Indian or mud rancho of the gaucho into an exquisite marble palace.

The old style of dwelling is the Roman, consisting of a ground floor alone, with azotea roof, wide and lofty folding doors and barred windows, and rooms of high pitch leading into one another from the inside, so that from the street, when the interior doors are open, a view may be obtained from one end of the house to the other. These rooms enclose one, two or three patios into which they open ; the first of which, paved with black and white marble from Italy, is almost severed from the second by the comedor (dining room), a cross room which leaves only a narrow exterior passage for ingress or egress ; the second and third are paved with either French tiles or bricks. The apartments flanking the first on two sides are devoted to reception and fitted up showily with Parisian furniture : those in the second are bedrooms and of the third servants' rooms and domestic offices. This azotea-house of the past is the most comfortable in existence, delivering from the tyranny of the staircase and providing plenty of fresh air by night and day ; if too hot, an awning can be drawn over the patio, and by closing the doors and window shutters, so as not to admit a ray of sunlight, the very reverse of the English plan, the rooms can be made as cool as a cellar ; living in such a dwelling is a perpetual picnic ; and as the front patio is filled with rare plants, its walls adorned with gaudy creepers and the fountain cools the atmosphere, the fragrance of flowers mingles with the vitality of the air to administer gratification to the senses ; whilst the railed azotea, looking down upon the street, invites to the evening stroll, a tête-à-tête with the cigar or to quizzing the foot-passengers. But the days of this style of residence are numbered ! fated the delightful Arabic roof ! doomed the dear old patio ! the fiat of omnipotent taste and fashion, deriving their inspiration from Paris, has gone forth and the demands of commerce are respected. Magnificent structures of two or three storeys, in the severest Italian style, faced with Greek pilasters, throwing out flying balconies and adorned with fantastic arabesque and profuse mouldings, are rapidly replacing the simple dwelling of the past, stamping out all trace of native architecture and transforming Buenos Aires, in spite of its straitened thoroughfares, into a European city of great splendour. In these palatial buildings, the ground floor is reserved for those grand bazaar-like shops, whose deep bowels, absorbing the ancient patios, are filled with the choicest goods of Paris and London and blazing with gas attract a crowd of gazers from amongst the evening loungers who nightly throng the fashionable streets of Florida, Victoria and Perú.

But if the town houses are rapidly acquiring a severe and lofty tone somewhat chilling to freedom and checking exuberance, the Quintas (suburban villas) remain in all their charming simplicity and sympathy. The environs of the city are studded with these delightful retreats for rural repose, which consist usually of a dwelling of moderate pretensions, surrounded by three or four acres of ground maintained in the highest state of cultivation under French and Italian gardeners. Here the English annuals flourish to a degree unknown in the Old Country and all varieties of European and semi-tropical flowers and fruits, with the exception of the *Primulaceæ* among flowers and those fruits belonging to the genera *Ribes* and *Rubus*, come to great perfection: strawberries, grapes, figs, peaches, apricots, nectarines, pears, pomegranates, and both sweet and water melons, are positively a drug. As the hawthorn

in England, so the Peach-blossom here, tinges the
landscape with its tender hue and sheds its luscious
fragrance through the air, to herald the approach
of Spring. All the forest trees of Europe succeed,
but those of quick growth, such as the Eucalyptus,
Paraiso, Willow, etc. are preferred, although they,
especially the first mentioned, sterilize the ground
completely: shrubs too, in particular rare and valuable
tropical ones, grace most of the quintas. But if the
gardens blaze with blossoms and flowers, the culinary
plants are very prolific and grow to a great size: the
potagerie is a department to which great attention is
paid, the ordinary vegetables of Europe are always
found on the table, and in addition, others such as
sweet-maize, yams and pumpkins. Sweet-maize (cho-
clo) when boiled is eaten from the cob, holding it
between the two hands, as a dog a bone, and notwithstanding the inelegance of the attitude, is a very delicately sweet morsel ; the various species of the pump-
kin are likewise much esteemed, one of which reaches
such an enormous size as to weigh more than 50 lbs.

Many families remain all the year round in their
quintas, but they are chiefly foreigners, as the natives
prefer the city as a winter, and the country only as a
summer residence.

For a people so devoted to pleasure as the Bonac-
renses, with such a multitude of foreigners in their
midst, especially of the gay French who are passionately fond of promenading in a throng, and a city
worse off even than London in the confinement of her

streets, it is absolutely necessary to be provided with
lungs, wherein the bulk of her population boxed up
during the day in offices and shops, may parade in
order to breathe the cool evening air, enjoy a little
simple recreation and gain health. To this end, thirteen
Plazas (public squares), averaging about four acres
each, and one public garden, are laid out, adorned
with flowers, shrubs, trees, walks and fountains, and
supplied with seats for the public convenience. Of
these the Plaza Victoria, so named in honor of the
defeat of the English in 1806, claims supreme attention, as situated in the centre of the city, containing
within its precincts the Cathedral and Archbishop's
palace, the Town Hall (Cabildo), Law and Police
courts and the two antique Moorish Recobas (arcades),
and as forming the site of all public spectacles. The
Cabildo with a date of 1710 was until lately, before
the opening of the Penitentiary, the great city prison,
and when a few years ago an adjoining cellar was
unearthed, large quantities of human hair were discovered, the sole remaining record of the times of the
Inquisition. Of the others, two only deserve notice,
the Plaza Constitucion at the South end of the city,
and the Once Setiembre at the West, averaging about
sixteen acres each: the former, the great wool mart
for southern estancias, the latter, for those to the
north and west; and here may sometimes be seen
hundreds of bullock carts piled with wool, hides and
skins, waiting for their contents to be inspected and
bought, for which purpose the brokers are astir early,
driving down to those localities in their tilburies even

before sunrise. All the Plazas form places of resort for the general public for promenading or business and unlike the squares in London are unenclosed and accessible to the people in every part.

As the character of a people may be partly determined from the nature of their food and how they cook and eat it, it is necessary to speak first of the markets and what they offer. From five to eight every morn· ing may be seen pretty well all the cooks in town, both male and female, wending their way to one or other of the six markets with which the city is furnished and returning with a changador (porter) laden with supplies of meat, fish, fowl, game, poultry, vegetables, eggs and fruits for the day's consumption ; as for laying in a stock, even of meat, for more than one day, such a thing is never dreamt of, as the Porteños are extremely sensitive to any thing at all stale, and for the same reason all poultry are purchased alive, a dead turkey, goose, pigeon or rabbit would not be looked at : so much does this custom permeate society that every pound of sugar or quart of wine and other like necessaries are obtained from the almacen (store) as required. The cooks are provided by the house stewards with money for the purpose and $100 (15/-) is the usual moderate daily expenditure on these articles for a medium-sized family, but the method offers great temptation to pilfering, which is not unfrequently taken advantage of. No butchers' nor greengrocers' stalls are allowed outside the markets, so the refuse is localised and the city kept cleaner : all the *abattoirs*

too are without its radius and heavy fines would be
impose 1 for slaughtering within. At these markets
there is always a full supply of mutton, beef, veal and
pork; the first of which costs about 6/- the carcase
without, or 8'- with the fat; the three last about 3½d
per lb.: the mutton is good but small, more like Welsh
in size, but inferior in flavour; the beef, insipid and
watery, does not please English palates, a disfavour
which is aggravated by the barbarous way in which
it is cut up (*); the veal is tasteless and the pork is or
ought to be eschewed, as the pigs are fed chiefly upon
the off.d of the killing-grounds. Several kinds of
fish, not exposed on marble slabs as in London, but
hung up on tenter-hooks, tempt the gourmand to expend 1/6 on 5 lbs., especially the Dorado (*Salminus
maxillosus*) of golden tint and not unlike salmon in
firmness, flavour and colour, growing to a size of even
100 lbs.; and the Pejeré (*Atherinichthys bonaerensis*)
which, delicate and white-fleshed, is very similar to
whiting in taste, and reaches a size of 5 or 6 lbs.; this
fish is striped longitudinally on each size the whole
length with a broad silver band, and its fry, when
treated similarly, can scarcely be distinguished from
white bait. According to the season, wild duck especially the Red-billed (1/6), a magnificent bird for the
table, Batatuz, Chorlos, Beccasine, large (1/-) and
small (6d) Partridge, Turkeys (5/-) very abundant

(*) As an instance, the sirloin is completely spoilt; the under-cut called
"lomo" is stripped from the vertebræ of the animal and sold for beefsteaks!

and fine eating, and Geese (4/-) which do not seem
to thrive, are very common ; and of Fowls (2/6) and
eggs (1,6 a dozen) there is an extraordinary consumption. Vegetables and fruits, cheap, abundant and excellent, are raised by the market gardeners in the
environs of the city, a hardworking race of Italians,
whose heavily-laden carts, may be heard rumbling
along the streets in the early morning on their way to
Covent Garden ; but the oranges, bananas and pine
apples are supplied chiefly by Brazil, and although
shipped green, nevertheless entail a loss of about five
per cent. on the first ; Montevideo too contributes by
steamer early strawberries and a most delicious liques-
cent water-pear of great size, equal to anything I ever
tasted in Europe. The early peaches are pared as an
apple, but the later the Freestones are delicious lumps,
which scarcely bear handling, but melt as soon as they
drop into the expectant mouth; oranges too are usually
stuck on a fork and pared with a very sharp knife and
the first is always presented to a lady at the table.

Closely allied to the market supply, are those of
bread, milk and butter; the bakers, who deliver the
first thoughout the city in carts, are a numerous fraternity and provide, from Argentine flour, all the
loaves known in Europe, besides the pan-criollo (flour
kneaded with milk), a delicately-white small round
one, which when fresh, yields an appetising bread.
Native made biscuits, like native made beer, have
driven the foreign from the market; but muffins and
crumpets, of which an Englishman preserves so lively

a remembrance, are not as yet down on the *boulan-
gerie* programme and await the advent of some enterprising Briton.   Milk and butter are furnished principally by robust-looking Basques, long files of whom
may be observed on horseback travelling many leagues
daily, irrespective of weather, along the public roads
converging to the city, and carrying six large tins
slung in leather saddlebags, so that the butter is
actually churned en route by the motion of the horse;
besides these however, cows and goats in numbers
patrol the streets morning and evening: but withal,
such a thing as cream, let alone Devonshire cream, is
never seen in this country.

As the Porteños, although no Sybarites, are yet
urgent in their demand for varied amusement and
that generally of simple character, the places and
opportunities for its indulgence are numerous; two
Opera Houses, five Theatres, the Coliseum Concert
Hall, a Skating Rink, many *Cafés Chantants*, the Florida Gardens, Palermo Park, two Race Courses, Flo-
ral Exhibitions and Cattle Shows, and a Rowing Club,
in turn minister to their gratification.   It sometimes
happens in the season that both Opera Houses are performing at the same time, but although the Opera
going public here is very numerous and respectable
as well as intelligent, to support two companies is
beyond their resources, The larger, the Colon, devoted
to Italian Opera, reminds one somewhat of huge
Drury, and although of course of lesser dimensions,
has a really fine well-lighted interior capable of seat-

ing 2,500 persons and when, as frequently the case, crammed with beauty, so brilliant is the *coup-d'œil*, that no stretch of the imagination is needed to remove the scene to London or Paris. The empresario (lessee) does his best by producing a *repertoire* that puts us on a level with the most favoured cities of Europe, and his companies, which are always respectable, frequently include a star of the second or third magnitude at least : and to such artists as show any ability the Argentines are exceedingly generous. The lesser is an elegant, comfortable, well-ventilated and lighted house of smaller capacity ; and out of the season both are let to various exhibitors. Of the theatres, one is appropiated to Spanish Zarzuela (Farce) by true Madrid companies, which is about the only opportunity presented of hearing Spanish spoken in its purity ; it is not however extensively patronised as Spanish low Comedy lacks incident, the players, dresses and scenery, are inferior, and the forte of the Porteños lies not in humour. Another is occasionally dedicated to the Spanish Drama, which likewise languishes, and at other times to political meetings ; a third to French *Opera-bouffe*, which always draws a full house ; and the last, the Politeama, a large and well-built structure in fact the largest of its kind in South America, was lately erected, as its name implies, for varied exhibitions, representations and entertainments ; an Italian circus at present occupies it.

All the theatres in Buenos Aires contrast very favourably with the close, ill-ventilated and uncom-

fortable London dens, into which managers there are
allowed to pack their audiences like sardines; the min-
imum of space and air, the maximum of discomfort
and heat, are not Argentine postulates; and the Opera
and Circus especially, to which the refined Bonarenses
are chiefly addicted, might well afford, in these particulars, a model for our friends at home.

The Coliseum, an elegantly proportioned Music
Hall, with good acoustic properties, adorned with
frescos of merit and capable of seating five hundred
people, is the home of classical music, where the Germans frequently delight society by the masterly way
in which they render high-class symphony. To gratify a lower taste, *Cafés Chantants* are found in almost
all the principal streets ; some however have been
closed on account of the noisy scenes they created and
the very broad innuendos in which they indulged; they
are pretty much the same in all civilized cities and as
the latest expression of a sensualistic cosmism, if not
capable of eradication, should be kept under strict
police surveillance and no young persons admitted.

Roller-Skating introduced some ten years since,
has at last become possessed of a building of its own,
and as it seems to have taken firm hold especially of
the juvenile portion of the population, and is still flourishing, will probably remain a permanent institution,
if Fashion, which is very fickle in the Plate, ordains
not otherwise.

Out-door recreation has been spoken of in connection with the Plazas, but the late afternoon drive

to Palermo Park and subsequent evening visit to the
Florida gardens eclipse the mere promenade as sun-
shine the glow-worm. Hither all Porteños who keep a
carriage or horse hasten to offer their evening sacrifice,
and in the glowing beams of the setting orb, all the
beauty and fashion of the cap'tal are focussed. A
drive of about three miles north from the city leads
to an antique-looking Moorish archway, on passing
which a lengthened vista of a mile an l a half is presented to the view along a beautiful well-watered macadamised road fifty yards wide flanked by footpaths
and lined throughout on both sides by Palms and
other rare trees; a grand avenue leading direct to the
majestic river. To see and be seen is the avowed
motto and rigidly and gracefully is it accomplished:
dashing forward, pursuing, drawing up, awaiting,
creeping beside, passing, crossing and all the other
arts, that coachmen instigated by flirts understand, are
practised, until the carriages at last arrange themselves in two parallel lines one on each side of the highway and a general pause ensues: many of the ladies
descend to promenade in the beautiful gardens adjoining, other prefer to remain as some favourite cava-
lier reins up at the carriage door.

As exclusive, nay almost as brilliant as Rotten
Row is the Palermo Park Road on the afternoon of a
Sunday or other feast day: no sniff of the "*oi polloi*,"
no republican cart or other lowtoned vehicle, invades
these precincts; the police are there to guard the
sacredness of the upper ten, the very dust is laid to

shield their beauteous skins, the prancing of the highbred cattle, the brilliantly appointed coaches to the
number of some hundreds, the cream-like complexions,
enveloped in the latest Parisian fashions, the flashing
eye, the air, the grace, the charm, the free masonry
of the restless Fan, which in the hands of the Porteña
is made to speak, ever fluttering, contracting, expanding; all point to a nobility of wealth and refinement
which lacks but the coronet to consummate. The
coachmen, chiefly French or blacks, although fault-
lessly got up, are very objectionable in the eyes of an
Englishman: they know not how to handle the rib-
bons, but seizing them in both paws, saw the horses'
mouths like an odontophore, smack their whips in
true postillon style and are continually irritating the
cattle. many of which costing £200 the pair are valuable. Equestriennes are very rare, the ladies although they practise riding in the camp, prefer in
town the carriage, in which their toilettes are not
disarranged, and which by long habit has become
their home, as they scarcely ever even visit on foot.

This park, situated about three miles from town,
close to the river, and which formed the old domain
of Rosas, was in his time filled with majestic trees
and rare shrubs and plants brought from all quarters
of the world. The vanity of standing well in the eyes
of Europeans was the motive of many of his measures;
he declared he would show them a park superior to
any in the Old World and this led him to expend his
country's means by laying under contribution the

whole earth to feed his ruling sentiment: further, so
carefully were the plants and trees nursed that numbers of prisoners, and there was no scarcity of such
during that reign of terror, sponge in hand, were kept
constantly employed in washing off the dust from the
leaves, so that no tree but what had one or more black
crows suspended in its vivid green : no wonder then
that in his time Palermo Park was one of the sights
of the Republic. Now however all the old hoary
trunks have been laid low with their master, others
have been planted and the gardens planned in modern
style, with artificial lakes, rustic bridges, mounds,
caves, walks and drives, intersprinkled with abundance
of flowers, and dotted here and there with houses,
enclosures and cages containing vicuñas, llamas, ostriches, rheas, capybaras, eagles, vultures, agoutis, pec-
caries, condors, guanacos, pumas, jaguars, monkeys,
Patagonian hares &c.; thus making it the nucleus, and
a fine one, for the establishment of Zoological gardens
on an extensive scale as, being confiscated property,
it is capable of indefinite extension. In the immediate
neighbourhood, nearer the water, but still within the
park boundary, lies the English cricket ground, whence
may be heard at intervals the joyous sounds of "well-
caught," "butter-fingers," the clapping of hands at
some unexpected mishap, or the sharp click of the
slogging hit, as our countrymen, heedless of the
galaxy of beauty almost in their very midst, pursue
the manly game that remains still a mystery to all
other nations. The Park likewise encloses on the
north-west the Rural Society's permanent Exhibition

buildings, artistically constructed of wood, a society
that has done much for the refinement of cattle, horses,
and sheep and still further merits the gratitude of all
holders of fine stock by the introduction of an Argentine stud-book. Further north, about a mile distant,
is the fine Hippodrome, with grand stand to match ;
this with another racecourse about five miles on the
south side of the city, affords the Bonarenses an opportunity every feast day of witnessing horseracing subject to European rules and also of indulging in the
national passion for betting on something like a fair
basis.

Through the very centre of the Park, on a level
crossing, runs the Campana railway, the great outlet
to the interior provinces; and separating the gardens
from the cricket-ground, the Northern line, likewise
on a level crossing, leading to the Tigre, a most delicious spot about 20 miles from the capital, abounding
in shady islands full of fruit, intersected by multitudinous streams, on which and in which, on Sundays
and Feast-days, many Britons disport themselves.
Here is the station of the English Boat Club and the
site of the annual November regatta ; whilst at the
south end of the metropolis, on the Riachuelo, the
Buenos Aires Rowing Club (likewise English) has
established itself and given birth to an offshoot, in the
shape of a native Marine Club, which threatens to
become a formidable rival to its parent.

One measure of civilization, as we have remarked
before, is the food ; another, the road. Hitherto the

majority of the highways near the capital, have been allowed to remain completely neglected and unrepaired ; now it is proposed, and no doubt will soon be carried out, to provide the public with a fine macadamised Boulevard 60 yards wide and lined on both sides with trees and footpaths, so as completely to encircle the city and divide the jurisdiction of the Province from that of Buenos Aires, which has lately become subject to the National authorities. This will furnish at the same time another fine drive and promenade for health seekers and necessitate a thorough organization of the whole of the Metropolitan roads, so as to cause them to reflect the advanced civilization of the capital.

Whilst the richer classes are enjoying the fashionable drive in the lap of luxury, those with humbler pretensions take advantage of the liberality of the tramways to obtain a mouthful of fresh evening air in the suburbs : for one fare (about 3d) the passenger, provided he does not alight from the car, may enjoy the round trip, and as one of these extends at least ten miles, it affords a sufficiently long course for the purpose.

The remaining place for outdoor recreation is the Florida Gardens, a quite modern but successful attempt to introduce hither the exterior musical life of Paris or Vienna. Although in the city, and laid out with flower beds and shrubs, with a covered central orchestra and reserved seats, there is still room for 4000 promenaders, which number is not unfrequently present. The moderate charge of 2,'- entitles to a chair and to the enjoyment of the first-class music under the direction of a Jullien, which combined with the ices and other refreshments, make this a very favourite resort.

CHAPTER IX

NATIVE INHABITANTS — FOREIGNERS

The present population of the city of Buenos Ayres is very cosmopolitan. Ham and Japheth are well represented, but Shem has not yet put in an appearance, although Chinese immigration has been mooted to provide labourers for mining operations. French, English, Italians, Germans, Belgians, Danes and Portuguese dispute the narrow pathway with the native, and foreign tongues, especially French and English, are heard in the streets almost as frequently as Spanish: nay the very air is rendered polyglot especially on feast-days when the flags of almost all nations conmingle.

The Porteños are jealous and very naturally of the wealth, power and position that foreigners are attaining and are endeavouring to frame measures whereby they may be either enticed or enforced to become naturalised, a step which at present is never meditated save by those in government employ or in the expectation of it; the fact is more faith is placed in the country than in its public men; and yet for-

eigners whilst extracting from it all the advantages in
their power, suffer the only means of amelioration to
lie idle in their hands. Compulsory military service
is one of the bugbears which deters many, but the
generality are not aware that from the epoch of natu-
ralization, a period of ten years' exemption is allowed.
In times of political disturbance, papeletas (protection
papers) are issued by the various consuls to their own
countrymen and these are generally respected by the
native authorities, not alone in the city, but throughout
the Republic.

The native population consists of the descendants
of the Old Spaniards through Indian marriages ; of
many families who have preserved purity of blood by
uniting with others equally untainted, either native or
foreign ; of a small but wealthy section who, by
continued intermarriage within prohibited degrees,
have had to pay the common penalty of deterioration
in mind and body ; and a heterogeneous assemblage
of African, Indian and Spanish stock. Every description of complexion may here be seen, from the creamy
white to the jettest black ; but an absolutely pure
white skin is a great rarity amongst the Porteños.

However notwithstanding the mixed type of the
native population, they have never relinquished the
main features of the Spanish character and may still
be described as an intelligent, polished, polite, hospitable, proud but not haughty, race ; devoted to
pleasure, possessing but little originality, but very
apt copyists, dependent even for their recreations on

European, especially Parisian, models. Individually possessing resource, which they seem to abandon when in concert, private business is conducted with capacity and energy, whilst joint-stock companies, committees and boards of administration languish and need the incorporation of the foreign element to add stability and vitality to their proceedings.

Morally and politically the Bonarenses have much to learn; the inviolability of a promise, the sacredness of life and property, are lessons not yet couned, whilst society throughout, abandoning the present, is based upon the shifting sands of a wearying procrastination; the obligation of today is lifted on to the shoulders of the morrow and mañana (tomorrow) like an overloaded Atlas, throws down his burden and buries alike duty and reputation. In politics too and although there are many men of undoubted elevated instincts, the majority look upon patriotism, not as founded upon noble principles and to be supported by great virtues, but as a Shibboleth by which to conceal, under the bombastic effusions of rhetoric, their scramble for place and power; and so their newspapers, with few exceptions, reflecting this, are little else but a tissue of personalities.

In the case of a people so gifted with natural æsthetic proclivities, so richly endowed with imagination and possessing so retentive a memory and a ready apprehension, what might not education effect, if properly directed? as it is, by the present course of proceeding, the taste remains uncultivated, the imagi-

nation unbridled, the judgement unformed, apprehension unquickened and the memory alone strength-
ened, whilst morality which should hold the reins is
left out in the cold ; and to this result the extensive
and unethical programmes of the University and National College contribute, by fostering a system of cram
in lieu of steady application, and ousting from her
throne the only true guide of the intellect. Although
Apollo indeed hath touched their tongues and oratory
is a natural gift, by which they speak well of many
things not much, talk of *alta metafisica* (high metaphy-
sics) and converse in diverse languages, the culture
of the Porteños is not deep, the Pierian spring is only
sipped ; unused to the lead to fathom the depths of
consecutive deduction, their plans of political and
social economy are often faulty, yet they handle
subjects with a charming sprightliness both of manner and diction ; and though from want of education
they find it difficult to distinguish exquisite flavours
or give an intelligent criticism on a work of art, none
the less are they endowed as a race with fine instincts
and exalted perceptions.

Personally, the Bonarenses form a stately, self-
possessed, well-knit, rather undersized, dark but
regular featured, well-dressed race, with small hands
and feet, quick, lively yet very decorous and graceful
in their movements, hyper temperate in their habits
and with an impressive *naïveté* of address that makes
them charming companions, but of abundant assu-
rance, equally ready to manage a Bank or command

an iron-clad, to propound a law or edit a newspaper: the extraordinary highbred courtesy of the old Spanish regime is however rapidly degenerating into the offhand nod and pow-wow of the mercantile code; today it certainly would provoke remark, at any rate, to see a gentleman stand hat in hand to allow a lady to pass on the narrow side walk; the modern custom, imported from Paris, is rather to stare persistently in her face. Two circumstances, connected with civic life in Buenos Aires, attract the notice of foreigners; the ease with which the social ladder is climbed "*Padre pulpero, hijo caballero!*" (the father an innkeeper, the son a gentleman!), but as the lower class, in manner and address are so much superior to the corresponding order in England, this excites no surprise, and elevated position sits facilely on parvenus. To witness the wondrous love of parents for their offspring is another matter that excites admiration; no shutting children up in a nursery with a governess! they are the constant companions, in and out of doors, in shopping, visiting or on pleasure trips, especially of their mothers, who watch their every motion with the fondest care. There is no doubt that family ties are stronger and that the communion between members of the same household are more intimate than is generally the case in Europe; yet too much of parental anxiety seems lavished upon mere externals; upon distinguished appearance and manners, dress, the acquisition of showy accomplishments and wealth, and an auspicious marriage; and too little upon the formation of character; indeed the moral

seems lost sight of equally in the home as in the
college education. The consequence is natural! children fostered from the birth as equals, and controlled
but feebly, become pert and forward and at last con-
temptuous of even parental direction. Boys of fifteen
or sixteen consider themselves men, assume their airs,
smoke, loll about the streets, enter the confiterias, play
billiards and absent themselves from home pretty
much as their inclination leads them. Smoking indeed
is so universal even amongst children that when I
landed for the first time in Montevideo, I was amazed
to see a little infant, scarcely able to walk, standing
in a doorway and puffing away at a huge cigar; at
first I took it as a joke, but on seeing him spit like a
man, humour was soon exchanged for pity and
disgust.

It is time now to speak of the ladies, but the
subject has its perils and like the Serpentine ice, is
marked dangerous. To say that the Porteñas, are
sprightly, gay, especially brilliant at repartee, fond of
pleasure, fashion and the toilet, very amiable and
charming, strictly observant of religious duties and
exceedingly charitable, is no more than their due: but
their culture, chiefly of the exterior, lies in the accomplishments, above all, in music and the study
of the English, French and Italian languages. When
Thalberg visited this city, a native lady begged of
him a few finishing lessons, but after listening to her
for a while at the piano, he declined, with the remark
that he could teach her nothing, and such talent is

very widely diffused; although in the rendering of operatic music, which alone finds favour here, brilliancy of execution is fostered at the expense of expression. The late Police band in this city, in thorough efficiency, reminded me of the Coldstreams', and Plaza Victoria was wont to be thronged on the evenings of its performance. It is a great pity that there are no Madame Rachels here to endow the ladies with the eternal bloom of youth, for at that period the figures of these etherial beings are remarkably fine and supple, their complexions lustrous and their features regular; with full flashing dark orbs and wondrously lavish silken black tresses, which no particle of grease or oil ever defiles, waists of gossamer and tiny hands and feet; but their carriage, naturally graceful in the extreme, is disfigured and reduced to a Chinese mince by those cramping high-heeled boots. As they advance in age however, they rapidly lose their form and through a too early marriage, sitting at the windows and riding in carriages, accept embonpoint as their lot, a monster which destroys in a measure corporal elegance, but is powerless to retard spiritual ripeness.

The Porteñas are extravagant in dress and amusements; English thriftiness is unknown and waste universal; so that marriages are not so frequent as they otherwise would be, and moreover young couples are only content to begin life as their parents end theirs. The ladies who talk in such a loud and high-pitched tone and with such energy and gesture as to lead a stranger to imagine they are quarrelling,

are greedy of admiration and against compliments
which would bring a tinge to the cheeks of an English lady, are proof; Cupid with a dash of Venus
hovers over society, flirtation is carried to the verge
of the proprieties, suicides from unrequited love are
not uncommon, phosphorous matches become the
elixir mortis, and the elopement of girls of tender age
is frequent. A curious custom which obtains amongst
the young and takes place annually on St. John's day,
the 24th of June, is that of choosing sweethearts for
the following year. Notwithstanding the gay and frivolous lives of many, the majority of the Porteñas,
not only make loving wives and tender mothers, but
with much self-abnegation, spend their leisure hours
in works of charity; numerous are the benevolent
institutions under their charge, supported by voluntary contributions; but one seems to be so unique, so
characteristic of these Christian women, as to be
worthy of distinct notice; it consists of taking charge
of the young children of the labouring classes whilst
their parents are absent at their daily work.

Life in Buenos Aires may be called the Daguerre-
otype of that in Paris and consists of a feverish hunt
after both business and pleasure. The occupation most
in request is government employ, although the emolument from the public offices is only moderate
from the President downwards: £500 per an. is
considered an average income, but a young man
can live economically on £200. The Exchange,
the Counting House and the Store absorb the majority

and from ten to five daily the city is one vast hive
wherein Mammon is exclusively worshipped. Of the
particular kind of home life to which Englishmen are
accustomed, there is but little in Buenos Aires; the
air is so pure and genial that much of one's existence
is passed out of doors and even when within doors,
there is no domestic hearth, no coziness, everything is
open to the day and retirement is unknown. Visiting
usually takes place in the evening, and the houses
remain open till ten or eleven o'clock ; but the stately
tertulia (evening reception) in which dancing is usual,
is generally limited to one night in the week; the old
method of calling attention by clapping the hands and
uttering an *Ave-Maria* at the street door has now
been supplanted by the modern electric-bell, which is
universal.

The ambition of private life partakes much of the
sensual and seems to be centred in the French man-
cook, high living, expensive wines, a fine house and
furniture, a fashionable coach, a box at the Opera, entrance to a Club, plenty of visitors, handsome dress,
and constant appearance in public; whilst a visit to
Paris is looked forward to as the goal of all earthly
desires ; and as French tailors and milliners abound,
the Bonaerenses have no difficulty in laying claim to
the distinction of being the best-dressed people in the
world. But whilst they thus enjoy a luxurious existence, the social amenities, guided perhaps by somewhat too severe an etiquette, are practised to the letter,
and there is a cheerful alacrity in paying those atten-
tions which society and friendship demand.

Home service is ministered to chiefly by blacks, creoles, Gallegos and Basques, who form the principal retinue attached to native houses; but the English generally engage Irish servants, who afford wide scope for annals from the pen of some South American Mrs· Skinningston. If good English servants would only emigrate to this country, they would be met on the mole with triumphant banners and relieve a great part of the foreign society here from the terrible incubus of incompetent and insolent attendance.

The Regent Street of the River Plate is "Calle Florida", which reminds one strikingly of the old picture of the Parade, Tonbridge Wells, in the time of Dr. Johnson, save the dowdy dress. Brilliantly lighted shops, gay women and sprightly cavaliers nightly throng the pathways, and the latter inundating every corner where there is standing room, peer into the faces of the fair sex as they pass (*), a custom very offensive to English taste, but which, with the attendant audible and complimentary remarks, is here taken as a matter of course. Contact with foreigners has civilized in one sense, but is rapidly destroying the simplicity of the native character. Whilst the streets are filled with promenaders, and on Opera nights with carriages, the confiterias (confectioners') and numerous cafés teem with those taking ices or sipping other light refreshments, or who indulge in the click

_____

(*) The señoritas (young ladies) go in front, with simpering mien and wandering eyes; the dueñas with severe expression following in the rear.

of the billiard balls; whilst the heavy gambler seeks the cover of the native Clubs; and although, as a rule, the pleasures of the Porteño are artless, in this latter respect, he has not yet shaken off the radical vice of the chief portion of the Latin race. Of the behaviour however of the Argentine community in public, it is impossible to speak in too glowing terms : all gatherings of whatsoever nature, political, social or commemorative, are alike marked by a love of order very uncommon elsewhere, and even when excited by party cries, although noisy, they still keep within the bounds of decorum ; good nature, politeness and consideration, characterise an Argentine crowd equally with an Argentine drawingroom.

If then the high degree of civilization of the Capital resembles, in some respects, that of the latter days of Rome, it is immeasurably superior in others ; in intellectual activity, refinement and culture ; here there are no barbaric displays, no downturned thumbs, no depraved exhibitions, nothing outwardly to offend good taste ; luxury there is, to which commercial activity and art are the necessary corollaries; the appreciation of what is excellent is dawning too and it needs but that the moralities should leave a deeper indent, to stamp the people with sterling worth, and add the key-stone to the social arch.

Turning to the foreign population of the city, they will be found in the aggregate to exceed the native in number ; but in speaking of immigration sufficient was advanced regarding the different classes and their

individual status: a few words however may be added
with reference to the position and prospects of the six
thousand of our own countrymen dwelling within its
walls. Since the time of such men as Lumb, Arm-
strong and other merchants of high standing and
supreme rectitude, it is a matter of concern that
English influence has not sustained that prestige which
belonged to it in days of yore, notwithstanding the
large amount of British capital embarked in various
enterprises. Every picture has its focus, so every
people; from an outpost, yet by one of themselves,
much may be seen, which escapes the ken of those in
the centre. Three classes of Englishmen put in
an appearance here: an educated middle class, a lower
orders of mechanics and some waifs and strays principally from the shipping. The two latter are not
included in the foreground and it is not necessary for
our purpose to advert to them further than to say, that
the mechanics are in general skilful and trustworthy,
but that the knights-errant have brought much
obloquy upon the English name. *Berracho* (drunk-
ard) was until lately a derisive term applied to our
whole race on the principle of "*Ex uno disce omnes*",
and natives commonly remarked that only an Englishman and a dog frequented the sunny side of the
street, pleasant companionship! fortunately we have
survived all that, and the following observations apply
solely to the higher stratum of Britons.

If a German, a Frenchman and an Englishman
were taken at random from this population, the com-

parison would in general undoubtedly be in favour of
the last mentioned in many points, such as physique,
manliness of bearing and integrity of individual character; but as undoubtedly prejudicial to him in,
knowledge of the world, self-reliance, adaptability and
that special education which fits for success in the business of life. Those qualities in which he maintains
superiority are due chiefly to a healthy and bracing
climate, exercise and good living, the general high
tone of English society and early home training : his
deficiencies arise from the restricted sphere of his youth
and consequent want of experience, overweening
conceit and the faults of his schools. Omitting the
Frenchman, as in this part of the world he does not
come into competition with the Englishman so directly
as does the German ; we find the latter gradually
ousting our countrymen from their hitherto unassail-
able position, and if the Teuton had a greater command
of capital, the English merchant would soon have to
retire to a completely secondary position. On arrival
in this country we find the German, speaking two,
sometimes three, languages in addition to his own, of
untiring industry and perseverance, received with
open arms by his clannish compatriots and entering
into business pursuits as though the employment was
not beneath him ; that is the obverse! now reverse the
coin ! and it is positively painful to witness the average Englishman endeavouring to stammer out a few
broken phrases in any idiom not spoken in Pall Mall ;
this no doubt is mainly the fault of his schools ; all
the years devoted to Latin elegiacs and Greek hexa-

pods, with all the taste they are supposed to convey,
do not at any rate loosen his tongue ; what independence and self-respect are not involved in being able
to address any European in his own language ! then it
is a fashion amongst them to affect to despise business,
and although a nation of shopkeepers, to look upon
its banner the ledger as a badge of servitude. Further
the island pride, the *"civis Romanus sum"* which
esteems everybody and everything not English inferior ; and the endeavour to uphold here the same
social distinctions as obtain at home, not only opposes,
in the one case, a barrier to his individual advance
but, in the other, renders English society without
cohesion, an unsympathising brotherhood which, split
into cliques, possesses all the jealous instincts of old-
maid coteries. The Scotch are free from most of these
faults, are clannish to a degree and by mutual support effect much ; but the Irish, although nestling
together adjacently, possess less cohesion and exhibit
even more internal jealousy than the English ; the St.
Patrick's society, a vast engine of benevolent design,
introduced a few years ago with a prolonged blast of
trumpets of extraordinarily loud pattern, soon met
with its *"hic jacet"* at the hands of its own friends
and supporters : but as President Roca exhibits great
sympathy with Erin and is using every means in his
power to foment Irish immigration, it is quite possible
he may succeed in striking a chord of union in breasts
to which it has hitherto been much of a stranger.

CHAPTER X.

INSTITUTIONS : THE CHURCH — EDUCATION — LAW — MEDICINE — PUBLIC PRESS AND LITERATURE — CLUBS — SOCIETIES POLITI- CAL AND CHARITABLE — HOSPITALS AND ASYLUMS — LOTTERIES — HOTELS — MUSEUM — BEGGARS' OPERA — POLICE — MUNICI PALITY.

In reviewing briefly the institutions of the capital the Catholic Church claims our first attention and respect. Although fortified with all the rites, ceremonial and pageantry which make it attractive in Europe; with a numerous clergy, churches, divinity college, monasteries and nunneries; with the sombre garments of the regular priests and the ascetic garb of the monks constantly flitting in and out amongst the people even in their busiest haunts, the Church here fails to enlist the sympathies of the male portion of the population, who remain unconcerned spectators of even its most solemn functions. If they do attend its services, it is as to an assembly, or to view the rows of ladies as they kneel on the carpet stretched the whole length of the central aisle ; but the general practice is to go only as far as the cathedral steps and there watch the arrival of the fair sex. The common

doctrine accepted by the majority of Porteños is that
the rites of the Church duly administered on a death-
bed atone for the sins and follies of life, and in this
belief they are suffered to remain. The feast-days
are observed as close holidays, in the early part of
which the steeple summons the faithful to devotion,
but the syren voice of pleasure, heard above the
clangour of church bells, attracts the majority by her
seductive charms ; in fact, Sunday is the great day
for recreation, all places of amusement, including the
Opera, then open their doors, and even auctioneers,
heedless of its sanctity hoist their Mammonish flags
and wield their godless hammers.

The general education of the Bonaerenses is con-
fided to the University, National College, Mercantile
Institute, Normal College, Jesuits' School, Military
and Naval Academies, Convents, Parish Schools and
numerous private establishments. Its nature and
extent have been indicated when speaking of the Republic ; but it may be further remarked that the University, which resembles a large English day-school
attended by nearly one thousand students, grants
degrees in Arts, Law, Medicine and Theology and
diplomas in Engineering and Surveying : but demands
a six years' preliminary course of Humanity, before
entering upon the more technical branches. These in
their turn occupy a further period of from four to six
years, of that to enter upon a professional career is
scarcely possible ¡before the age of 25. The programmes are extensive and rapidly passed over by *vivâ-*

voce instruction, terminated by yearly examinations, and do not serve as engines of education in its higher sense, but as the National Government has just issued an edict for the reformation of the University we may confidently expect a change for the better. The professors, mustering a goodly corps of 60, are for the most part foreigners engaged at the very moderate stipend of 250 £ per an., an emolument which they are obliged to supplement by private tuition, or by merging two or more professorships into one. As the University, with the other institutions of the capital, has lately been placed under National control, it is most probable that the National College, for which there is now little need, will not long continue an independent existence but that the Mercantile Institute will gather fresh strength to pursue its useful career. The Normal and Naval and Military Colleges, ably conducted as they are, but purely technical need not detain us; and as for the private schools, unable to command high professional attainments or to enter into competition with the public, at which instruction is gratis, they either languish or await dissolution.

The system of education however most in vogue amongst the upper class of the Porteños is that of family instruction by private Tutors, both girls and boys are thus taught together ; the bad atmosphere of schools is avoided, and such good results secured, as are otherwise unattainable : but as the University course is compulsory for all those destined for professional pursuits, home training in the case of boys is necessarily limited to the earlier years. The Jesuits, although the law of their expulsion is still unrepealed, and but a very few years ago their buildings were attacked by an infuriated mob and burnt, a scene constantly in danger of repetition, have succeeded in reerecting them and are now maintaining that reputation as teachers, which has so characterized the order; some of the convents too afford a very strict and superior education for girls, which as yet has not succeeded in gaining much support, although apparently richly deserving it.

The study of law seems to exercise such fascination over the majority of students, and the number of doctors in this branch is so astounding, that sometimes they have to resort to equivocal means to obtain clients, as the following current story illustrates. A countryman came into town to consult a legal adviser as to whether he should enter an action upon some point on which he felt himself aggrieved. He was ushered into a studio filled with learned looking tomes. "Oh yes!" replied the man of law, "of course you ought! don't you see all those books there?" pointing to a cabinet bursting with legal lore; "all those are in your favour!" The client took the doctor's advice and lost the suit; upon which he returned to upbraid his counsellor, who answered, "true! I told you all those volumes were in your favour, but omitted to inform you that those on the opposite side, more numerous still, were antagonistic to your claim."

In almost all Argentine undertakings, professions

or business, special fitness based upon technical training is disregarded; the scientific and practical are
united in the same person, and the doctrine of the
subdivision of labour looked upon as an Old World
fable: a druggist will be a professor of chemistry; a
seller of optical instruments, a lecturer on light;
a carpenter will undertake to build a house; a con-
fectioner to provide a banquet; a soldier to command
an ironclad; a café-waiter becomes an officer: a
lawyer will assume government finance or glide into
the seat of a bank manager, and so on; the same
happens in the legal profession, which here is not
subject to such ramifications as in England, but comprises only two branches the *abogados* (lawyers proper).
and the *escribanos* (conveyancers). The abogados, to
number of 450, are equally ready to counsel, plead,
collect evidence, or in fact conduct a suit to its termination unaided; whilst the escribanos, 200 in
number, are looking after property, arranging its
transfer and settlement, and the making and testing
the validity of, wills. The higher justiciary forms a
superior tribunal of ten judges, who decide upon the
cases that come up for judgement from the inferior
courts: but the proceedings are closed to the public, no
viva-voce cross examination, that crucial test, all
testimony is written; no actual trial by jury; and
talk about the English Court of Chancery and its
delays, the suits here are frequently as protracted and
infinitely more uncertain.

Medicine is scarcely less in favour than Law

with youthful aspirants, and the profession is already
overstocked with at least 200 physicians in full practice : indeed no city in the world ought to present
greater encouragement to Insurance offices than Buenos Aires, considering the number of persons paid to
take care of life and property, and it is a fact, that
though in excess, they do a remarkably profitable
business. No legal caste exists in Medicine ; all
practitioners are equally obliged to possess the degree
of M. D. and are supposed to be at the same time
skilful as pathologists, surgeons and accoucheurs ; the
duty of the apothecary is here divorced from that of
the physician, who never makes up his own prescriptions, and the general consultation fee, at the studio,
is 5l.

The medical course for students is severe and
includes Hospital practice, but many after concluding
it, visit the European schools before settling down
amongst their own countrymen. The Faculty, consisting of ten professors, possesses a large and complete institute provided with lecture rooms, library,
a school of pharmacy and natural history, and a
museum, besides a noble hall in which degrees are
conferred ; and foreigners, no matter what distinctions or diplomas they bring, are not allowed to
practise without first undergoing a strict examination,
especially in Spanish, before this learned board. To
quacks, and the allopathists include under this term
the homœopathists, no mercy is shown in the city,
although the *curanderos*, who are really no worse than,

if so bad as, the corresponding class in England, still
flourish in the provinces. One of the English fraternity was brought up before the Derby magistrates, a
few years ago, charged with administering some
deleterious stuff that caused the death of a woman
On being pressed to declare the constituents of the
pills he prescribed, a long silence ensued, but in the
sequel he confessed mysteriously that it was " soap
and antibilious ! " In the same quarter and about the
same time, another quack was found ordering a
" lump of coal dissolved in milk ! " We have not yet
reached this ingenious stretch of quackery in the
Argentine Republic, as the curanderos are nothing
but Herbalists, whose pharmacopœia frequently includes very valuable remedies, as yet unknown to the
Faculty.

Taking example by the United States, the political type of the Porteños, as Paris is their social, the
native press of the capital is very fertile. Thirteen
daily newspapers, or including the illustrated and
other weeklies, forty five in all, form here the third
estate, but not a moral power as in Europe; an immense mass of fugitive reading which soon grows
wearisome to the foreigner on account of its verbosity
and personality. Besides these, each foreign community supports its own organs, some of which are
ably conducted, notably so the English and French ;
the English " Standard " and the French " Le Cour-
rier de la Plata " would vie in tone with any country
newspapers in England or France, whilst immeasura-

lily superior in their monetary articles. The original contributions to the native press are frequently especially brilliant in the facile use of rhetorical figure and their light, easy, graceful style, but ordinarily display a want of vigorous, masculine, matured intellect.

The following forms part of an article taken at random, from the Prensa, an opposition organ, of the 18th of February 1881 ; a translation of which is appended in order to give the English reader a notion of the character of Argentine newspaper literature, as far as can be done by a limited extract : the Prensa, upon whom Mr. Reid's mantle has fallen, is urging Naval Reform :—

Es un profundo error el creer que los gobiernos lo saben todo y que no han menester que les dén noticias y les hagan indicaciones sobre temas de administracion pública. Desde que existen gobiernos y mientras subsistan por todos los siglos, necesitarán de la colaboracion de los hombres independientes y de rectas intenciones. Aun mas : un buen gobierno no desperdicia el material diario que le suministra la oposicion, por ruda y apasionada que sea ; la oposicion es una pieza esencial en la máquina administrativa, ella estímula, enfrena y vigoriza la accion gubernativa, en último resultado. Un buen gobierno sale el modo cómo se de arma una oposicion, que no es otro que entregando al desprecio sus errores, aprovechando sus opiniones y sus exigencias para practicar el bien

It is a remarkable mistake to believe that governments know everything, and that there is no necessity to prompt and supply them with suggestions on points of public administration. As from the very first moment of their existence, so for centuries to come they will need the cooperation of men of independent and upright principles. Even further ; a good government will never fling to the winds the daily convictions that emanate from the opposition, however crude and biassed they may appear ; the opposition form an essential rôle in the administrative machine ; it stimulates, curbs and invigorates governmental action to the last degree. The method of disarming an opposition is well recognised by every virtuous government ; it is no other than scorning all irregularity

general. Si la opinion del adver-
sario sistemático es utilizable ¿qué
diremos de los juicios independientes y desapasionados, engen-
drados por el sincero amor al bien-
estar del pais ?

Los gobernantes se ven asediados
á todas horas por una multitud de
personas complacientes, empeñadas
en agradarlos, descubriéndoles cie-
los límpidos suavemente teñidos de
rosa, amurallándolos con un círculo
de fierro que los aleja del contacto
del mundo real con todos los de-
fectos, vicios y miserias, engendros
legítimos de las flaquezas humanas.

and excess, supporting advanced
opinions and putting a strict limit
to waste, so as to conduce to the
general welfare. If the convictions
of the systematic adversary are
capable of producing benefit, what
shall be said of those independent
and impartial judgements, the offspring of sincere love for the well-
being of the country ?

These persons who assume the
prerogative of government find themselves continually besieged by a
throng of admirers, whose object it
is to render them self-satisfied, to
disclose to their gaze a clear horizon
delicately tinged with rose, to surround them with a wall of iron so
as to separate them from all contact with the real world with all
the defects, vices and miseries, the
logical results of human weakness.

The literature of the Porteños exactly reflects their
idiosyncracy : witty, lively, superficial, polished, the
exponent of sentiment rather than the matrix of deep
thought, it indicates the sway of words, and the
sovereignty of rhetoric over logic ; if however not
clothed with grandeur, it is decked with beauty, the
pose of attitude and drapery are its, the swelling
muscle and the expanding nostril, but philosophy
whose latent fire dwells within is degraded to mere
emotion.

Take their authors and distil their works : a few
flowers, fragrant 'tis true, remain in the alembic, but
the first blast of the purger renders to their elements
the subtle, instable and etherial compounds. So poetical

however are the people that their prose differs little
from poetry except in the metre : a fact which will be
observed in the following extract from one of their
best living authors, Sarmiento : —

ESCENA CAMPESTRE

Yo he presenciado una escena
campestre, digna de los tiempos
primitivos del mundo anteriores á
la institucion del sacerdocio. Ha-
llábame en 1838 en la Sierra de
San Luis, en casa de un estanciero
cuyas dos ocupaciones favoritas eran
rezar y jugar. Habia edificado una
capilla en la que los domingos por
la tarde rezaba él mismo el rosario,
para suplir el sacerdote y al oficio
divino de que por años habian care-
cido.

Era aquel un cuadro homérico : el
sol llegaba al ocaso; las majadas
que volvian al redil hendian el aire
con sus confusos balidos : el dueño
de casa, hombre de sesenta años, de
una fisonomia noble, en que la raza
europea para se ostentaba por la
blancura del cútis, los ojos azules,
la frente espaciosa y despejada, hacia coro, á que contestaban una do-
cena de mujeres y algunos more-
tones cuyos caballos, no bien do-
mados aun, estaban amarrados cerca
de la puerta de la capilla. Con-
cluido el rosario, hizo un fervoroso
ofrecimiento. Jamás he oido voz
mas llena de uncion, fervor mas
puro, fé mas firme, ni oracion mas
bella, mas adecuada á las circuns-
tancias que la que recitó. Pedia en
ella á Dios, lluvia para los campos,
fecundidad para los ganados, paz

A COUNTRY SCENE.

I was once present at a country
scene, worthy of the early ages of
the world, before the institution of
the priesthood. In the year 1838
whilst travelling on the Sierras of
San Luis, I happened to visit the
house of an estanciero, whose two
favourite occupations were praying
and gambling. He had erected a
chapel in which on Sunday after-
noons he personally conducted service, in order to supply the place of
the priest and that divine worship
of which they had been deprived
for years. That was indeed an
Homeric picture! the sun was
about to set : the flocks that were
on their return to the fold rent the
air with their confused bleating :
the patriarch, a man of seventy winters, of a noble cast of countenance,
pure European extraction, as evidenced by the fairness of his skin,
blue eyes, spacious and unwrinkled
forehead, sang the service, the re-
sponses to which were given by a
dozen women and a few youths,
whose horses not yet well tamed
were secured around the chapel
door. When the rosary was con-
cluded, a fervent prayer was offered up. Never have I listened to a
voice fuller of unction, a purer
fervour, a firmer faith nor a petition
more beautiful and suitable to the

para la República, seguridad para
los caminantes......

Yo soy muy propenso á llorar, y
aquella vez lloró hasta sollozar,
porque el sentimiento relijioso se
habia despertado en mi alma con
exaltacion y como una sensacion
desconocida, porque nunca he visto
escena mas religiosa; creí estar en
los tiempos de Abrahan, en su presencia, en la de Dios y de la natu-
raleza que lo revela; la voz de aquel
hombre candoroso é inocente me
hacia vibrar todas las fibras, y me
penetraba hasta la médula de los
huesos.

SARMIENTO.

circumstances than the one he pious-
ly uttered. In it he besought God
for rain for the earth, fecundity
for the cattle, peace for the Republic and security for travellers......

I am very prone to tears, and at
that time I wept to sobbing, as religious sentiment was strongly awakened in my soul to a degree hitherto
unknown, for never had I witnessed a more holy spectacle: I thought
I was in the times of Abraham, in
his very presence, in that of God
and of nature his reflection; the
voice of that hoary and pure-min-
ded man made all my nerves quiver
and penetrated even to the marrow
of my bones.

So redolent is the air of the River Plate with
literary instinct, such petted children of the Muses are
the Porteños, and poetic inspiration so widely diffused,
that besides a galaxy of authors such as Dominguez,
Gutierrez, Gomez, Marmol, Alberdi, Sarmiento, Mitre,
Avellaneda, Calvo, Carranza, Cané, Andrade, &c , some
of whom in prose, some in verse, have enriched their
country's literature; even the very postmen find no
difficulty in climbing the rugged steps of Parnassus
and annually lisp in verse for Christmas-boxes.

This general " ore rotundo " is no doubt aided
by the sonorousness and rhyming facilities of the language, especially in the construction of the more artificial forms of poetry such as the sonnet, which is
much affected here; but simplicity and elegance, both
of thought and expression, are characteristic of Ar-

gentine writers, who bedeck the meanest subject with wondrous grace and interest.

Two examples follow: "An ode to the Ombú" from the pen of Luis L. Dominguez; the second, the "Postman's Lay" which will bear favourable comparison with any thing yet contributed by the historic Literary Dustman of London.

El Ombú	Literal Translation
Cada comarca en la tierra	Every region of the earth
Tiene un rasgo prominente,	Has some prominent feature,
El Brasil su sol ardiente,	Brazil her scorching sun.
Minas de plata el Perú,	Silver mines Perú,
Montevideo su Cerro,	Montevideo her Mount,
Buenos Aires—Patria hermosa,—	Buenos Aires—lovely country—
Tiene su Pampa grandiosa ;	Has her magnificent pampa ;
La Pampa tiene el Ombú.	The Pampa its Ombú.
Esa llanura estendida,	That extensive plain,
Inmenso piélago verde,	Immense verdant ocean,
Donde la vista se pierde	Where the view is lost
Sin tener donde posar,	Without having anything on which [to repose,
Es la Pampa misteriosa	Is the Pampa, a mystery
Todavia para el hombre,	Still to man,
Que á una raza dà su nombre	Which gives its name to a race
Que nadie pudo domar.	That no one has been able to tame.
No tiene grandes raudales	It has no majestic torrents
Que fecunden sus entrañas ;	To fertilize its bosom ;
Pero lagos y espadañas,	But lakes and rushes
Inundan toda su faz,	Cover its whole surface,
Que dan paja para el rancho,	Which yield thatch for the rancho.
Para el vestido dan pieles,	Skins for clothing,
Agua dan á los corceles	Water for the steeds,
Y guarida á la torcaz.	And afford shelter for the fowl.
Su gran manto de esmeralda	Its grand emerald mantle
Esmalta modestas flores	Is enameled with modest flowers
De aromáticos olores	Of aromatic odours
Y de risueño matiz.—	And of pleasing and variegated
El bibí, los macachines,	The bibí, the macachins, [tints.—
El trébol, la margarita	The trefoil, the daisy
Mezclan su aroma esquisita	Intermingle their exquisite scents
Sobre el lucido tapaz.	Upon the glowing turf.
No tiene bosques frondosos	It has no leafy groves
Ni hermosas aves en ellos ;	Nor in them lovely feathered dwe-
Pero sí pájaros bellos	But aye! fine birds [llers ;

Hijos de la soledad,	Children of the solitude,
Que siendo únicos testigos	Who being the only companions
Del que habita esas rejiones,	Of him who inhabits these regions,
Adivinan sus pasiones	Divine his sufferings
Y acompañan su horfandad.	And share his exile.
Así, nuncio de la muerte	Thus, the messenger of death
Es el cuervo ó el carancho ;—*	Is the raven or the carancho ;—
Si la peste amaga el rancho,	If pestilence threatens the rancho,
Sobre el techo el buho está;—	Upon the roof sits the owl—
Y meciéndose en las nubes	And sporting in the clouds
Y el desierto dominando,	And domineering the desert,
Las horas está cantando	Is chiming the hours
El vigilante chajá.	The watchful chajá.
No hay allí bosques frondosos	Here are no leafy woods,
Pero alguna vez asoma	But sometimes there looms,
En la cumbre de una loma	On the top of an eminence
Que se alcanza á divisar,	Which is descried,
El ombú solemne, aislado,	The solemn, isolated Ombú,
De gallarda airosa planta,	Of graceful and airy appearance,
Que á las nubes se levanta	Which rises to the heavens
Como faro de aquel mar.	Like a beacon of that sea.
El ombú! Ninguno sabe	The Ombú! no one knows
En qué tiempo, ni qué mano	At what time, nor what hand
En el centro de aquel llano	In the centre of that plain
Su semilla derramó.	Scattered its seed.
Mas su tronco tan ñudoso,	But its trunk so gnarled,
Su corteza tan roida,	Its bark so rugged,
Bien indican que su vida	Clearly indicate that its life
Cien inviernos resistió.	Has resisted a hundred winters.
Al mirar como derrama	On viewing how it spreads
Su raiz sobre la tierra,	Its root along the soil,
Y sus dientes allí entierra	And how it buries its teeth in it
Y se afirma con afan,	And laboriously strengthens its grip,
Parece que alguien le dijo	It seems as though some being
	[warned it
Cuando se alzaba altanero:	When it was soaring so loftily:
Ten cuidado del Pampero,	Take care of the Pampero,
Que es tremendo su huracan.	For its hurricane is overwhelming.
Puesto en medio del desierto,	Placed in the midst of the desert,
El Ombú, como un amigo	The Ombú, like a friend,
Presta á todos el abrigo	Lends to all the shelter
De sus ramas con amor:	Of its branches lovingly:
Hace techo de sus hojas	It makes a roof of its leaves
Que no filtra el aguacero,	Which permits not the showers to
	[penetrate,

* The carancho after uttering its harsh grati gory of "traro, traro!" suddenly jerks back its head completely on to its back, thus stretching its trachea to its utmost tension, in order to croak forth a strong hoarse guttural of dire portent.

Y á su sombra el sol de Enero
Templa el rayo abrasador.

And within its shade the January
Moderates its burning ray.   [sun

Cual museo de la Pampa
Muchas razas él cobija:
La rastrera lagartija
Hace cuevas á su pié,
Todo pájaro hace nido
Del jigante en su cabeza:
Y un enjambre en su corteza
De insectos varios, se vé.

Like a museum of the Pampa
It shelters many specimens;
The creeping lizard
Scoops its hole at its foot.
Every class of bird builds
On its giant top;
And in its bark a swarm
Of various insects is seen.

Y al teñir la aurora el cielo
De rubí, topacio y oro,
De allí sube á Dios el coro
Que le entona al despertar
Esa Pampa, misteriosa
Todavía para el hombre,
Que á una raza dá su nombre
Que nadie pudo domar.

And when the dawn tinges the sky
With ruby, topaz and gold,
Thence arises to God the chorus
Which entones to him, on awaken-
That Pampa, mysterious   (ing,
Still to man,
Which endows with its name a race
That no one has been able to tame.

Desde esa turba salvaje
Que en las llanuras se oculta
Hasta la porcion mas culta
De la humana sociedad,
Como un linde está la Pampa
Sus dominios dividiendo
Que vá el bárbaro cediendo
Palmo á palmo á la Ciudad.

From that savage crowd
Which in the plains lies hidden
To the more civilized portion
Of human society,
Like a boundary is the Pampa
Dividing their dominions,
Which the barbarian keeps yielding
Inch by inch to the City.

Y el rasgo mas prominente
De esa tierra donde mora
El salvaje que no adora
Otro Dios que el " Valichú." *
Que en 'chamal' y poncho envuel-
Con los 'laques' en la mano   (to,
Vá sembrando por el llano
Mudo horror, es el Ombú.

And the most prominent feature
Of that land wherein dwells
The savage who adores
No other God than " Valichú," (el,
Who in chiripá and poncho envelop-
With the boleadores * in hand
Goes sowing through the plain
Mute horror, is the Ombú.

¡Cuánta escena vió en silencio!

Cuántas veces ha escuchado
Que en sus hojas ha guardado
Con eterna lealtad!
El estrépito de guerra
Su quietud ha interrumpido;
A su pié se ha combatido
Por amor y libertad.

How many a scene has it witnessed
   (in silence!
How many tales has it listened to
Which in its leaves it has locked up
With eternal loyalty!
The clamour of war
Its repose has broken in upon:
At its feet struggles
For love and liberty.

---

* Valichú or more properly Hualichu
the Devil. The Pampa Indians although
they believe in a Supreme Good God
(Guarcchen) do not worship him, but of
rather like the Africans, are driven to
fear and pay homage to the Spirit of
Evil.

* Three stone balls joined by thongs
to a common centre, which when dis-
charged from the whirling hand, with
their wabbling gyratory threatening
motion, serve to entangle the legs of
animals.

En su tronco se leen cifras
Grabadas con el cuchillo,
Quizá por algun caudillo
Que á los indios venció allí :
Por uno de esos valientes
Dignos de fama y de gloria,
Y que no dejan memoria
Porque nacieron aquí !......

On its trunk may be read characters
Engraven with the knife,
Maybe by some chief   (spot ;
Who conquered the Indians at this
By one of those brave men
Worthy of fame and glory,
And who leave no memorial
Because they were born here !......

A su sombra melancólica
En una noche serena
Amorosa Cantilena
Tal vez un gaucho cantó :
Y tan tierna su guitarra
Acompañó sus congojas,
Que el Ombú de entre sus hojas
Tomó rocío y lloró.

In its melancholy shade
On a calm evening,
Some amorous ballad
Perhaps a gaucho has been singing;
And so tenderly his guitar
Accompanied his heart-throbs,
That the Ombú from between its
Distilled the dew and wept. (leaves

Sobre su tronco sentado
El señor de aquella tierra
De su ganado la yerra
Presencia alegre tal vez :
O tomando el " matecito "
Bajo sus ramos frondosos
Pone en paz á dos esposos,
O en las carreras es juez.

Upon its trunk seated,
The owner of that property
Of his flock the support,   (himself:
At times good-humouredly presents
Either sipping from the maté-bowl
Beneath its foliaceous branches
He sets at one two rivals,
Or acts as judge in the races.

A su pié trazan sus planes,
Haciendo círculo al fuego,
Los que van á salir luego
A correr el avestruz......
Y quizá para recuerdo
De que allí murió un cristiano,
Levantó piadosa mano
Bajo su copa una cruz.

At its foot draw up their plans,
Making a circle around the fire,
Those who are about soon to set out
To hunt the ostrich......
And perhaps as a memento
That here died a christian,
Some pious hand has erected
Beneath its bower a cross.

Y si en pos de amarga ausencia
Vuelve el gaucho á su partido,
Echa penas al olvido
Cuando alcanza á divisar
El Ombú, solemne, aislado,
De gallarda, airosa planta.
Que á las nubes se levanta
Como faro de aquel mar.

And if after a bitter absence (trict,
Returns the gaucho to his native dis-
He buries all his troubles in obli-
When he descries   (vion
The Ombú, solemn, isolated,
Graceful, airy tree,
Which to the clouds rises
Like a beacon of that sea.

LUIS L. DOMINGUEZ.

Aguinaldo
El Cartero á sus Clientes.

Apenas el sol estiende
Su cabellera dorada
Por las calles ó barrancos
De la gran ciudad del Plata ;

Christmas-box
The Postman to his Clients.

Scarcely does the sun shed
His golden rays
Over the streets and heights
Of the great city of the Plate ;

Cuando con paso veloz,	When with swift step,
Y de papel una carga,	And a load of paper,
Sale este pobre Cartero	Issues forth this poor letter-carrier
De la de Correos casa :	From the General Post-office.
Diligente el rumbo toma	Diligently pursuing his road
Sube escalones y baja,	He ascends and descends stairs,
Haciendo mas ejercicio	Taking more exercise (ties.
Que si aprendiera gimnasia.	Than if he were practising gymnas-
Ni el " Pampero " le detiene	Neither the Pampero stops
Ni la lluvia le acobarda,	Nor the rain intimidates him,
Y si de tierra hay tormenta	And if there be a dust-storm
Cierra los ojos y avanza.	He shuts his eyes and advances.
Se detiene en cada puerta,	He is detained at every door,
Donde veinte veces llama,	Where he knocks twenty times,
Hasta que un vecino sale	Until some neighbour comes out
A recibirle la carta.	And takes the letter from him.
Lo que suda ó lo que toce,	All his sweating and rapping,
Lo que grita ó lo que rabia,	Shouting and hurrying,
No se puede comparar	Cannot be compared
Con lo que en botines gasta.	With what he spends in shoe-
	[leather.
Ahora bien, este mortal	Well then! this poor fellow
Que por servirte se afana	Who toils to serve you
Te desea de buen grado	Wishes with all his heart (mas.
Que pases muy feliz Pascua.	You may pass a very happy Christ-
¿ Comprenderás la indirecta	Will you take the hint ! (said ?
O te llamarás andana ?	Or will you deny what has been
Es verdad que habiendo crisis	The fact is that in consequence of
	(the crisis
Anda escasilla la plata.	Cash is very scarce indeed.
Pero aunque me dés papel	But although you give me only pa-
No te diré una palabra,	Not a word shall escape me. (per,
Que en cuestiones de aguinaldo	For in the matter of the Christmas-
Siendo moneda, me basta.	Being money, it is sufficing.) (box,
No olvides que mi deseo	Don't forget that my wish is
Es que pases feliz Pascua ;	You may pass a happy Christmas :
Con que así, suelta la mosca	So that the fly may have a chance
Que espera mi dama-juana.	To sip at a demijohn of mine.
EL CARTERO.	THE POSTMAN.

Quitting the subject of Literature, let us next turn our attention to the Clubs and Societies.

The Clubs in Buenos Aires are not endowed with so distinctive a character, externally or internally, as those in London, nor are they of so high a tone, and although sixteen in number, the stranger would in vain look for them, as their habitats are modest and no isolated piles tell of luxurious wrapt seclusion.

Four native, chiefly political, occupy the first rank, of which the two most select, the Progreso and La Plata, give most sumptuous balls in the season, especially at Carnival time, invitations to which are eagerly sought; they are magnificently fitted up, but permit nightly heavy gambling.

As Carnival has been mentioned, it may be well, *en passant*, to say a few words upon that Institution. With what expectation, with what beating of the heart, is not this joyous season awaited, whose advent bears on its wings such delight to the whole population! For the three days and night of its continuance the whole city is in a delirium of pleasure; and outside Rome and Venice, possibly there is no similar spectacle to compare with that of Buenos Aires. The houses are all decorated and most illuminated with various devices: the greater part of the *corso* (course) is spanned with lofty arches of piping, on which innumerable gas lamps are fixed, shedding over the city a brilliancy almost equal to day, which viewed from the balconies appears one continuous blaze. The flying balconies with which almost every house is provided, all draped, are lined throughout, as are the open windows, with crowd of elegantly dressed women, who shower bonbons and flowers upon the public, especially the carriage occupants, or deluge them with scent from pomitos (scent fountains). Masqueraders traverse the streets, entering every house by the open portals, scattering fun and odoriferous waters in their train and cracking jokes with all the neighbours.

A general combat between the sexes succeeds; in street and road, in carriages and out of carriages, from balcony and window to street, from street to balcony and window ; flowers, confites, and scented water fly in every direction : nay not only so, but as it is the custom for those living on the route to invite all their friends for the purpose of playing Carnival, gay countless gatherings may be viewed through the open windows, in brilliantly lighted saloons, wetting one another to the skin ; and as the fun grows fast and furious, terrific single combats, in which the ladies do not always get the worst of it. As an unlimited supply of pomitos is provided for friends, some families spend as much as 30,000$ (£200) upon them, and the total outlay for the three days upon these scent fountains cannot be much less than from thirty to forty thousand pounds.

But the great animation of Carnival arises from the sparkling panorama, the milky way, of so dense a throng, fully one thousand, of finely-decked carriages and caparisoned horses, laden with the dazzling toilettes of multitudes of Hebes who, pursued by cavaliers on foot, dare to the encounter and loyally dispute the

laurels by the aid of pomitos and glass shields. With
these are interspersed cavalcades of harlequins, pun-
chinellos and other fantastics caricaturing well known
politicians, clubs on foot in splendid attire preceded
by bands of music, and gaily adorned waggons containing families of grotesque mascaras who, launching
their satire and flour bags together upon the gazers,
with

> Quips and cranks and wanton wiles
> Nods and becks and wreathed smiles

convulse the bystanders with merriment.

The public demonstrations are succeeded by balls
in the private houses and clubs, and but little rest is
taken during those three days and nights of intense
excitement, which are scarcely a suitable preparation
for the immediate solemnities of Lent.

The Strangers' Club, the entrance free to which is
about £ 8 and monthly contribution £ 2, is chiefly
composed of English and German Heads of houses,
and is in a flourishing condition; but the United, a
purely English association, started for the benefit of
Clerks, can barely keep the wolf from the door,
owing to the fact that few of that class remain in town
at night and so are unable to support it. Many of the
members of the Strangers' and the United, breakfast
and dine in them, and both are fitted up with libraries, billiard, card, chess and reading rooms. Besides
the French who possess a pure and well-ordered Club
for their own countrymen, no other nationality has succeeded in establishing such; for although the Germans

have nine or ten which are so called, they are rather associations, devoted either to music, gymnastics or philanthropy; and the same may be said of the various social ligaments which bind together Italians, Swiss and Belgians: indeed the number of societies, native and foreign, in Buenos Aires is simply wonderful, what with the scientific and literary, the Fine Arts' and Musical, the Agricultural and Horticultural, Pigeon Shooting and Rifle practice &c. but to the honour of human nature, the majority take a benevolent form. Here too are found Trade guilds, Freemasons, Foresters and one or two other secret bodies, pursuing modestly yet penumbrously their various works of charity; but philanthropy finds its noblest expression in two native Hospitals, besides the English, French, German and Italian: a *Cuna* or Foundling; Poor Asylum; Orphanages: a female Retreat; and Deaf and Dumb Institute. The *Sociedad de Beneficenzia* (Benevolent Society) composel of charitable native ladies, takes entire charge of the Women's Hospital, Foundling, Orphanages and the State School for girls, and formerly derived its income from a public lottery established under Municipal direction; however this source of support has of late years been cut off, but is about to be reestablished under National supervision, so that the Society has been obliged to fall back chiefly upon voluntary contributions.

Wherever the Spaniard wends his steps, the lottery as a matter of course follows, and notwithstanding that the odds are about 13 to 1 against any

return for investment, he regularly puts by a certain
portion of his income for the weekly temptation of
Fortune and usually takes the same number on his
ticket. No lotteries are now played in the Argentine
Republic, such being declared illegal in the Province
of Buenos Aires; but the neighbouring Republic
Uruguay, has two in operation, the administration of
which, although viewed with suspicion, suffices to
draw large sums of money weekly from this city.
The chief prize varies in general from £800 to £4000,
but at Christmas it is usual to institute a monster
hazard of £20000; and whole tickets subdivided into
fourths or fifths may be purchased for from 10/. to a
sovereign. Foreigners, especially the English, are
shy of confessing when Fortune smiles upon them in
this way, but the natives glory openly in their good
luck.

The city Hotels although numerous are not deserving of much notice, as they all, with three exceptions, partake too much of the restaurant or café type,
and are neither imposing nor very cleanly-looking
externally or internally. All receive boarders (pen-
sionistas) and for about £5 per month, provide
breakfast and dinner, with *vin ordinaire* gratis; adding the extras and a 7/6 fee to the waiter, this
amounts at the utmost to about 2/. a meal, which must
be considered very reasonable. The food is abundant,
varied and well-cooked in the French style, and garlic
and grease, those culinary abominations, rigidly
excluded. Two or three higher class cafés however

exist which do not admit boarders, and therein may be
enjoyed a dinner equal to anything in Europe and
at about the same cost. Almost the whole of the
bachelor residents take their two daily meals at one or
other of the hundreds of restaurants and it would
surprise our friends at home, who are generally
satisfied with a few cubic inches of toast, a mite of
bacon and one egg, washed down with a modest cup
of tea, to witness the substantial breakfasts which from
ten to twelve are here disposed of: *caldo* (broth);
cold meats; Stews; Grilled and Fried Meats; Potatoes
in various forms; Salads; eggs, cheese or omelette;
fruits; with wine ad lib. ; all settled by a cup of the
strongest Brazilian coffee, which when mixed with the
Bolivian berry (Yungas) is finer than Mocha : the
truth is, Brillat Savarin counts his disciples in thou-
ands and gastronomy, as practised in Buenos Aires,
may be dignified as a Fine Art : a fact further evidenced by those monstrous and wonderfully architectural
piles of confectionary which, dressed with fruit and
flowers, are carried on salvers from house to house as
presents to grace the various domestic festivals.

We now proceed to a more dignified subject, the
Museum ; but shall have to hasten to close the City
annals, having already transgressed the limits of our
space.

This institution, notwithstanding its locale, which
is the worst that could be chosen, cribbed, cabined
and confined, without light or air, in the upper storey
of the plot adjoining the University, is yet an honor

to the country. There is a tendency in this city to
restriction in public exhibitions ; to exclude European
products and to foster and bring prominently forward
only Argentine: the proposed Exhibition of 1881
was of this narrow nature and so with the Museum,
whose mission is to illustrate the natural history solely
of this Republic ; a remnant of the same spirit that
dictates to the economist the wisdom of a tariff of
protection. The Museum of Buenos Aires is doubtless rich, perhaps richer than any other, in palæologic
edentate osteology : those huge monsters which once
lazily trod its surface, are brought from their oozy
tombs by the wand of science, to astonish mankind by
their massiveness and uncouth forms, to attest zoologic
degeneracy and themselves to witness how the mighty
are fallen in the puny pigmy forms that now surround us. Fancy with what contempt must the huge
" *Glyptodon clavipes* " look down upon his tiny modern
representatives the " *Dasypus peba* " or the still
smaller " *Chlamydophorus truncatus* "; the gigantic
Megatherium twenty feet long and with bones more
massive than an elephant, or his ancient brother the
Mylodon somewhat less ponderous, with what a
derisive smile must they not view the efforts of their
feeble modern vicar the " *Bradypus tridactylus* ": and
so of the rest.

In its handsome cases are found the remains of
extinct tertiary animals, which besides the Glyptodon,
Megatherium and part of a Toxodon, include imperfect
specimens of a Scelidotherium and of three species of

Mylodon, and the fossil teeth of an antediluvian horse; a fine collection of recent Mammalia, in which the Armadillos the *Canis jubatus*, and two species of Chlamydophorus deserve notice; 1800 ornithological specimens and a magnificent entomological display, chiefly Brazilian; some skeletons of recent cetacea, including the *Epiodon*, line the vestibule; mineral wealth is well represented by a tempting show of ores; and a very curious picture, occupying the whole of an end wall, wrought on wooden tablets inlaid with mother-of-pearl, and accompanied by a commentary in Spanish, reveals to the visitor the details of the conquest of Mexico by Cortez, and is evidently the work of Indian artists.

The stranger would hardly expect to find buried here amongst his ponderous tomes, one of Europe's savans: yet so it is, the curator Dr. Hermann Burmeister. whose twenty years' residence in the Argentine Republic has not dimmed but enhanced the lustre of his fame, is a philosopher who has already celebrated his golden wedding to science: spare and tall, eagle-eyed, fibrous, his whole frame bristling with intellectual energy; such is the courteous but independent autocrat, whose figure stands out amongst the literati of South America, as did Saul's amongst the Israelites.

A few decades since it was the custom for mendicants to ply their trade on horseback and be licensed by the police; at present their numbers are so wonderfully increased, that if this mode of visiting were

still practised (some slay in chariots), it would be
impossible to be a moment free from their impor-
tunities; as it is, the knocker is assailed pretty frequently during the day and the "*Por amor de Dios*"
(for the love of God) sounds through the premises in
various whining tones. Now true distress arising
from bodily infirmity or inability to procure work,
every Christian would willingly compassionate, but
the case is far otherwise here : begging is taken up as
a profitable speculation and every Saturday is the
great field-day on which the halls of the richer part
of the community, as well as the other private dwellings, shops and stores are invaded by a throng of
sturdy and pertinacious beggars, clothed in the filthiest
rags obtainable from the *basura*, and some of whom,
especially the negresses, sport a cigar in the mouth.
If however this infliction were only hebdomadal or
otherwise periodic as formerly, it might be borne with
equanimity ; but the Beggars' Opera has now a daily,
nay hourly function, owing to the immense influx into
their ranks : it seems as though the Italian Municipal-
ities were emptying their dregs upon us, or that
paupers are farmed and made a regular article of
import : the fact is, illegitimate mendicity is fast
becoming a vice in Buenos Aires and needs police
supervision. Notwithstanding the magnificent asylum
for the real poor, and the abundance of work for those
who desire it, as long as the patricians provide through
their housestewards a stream of $ 5 notes for
indiscriminate distribution, it is not likely the number
of claimants will undergo diminution, and so in a

city where there is little need for begging save
amongst the maimed and aged, a race of *lazzaroni* will
be perpetuated. Men even in the receipt of good
wages, as opportunity occurs, sometimes doff the garb
of the fraternity of *Saint Lazarus*: thus, a coachman
of one of the first families in Buenos Aires, on the
departure of his employers for the usual summer trip
to the estancia, used to be left in charge of the town
house, but although still in service and with a pay of
$ 1000 (£ 7) a month, patrolled the city soliciting
alms, and it was his boast that he made more in this
way than by his regular employment.

As the old style of architecture has merged into
the new, and the maté bowl been exchanged for the
tea-cup (*), so the time of the old Charlies is gone for
ever; they were the exact counterpart of their fellow
genus in the London of 50 years ago, and after patrolling their beat and calling out in all the various tones
of the watchman's gamut *"Las once y media, noche
serena!*(half past eleven, fine night!), which was the
last sound that issued from their wheezy lungs that
night and gave them their soubriquet of "serenos",
used poor tottering old creatures to hang up their
lanterns on the nearest street post, seek a snug corner
and compose themselves to rest. Not so however now!
the chrysalis (sereno) has emerged into the butterfly
(vigilante), the sleepy into the wide-awake. The peace
of the city is maintained by a body of about 900 police

(*) The quantity of tea consumed in this city is enormous and the
natives pay as high as 10 . a lb. for it.

who are stationed on duty night and day, in the centres of the *boca-calles* (crossings), so that they have
full view of the four cardinal points, Armed with
the dirk, and some with the revolver, they do not
scruple to use either in case of any liberty being taken;
but their office is much of a sinecure in comparison
with that of their London brethren, as there are but
few drunken brawls here: a murder now and then
takes place, but such an unaccountable indifference on
that point reigns amongst all classes, that conduct
unbefitting a gentleman would be considered much
more scandalous in the public streets than running a
knife through the heart of a rival. The physique of
the corps is such as would not inspire terror in the
breast of a European criminal, but in this city the
sight of one such uniform in a crowd is sufficient;
sprightly, well-dressed and well-cinched, the police of
Buenos Aires, although somewhat useless in case of
robbery, are very determined in a scuffle, invariably
pouncing upon the wrong man, so that it is extremely
dangerous to interfere in a street or other quarrel. A
few years ago, a Post Captain in the English navy,
passing through the streets of Montevideo one evening, heard a woman's screams proceeding from an upper
storey; sailor-like he hesitated not a moment to spring
up the stairs to the rescue and found himself in
presence of a man who was bent upon killing a
woman; scarcely had he time to throw himself upon
the would-be murderer. before the spear of a valiant
sereno was lunged into his back, and from the wound
he died.

A hard case is that of the engine drivers! As all the railways run on pretty nearly a dead level and the crossings are numerous, strict rules are laid down to prevent persons walking on the line; however nothing in the shape of prohibition or fine will keep them off, and the consequence is they frequently get killed, a misfortune entirely their own fault; but the police instantly pounce upon the poor driver and consign him to prison whence, as there is no "*habcas corpus*", he may think himself lucky to be released in six or eight months: many drivers on seeing such an accident inevitable, leap off their engines and hide for a time.

During the reign of Governor Tejedor when the police were subject to provincial jurisdiction, they were drilled in the use of the rifle and bayonet, evidently for the purpose of aiding in the liberation of the province: he sowed armed men and they sprang up dragons' teeth; now however that their allegiance is due to the National authorities, their teeth have been drawn, their military exercises abandoned and the corps has lapsed into its purely civilian *rôle*.

A few words on the Lord Mayor and Aldermen of the city must close the chapter.

Here as elsewhere the Municipality as a body is not held in much esteem, as it treads merely on the lowest rungs of the Government ladder, and its action is generally vexatious. Foreigners are eligible to serve on the board, and some few attempts, on the part of Englishmen and Germans, have been made to occupy

civic chairs, but resignation quickly follows, and in
the absence of direct testimony we are led to surmise
that the atmosphere of the Townhall is too hot for
European constitutions. A President and twenty
members, subdivided into various committees, take
charge of offices of an Ædilic nature, such as lighting,
paving, street sweeping, water supply, buildings,
weights and measures, health, morals, public worship,
&c., impose taxes and levy fines, producing probably
an income of £ 100,000 a year, which is by no means
sufficient to cover expenses; so our city Fathers are
always impecunious, begging, borrowing, and funding
their debts, the coupons on which are ever in arrear.
No doubt the present government, whose vigorous
broom no cobweb escapes, will soon have something
to say to the effete corporation of Buenos Aires.

CHAPTER XI.

BUENOS AIRES

MEANS OF TRAVEL AND COMMUNICATION—RAILWAYS—TRAM-
WAYS—POST OFFICE—TELEGRAPH—TELEPHONE—STEAM-
BOAT—DILIGENCE—HACK-COACHES AND HACKS.

As to internal and external means of locomotion
and communication, Buenos Aires is, in some respects,
on a level with the most favoured cities; in others,
far in advance. Five lines of railway radiate from the
Capital, north, west and south, four of which the
Southern, Northern, Campana and Ensenada with its
branch to the Boca, have a common central terminus
on the barranca facing the river; but the fifth, the
Western with its branch to Chacarita, starts from the
Plaza Once, about two miles thence. The Southern,
an English line whose shares are at a high premium
and difficult to be obtained, lays open to the traveller
the south camps of Buenos Aires for a distance of
about 200 miles as far as Azul and Ayacucho besides
passing through some important towns as Chascomus
and Dolores; its goal however is not yet reached, and
no doubt in a few years a further stride of 200 miles
will be taken to Bahia Blanca, a port on the South
Atlantic which finds favour as the future capital of the
Province. The Northern, likewise of English parentage, but a much abused and long-suffering line,

incapable of extension, is left without a future, owing to the remarkable obtuseness of those who planned its route on the low-lying shore of a river subject to overflow, when high ground presents itself in the immediate neighbourhood. Although pleasure seekers grumble at the want of punctuality and absence of cleanliness and comfort, they use the line in preference to all others as it leads through a very picturesque country, studded with charming quintas, and ultimately to the Tigre, a distance of 20 miles, the usual site of pic-nics, regattas and moonlight Venetian processions. Enjoying but little cargo traffic, and cut off by the Campana line, from the river it hugs so fondly, nothing but the superhuman exertions of its present able manager have saved this railway from shipwreck.

To those whom business or pleasure summons to the distant upper provinces, the Campana line will be found to offer a comfortable, speedy and cleanly mode of transit. This railway, owned by an English company, was constructed merely to tap the traffic from the vast interior and for this purpose stretches its iron way 50 miles from the capital to the port on the Paraná which gives it its name. A train runs daily with the exception of Friday to meet one of the company's steamers in waiting there to convey passengers to Rosario and thence to all parts ; but the local traffic is insignificant and the route throughout uninviting, though in all its appointments this line makes a near approach to a well-conducted English one.

The far-seeing Wheelwright it was that planned

and by means of English capital carried out the line,
by which a visit may be made to Ensenada, a distance
of 35 miles from town, where lies the nearest natural
port to the city and the one used by the Spaniards for
two centuries. His object was to make that spot the
harbour for the capital and probably his experienced
eye was not at fault, as such a plan might be of all
others the most feasible and economical; but the
Porteños will never consent to remove the long line of
shipping from their own offing; although any works
undertaken at Ensenada would most probably be rendered subsidiary to Bateman's scheme which has
every prospect of being carried out in front of the
city: a bar appears to exist there which needs removal
and then no doubt with small additional expense a safe
and commodious harbour for a thousand seagoing
vessels might be constructed. The scheme however
does not meet with much support, and the Railway
languishes in consequence. At Punta Lara, three or
four miles this side of Ensenada, the company have
erected a fine substantial wooden pier nine hundred
yards in length, alongside of which vessels drawing
16 ft., may load and discharge at all states of the tide;
and as the Bonarenses sigh in summer for a bathing
place, here is one ready made to their hands, some 30
miles from the capital, with a railway passing through
it; whose sands in hardness and extent rival those of
the most favourite English watering-places; where a
southeast delicious breeze, smelling briny and coming
direct from the mouth of the river, is prevalent;
where the waves and swell are identical with those of

the ocean, although the water is fresh; where the fine bay offers a beautiful marine view or invites to a fishing excursion rewarded by pejeres as long as your arm or corbines strong enough to drag an Isaac Walton into the water; where the shore rapidly shelves to give at once a fine bath and a dive and the pier affords a splendid promenade; in fine a spot which a little enterprise might soon convert into a local Brighton. On the whole, the Ensenada railway, passing through a grazing district and flanked on the left, at some distance, by a low marshy coast line is not picturesque, yet in the neighbourhood of Quilmes the eye is agreeably relieved by numerous fine quintas and other evidences of cultivation and refinement; whilst on nearing Punta Lara, one of the grandest properties in the country arrests the attention. Here a native gentleman, Pereira, has laid out a quarter of a million sterling in pure adornment and in the acclimatisation of both rare animals and plants, which he strictly preserves; and on alighting at Ensenada, the terminus of the line, many fine Saladeros present themselves which, in full working order, well repay a visit.

The two remaining branches the Boca and Chacarita, that start the one from the common city terminus, the other from the Once, are both short local enterprises, extending not more than four or five miles, the former of which, belonging to an English Company, connects the capital with the mouth of the Riachuelo, on whose banks a colony of Italian boatmen and boatbuilders and numerous shops and cafés exist,

and in whose waters lie as thick as black-berries the
coasting and fishing craft, which bring from the
Upper Paraná oranges and other fruits, firewood,
charcoal and potatoes, or cargos of the finny tribe from
the roads : a pretentious little stream which, with its
breadth of scarce fifty yards and maximum depth of
ten or twelve, aspires to be considered the port of
Buenos Aires and under the direction of a native
engineer who has borrowed half of one of Bateman's
ideas, government has already sunk two or three
hundred thousand pounds and seems likely to squan-
der more on a pure chimæra.   For a few years past
it has rained port-schemes, but none of them comprehend a single original conception; they are all inspired by the ghost of the famous English hydraulist·
The life and activity of the Boca district, with its well
paved and well lighted streets and its promenades, are
surprising, especially on feast days when families
from town mingle with crowds of the indigenous,
ramble on the river banks or secure bargains in fruit
or fish taken straight from the hold.

From the previous gay and busy scene, we turn
to a sad and lifeless one.   The Chacarita, a government branch of the Western, transports a cargo of
dead to the mortuary.   Here lie in the Cemetery the
plague victims, a holocaust of 23,000 which the city
offered up to the malicious fiend on his last visit in
1871 and it is still used as one of the outlying burial-
grounds.   Apart from this, it is a pleasant little line
and when duty, affection or pleasure leads to sepul-

chral decoration or a visit to the military encampment in the neighbourhood, it affords another agreeable outlet for the panting population of the densely-crowded metropolis.

The last of the home railways, the Western, and the first constructed in the Republic, has its terminus at the Plaza Once, so that a coach or tramway is necessary to reach it ; formerly it started from the Plaza Parque, within the city, the trains passing through a mile or so of densely inhabited streets, with great danger to life. By means of this railroad and its three branches, to Lobos, Pergamino and Rojas, the rich grazing and agricultural western camps of Buenos Aires, as well as several important towns, such as Mercedes and Chivilcoy are visited ; and although at present the career of the main-trunk line terminates at Bragado, 133 miles distant from the capital, many other feeders are in course of projection, and ultimately no doubt the network will be completed by a junction with the Andine at Rio Cuarto. This western line, the property of the Provincial Government, enjoys the reputation of being the best managed in the Republic ; and if in addition to the punctuality, comfort, civility and very moderate charges of its service, we inspect its balance sheet and find a net profit of 8 per cent., the half of which is mortgaged, and that with the remaining half it has been able to construct its branches, no one can withhold admiration from so surprisingly archetypic an administration. No wonder then that whilst the English railways have to suffer much hostile criticism from the native press, the Government line, like an Adonis, lives in an atmosphere superior to it; the fact is, the Argentines are impatient to obtain the control over all large foreign public enterprises within their territory, especially the railways, and having expressly inserted in their law of construction a clause entitling them to expropriate on payment of 20 per cent. above their cost, the newspapers frequently hound on the government to take advantage of the provision. In the case of one English line, it would be to the manifest advantage of the shareholders that such action should take place.

Due to the absence of engineering difficulties, all the lines have been and are constructed very cheaply, in no case exceeding £10000 per mile, with the exception of the Northern and Boca, where after repeated expense was incurred from the invasion of the river, in the immediate neighbourhood of the city, it was found absolutely necessary to carry the lines on iron viaducts.

English cars are used on all the lines, but those generally preferred are the long American saloons, as they afford more air, the guard traverses the central aisle and a larger company can be gathered together to promote conversation and sociality. A low rate of speed, averaging from 20 to 25 miles per hour, is combined with moderate fares, the maximum of which is 2½d. per mile, first class. The comfort of the passengers is usually studied and the guards are generally very polite and attentive; but one of the greatest inconveniences of railway travelling in the Plate is the dust which is excessive and so very fine and penetrating, that dust-coats are an absolute necessity.

Owing to the strong objection of Argentine generally to traverse any distance however insignificant on foot, the Tramways on their introduction in 1871 were found exactly suitable to native habits and in consequence spread so quickly and extensively that now Buenos Aires possesses a greater length of rails (150 miles) than any other city in the world; the present network is so completely bewildering that Kidd's Guide, the local Bradshaw, has started up to unfold its mysteries. These tramways have brought one great improvement in their train; the Municipality seeing their opportunity, arising from the eagerness of empresarios, made it a preliminary condition before granting a concession to traverse any route in the city that the concessionaire should pave the whole of the streets included in the course with *adoquines* (square cut blocks of granite), so that the central part of the metropolis has been laid down without burdening the civic finances; in the case of one contractor who undertook to construct a line of five miles to Belgrano, the condition of granting the concession was that he should macadamize the road the whole distance, an onerous obligation which fairly broke his back. The cars are very light and comfortable, holding about 30 people, and the fare to any part of the city is 2$ (3d.), but to the environs 3$, 4$ or 5$ according to distance: the number of travellers annually car-

ried by the five city companies reaches the astonishing
figure of fifteen millions, and what speaks to the care-
fulness of the drivers is that although the rails are
laid close to the kerb, very few accidents indeed
occur.

The enormous difficulties arising from immense
distances, sparseness of population and the rough physical features of much of the Argentine soil, render
the interior Post-Office service one full of hazard and
obstacles. The poor postmen, in all weathers, and at
great speed, have to climb mountains, swim streams,
cross deserts and otherwise endure great hardships :
but the National Government does all in its power to
mitigate suffering and remove impediments by maintaining in repair roadways and bridges, for which
there is a special credit launched on the market,
whose scrip bears an annual interest of 8 per cent ;
and it is really wonderful with what exactness the
duties are performed ; it is a very rare circumstance
indeed to lose a letter, although newspapers are not
subject to the same care. The land services to Chili
and Bolivia entail great peril upon the letter carriers,
especially the former, when in the winter twelve or
fourteen days are required to cross the Andes on foot
in snow shoes; and many is the poor fellow swallowed
up, correspondence and all, by the sudden snow storms
accompanied by violent hurricanes. The Republic
having joined the Postal league, is enabled to release
foreign correspondence from its former heavy charges
and now for 6d., a letter can be posted to all parts of

Europe and those other countries included in that association; whilst from one end of the republic to the other 3d. is the cost of a similar missive.   About ten millions of postal matter pass annually through the central office and every year it is increasing.   The facilities for postal transmission within the city boundaries are very great; pillars are erected at intervals and several times a day, even to late at night, deliveries take place, whilst for the interior, mail bags are daily made up and almost as frequently for Europe; and yet answers are many times received from the latter before a reply from some distant part of the republic puts in an appearance.   There is no doubt that the Argentine Post Office is well organised, and considering the vast obstacles to be encountered, that its service is exceedingly well administered : the systems of Book-post, Postal cards, Registered letters and all the others regulations of St. Martin's le Grand are in full operation here and very well patronised.

Thanks to the spirited administration of President Sarmiento (1868 – 1874), the whole of the Republic was spanned by the electric wires, a measure which benefitted it in two ways; as it equalized the advantages of the Provincianos and Porteños, between which two classes there has ever been jealousy; and put an end for ever to intestine provincial squabbles that were rendered feasible solely by the want of ready communication with the central focus of power.

Such a revolution in the means of intercourse is easily recorded ; but in a country like this no European can conceive the difficulties that had to be, and still have to be, overcome in the physical obstacles of the vast region, as well as the obstinate opposition of the people in the interior. To reticulate a kingdom such as England with Æolian wires and to maintain them in working condition, are matters comparatively simple : but although here it is a question of exceeding difficulty, enormus daily expense and administrative capacity, 10000 miles of wire have been already suspended and every regulation of the most advanced countries adopted, with the exception of the employ-ment of female clerks. To flash a message of ten words to any part of the Republic for a little more than a shilling, to Chili for ten shillings, to Bolivia for 7/6, or to London for £5, are advantages capable of satisfying the demands of commercial or private necessity. Nor is this all, further facility for the quick transmission of intelligence is afforded by the Telephone by which all the public offices are now connected ; the President daily converses by this means with his Ministers before arrival in town from his quinta in the suburbs ; and the time seems looming when man will scarcely need bodily presence and activity, but the subtlety of ethereal intercourse ban-ishing corporeality he will begin his immortality on this side the grave.

The great fluvial highways of this country are traversed by numerous steamboats, but the lesser streams have not, as yet, been generally rendered navigable.   Although, as was early remarked in this

work, the republic is on the whole badly watered,
nothing but capital is required to divert by artificial
means some portion of the superabundance of the gifts
of Aquarius, so as to irrigate and connect the vast
interior. Daily steam service takes place to Montevideo and Rosario; every few days to Corrientes,
Concordia and Asuncion and all intermediate ports;
and when the rivers are high the upper parts of the
Paraná and Uruguay may be visited by the same
means. Bahia Blanca, Patagones and Chubut enjoy
bi-monthy communication with the capital, owing to
the liberality of the government in converting a new
and magnificent troopship, lately received from England, into a packet for those distant parts; but the
Falkland isles are as yet left out in the cold and seem
to remain satisfied with a monthly sailing-packet service to and from Montevideo and the casual call of H.
M's vessels. Travelling by the riverine and coast
steamers is rendered agreeable by the sumptuous style
in which they are fitted up, the excellence and abundance of the cuisine, and the reasonableness of the
fares. A ticket to Rosario, a passage of 18 hours,
including the railway and dinner on board, costs no
more than 38/.; to Montevideo, in 12 hours, 30/.;
and to Corrientes, 3 days, about £ 5, whilst the fare
to Bahia Blanca or Patagones is about £ 6 or to Chubut £ 9. The monster, decked, Mississippi steamers
tried a few years ago to gain a footing here for riverine service, but Nemesis hoisted her flag at the main,
misfortune tracked their keels, and most of them
being either burnt or wrecked, the Argentine public,

ever distrustful of the waves, became afraid of them,
and now pin their faith to the less pretentious but
safer English craft. With regard to oceanic steam
service, the eye has only to wander to the distant
horizon, to observe the mast heads of a fleet of noble
ships embracing representatives from the Royal Mail,
Pacific, Lamport and Holt's, Scotch, German, French
and Italian companies, which vie with each other in
courting the passenger and merchandise traffic to and
from Europe ; so that scarcely a day passes without
the departure or arrival of one such, nay at times two
or even three on the same day, and most of them land
their patrons on European soil within the month, at a
universal fare of £ 35.

In this country the Diligence better deserves its
name than in many parts of Europe, as, yoked with
eight or ten horses or mules, the pace is generally good,
and when the road permits, ascends to a continued
gallop: nevertheless the vehicle itself, as well as the accommodation it offers, are by no means inviting to the
European eye, although very suitable to this incipient
region ; unwashed, dust-laden mud-bespattered, with
ungroomed horses, harness of the roughest, springs
made to jolt, doors and windows not to open or close
and drivers of the seediest, it requires great determination to entrust oneself for a day or two to the coffin-
like omnibus; but after all, it is Hobson's choice,
unless the traveller prefers an independent life on
horseback, with a bed on the open camp, the recado
for pillow, his sleep disturbed by nipping cold, the

sniffing of the barking fox or the sinister eyes of the
wicked carancho; as it is, every town in the Province
of Buenos Aires, being connected with the cap'tal by
Diligence either directly or by means of the train and
diligence, homo intercourse is neither difficult nor
expensive, although the annoyances of heat and dust
are well-nigh intolerable at times; a dense cloud of
the latter, enveloping the whole procession, always
accompanies and hides the cavalcade from mortal sight
and forces the traveller to taste the ashes of his
fathers before his time.

Besides the tramways, locomotion to the different
points of the city is assisted by the numerous pair-
horse hackney coaches stationed in every Plaza.
These stands are licensed by the Municipality at a
high rate and in consequence the fares are considerable, from 3/. to 4/. an hour, but neither the vehicles
nor the jarveys bear that indescribable appearance of
seediness, that air of approximate dissolution, so universal in London. Here it is a dignified though
unpleasant mode of travelling; dignified as the whole
appointment indicates a private turn-out; unpleasant,
because of the jolting from the execrable pavement;
but as the guage of the tramways, which now pass
through almost every street, is foolishly identical with
that of all other vehicles, coaches wear the companies'
metals to avoid injury to their own springs. "One
touch of nature makes the whole world kin!" what is
it in the nature or calling of cabby to make him universally extortionate? a street Arab whose hand is

against every man? just as in London, he holds out
the sixpence for the inspection of his fare, seeking in
meek irony to know, what it is; so here, no municipal regulations as to charges ever satisfy him, and
country cousins are especially victimised by his exorbitant claims.   A few years ago the eyes of the
English were gratified at the sudden apparition of a
real Hansome in the streets of Buenos Aires, which
stood its ground for a few months, but ultimately
withdrew, a sacrifice to competition and chaff.   If
however a quicker mode of transit is sought, the
numerous *caballerizas* (livery stables) will supply at
any moment a good saddle horse for 6/. a day; and
this mode is generally employed by collecting clerks
to farm the weekly Saturday accounts; talking of
stables, almost all the stately mansions in the capital
have their own within, so that the odour from them
permeates the whole premises, an arrangement which
the Sanitary Commissioners ought at once and for
ever to dispense with.

CHAPTER XII.

BUENOS AIRES

TRADE — BANKS — BOLSA AND PUBLIC FUNDS — MONETARY SYSTEMS AND MINT — IMPOSTS — WEIGHTS AND MEASURES.

The Argentines as a nation are not given to commercial pursuits and so it happens that the import and export trades of the capital, which may amount in the aggregate to about £ 30,000.000, have fallen almost entirely into the hands of foreigners, who have provided the capital necessary to develop these as well as pretty well all other industrial enterprises. Few houses however are limited strictly to one of the two branches; most of the importers ship this country's treasures, such as wool, hides, skins, tallow, wheat, maize, saladero produce, mules, ores or woods, either on their own account or on commission. The trade of the city is subject to much fluctuation, not only according to season, but as the result of political disturbance or speculation; so that at one time prostrate, at another in the height of fever, it is perpetually oscillating between the two extremes of actual failure from depletion, or threatened crisis from surfeit. It is probable however that civic agitation has received a serious check if not its permanent quietus, so that danger from this source may not be apprehended in

future ; and well would it be if the other were equally
shorn of its peril. The country has but just recovered
from a very severe crisis lasting several years and
produced by over trading, and it is much to be feared
that a similar state of affairs will soon recur, from the
present enormous importation, which is out of all proportion to the requirements of the population ; infla-
tion and collapse lie very contiguous. So common is
it, that inability to meet engagements is thought but
little of here, and to be whitewashed several times, if
it does not impart lustre to the commercial career,
scarcely adds a speck to its reputation ; yet there are
firms which have stood like oaks bending to every
storm though never breaking and which now after half
a century of service, still viridescent, still occupying
the first rank, are a standing rebuke to the general
haste to get rich, to that accelerating process which,
more frequently than not, leads to disaster. The dry-
goods' and hardware houses are the wealthiest : but
the importation of eatables and drinkables is subject to
many disadvantages, as adulteration and falsifi-
cation, which are practised to such an amazing extent
in Buenos Aires, especially in wines and spirits, that
it is utterly impossible to get either pure retail.
French wine, so universally consumed, is the most
adulterated of all ; subject before it leaves Bordeaux
to the process known as "plâtrage", that is sprinkling
the grapes with gypsum to give fictitious age by suddenly withdrawing the astringency, an operation
which, in addition, by the interchange of elements
with the potassa salts of the must, produces "potassium

sulphate" a drastic purgative ; the wine arrives hither
to undergo further doctoring, by the introduction of
logwood decoction to impart colour and other ingredients to restore some of the lost astringency. The
same means are successful with the coarse Spanish
wines, which are for this purpose bought largely by
the Bordeaux merchants and, after manipulation, passed off as the produce of their own hill-districts.

The case is even worse with the liqueurs ; as
alcohol is largely distilled from maize and other sources, and is very cheap, they are boldly manufactured,
by simply adding a little flavouring, so that harsh
spirits of wine is the only stimulant sold retail. In the
case of the wines, they are not altogether an unmixed
evil (in two senses), as they act at least as cathartics
and perhaps thus keep the population in healte.

The export trade however is not a whit behind the
import in activity and so wonderfully is the country
opening up that, notwithstanding the general luxury
and waste, a balance in its favour will soon be recorded, the criterion of prosperity according to the
economists. A cowd of merchants, *barraqueros* (storers
of produce), brokers and middle-men, for the half of
whom there it scarcely legitimate business, vie with
each other in bulling the market and n any are the
bargains that become roast chestnuts in the hands of
the speculators.

As regards manufactures, many trials have been
made in Silk, Cloth, Glass, Paper, Boots, Gloves, &c.,

and although backed up by capital or government subvention have universally failed, with the exception of Breweries, Distilleries and Biscuit factories, owing to the absence of, or exorbitant remuneration demanded for skilled labour (*) and the excessive dearness of fuel (Coal £3 to £4 a ton). British capital has suffered so much of late years in private enterprises in this country, that it is now somewhat shy of bolstering up such undertakings, although for public purposes and under authoritative guarantee, the offers are always in excess of the need.

The number of insurance offices is always a good trade barometer and as the increase in their ranks has been so great lately, it serves as an indication of commercial prosperity: all the best London offices are represented by first-class agencies and the business they do is of a highly remunerative character, especially in Fire, as the houses are so built as to be practically incombustible, although goodness knows they are tested in this way to the utmost limit of endurance; every child even carries phosphorous matches which are continually being struck to light the universal cigarette and are then thrown carelessly alight on the floor. Trade generally is much hampered by the want of a port, for as the lighters have to go out 15 miles to load and unload in open exposed roadsteads, much time is wasted and damage and loss sustained;

(*) The question of skilled technical labour has lately engaged the serious attention of the National authorities, who have just established a grand school of Mechanical Arts, for the training of Argentines in the use of machine tools.

for a rich city like Buenos Aires, the evil is crying and shows that commercial shrewdness is only skin deep.

Of the six banks at present existing in the Capital, the Provincial with an effective capital of two millions sterling, is the acknowledged king, as well from government support, fiscal priviledges, and the right of emission as from the extent of its beneficial operations : it controls the price of gold, establishes the rate of exchange and has become a powerful rival of, if not dictator to, foreign capital. Established under the ægis of the Provincial Government, which nominates its directory, its operations are conducted with a view to foster commerce by liberal discounts at a low rate, and as it is the only bank where labour is accredited, any restriction of the sphere of its operations would be felt injuriously.

The National Bank started in a time of crisis, with a nominal capital of five millions sterling, in order to provide the interior of the country with the same monetary facilities as the littoral, seems destined under the present National Government to rise at the expense of the Provincial : two-thirds of its directory are nominated by the shareholders and the remaining third by the National authorities and its scrip subject, to much fluctuation, is quoted and dealt in on the Exchange. The Hypothecary (mortgage) Bank, an offshoot of the Provincial, issues loans on property to the extent of 50 per cent. of its value, and acts as a savings' Bank of its own scrip (*cedulas*) which bears an interest of 8 per cent. and whose average quotation on the exchange is about 85. The English and Italian joint stock undertakings and Carabassa's private bank complete the list; four others which were considered strong, the Mercantile, Argentine, Maua and Belgo-German have disappeared from the scene; so that Lombard Street is by no means crowded, and as the business is not only lucrative, but with good, not dilet-tante management, very secure, we may hope soon to see an increase in the number of strong-rooms. At present the general bank rate for borrowers is about 8 per cent. and the interest allowed on deposits 3 per cent. whilst the rate of exchange is 49½ pence to the patacon.

The *Bolsa* (Exchange, literally purse) is, like most other similar institutions throughout the world, the centre of the activity and business operations of the city between the legal hours of 12 and 2; although till 4 p m. when it is finally closed, the throng does not much dim'nish: and yet European Exchanges cannot compare, at any rate outwardly, with the high pressure that is here produced by the struggles of 300 brokers to create fictitious value. The London Stock Exchange with its variations of eighths and sixteenths would not feed the hungry crowd of bulls and bears that daily lines our hall. The stocks dealt in are all of home creation, consisting of National, Provincial and Municipal bonds, National and Pro-vincial Treasury bills, Mortgage Cedulas, National Bank shares, the different Railway, Tramway and

Gas scrip, Roads and Bridges, and sundry Telegraph lines, representing an aggregate amount in circulation of about 2¼ millions sterling, and which originally issued as 6, 8 or 9 per cent. stocks, are now bought at prices to yield dividends of from 7 to 9 per cent. which is very moderate indeed for this country. As the patacon is not fixed, paper money being inconvertible at present, besides dabbling in stocks with a daily fluctuation of one or two per cent., the oscillation of gold to the amount of ten or twenty cents. each way, engrosses the attention of the two opposing classes, one of which desires cheap, the other dear gold, amongst the latter of which are the produce shippers, as with gold under 30, exportation is at present almost stopped; and so this game at see-saw is a diurnal pastime in the Temple of Plutus, where "*le palais de la Renommée*" itself is rivalled in point of rumours and canards to influence prices. Here the various gold, stock, comestible, produce and ship brokers elbow merchants, sea captains and proposers of various schemes to enrich, and make the marble floor reecho with their nimble tread in pursuit of percentages and differences.

The existing money of the city and Province of Buenos Aires is the *peso* (paper dollar) worth at present about 1½d., although formerly its value was identical with that of the United States dollar. Gold is not used as a circulating medium, but only to aid speculation, no money can be made in it, and the banks will scarcely receive it in deposit; certainly all who have used paper money prefer it to heavy coin, and if its value were only permanent and itself convertible, nothing more could be desired. The fixed but imaginary unit of monetary value is the gold patacon or hard dollar 4,88 of which go to the Sovereign and all gold transactions and accounts are kept in this unit. But all other parts of the Republic, having been deprived of the right of coining which existed twenty years ago, are in a state of great monetary confusion; the Provincial Banks have the priviledge of a paper emission which is usually excessively depreciated, foreign silver and gold, Bolivian, Chilian, Peruvian and Brazilian are current, especially the debased silver Bolivian dollar, worth about 22 pesos of capital money, and the Chilian gold Condor of 9,25 hard dollars (£ 1.18.0). The numerous moneys of the interior render travelling there both unpleasant and expensive, as every change is for the worse, loss occurs on each transaction and the question is who is the gainer. In order therefore to create fiscal order out of monetary chaos, Congress passed a uniform currency law in 1875, and the National government has erected a fine Mint, at which operations are about to commence to provide the Republic with the following coinage :

GOLD $\frac{900}{1000}$ FINE

The Double Colon, worth about £ 4.2, weight 33,333 grammes

" Colon, " " £ 2.1, " 16,666 "

" Half Colon " £ 1.0,6. 8,333 "

SILVER $\frac{900}{1000}$ FINE

The Dollar, worth about	4/1,	weight	27,110 grammes
" Fifty-cents'	s. 2.0½,	"	12,500 "
" Twenty-cents'	9¾d,	"	5,000 "
" Ten-cents'	4¾d.	"	2,500 "
" Five-cents'	2½d,	"	1,250

BRONZE { 95 per cent Copper / 4 " " Tin / 1 " " Zinc

The Two-cents' piece, worth about	1d,	weight	10 grammes
" One-cent	½d,	"	5 "

In an early chapter of this work, the means employed by the National Government to secure a revenue, were discussed, and Custom Houses and Public Lands indicated as the chief sources of the Ways and Means; no doubt in time to come, Stamps, the Post Office, Telegraphs and various railways already constructed, or in course of construction, will help to swell the National coffers, but at present the Treasury cannot count upon any but the two former very variable springs, of which one is far from exhaustless.

How often, no doubt, in their pecuniary troubles and virtuous self-sacrifice, have not the eyes of President and Chancellor wandered over the vast field, especially of this city and province, wherein lie exposed such evidences of wealth and which is so ripe for taxation, with the desire that with the tips of their fingers merely, they might be allowed to scrape together some of the superfluity presented to their gaze! but no, it would be an act of contravention of the constitution for Congress to levy direct imposts, which is strictly a Provincial prerogative; so the National

executive has had to withdraw its itching palm and
remain satisfied with fostering by every method
within reach its dual, soon to become plural, resources;
and it is evident that immigration, by disposing of the
public lands and augmenting at once producing power
and consumption, is the great panacea for what cannot
be styled other than frail finance. The Custom House
tariff involves, on the average, about 35 per cent. on
invoice prices and some months, that in the capital
yields as much as £ 300,000.

A property tax (*Contribucion directa*) of 5 per
mill. imposed by the province, an annual *Patente*
(license) for carrying on business within the city, which
is severe on some classes as banks. (£ 200), and the
usual municipal rates, have to be borne, but otherwise
the people are lightly taxed.

The old Spanish weights and measures which,
like the language, have undergone great changes in
different parts of this country since their first introduction, vied with the monetary system in producing
such confusion as at last to arouse the government to
attempt remedial measures. People generally imagined that the English system was tolerably complex,
but the Argentine Republic, a comparatively new
member of the fraternity of nations, bears on its young
shoulders even greater anomalies, the remains of that
yoke, which she is fast severing in her anxiety to rise
into the foremost rank by progress and intelligence.
After a few years preliminary warning, a law has at
length been promulgated, declaring the ancient system

of weights and measures at an end and substituting in their stead, the French metric code; but the people are not yet educated up to this standard, and it will take a century at least to effect a complete change.

The chief weights and measures at present in use with their English equivalents, are the following :—

LENGTHS

The Unit for—

Small	lengths is the	*Vara*	=	,947 Eng. Yards	
Medium	"	*Cuadra* (150 varas)	=142,050	"	"
Great distances	"	*League* (40 cuadras) =	3,228	" Miles	

LIQUIDS

The Unit for—

Small quantities is the	*Cuarta* (quart)	=	1.050 Eng. Pints	
Medium " "	*Frasco*	=	4,200	" "
" " or the	*Galon* (gallon)	=	6,720	" "
Large " is the	*Barril* (barrel)	= 16,800	" Gallons	
" " or the	*Pipa* (pipe)	=100,800	" "	

WEIGHTS

The Unit for—

Small weights is the	*Libra* (pound)	=	1,013 Eng. lbs. Avoir.		
Medium " "	*Arroba* (25 libras)	= 25,323	" " "	
Large "	*Tonelada* (Ton)	=	,904 " Ton	

AGRARIAN MEASUREMENT

The Unit for—

Small superficies is the	*Cuadra* or *Manzana*	=	4,169 Eng. Acres	
Large " "	*Square League*	= 10,422	" Square Miles	

CHAPTER XIII.

BUENOS AIRES

CLIMATE — HEALTH AND SANITARY LAWS — DISEASE AND
MORTALITY — MORTUARIES — CREMATION.

How brightly azure by day, how brilliantly beautiful by night, the firmament that hangs as a canopy
over the favoured city of Buenos Aires! Orion with
its companion constellations of Canis major and minor,
the Southern Cross, the Milky way and Magellan's
clouds, provide a starry illumination in which, Sirius,
Procyon, Rigel, and Betelgueux glow as incandescent
suns. Here no atmosphere tainted with manufacturing refuse, no soot begriming the features and tar-
nishing the work of the architect, but a soft transparent
ether perpetually fanning the cheek with its gentle
zephyr; and although the sun's rays scorch by day,
and fans and sunshades are much in request, the
evenings and mornings revel in grateful coolness.
And when at times the ambient air becomes well
nigh insufferable from the northern Zonda blasts,
straight from his cavern on the Andes comes the
mighty Pampero to refresh humanity and equalize the
temperature. That the "airs are good" is testified
alike by the very name the city has borne for three

centuries and by the number of macrobians dwelling
in it, on an average perhaps one centenarian for every
ten thousand of its inhabitants. The Bonaerenses live
surrounded by an atmosphere, salubrious and invigorating as it is clear and blue, and in which

The mean annual barometric pressure is 29,965 inches

" average " Temperature............ 71° Fahr. and

"   "   " Rain-fall .... 33,335 inches.

As nature has done so much in climate for the
capital, it is only to be expected that the inhahitants
should do their part by cleanlines of site, dwelling
and person to preserve the queen city in a Sanitary
condition. Unfortunately relying too much upon
past immunity and forgetting the dreadful scourge
that visited Buenos Aires in 1727, when the cadavers
were lassoed to the horses' tails and dragged to the
outskirts for burial, laxity and reliance upon natural
advantages characterized the Bonaerenses, until three
comparatively late epidemics, introduced from Brazil,
two of cholera and one of Yellow Fever, following
closely upon one another, awoke them from a fatal
lethargy, and inspired them with a sudden zeal for
purification, which eventuated in a magnificent port,
water-supply and sewerage scheme, for which the
money was actually voted, but spent instead on ironclads. The site therefore as yet remains in " statu
quo"; as regards the dwellings, although built with
rooms, doors and windows of high pitch, so as to
admit plenty of light and air and thus contrasting
with the closeness and stuffiness of European apart-

ments, badly-burnt bricks made of clay impregnated with salts and cemented with river mud saturated likewise with saline matter, render the walls little else than efflorescent sponges, barometric planes which, in the absence of fires even in winter, are a starling menace to health; if they were kept clean however, that would be a redeeming point; yet although the front part open to visitors is the pink of perfection, a model of propriety, a peep into the back patio reveals to nostril and eye foul sinks, sewers and other exposed filthy receptacles whose mephitic emanations combined with the carbonic oxide of the thousands of braziers, in which charcoal is consumed for cooking and ironing, defile the inner atmosphere of the city, and drive the inhabitants to seek, according to the advice of physicians, the upper storeys as dormitories. Not only so, but densely crowded *conventillos* (clusters of rooms) filled chiefly with Italians, abound even in the heart of the city, whose tenants have little facility and perhaps less inclination to keep them clean.

A residence near the river is considered unhealthy by reason of the evaporation from such a vast body of shallow fresh water, as well as the vapours that arise from the extensive, exposed, moistened coast of low water, which become evident in winter by mantling the city in early morning with a dense sheet of fog, soon to be dissipated however by the rising sun. So likewise houses and rooms with a southern aspect are always damp in the fall of the year, a fact rendered patent to the wayfarer, as he sees those sides of the streets looking southwards steeped in moisture till midday, whilst the opposite are perpetually dry.

Of all the habits most conducive to a healthy condition, personal cleanliness claims the highest consideration and in this respect, the upper classes in Buenos Aires may well challenge competition : as all the houses of any pretension are fitted up with a bathroom attached to the "*aguas corrientes*" (water works), every member of the family takes advantage of it throughout the year, so that daily cold water ablution, and in the summer-time even two or three times a day, is the universal custom from the father to the least chick; but once descend below this grade, the stratum of the great unwashed is reached, a race of pachyderms sadly in need of honest Mrs. Partington's mop and pail.

A scene I witnessed on board the steamer that brought our family to this country, first opened my eyes as to what might be expected in the lavatory department : even French washing arrangements are not usually on too profuse a scale, but the Latin race as a whole can scarcely be induced to try water for any other purpose than drinking. The steamer was on its passage from Bahia to Rio, and had embarked several Brazilian gentlemen, the daily ablution of one of whom I had an opportunity of observing. He stood at the bottom of the companion with a tumbler of water in the left hand, dipped the tips of the fingers of his right therein, smeared the moistened extremities over his black bristly features, repeated the operation twice or thrice, *drank off* the remainder of the liquid, wiped his face with his pocket handkerchief and nimbly jumped up the ladder as though powerfully refreshed. The fact is the city does not receive fair play from its inhabitants in matters sanatorial, and will never be able to reduce its deathrate, until, stone or English bricks cemented with lime and pure sand be used for building, conventillos swept away, sewerage prohibited from being vomited into the river directly in front of it, horses from taking their matutinal tub therein (*), washerwomen driven from their stronghold on the river banks, works to carry off noxious matter completed, and people generally educated to the necessity of greater cleanliness in person and residence; for although negros are proof against any amount of dirt, those of European descent soon furnish victims to the want of proper sanitary precautions.

Nature however kindly supplements man's neglect, and as with the Pampero she sweeps the regions of the air and instils new life into it, so with the Deluge she searches the innermost corners of corruption, carrying away all city impurities into the vast cloaca of the River Plate, so that Buenos Aires is never so healthy as in the rainy season: and if sometimes the inconveniences of a drenching shower have

---

(*) A curious sight it is to witness the distant moving black spots, indicating a troop of horses swimming, with a man standing upright circus-fashion on the back of one and guiding the whole by his shouts; these men not unfrequently get drowned.

to be endured, never are the boots penetrated, the feet numbed and the whole frame chilled by having to wade through that dreadful London slush, consequent upon thawing snow. The only snow that falls in this city, and which seen at a distance resembles it, is that of the delicate, white filaments of the thistle down and that even finer glistening gossamer, bearing each their aëronauts, the former a seed, the latter a tiny spider.

In the first chapter of this work, when treating of the health of the littoral, much was advanced that of course applies to the capital, but at the risk of repetition, it is necessary to remark that nature avenges excess quicker here than in Europe; the digestive organs are liable to be easily disordered ; the air does not seem to favour the healing of wounds ; lockjaw is not infrequent, tumours and abcesses common. Almost every infant is subject to a violent and very fatal form of indigestion which, combined with the parental neglect so common amongst the lower order, makes baby mortality excessive. Small-pox, augmented of late by the introduction of so many Indian children into city service, demanded last year a holocaust of 832 victims or 0,333 per cent. of the population ; of lung diseases, which are unfortunately by no means rare and on the increase, owing to sudden changes of temperature, damp residences and supremely tight lacing, consumption claimed 774 or 0,309 per cent. and pneumonia 462 or 0,185 per cent.

Even in the hottest season, neither Siriasis in

man, nor Hydrophobia in dogs is widespread; the inhabitants take great care not to expose themselves unnecessarily to the direct rays of the sun and then only with a silk handkerchief to protect the nape of the neck ; and as for the dogs, the breed is so inferior as not to subject them ordinarily to a disease so aristocratic and which like gout in man only attacks good blood. Talking of dogs, they are kept here for three purposes; to guard houses, to rid rooms of vermin, and to act as a warming pan : the first object needs no comment, but the second and third are unique and confined to this city. The English idea is to prevent the entrance of the canine species into rooms as, like the Russian ambassadors in the time of Queen Anne, they shed vermin (but not pearls), the opposite belief obtains in Buenos Aires where the thickcoated especially are encouraged in the houses to attract and carry out the fleas : it would require a Diophantine analysis to determine which view is correct : but to use a dog as a hot water bottle is extraordinary ! for this purpose, the lower class of women select a hairless smooth-skinned Chinese breed and popping the unfortunate between the sheets, extract all the warmth they can from its carcase, on a cold winter's night.

Dry smoking, especially of cigarettes made from coarse, black, Brazilian tobacco, is a fruitful source both of apoplexy and paralysis : the English, in their fondness for strong flavours in everything, generally prefer these to others manufactured from the lighter and more wholesome kinds: but by the natives they

are termed "peons' smoke", that is only fit for labourers. It has been remarked before that the blacks are
very subject to small-pox, but in addition it may be
added that they form a large proportion of the inmates
of the lunatic asylum, as a harmless kind of insanity,
which very seldom results in actual madness, is very
prevalent amongst them. In minor matters, the Porteños enjoy good sight even to advanced age and it is
rare to see them use spectacles or even eye-glasses ;
but the ladies for ever sucking sweetmeats have to pay
the penalty of bad teeth and are constant attendants
upon the dentists : Buenos Aires may be styled, the
" *Paraiso de los Dentistas* " (Dentists' Paradise).

The children born in this city, both of whose
parents are Europeans are always delicate, whilst those
of mixed descent are strong and healthy ; so likewise
when European children are brought hither at a tender age, they seldom become vigorous.

The home province alone maintains a Registrar
General of Births, Deaths and Marriages, whose sta-
tistics however, in times of difficulty, are not always
reliable, as was seen during the prevalence of the
yellow fever, when the number of victims was the
subject of dispute and ranged according to different
accounts from sixteen to twenty-three thousand, but
the latter estimate is now generally considered correct. No such officer has as yet been appointed for
the whole republic, in fact, the creation of several
new national bureaux, involving numerical statement
and tabular arrangement, cannot long be deferred ;

and as now our citizens' ears have been cut, (*) they may expect to be submitted to rigorous arithmetical analysis. From the Registrar General's return we gather that the death rate for the city, in spite of all the artificial disadvantages which have been enumerated, is only 26 per mill.; also that 106 boys are born to 100 girls and thus the New World has inversed the problem of the inequality of the sexes; that children form 50 per cent. of the mortality; and that marriages are ten times more numerous amongst foreigners than amongst natives: in fact, that the inferior orders of native women scarcely ever marry.

The city Mortuaries are three in number; the Recoleta, Chacarita and British Cemeteries. The Recoleta, lying at the North end of the city on a picturesque site overlooking the river, is the West-Minster Abbey of the Plate, wherein rest the ashes of its chosen dead. From yonder splendid mausoleum which guards the remains of Rivadavia, would that some Pythoness could evoke the living form of that eminent statesman to behold the wondrous progress of the Republic since the 7th of February 1825 when he became its first President; and with astonishment to find that upwards of half a century had elapsed, ere his golden unitarian dream was accomplished. Towering 30 feet stands the Corinthian shaft which surmounts the tomb of the Argentine Nelson, Admiral Brown, at the base of which

---

(*) If a horse's ears are cut, or one of them, it becomes "ipso facto" the property of government, so to spite estancieros, peons frequently resort to this method of revenge.

are cast relievos detailing his various victories over the Brazilians. Although adorned with many other noble monuments, the whole atmosphere is too redolent of the winding sheet, as in many of the vaults facial remains can be viewed through glass squares in the coffin lids. The Chacarita cemetery, without the city, is neatly laid out and adorned, but the British, lying within, amidst a dense population, is subject to be closed at any moment by municipal decree and only awaits another site to be transferred. In this Protestant God's-acre are united with English dust, the ashes of Scotch and Americans, French, Swiss and Germans; and although marble and gravel, trees and shrubs, lend their aid to lessen the severity of the scene, it is a melancholy spot telling of accident by flood and field, by fire and civil discord, and above all melancholy, in that the loved head which ought to have been tenderly laid in the family vault at home, lies here expatriated till the last trump unites all stragglers. Grave stones tell the truth scarce forty years! here half that time suffices to resolve to its elements many a memento: and in the absence of vaults, the ground can be dug and redug interminably after an interval of five years.

Cremation has been discussed in this city, but stands no chance of ever being brought into extensive practice: such a custom was all very well for pagans with little or no notion of the dignity of the human body, and who were not even instigated thereto by any conception relative to health; but Christians will remain content to commit dust to dust and not fire, let the Sanatory chemists prate as they may : to incinerate the human form of a parent, wife or child is to destroy the sentiment of a life, nay to condense the hopes of an eternity into a handful of urnal relics.

As the mortuary forms a necessary termination to the busy scenes of human life and activity such as have been described, it provides likewise an apt Colophon to this branch of our subject ; and so, gentle reader, after having brought you thus far pleasantly I trust, and placed before you as graphic a picture, as my capacity admits, of the Argentine Republic generally and of its Capital Buenos Aires in somewhat greater detail, I must ask you to accompany me in some of the various trips into the interior, which were undertaken principally for the purpose of becoming acquainted with the fauna of those regions, the cameos of which will complete the present volume and form the sole topic of the second.

CHAPTER XIV.

At the commencement of a late hot season, in order to sniff the hill breezes, I started from Buenos Aires to reach the glorious mountain ranges in the neighbourhood of Córdova. A little over two-hours' journey by rail brought us to Campana, a port on the right bank of the river Paraná, where we found the commodious steamer "Proveedor" in waiting, and were soon under weigh for Rosario, the third city in point of population, but the second in importance, of the Argentine Republic. The fare from the metropolis was £2.10, including rail and steamer, dinner and berth, and the distance about 200 miles. On retiring for the night, after a sumptuous dinner and a cigar and coffee on deck, my chief anxiety was on the score of mosquitos, as these Dipterous plagues are unusually large and bloodthirsty on the river Paraná; so, of two empty berths, I chose the lower, opening the curtains and allowing the sanguinary culices free access to my person. When all the bloodsuckers were assembled and their lancets and appetites whetted in anticipation of a feast upon their apparently willing victim, he suddenly sprang up, closed the curtains and leaped into the upper bunk, to the no small chagrin of the imprisoned buzzers. The Culicides form a very numerous family in this neotropical region; some flying by day, others by night, and of the two it is impossible to say which is the more tormenting; one species however, I have remarked, whose bodies emit an exquisite perfume; for riding with a friend one day in the neighbourhood of Quilmes, a few leagues from Buenos Aires, we both observed a delicious fragrance, proceeding as we imagined from flowers in the hedge by the road side. Dismounting several times we were disappointed in discovering such, until happening to slay one or two mosquitos on my cheek : " *Eureka!* " cried I, and from that moment we enjoyed a perpetual bouquet, to our no small astonishment.

In this country, in which following the lead of the seasons everything European seems reversed, the principal part of the riverine passenger traffic is prosecuted by night. This militates much, from a tourist point of view, against the thorough appreciation of its fluvial and ripal scenery, which here presents a noble Ægean twenty miles in breadth studded with innumerable islands clothed with verdure and foliage to the water's edge; so distant indeed are the river banks that for hundreds of miles no point can be found at which a glimpse of both can be caught at the same time; and those beauteous islands filled with orange groves, peach montes, apple and pear orchards, poplar, willow and plane trees and charcoal furnaces, that supply the city with early fruit, vegetables and fuel and are besides the home of the Carpincho, and its enemies the Puma and Jaguar, with serpents in abundance. When the river is high, it is no very uncommon circumstance to see the whole surface of this archipelago covered with the debris (*camelotas*) of these mud-formed islands, buoyed up by matted roots and carrying their living freights of hungry Carnivora and hissing Ophidia even down to the shores of Buenos Aires. We wend our way through this insular network, and then coasting along the low barrancas of tosca that line the right bank of the mighty estuary, reach Rosario at ten o'clock on the following morning: but as the water was high, the mole had vanished, and the passengers had to land on terra firma direct from the deck of the steamer. The sudden inundation of the Paraná is a perpetual source of danger to the houses on its beach and although the upper riverine towns are built high enough to escape that source of peril, a sudden rise of the estuary waters accompanied by a strong and continued east wind might be sufficient to threaten the existence of Buenos Aires. Rosario being a national port, of course possesses the inevitable *aduana* (custom-house), but thanks to the exceedingly well-planned regulations in force, the miseries usually attendant upon passing this ordeal, are here much mitigated.

This town holds the second rank in the Republic for commerce and importance, due to the natural advantages of its site: placed at the western elbow of a bend in the Paraná, where the tosca cliff rises 40 feet and a natural basin of deep water in front admits

ocean steamers at all states of the tide to a secure anchorage whatever may be the weather, it has become
the natural depot for all the provinces west of the
river and the grand commission agent for eleven
states. Devoted to commerce, which is mainly in the
hands of foreigners, it draws its supplies of Tobacco,
Woods, Sugar, Cotton, Hides, Skins, Wheat, Wines,
Dried Fruits, Bones, Minerals, &c., from the upper
and western districts, yielding in return the various
products of European luxury; and so cheap are these
articles from the interior, that Tucuman cedar, a
beautiful wood for durability and appearance is cheap-
er than pine; in fact Rosario holds exactly the same
relative position now, as Genoa and Venice in the
middle ages, and is rapidly copying them in its bold
and lofty architecture. Since the war between Chili,
Peru and Bolivia commenced, Rosario has been the
high road for Bolivian products and immense quantities of silver ore and cinchona bark &c, have found
their way down hither via Jujuy and Tucuman and
when the railway, in course of construction to Salta
and Jujuy, is finished, great will be the increase in
native as well as Bolivian exports. Now that the Rosario terminus of the Central Argentine is connected
with the mole and harbour, and its other Cordova extremity with the Tucuman line, nothing remains
but to await the time when Rioja, Catamarca, Salta
and Jujuy shall be united in one great iron band,
and then the interests of Rosario will culminate at the
expense of Buenos Aires and she will become the
grand emporium for the whole of the interior.

Rosario, although possessing all the elements of civilized life in the shape of Government, Foreign consuls, Theatres, Clubs, Hotels, Newspapers, Hospitals and other charitable institutions, Churches, and Markets where food of the best, especially magnificent fish from the Paraná, is exposed for sale, has however no element of beauty in it; the only picturesqueness it ever possessed was adventitious and due to the numerous caravans of bullock-carts, which made it a general rendezvous from the North, West and South : the railway however has struck the caravan off the rolls and inspired movement with life and activity.

Alternately a prey to dust and mud, there is an East-end look about the city that renders it not a very desirable residence for the traveller; although the houses which are still mostly of ground-floor with azotea roof and adorned with fine gardens and spacious *patios* (air spiracles) are in course of rapid conversion into showy structures of two or even three storeys with fine shops and plate-glass windows. In the construction of the buildings, both bricks and mortar are of superior quality; the latter sets as hard as Roman cement, due to the exceeding fineness and strength of the lime and the purity of the river sand : in fact, a London bricklayer declared that there is no such lime in Europe, and we may well credit the assertion, as that from Córdova is manufactured from pure marble : here are no damp or efflorescent walls to contribute to that rapid increase of pulmonary disease so painfully evident throughout the plains of Buenos Aires. One church suffices for the catholic population, whilst two minister to the wants of the Protestant, thus reversing the customary proportion: the English are very proud of their elegant little temple, not only on account of its intrinsic beauty, and freedom from debt, but from the fact that it has been erected and fitted up entirely with material from the neighbourhood, a result due to the cooperation of the numerous and respectable corps of employés in the extensive works of the Central Argentine Railway situated in Rosario. Amongst Argentine cities, but a short while ago, Rosario had attained an unenviable notoriety for the hatching of political plots; in fact a dozen revolutions have been known to succeed one another in the short space of two or three years; now however, commerce seems to be asserting her supremacy over the fire-eating politicians, and peace and plenty are flowing in her train.

Two or three days' sweltering in the unmitigated heat, glare and choking dust of this city, the former accentuated by the universal custom of whitewashing the exterior of all buildings; devoured by fleas, for the culices of the river have only been exchanged for the pulices of the town; and tormented by the sight of mangy dogs and locusts, combine to make one sigh for the promised refreshing breezes of the Cordovese heights; and were it not that the Rosarinos possess the knack of true hospitality, the city would leave but few fond reminiscences behind.

On then for the learned city of Córdova! our

train starts punctually at 6 a.m, by railway time
which, throughout the line, is identical with that of the
Observatory at Córdova ; and after a sleepless night,
asphyxiated by the dreadful sultriness and persecuted
by a determined corps of representatives from the
whole thirty species of hoppers, it demands considerable resolution to rise in time, pay the £3 fare, and
jump into a car : the Pampa engine roars and off we
speed to accomplish the 257 miles in fifteen hours, a
tedious journey enough even with every comfort, considering that a stoppage is made at every one of the
twenty stations, and only one solitary half-hour allowed
at Carcarañá for breakfast ; but with cane-bottomed
seats, a broiling sun, closed windows and yet stifling
dust, one's powers of endurance are severely put to
the test. And yet, on a late occasion, a countrywo-
man of ours, an authoress of repute, visiting the Republic for the first time and crossing these Pampas
actually preferred to ride on the cowcatcher, in the
midst of a pitiless Pampero, her dress and locks
streaming in the wind, whilst the worthy engineer of
the line, a victim to gallantry, was obliged to share her
company on that dangerous and exposed seat. To
counteract somewhat the inconveniences of the road, I
had provided myself with a supply of Iced Claret Cup,
a nectar which was pronounced a superb remedy for that
impalpable and mantling dust-mist of comminuted
tosca, which enveloping the whole train, renders invi-
sible all save the roaring, one-eyed Cyclops in front.
A stretch of forty miles from Rosario brings us to the
station of Carcarañá, where there is a fine hotel adjoin-

ing and much comfort; to take advantage of which
and avoid the early hurry at Rosario, I should strongly
recommend travellers to take the afternoon train from
that city, and dine, sleep and breakfast at Carcarañá
in readiness for that of the following morning which
comes up about 9 a.m. Three distinct climatic regions
are passed through between Rosario and Córdova,
corresponding to the three zones of vegetation; that of
the Cardo or white artichoke: of the Cardo castilla or
giant thistle; and of the Algarroba woods: and
oftentimes, starting from the former city with the
thermometer at 90 Fahr., a great coat is needed before
reaching the latter.

After skirting the numerous and flourishing colonies, planted by the Central Argentine Land company
alongside the railway, and viewing with satisfaction
evidence of their prosperity in the splendid crops of
wheat and maize, the snug dwellings, the stacks, the
farmyards and poultry, and the busy agricultural
operations telling sweetly of industry and its rewards,
we gradually emerge upon that trackless, treeless
land-ocean, the Pampas. These immense, solitary,
silent, grassy plains would seem to confound all ideas
of time and space, were it not for the presence of the
exact machinistic locomotive and the mathematically
rigid and flashing rails, which choke at once all
sentiment.

The Pampas present completely different appearances in different seasons: sometimes when, through
the ignition of the dry herbage of past years, the

dreadful prairie fires have swept their lambent flames over the length and breadth of the land, the eye surveys nothing but blackness ; at others, a beautiful clear vivid green announces nature's new suit ; later on, the sober quaker brown speaking of mature growth, and lastly the dazzling silver of hoary age with its legacy of ripe seed.

Countless herds of wild cattle, horses, rheas, guanacos and deer roam at will over these illimitable pastures and graze on the indigenous fodder, flavoured by the succulent parslane and milky spurge, the scarlet verbena and various compositæ and leguminosæ. It is no uncommon circumstance for ostriches, with the curiosity and stupidity of the race, to attempt, on crossing the line, to interview the train, which they do by turning sharply round and facing it, when instant destruction overtakes them ; at other times, the ponderous machine like a huge Juggernaut weary with the slaughter of countless millions of locusts, comes to a stand; the wheels clogged with their bodies and unable further to bite the rails all slippery with orthopterous oil. The attempts to destroy or even mitigate this pest, *Acridium paranense*, by rewards for their eggs and diligent gathering of their bodies, very much resembles the efforts of Mrs. Partington to mop up the Atlantic, so long as there exist deserts in the north of this country, where they are bred; turn water into these, make them blossom as the rose, pour population into them and locusts and other plagues will vanish as if by magic.

Every few minutes we strain our eyes to catch a glimpse of the distant sierras, until at last, just before sunset, when about sixty miles from Córdova, we descry them like a line of neutral-tinted clouds on the horizon, with their jagged summits here and there tinged with the rays of the now rapidly declining orb.

Then, as the shades of evening creep on, the fiery locomotive, rumbling like thunder, drags its submissive convoy across that noble viaduct which, 1260 feet in length, crosses the Rio Segundo by thirty-six spans : soon the moon rises, summoning the wily fox from his recess, and bidding the moth, beetle, owl and bat, speed on their various errands of love or prey ; and yet a litte while, and we can distinguish the lights of the city of the Jesuits, nestling in a hollow at the foot of the spur-like ranges which shoot from the distant Cordilleras; its domes, minarets and towers are bathed in a sea of brilliancy, a glorious picture! which the experience of the succeeding day does not altogether dispel. At a little before 10 p.m. after a hard battle with the unwashed genus *peon* (porter), which here, as at Rosario, forms a jostling and insolent class, I find myself located in a very fine-looking hotel within half a square of the central Plaza ; and snatching a hasty supper, retire to seek, not the downy pillow, as European travellers love to describe it, but the hard woollen *almohada* (bolster); you may punch, squeeze, toss and shake it, the pommeling renders the matted mass only the more obdurate; but as Wool is one of the chief "*frutas del pais*", a source of the country's wealth, it must be spoken of with respect, and how much that staple enters into the thoughts and conversation of every class in the Lanigerine Republic, may be gathered from the following story. A right-reverend protestant prelate visiting the camp a short while ago, fell in with another protestant clergyman, but of a different persuasion, and amongst other questions, enquired the state of his flock; the worthy minister, putting an ovine construction upon a spiritual enquiry, replied " They have all got the scab ".

The morning broke in sub-tropical splendour, revealing a sapphire vault and presenting a distant view of those purple heights so enchanting to the dweller on the plains.

The quaint city of Córdova, with its 40,000 inhabitants, lies 500 miles N.W. of Buenos Aires, in Lat. 31°24′ S. and Long 64°10′ W., midway between the two oceans, and although at an altitude of 1248 feet above sea level, its site is on a bed of granitic sand in a small valley scooped out by the Rio Primero which, although of little depth, has a times a velocity sufficient to sweep everything before it, as evidenced by its old banks that, skirting the north and south of the city, form barrancas rising to the height of from thirty to a hundred feet. Here dwells the centre of the learning, piety and laziness of the republic ; here too, banished from its other regions, are found to linger dogmatism and exclusiveness, the last

shreds of that mediæval bigotry, which the intellectual
activity of the present age has doomed to oblivion.

The climate is fine and dry, the town well and
handsomely built, with a road pavement which it is a
positive pleasure to traverse after the jolting received
in the streets of Buenos Aires, and the Quintas, especially on the western side, revel in eternal bloom and
freshness by means of irrigating canals. The public
buildings including the Cathedral, of composite style
with fine dome, whose interior is ornamented with
pilasters of fine marble from the sierras, the Cabildo,
seventeen gloomy Moorish-looking churches, three
Monasteries, two Convents, University, Observatory,
and numerous charitable institutions, are all massively
built though, in general, with little pretension to architectural beauty. If however the churches cannot
boast much external grandeur, on their interior has
been lavished a degree of ornament almost unknown
elsewhere in this country. The pictures, plate and gilt
decorations are very valuable and in good taste and
the ceremonies on high festivals gorgeous. The Old
Jesuit church presents a magnificent interior, bearing
a very lofty, finely-carved roof of Tucuman cedar, put
together without a nail. A noble-looking, patriarchal
priest was kind enough to act a cicerone, drawing my
attention with great gravity and politeness to the different points of interest, especially the paintings and
statuary, which adorn the walls and niches. Here
may be seen a Raphael by the side of a Michael An-
gelo. Not alone the interior, but the vestry likewise,

is crowded with valuable works of art, paintings,
screens and images: verily the Cordovese are no icon-
oclasts and guard these treasures with scrupulous
care. To the adjoining monastery, I next directed my
steps, ascending first to the library, on the stairs of
which, two life-size effigies, very much resembling
God and Magog, confront us: these are exquisitely
carved in wood by early Indian converts and would
not disgrace Geneva. How is it that the work of Indian fingers is always full of grace and truth? such
taste in form and colour! the Indian is a child of nature, untrammeled by scholastic canons, seeking to in-
terpret from within, those perceptions of the beautiful,
which are the natural result of man's organization.
The library is still rich in rare works, especially MSS.
in the various Indian tongues, although most of its
manuscripts and books have been sent to Buenos Aires, or presented to the University of Córdova or gone
the way of the butter-men. The prior next allowed
me to visit the crypt which, to my astonishment, forms
veritable catacombs. Descending to the church again
and standing before the altar, eight men prepared to
raise the massive marble slab lying at its base. A
yawning gulf, from which issued a sepulchral blast,
invited us to communion with the dead: so disappearing slowly within the aperture we found galleries
in which lie buried (?) all the monks who have died
at the monastery since its foundation, and a ghastly
sight it was! Traversing the passages, you see on the
right hand and on the left successive mounds of earth
from each of which protrude a human skull and cross-

bones, a grim epitaph, the relics of the superior officers. One gallery leads to a case containing the
relics of the founder, and further on, an iron grating
exposes to view piles upon piles of human bones,
where were shot the sole remains of those Jesuit
Fathers, the rank and file, who trod the aisles above
for centuries. We are glad to escape from an air so
redolent of corruption; the picture of which will for
ever dwell on my mental retina.

But if the churches and monasteries speak of the
past, the University and Observatory declare the present, and an active present it is in both cases, although
due entirely to foreign intellect. The former with its
distinguished staff of professors, some of whom are of
European reputation, and with its schools of Science,
Arts, Law and Medicine, its Museums and Library,
constitutes a nucleus or central authority, a veritable
Lagado, whence issue and to which are referred, all
scientific questions and investigations that have for
their object the development of the Republic. Such
men as Lorentz, Wyneberg, Hieronymus, Döring, and
Stelzner have laboured and still do labour at this
great work.

The Observatory, whose site is on an eminence
just without the city and whose floor exceeds in
"apogee" the highest church spire in the city, much
to the chagrin of the Holy Fathers, has been established in Córdova, on account of the dryness of the
atmosphere and general clearness of the heavens.
Here the American savant Dr. Gould has sustained

that high reputation which preceded him, in the
exactness of all his observations and the patient and
skilful labour evinced in that classical work the "*Ura-
nometria Argentina*"; he was one of those selected to
undertake the observation of certain stars, wherewith
to compare the positions of the planet Mars, in order
to obtain the Solar parallax more closely, with a view
to determine with greater precision the distance of the
earth. The Córdova observations were acknowledged
to be more accurate than those from any other source;
and what adds to the utility of its observatory is that
it acts as a central department of Metereology, whither
all the daily registrations, from the various stations
scattered throughout the Republic, regularly con-
verge.

As the site of Córdova is necessarily restricted by
the dimensions of the limited basin that contains it,
the city bears somewhat of a European aspect, a similarity which is enhanced by its beautiful environs, the
dress and culture of its inhabitants, and the excessive
number of its churches : and yet the culture of the
Cordovese is of that passive, Platonic and Donnish
kind, which is rather obstructive than progressive, the
result of enfeebled age rather than of vigorous youth ;
that would repel the railway whistle, the tram-car and
all other signs of modern advance, and rest in the
ancient siesta and that ample inheritance bequeathed
them by the Jesuits : and in these respects, strictly
conservative Córdova is in marked contrast to such
cities as Mendoza, where all is activity, progress,

modern improvement and production. As has been
before mentioned, at the north and south ends of the
straight streets rise barrancas; towards the west the
view rests upon the Sierras; whilst on the east, the
city is bounded by the Rio Primero, sluices from which
feed a large and deep lake in the centre of the
town, whence permeate in every direction streamlets
of pure limpid running water, cooling the scorched
air and cleansing the roadways. Around this lake run
wide *Boulevards* (the Alameda), which until lately
were fringed with noble willows and poplars, the
growth of five generations, affording a cool and shady
retreat; but unfortunately whilst I was in the neighbourhood, these were all destroyed in one day by a
most terrific hurricane. Of their Alameda, the fashionable evening lounge, the Cordovese are justly
proud, and as the entire plaza is lined with seats, the
population turns out *en masse* to revel in its freshness
and listen to the strains of martial music. From the
centre of the lake rises a small island, furnished with
a confiteria ready to supply all the different varieties
of modern iced drinks and the transit to and fro takes
place in boats. In the earlier chapters devoted to
Buenos Aires, mention was made of the wide-spread
system of mendicity in vogue there; but in Córdova
it rises into an institution. Strange it is in one sense,
that where the outward forms of Christianity prevail
in excess, the following of whose precepts would di-
minish if not eradicate it, there pauperism puts on her
most loathsome rags and utters her most piteous cries;
it is so partly in England even, where the purlieus of

the Cathedrals harbour the most squalid of populations; yet the paradox vanishes when intrusive insolent beggary, as practised in Córdova, is seen to be
but a drama in which one section of the community
plays upon the fears of the other. Leisurely promenading the streets one day, I observed a wheelbarrow
approaching, trundled by a sturdy, navvy-looking
man, whilst an individual of equally robust appearance, but enveloped in beastly rags and stretched at
his ease, occupied the box seat. I watched the barrowcade, and to look at these able-bodied fellows, you
would declare them worth 4/6 a day each to Messrs.
Brassey, Peto and Betts: when they approached a
respectable-looking residence, the trundler put down
his load and disposed himself unconcernedly to rest
upon the handles, whilst the melo-dramatic mendicant,
whom it would be a sin to dignify by the title of Lazarus, forthwith sat up, assumed divers tortuous and
painful attitudes, and moaned the usual "Por amor
de Dios", ending by a gamut of discordant howls
and dismal cries. Locomotion about the city is a positive pleasure, not alone from the excellent pavement,
but the luxury of the hack carriages that completely
put to shame the peststricken, shady cabs of London,
and which to the number of 20 or 30 afford ample
means of local travelling to the higher classes, as the
tramway, which has at last been introduced in spite
of the Dons, to the lower. The suburbs too are such
as to invite rambling, on which occasions, in striking
contrast to the habits of the city, may be seen, in the
shanties of the Indians especially, lively evidence of

industry; they will pluck the coarse grass or rush, and in your presence manufacture, for a trifle, any shape I basket you may require ; and as for the thong-plaiting, I have never seen such fine and handsome work in Europe.

Córdova possesses several hotels, the best of which I found to be the Hotel Paris, half a square from the central Plaza, where a very liberal table and good service are maintained, at a monthly expense of about £8 for board and lodging. Although the province contains 2,63 horned cattle, 75 horses and mu·les, and 3,84 sheep and goats per head of the population, sheep are not easy to rear on account of the difficulty of finding suitable indigenous grass, so the traveller has to rest content with kid, roast kid forming the universal substitute for roast mutton ; and in the early morning, troops of such, with their legs tied, are brought in by country women and laid in the patio, where the poor innocents, as though aware of their fate, render the air alive with their shrill bleat-ings and effectually banish sleep. The domestic pets of this remarkable city are not such as would be deem-ed desirable in European households ; when you en-ter a dwelling, a growling puma or bounding deer, a stalking ostrich or a spitting guanaco, a pouncing eagle or perchance a shambling anteater, salutes you.

CHAPTER XV.

The heat of Córdova being insupportable, in spite of its water-vascular system, a three days' residence there sufficed to bring to maturity the resolution I had formed of visiting the distant peaks; so being recommended to the inside of the first range, to a village called Cosquin, founded by the Indians, and distant thirty miles, a carriage was engaged for the moderate sum of sixteen Bolivianos (about £ 2.10), to transport thither a friend, myself and baggage.

After leaving the city, the road gradually ascends for three leagues over a bed of tosca which, in wet weather is almost impassable, but in dry, forms a hard compact mass; the vegetation is scanty, consisting of dwarf scrubby brushwood, until the Caldera or limestone region is reached, when, leaving on the north the ruins of the South American Ben Rhydding, a sanatorium founded by the philanthropist Wheelwright for the benefit of consumptive patients, and proceeding westward, the scene, which has hitherto presented a rising plateau barren both of fauna and flora, now changes and the granitic formation, succeeding the tosca and limestone, discloses well-wooded ridges paved with boulders and the debris of mica and feldspar, yielding throughout the year a dry, yet rough road.

Ascending the first ridge we are rewarded, by a fine panorama of the valley through which the Rio San Roque winds, on whose banks stands the half-way house, where we halt for a light meal washed down by that universal mountain beverage, goats' milk : clouds of parrots (*Conurus murinus*) and humming birds (*Trochilus flavifrons*), here clip the air and render it alive with scream and hum. Anxious to reach our destination, we set off to climb the summit of the same range by a road cut here and there through the solid rock, surmounting which, the well-wooded, well-cultivated and fruitful valley of Cosquin lies revealed, occupying an area of about nine miles by two, and containing in its bosom the tortuous and rapid Rio Primero. At about half past ten a.m. we descry a snug mill, enveloped in trees and posted at the very edge of the eddying stream, an hostelry destined to be my residence for the next few months, and the journey to which had cost us six hours' jolting in a cramped carriage over very rough roads, that would have been unendurable but for the glories of the scenery, which drew from me continual expressions of delight. The jovial miller *Don Juan* appears and bids us welcome, and assisting us to dismount we are quickly housed and seated at a breakfast, to do justice to which, the early drive and mountain air coupled with the remarkable cleanliness of everything in this remote nook of civilization, stimulate us. A limpid mountain stream, furnishing an invigorating matutinal bath; a spring of unrivalled crystal water; a pure unclouded azure; an exceedingly dry and light air, the result of distance from the littoral, elevation and absence of lakes or rivers of any size; abundance of food, plain but wholesome, and consisting amongst other dishes, of wheaten soup, *caldo* (broth), *puchero* (boiled meat), *guiso* (stew), fricasseed parrot, owl *ragoût*, grilled beef, roast kid and homemade bread, with French or Spanish wines at a shilling a quart, or goats' milk gratis: an abundance of large and small game, and a very plethora of specimens for the cabinet; announced a Goshen, where we had been led to expect a desert and in every way surpassed my anticipations either as sportsman or naturalist. Settled then thus, my object was to combine the pursuit of health with devotion to my favourite study and to employ my leisure in the collection of such specimens of the fauna of the Sierras as necessitated not much exertion on my part. The large game with one exception, I did not feel equal to combat: of these the Guanaco (*Auchenia huanaco*), Peccary (*Dicotyles tajaçu*). Puma (*Felis concolor*), Jaguar (*Felis onça*), Gato Montés (*Felis Geoffroyi*), Fox (*Canis Azaræ*), and Condor (*Sarcorhamphus gryphus*), are tolerably numerous on the hills and in the dense woods: whilst skirting the banks of the Rio Primero, solitary specimens of the screaming Chajá (*Chauna chavaria*) are met with. The natives assert that both the " Vibora de

Cascabel" or Rattlesnake (*Crotalus horridus*) and the Ampelagua or Anaconda (*Eunectes murinus*), as well as the "Vibora de la Cruz" (*Trigonocephalus alternatus*), inhabit the surrounding ranges. Of partridges two species the Nothuræ; the *Falco femoralis*; several species of Owls; many of Parrots; and more than a hundred of the Insecta, are some of the chief forms of life that present themselves most commonly; whilst the dead shells of the Mollusca, principally Helices, cover the sierras in immense quantities.

Considering the opportunities at my disposal, and the abundance of the Aves and Reptilia in particular, my bag was very poor, but consisted of:—Cheiroptera, two species; Dasypodidæ, one; Vulturidæ, two; Falconidæ, thee; Strigidæ, two; Hirundinidæ, three; Alcedinidæ, two; Trochilidæ, two; Certhiidæ, one; Psittacidæ, three; Picidæ, three; Columbidæ, four; Tinamidæ, two; Anatidæ, two; Colymbidæ, one; Sauria, three; Ophidia, seven; Amphibia, three; Pisces, two. With regard to the Sauria, one species the Chelke (*Enyalus letirepo*), has been hitherto almost unknown in Europe; it is a rock lizard, measuring about nine inches from the tip of the snout to the extremity of the tail and of which the natives stand in utter dread on account of its supposed venomous and aggressive nature; they refuse even to dismount in the neighbourhood where one is supposed to be, and accredit it with the power of jumping on to cattle and biting them, so as to cause the flesh to rot off before death ensues. To dispel their fears by illustrating its harmless character was almost hopeless ; nevertheless taking a large glass vase, a live vigorous chelke was introduced and immediately afterwards a young lively chicken, when with all our efforts to provoke the Saurian to attack the expected victim, it remained un-harmed to the last. I was fortunate enough to secure, amongst the Ophidia, a specimen of that beautiful snake known in the Córdova museum by the syno-nym of *Coronella Bachmanni*, a species of Oxyropus, and the second known as yet ; besides a remarkably handsome serpent of brilliant hues, scarlet, black and yellow, the *Herpeton pulcher*, of which I managed to obtain four specimens.

Lazily reclining one day in the shade and watch-ing the butterflies, I noticed that one species *Colias Lesbia* took possession of an alfalfa field, and as soon as any interloper of a different species so much as popped its head over the enclosure, the whole corps instantly took up the cudgels and pursued the tres-passer and having succeeded in driving him away, returned to their feast, which, not long after, they quitted in a body in order to cool their feet in the neighbouring wet sand : is it possible that nectar becomes converted into a heating stimulant in the in-ternal laboratory of the butterfly ?

On another occasion, directing my gaze upward to a cloud of locusts, of which there are several species here, I observed that none of them flew with their bodies longitudinally in the direction of the wind, so that the whole mass was driven obliquely forward ; a lesson in

dynamics, for the angle at which this would be possible must be small, considering where their wing
power and centre of gravity are situated. These
locusts are a terrible scourge to the neighbourhood;
wherever they settle, an equivalent to winter is the
result. Parrots are extremely abundant throughout
the Sierras, and very destructive to crops : and so on
each patch of ground where wheat or maize is cultivated, a boy is stationed to frighten them off by shouting, and this being continued the whole length of the
valley, some leagues, the effect of the chorus of scare-
crows is very curious. The cunning birds however,
are a match for their noisy tormentors ; for, gliding
down to the bottom of the stem, through that they
bite, the stalk falls, and so unseen the *loros* leisurely
consume the grain : in winter, they live mostly in the
woods, where they feed on the kernels of wild fruits
that strew the ground in rich abundance : holes in the
cliffs along the river banks serve them for breeding
places and four or five eggs are usually found in each
nest, which is concealed at the extremity of a tunnel
two or even three yards deep, and the young are
justly esteemed a great delicacy, resembling in flavour
roast sucking pig and equally rich. Walking even in
the neighbourhood of the cliffs in the breeding season is hazardous, as the old birds in myriads, resent
the intrusion, wheeling round the wanderer's head in
rapidly narrowing circles and flapping their wings in
his face, all the while uttering shrill and deafening
shrieks : still more perilous is the attempt to sack their
nests which, besides other dangers, involves a giddy

dangling in the air, suspended by a rope over precipices which in some cases are 400 feet high. Eagles
too are good judges of flavour and steem the taste
of parrot ; for casting the eye upward, there sits his
ever vigilant majesty on a projecting pinnacle, ready
to swoop upon any unfortunate stray psittac.

On the plains of Cordova, wild tobacco (*Nico-
tiana rustica*) is very abundant, but the cultivated
plant is reared successfully in Cosquin, though to no
very great extent, and the leaves sold at the rate of
five bolivianos (15/.) the arroba of 25 lbs.; one thousand plants produce about ten arrobas and when
bought young for transplanting involve an outlay of a
bolivian per mill. The whole of the produce is consumed in the province and the native made cigars, at
about four for a penny, do very well for a postpran-
dial smoke, although lacking the flavour of those
manufactured by the squaw or Indian wife of George
Falkner, a boatman on the river Paraná. This dark
beauty always acts as cockswain on her husband's
riverine expeditions, and occupies her leisure moments
in the boat by twisting cigars for the gentlemen fares,
using the saliva of her mouth as an emollient and her
nude femur as the rolling board, the usual custom
with Indian women, and feels herself mightily in-
sulted if any demur is made in accepting and lighting
her savoury oblation.

But though in these fruitful valleys, the cereals,
various fruits and tobacco are raised almost spon-
taneously and to a certain amount ; yet, flax, cochineal,

castor oil, silk and innumerable other products might
be added with profit; and as for vines, if the same
advantages in soil, climate and site were presented in
Europe, the heights, instead of lying barren, would
soon be covered with smiling vineyards; but until the
present race gives way to one more vigorous, Nature
in vain lavishes her treasures. What can be expected
of people who have absolutely no idea of the value of
time? who poor and ignorant are enveloped in the
present and have just sufficient instinct, and barely
that, to provide for its actual pressing necessities?
Why, daily come women to the mill on foot, trudging
distances of leagues, carrying on their heads a few
pounds of grain to be ground, and after waiting perhaps two or three days lying about in the sun and
sleeping on the open ground at night, when their
meal is ready, leave a tithe for expenses, as they have
no money, and contentedly and leisurely jog homewards with their lightened load. In pity to them, I
have sometimes descended from my lodgings and set
the wheel in gear to grind their modicum and set them
at liberty; it's all one! If you offer such people
money to do anything quickly, although reckoned a
power amongst civilized races, here amongst a people
descended from the Comechingones, a branch of the
Quichua Indians, it is completely impotent: and such
is the case throughout the Republic with people of
mixed Indian stock. And yet I have found this same
listless people, wonderfully alive to the appreciation of
natural phenomena: is it not always so with the
ignorant and superstitious? do not their fears sharpen

their perceptions and make them alert to unusual
events which strike upon their senses? thus in this
valley of Cosquin, where hail falls at times of fabulous size, they will distinguish its pattering on the
granite rocks at a distance of six miles and foretell its
approach with accuracy, when to my ear not the
slightest sound was audible.

Here as throughout the Upper Provinces, the
Chilian is accredited with much the same simple character as Pat in Britain; in fact, the outrageous va-
garies with which he is charged are due to the undoubted jealousy and contempt with which he is universally
regarded; so, a Chilian sports-man crossed over to the
Argentine plains to hunt the Rhea, but not being accustomed to the sport, went forth to the chase with dogs,
and eventually succeeded in catching one. In high glee
at his first successful essay, he unclasped his silver-
ornamented belt and proceeded to lash its wings to
prevent it flying (!) away. Thereupon he sat down
to contemplate his capture and enjoy the usual South
American solace. The cigarette is produced and made
up, the matchbox opened, the light awaits the magic
summons to flash, when happening to lift his dreamy
eyes, he beholds to his dismay the Rhea airing her
fleet heels on the horizon, and what is worse than all,
bearing off to her distant home the ancestral silver
girdle. Sometimes however, the Chilian is debited
with smartness:—In the marshy plateaux of Chili,
the frosts are often very severe in winter, and the Fla-
mingoes and other waders roosting in their midst are

entrapped by the ice which quickly imprisons them:
the inhabitants aware of this, save their powder and
shot by sallying out in the early morning and captur-
ing them. In the same way in England, on high exposed ground authenticated instances have been
known of a similar fate overtaking hares; whilst the
Abbé Huc in his "*Les souvenirs d'un voyage dans la
Tartarie et le Thibet*" describes himself, on his journey to Lasso, as crossing a Thibetian river capable
of bearing his cavalcade, and observing a number of
small black objects protruding through the ice, found
them to be the noses of a herd of wild cattle (Yak),
which had been entrapped by the sudden congelation
of the water, at the time of passing from one bank to
the other.

At times a shaft is aimed against their spiritual
advisers :— A priest guiltless of any knowledge of
fractions, but just to a degree, was visited by a native
who, confessing to three thefts, was anxious for abso-
lution, which the worthy father granted on condition
of certain penances. A friend of the absolved, a bird
of the same feather, then consulted his reverence, confessing to five sins of a like nature and now the
ecclesiastic was non-plussed, not knowing how to ap-
portion the chastisement according to the quota of the
previous applicant; so, after dwelling upon the matter, "Go" says he, "and commit one more, and
then come to me for remission".

CHAPTER XVI.

TRIP TO CORDOVA

VISIT TO COSQUIN — CONDOR HUNTING.

After some few weeks spent in leisurely surveying animal life in the neighbourhood of the mill, the
thought occurred to me that it was time to organise
an expedition into the region of the Condor, the king
of the skies ; so, with the assistance of a native friend,
arrangements were soon completed for that purpose,
and a start made from his house early on the succee
ding morning.

Our party consisted of two native gentlemen and
myself, mounted on horseback, accompanied by two
peons on mules carrying bedding and other necessaries. An old sportsman would have despised our
arms, but not the panniers which were loaded with the
good things of this life. As damp ammunition rendered my rifle unserviceable, another gentleman lent
me his, but unfortunately could only produce three
cartridges ; a double-barrelled fowling piece carried by
the other native and a revolver stuck in my belt, completed our insignificant armoury. Well might we
look forward with some anxiety to the issue of the

campaign, with such slender means of attack ; but,
having heard of the skill of the natives with the lasso,
determined to proceed; and the sequel will show how
that formidable weapon is more than a match for this
enormous and powerful vulture. Our route lay through
the village of Cosquin, across the river, and after travelling a league on the high road to San Juan, we
branched off eastwards.   Here entering the dense
woods of Tala (*Cellis sellowiana*), Algarroba (**Prosopis
algarroba**) and other members of the Mimosa family,
that cover the gentle slopes rising one above another
to the foot of the mountains, and following the cattle
tracks, we had great difficulty in preserving our skins
and clothes whole, from the almost impassable barrier
of formidable thorns that arrested our progress. Another league, always in Indian file, brought us to the
foot of the mountains, a bold and towering granitic
range flanked by a rushing torrent which it was necessary to cross.   Thence our route lay still upward,
through dense forests of noble and lofty trees, and
over a thick carpet of sweetly-scented medicinal herbs,
the characteristic vegetation of the Sierras, which,
crushed by the horses' hoofs, loaded the air with a
rich never failing mountain bouquet.   For the animals the labour is severe ! for besides having to cross
impetuous streams every few minutes, slippery granitic boulders elevating their giant ashen backs some
few feet above the level, block the path, and to cross
these rocky shoals, the rider was obliged to assume
the undignified attitude of Johnny Gilpin. A sudden
turn in the track and emerging on to a flat open space

we pull up to feast our eyes on the glorious picture;
hill and dale, forest and thicket, rock and boulder,
herbage and stream, melting from an abrupt coarse-
featured foreground palpability, through every stage
of gradation, to that airy purple gauze, which sepa-
rates the physical from the ideal : no sound to break
the solemn stillness, save the distant roar of tumbling
water or the plaintive cooing of some solitary dove!
Here both nature and our own bodily inclination invite to rest : and what fitter spot for horse or man?
Luxuriant herbage for the former; to delight the
latter, the sombre and grateful shade of the towering
Quebracho (*Aspidosperma quebracho*), Algarrobo, Espinillo (*Acacia cavenia*), Tintitaco, and Chañar (*Gour-
liaca decorticans*), the last of which produces a sweet
and savory fruit not unlike the date in flavour; a bubbling brook coursing at our feet, a background of
picturesque lichen-covered boulders, half hiding their
bulky forms in the shady foliage, and a velvet bed of
moss offering its services for the midday siesta.   Lazily
reclining "*sub tegmine fagi*" and watching those richly
ornamented flying flowers chasing one another through
space; images of grandeur, solitariness, home and
distant friends, form a perpetually varying mental
kaleidoscope; but time is inexorable, and we rise to
resume the journey.

The woods now retreat, leaving us to traverse ground
covered with coarse tufty grass springing from between
the stones.   Absence of life is characteristic of this
elevated region, for, with the exception of here and
there an eagle perched on some giddy rocky eminence,

or a noble condor circling high with immovable,
expanded wings, a mere speck in the lofty air, nothing
relieves the monotony of this oppressive muteness;
and yet how the earth sparkles, as though sown with
brilliants, for flashing in every direction lies the
inexhaustible mica-schist.

One summit is now surmounted; and stretched out
at a sickening depth below lies the valley of Cosquin,
with the Rio Primero like a silver thread winding
through it; the magnificence of the panorama quite
recompenses the difficulties of the ascent. On the
opposite side of the valley, a succession of well-wooded
hills extends one above another to the foot of the
second range which rises to the height of 8000 feet
and is distant about twelve miles from the first on
which we stand.

Our object was to reach an *estancia* (cattle-farm)
situated in the interior of the first range, which here
averages a breadth of from four to five miles and a
height of 3500 feet: this necessitates more climbing
and we set forward to accomplish it.

Minerals are not abundant on this chain, although
one or two abandoned mines were passed, which from
specimens of copper pyrites picked up, must be rich
in that metal; but in the other ranges, gold, horn and
native silver, copper, lead, white, rose and green
marbles, spinelle, garnet, chondrodite, woollastonite,
titanite &c. are common and need only intelligent
labour to develop. Guanacos exist, but are shy,

although the Peccary (*Dicotyles torquatus*) is exceedingly numerous in the accessible woods below.

Mounting still upwards we reached the splendid
pasture lands of the summits, presenting gently sloping
terraces, with extensive valleys threading in and out,
flanked by charming glens. Rich grass is abundant,
but neither tree nor shrub meets our view. The cattle
begin to show themselves, and presently we arrive at
the stone-wall boundaries which mark the limits of
each "*estancia*". So light and clear is the air that it
imparts a positive sensation of delight to breathe it,
and fatigue is forgotten. At the first estancia house
we dismounted and after the usual "*Ave Maria*", were
received with the customary native politeness towards
travellers : maté was handed round and then our peons
were despatched to give notice of our arrival to the
estanciero, Señor Torres, on whose property we had
arranged to have the hunt: the messengers were dilatory
however, and so we reached the goal before them,
receiving a welcome of the utmost warmth from our
host. The estancia house, a very picturesque old
building, faced by a hoary trained vine, has a patio in
front, bounded by a trickling rivulet, shaded by
patriarchal willows. An orchard of twenty-five acres
filled with various thriving fruit trees stands adjoining, and a few barns and other out-buildings, alfalfa
and wheat-fields, complete the exterior picture. No
long time elapsed, ere we were seated at a breakfast
table well supplied with abundant fare, to which it is
scarcely necessary to add we did extreme justice

after a six hours' ride up the mountains over very steep and broken country. The usual siesta followed, and then a consultation as to the morrow. Señor Torres kindly offered to slaughter an old mare as bait and having decided to kill the animal that night, we completed arrangements by rubbing over the carcase the 20 lbs. of salt brought with us for that purpose. The object of this is to quicken the digestion of the condor, so that he may not be able to disgorge his food, an invariable practice with this monster when disturbed at his meals: the bird's instinct teaches him that by this means his specific gravity is diminished and his chance enhanced of rising more speedily from the ground. Satisfied that everything was in order for the next day, we retired to the shady orchard, there to regale ourselves with luscious fruit, and about dusk reentered the house for a dance until 10 p.m. when a late dinner was served, the *"pièce de resistance"* of which was, as usual, roast kid. All the dishes of the sierras, if not to the taste of the epicure, form welcome additions to the carte of the traveller. Thoroughly exhausted, yet with feverish pulse, we now retired for the night; two moments sufficed to woo the fickle god, who prolonged our sleep till cockcrow : one such magic summons was sufficient, so springing from our *catres* (trestle bedsteads) and singing out lustily for a peon, we hurried him away to reconnoitre, but no condors were yet visible ; this gluttonous vulture, like its human congener, is a very late riser. After the despatch of two or three other messengers, we had the satisfaction of learning, about 9 a. m. that our quarry

had sighted the bait; in fact, we had no need of further reports as the Sarcorhamphi announced themselves
from every quarter of the horizon, looming up in
successive lines. And now all was hurry and confusion,
saddling, tightening girths, coiling lassos and handling
arms; for when once the condors make their appearance, very little grace is allowed; less than half an
hour suffices to pick clean the bones of an ox or horse.
In about ten minutes we were ready to start for the
field of battle, which was selected with good general-
ship, not far distant, the bait having been placed on
the gentle declivity of a grassy knoll free from stones,
whose summit shielded our approach from view.
Reaching the elevation and putting spurs to our horses,
we charged right down upon the assembled condors.
Imagine the scene of dismay that then ensued at the
royal banquet table, when more than fifty magnificent
kings flapped their huge wings and endeavoured to
rise. I had only just time to throw myself off my
horse, when like the rushing of a mighty wind the condors flew past; the strange scene flurried me, as Linnæus
says,

In terram devolans, susurro attonitos et surdos fere reddit homines

and like a young soldier on a real field of battle, discharging my three solitary bullets in quick succesion
without taking aim, was mortified to find their wing
feathers alone struck, which did not stop their progress : nay, as the birds sped over, they gave us a
disgusting *hasta luego!* (parting salute) in the shape
of a perfect hail of undigested carrion, disgorged to
to accelerate their flight ; our salt was evidently, not

strong enough! Suddenly a loud shout of "*viva!*"
was heard and looking round, I perceived a fine
condor struggling on the ground, in the meshes of one
of the peons' lassos; one other was similarly entangled by our host, but the beast managed to slip the
knot and escape. Our capture was a male bird,
young and in very good plumage, measuring over ten
feet across the wings. *Don Palemon* had no better
luck with his fowling piece than I with my rifle, firing
two shots without effect. Some of the Condors having settled on a neighbouring eminence, two of us
gave chase : *Don Enrique* fired two unsuccessful shots,
and I in very vexation at not having a better weapon,
peppered away uselessly with the revolver. All the
game had now taken to flight, circling high above
our heads, no doubt awaiting our departure to continue their meal and as all chance of further sport for
that day had vanished, we wisely set our faces homewards for dinner. Time did not permit us to extend
the programme, as was intended, to the sacking of
Condors' nests, a difficult and dangerous feat. About
a league distant stands a precipice, on a ledge of which,
two hundred feet deep, they love to build, and to
reach this otherwise inaccessible spot a rope is used,
by which the hunter is suspended dangling in the
air; and woe to the daring plunderer, if the old birds
should return during the burglarious attempt. The
nest is usually composed of a few sticks merely
and contains two eggs, each about four inches long.
I managed to construct a leather hood for our prisoner
and having tied his legs and wings, deposited him

safely in one of the panniers; and then, all being in readiness, we bade adieu to the kind family which had entertained us so hospitably for two days; and as our host himself acted as our guide, the descent was rapid. Passing round the crest of a eminence, three condors were espied, evidently about to attack a calf grazing with a few head of cattle in the hollow beneath us; now these birds are notoriously inquisitive and one of them sailing up to interview us, quickly got into trouble; for *Don Enrique*, who was carrying the gun charged with swan-shot, jumped off his horse and brought down the intruder with thundering rush at our feet: so the other pannier was now loaded and off we trudged to the next brow, where our guide parted from us, after giving special directions as to the road to be followed. It seems to me that shot is more fatal to the condor than the bullet, as the skin is so closely covered with hard glossy plumage, that the latter is more liable to glance off. Condor hunters are specially welcomed in the sierras, as the birds commit such dreadful havoc amongst the herds: their plan is to select a calf, four or five months old, and wait until the mother is at some distance, then suddenly swooping down and striking the animal to the ground, to rip out its tongue either as a *"bonne bouche"* or to prevent the utterance of any signal of alarm, and in a few minutes nothing is left but the skeleton.

Our homeward descent was continued without any other adventure, save the temporary loss of one of our companions in the woods: our whistles were used

continually but unsuccessfully for an hour, and then
by sheer accident he again crossed our path, having
been riding in every direction, misled by a will-ó-the
wisp in the shape of a bird whose notes strongly
resemble the sound of a whistle. A short halt was
made for maté and a cigarette at a rancho, the people
in which, whilst expressing their delight at our success,
wished to know whether we were going to make use
of the condors to concoct some *remedio* (medicinal
remedy). having no idea of the value or object of
Natural-history pursuits; in fact, by them a naturalist
is considered a species of quack-doctor, who collects
specimens for the alchemist's retort. At Cosquin one
evening, an old woman presented herself as I sat at
dinner, beseeching me for a piece of candle-end as a
remedio; but for what it could be a remedy, except for
darkness, I was a loss to conceive. At sundown we
arrived safely at our journey's end, a little fatigued,
but thoroughly well pleased with this our first Condor
hunt on the sierras of Cordova.

My first object on reaching Cosquin, was to secure
the live prize ; so, taking strips of raw hide, I proceeded to bind the fierce Sarcorhamphus to a post, until a
suitable cage could be built; a task both difficult and
dangerous : but when satisfactorily accomplished, raw
meat and water were offered the prisoner, both of
which he greedily accepted. A day or two subsequently
on rising in the morning, what was my surprise to
find that during the night the beast had actually
gnawed through the thick wet hide, and having just

succeeded in freeing himself, was about to launch his
pinions on his native element. Rushing up to him
for the purpose of securing the end of the thong, he
with open snapping beak and outstretched flapping
wings dealt me a staggering blow full on the chest;
but fortunately happening to have a stick in my hand,
I struck the condor with all my might full on the
crown of his head a blow certainly sufficient to fell a
large dog, but of this he took no notice except to prepare for a fresh assault, on which I thought better of
it and literally took to my heels : and from my experience on this occasion I am convinced that one
enraged condor is more than a match for an unarmed
man and that two would speedily put him to death.
Some peons hearing the affray hastened up with a
lasso and recaptured the dangerous bird, which was
then fettered more securely, and had the occurrence
not taken place in the midst of an orchard thick with
trees which prevented the vulture rising, he would
have bid goodbye at once to his tormentois. There
are evidently two species of Condor, the Condor negro
or black, and the Condor pardo or dark brown, and it
is a mistake to imagine that when the brown species
gains his beautiful neck-ruff, the plumage is gradually
darkened : both my specimens were of the latter kind.
The vexed question as to whether the Condor is led to
his carrion by sight or smell, I tested very simply by
wrapping up a lump of meat in one fold of a newspaper,
and presenting it to him at the usual dinner hour and
when therefore I knew him to be hungry ; of this he
took no notice whatever, although urged in every

possible way; but immediately the wrapper was removed and the flesh exposed to view, he pounced upon it ravenously.

My menagerie was now stocked with two live Condors, a young one having been purchased, an eagle, two black vultures (*Cathartes fœtens*), four caranchos (*Polyborus brasiliensis*), a fox, several parrots and a Dasypus: the fox owing to the bad example set him by the condor, managed in one night to gnaw his way through a half inch hard wooden box and escape. The few days that now intervened before my return to Cordova were employed chiefly in collecting specimens of the hard and useful woods with which the sierras abound; most of which, being tough, close grained, heavy, coloured and susceptible of high polish are suitable for cabinet work, whilst several are permanently scented, and all easy of access and would be a very agreeable change from the everlasting mahogany and walnut of our dining rooms. The following is a list of the native names of the twenty-one specimens I obtained; the scientific nomenclature attached to some of these I give with diffidence : — Coco (*Xanthoxylon coco*); Garabato (*Acacia lucumanensis*); Algarrobo (*Prosopis alba*); Picillin (*Condalia microphylla*); Molle (*Lithræi Gillesii*); Tala (*Celtis Sellowiana*); Moradillo; Sauce Colorado; Manzana del campo (*Will apple*); Chañar (*Gurliaca decorticans*); Talilla (*Duranta Lorentzii*); Quebracho colorado (*Loxopterygium Lorentzii*); Quebracho blanco (*Aspidosperma quebracho*); Uña de Gato, a variety of

Chañar; Fiamato; Garilla (*Larrea divaricata*); Espinillo (*Acacia cavenia*); Durazno del Campo (*Wild peach*); Tintitaco; Atamisqui (*Atamisquea marginata*); Alamo (*Poplar*).

And now it was time to pack up and return to the city of doctors, my impedimenta seriously increased by the addition of the live stock. On the journey I narrowly escaped one of the most destructive storms ever known in these parts: so violent was the hurricane that the thick iron crosses on the church steeples were bent down at right angles, roofs blown off, heavy metal garden seats spirited away fifty feet into the air, and worst of all, the beautiful Alameda, the pride of the Cordovese, ruined. When I went to view it the next morning, it was a complete wreck; all the fine old trees torn up by the roots and lying across one another in confused heaps; a loss which a century will not repair. As soon as the Rector of the University heard of my arrival, he kindly made an addition to my family, by entrusting me with a live puma, with which I became so familiar as to be allowed to fondle it as a kitten.

At this time, a remarkable instance of direct attack by diptera upon the human subject was brought to my notice in the city. A young girl's face became suddenly much inflamed and swollen, especially about the nose, eyes and cheekbones; the case was mysterious, and the faculty in perplexity, until at last one of the medical men made use of an astringent injection up the nostrils, when to the astonishment of everybody, more than fifty caterpillars came tumbling out. On being questioned, the patient remembered that, a few days before, a fly had entered her nostrils, and no doubt had fixed upon this singular cavern wherein to deposit its eggs, which were hatched and produced the larvæ. The patient lay for a long while in a very precarious condition. On a subsequent visit to Buenos Aires, I presented my menagerie to the Palermo Park Zoological gardens, in the outskirts of that city, an establishment which, in the present era of progress and under the fostering care of an enlightened government, will rise to be not only an ornament to the city, but an honor to the country.

CHAPTER XVII.

TRIP TO CORDOVA — VISIT TO JESUS MARIA

In America especially, wherever the footprints of the early Jesuits are discerned, there may be discovered remains of a civilization far in advance of their contemporaries. The society from the time of Loyola, cannot be denied a great faculty for organization, especially in dealing with uncivilized races, with man in his civil as well as absolute youth : and yet it is this very advance, material and moral, that has contributed to its decadence. Centres of thriving industry and peace, subservient to other and purer laws than those of worldly ambition, have always provoked the jealousy of mere politicians: witness the number of deserted missions throughout the upper Provinces of the Argentine Republic. It is due in a great measure to these self-denying yet persecuted apostles, that the Interior of this country is not now sunk in a state of barbarism, that there is any semblance of restraint to the passions of men, and that Christianity is both preached and practised therein.

Jesus Maria, that erstwhile stronghold of the Jesuits, is thus a spot that provokes strong interest, and so, as it lies in the neighbourhood of Cordova, I

determined to pay it a visit. At half past six on the
morning of the 4th. of November then, a carriage was
at the door of the Hotel Paris to convey two companions and myself to the terminus of the Tucuman
railway.(*) We soon rattled over the ten or twelve
squares intervening, crossing the beautiful Rio Primero by the ford, as the Sarmiento bridge was some
time ago carried away by a freshet, but has now been
rebuilt. The station is reached, and as this is a Government line, we naturally expect everything to
reflect grandeur, solidity and order: but a smile of
disappointment creeps over our features as we survey
the diminutive dimensions and inferior condition of
everything around. The temporary station is a mere
wooden shed, the guage very narrow and the carriages
and engines of the smallest: insignificance is stamped
on everything and we are suddenly transported to
Lilliput. "Surely," said we, "this is the land of the
Pigmies." I was forcibly reminded of the children's
toy-railways exhibited in the shop-windows of the
capital, the comparison no doubt heightened by the
colossal nature of all the works on the Central Argentine. The natives themselves are in high dudgeon
about the condition of this North Central line: they
affirm that it was arranged to be laid of the same
guage as the others already constructed in the Republic, but that by some jugglery between the existing

---

(*) Since this was written the Tucuman line has been prolonged to
the fine station of the Central Argentine.

government and the contractor Count Telfener, the guage was altered, by which means the one and the other were enriched. There is no doubt, inferior material was used throughout its construction and, in my opinion, a few years more will necessitate the replacing of the metals and the substitution of a broader guage: with European errors to warn them, it certainly does seem short-sighted policy to have more than one guage in the country.

Taking a return ticket which is serviceable for five days, we started at 7 a. m., ascending, through cuttings, the barranca skirting one side of the city, through which we now and then catch glimpses of its cupolas and minnarets, and in the distance lie the blue sierras. As we stretch northwards, the ground becomes more even and clothed with prickly shrubs and Pampa grass and contrary to my expectations, the motion of the cars and the speed left nothing to be desired. Soon, passing by numerous estancias, we enter dense forests of very fine trees, principally Algarrobo, Quebracho and Tala, embracing villages consisting of mud ranchos, which look very picturesque nestling amongst the foliage. General Paz, nicknamed *Chocolate*, the first station from Cordova, is reached by 8-20 and presents a shabby appearance: but if the wooden hut is not to our taste, the hot chocolate and cakes, vended by native women, are; and so the five minutes allowed by our diminutive but snorting and impatient steed, scarce suffice to discuss their merits. The line now running parallel

to and flanking the sierras, at a distance of a league
or so, a very fine view of their bold outline is presented and very shortly we find ourselves traversing
the Italian colony of Caroya, 30 miles from Cordova.
This colony is planted on a fine territory belonging to
the government of the Province, embracing fifty
square leagues, well-wooded, watered and pastured,
and such that with the most ordinary precautions,
thousands of hard working emigrants might secure
competence for themselves and be a source of wealth
to the country; but such is the short-sighted jealous
policy of those in power, that obstacles are thrown in
the way of success and the colony bids fair to imitate
many others, instituted on like unsatisfactory bases,
and dissolve into chaos. So exasperated were the
settlers at one period, that after having undergone the
labour of clearing the ground, erecting dwellings and
planting crops on the strength of unfulfilled promises,
they at last threatened to fly to arms to establish their
just rights. The fine estancia-house of Caroya next
meets the eye, and within a little, after a ride of one
hour and fifty minutes, we glide into the really well-
built and pretty station of Jesus Maria, surprised to
find it surrounded by goods' deposits and other buildings indicating considerable animation. The hotel
accommodation however is poor, only on a level, in
outward appearance, with an ordinary fonda (low restaurant) in the metropolis, and yet infinitely superior
in internal cleanliness: the baths, a point of the first
consideration throughout the province, quite surprised
me; to the credit of the Cordovese it may be remarked,

that in spite of their many faults, they do set a good example to the rest of the Republic, being both godly and clean.

The straggling town of Jesus Maria is built partly on a hill slope and consists mainly of mud huts, although it contains many good substantial brick houses; and seems destined to recover a great part of its pristine importance. The irrigation is simple and perfect; through the centre of the town runs the old river-bed, the stream of which having been diverted from a point above it, is made to flow through aqueducts, affording an abundant supply of crystal water to every house and garden, besides motive power sufficient to work an unlimited number of flour and saw mills.

Founded 300 years ago, Jesus Maria was one of the first strongholds of the Jesuits in this country, and numerous massive stone ruins remain to attest the power and wealth of those earnest pioneers. Situated on the higher ground across the river, stand and will stand for many successive generations, their yet living mementos, the old church and town, which indestructible as the rock whence they were dug and built of stone throughout, present a truly Derbyshire-like appearance. On one side lies the massive old monastery with its cloisters and cells, and at the back of this an immense oblong building more than 200 feet long, the ancient purpose of which I could not discover, but now rented as a corral (cattle enclosure). The old mill too, whose flour the venerable Fathers munched three centuries ago, still serves its original design for

more modern but less pious months; although some
recent additions have been made to it, as attests the
exceedingly well carved face over the main entrance,
with date 1760. When the Jesuits were in the zenith
of their power, they held in sway here as many as 3000
slaves, which will account for their many massive
works. Their ancient quinta adjoining, with its orchard and garden grounds, is still a very lovely place,
abounding in orange groves and magnificent walnut
trees which, attaining a height of a hundred feet and a
girth of 18 f. 2 in. as measured by myself, are without
doubt the finest of this class in the republic: and in
the midst of this lovely forest stands revealed a
stone tower in ruins, with a subterranean dungeon
telling of woe.

Under the cool shade of these patriarchs and
surrounded by bubbling rivulets and apples of gold,
we sat and conversed of these things.

After a residence of two days in this interesting
spot, a complete mine of antiquated lore awaiting development at the hands of some future Walter Scott,
we turned our steps once more Cordovawards, but
were almost alarmed and made to hesitate by the numerous stories afloat of the frequent dastardly attempts
to upset the trains on the Tucuman line ; a Cordovese
mania indicating hostility to modern improvements,
from which the Central Argentine had likewise to
suffer, for some time after it was opened. In Cordova,
I heard the same accounts and certainly many persons
were thereby deterred from travelling on that railway.

On the other hand it was asserted that no foundation really existed for such reports but that the government originated them as a device to shield themselves from censure for the notoriously bad condition of the road: the sequel however will clear the government from imputation. Disregarding then these warnings, we entrusted our precious lives once more to the stunted Cyclops and all went well until having passed General Paz and when within a league and a half of Cordova, the shrieks of the engine were shared by the passengers who, in their alarm, rushed to the doors and bounding down the steps were on the line in a moment. There lay two heavy sleepers of *quebracho colorado*, two and a half yards long and more than a foot thick, right athwart the metals, with a deep open culvert a few feet in advance, to reveal a diabolism almost without parallel in a country professing to be civilized. The engine just managed to pull up in time, or in place of this account, a Tay-bridge disaster would have been chronicled. I need not say that the passengers, thirty in number, were very much enraged and signed a declaration to the government on the spot, meanwhile talking loudly of Lynch-law.

Happily this epoch of destructive monomania has now passed away and the Cordovese have accepted the situation and suffer themselves to be borne on the tide of modern progress; so that ere long their city will become as noted for its material and industrial pursuits, as at present it is for dignified and learned ease.

On my return to the capital, a very brief experience of its formal life sufficed to arouse within me the instincts of the nomad, and so packing up once more, I lost no time in starting "Westward Ho!" for the Andes, whose majestic heads had long filled my youthful imagination with cameos which I longed to realize, the description of which will entail upon the reader the perusal of the several chapters which complete the present volume.

CHAPTER XVIII.

TRIP TO MENDOZA.

In a previous chapter detailing the route to Cordova will be found a description of the line as far as Villa María, at which point we branch off on to the Andine Railway, a government enterprise of the same guage as the Central Argentine. Well! in pouring rain, a very unusual circumstance in this quarter of the world, we arrived at the junction of Villa María, a name much honoured in this as in all other Catholic countries, for places as well as people, nay for men as well as women ; thus Mr. Santa María sounds strangely to English ears. In the refreshment room attached to the station I dined, and afterwards crossed the line to an inn kept by an Irishman, where I turned in and slept away the inclemency. The next morning broke fine, but the mud was indescribable; in the Argentine Republic mud and dust reign alternately. Villa María, 491 feet above sea level, is one of the most important stations on the Central Argentine Railway, due greatly to its forming the junction with the Andine line. The town lies about a mile and a half away, the usual provincial town, the river Tercero passing between it and the railway sta-

tion : here there is a ferryboat, but woe to the unlucky
wight who wants to cross in a flooded season, as
Charon's charges rise with the tide. The materials
for a fine bridge are visible, lying rotting on the banks,
as the piers were found too short ; an instance of the
folly of ordering from Europe what might be more
readily produced on the spot.

From Villa María, whose time differs from that
of the metropolis by twenty-five minutes, to Villa
Mercedes the present terminus of the Andine line, is
a distance of 158 miles by railway and punctual to the
minute off we start to accomplish it. The change of
cars from the Central Argentine to the Andine was
hailed with pleasure, as the trains on the latter line
are composite, made up both of English and American
coaches, and in addition are fitted with lavatories and
other conveniences conducing to personal comfort,
besides being kept scrupulously clean : here too is
seen an innovation which strongly reminded me of
Herne Bay pier, wind trolleys equipped with a Sampan
sail traverse the line at a speed of sometimes twenty
miles an hour. We cross the Rio Tercero by a very
fine iron structure, the river in its then flooded condition presenting a broad expanse of water. The woods
are left behind, and the open camp succeeds, studded
with numerous lagoons, some of them a quarter of a
mile long, whose surfaces are literally alive with duck
and geese. About 5.30 p. m. Velez Sarsfield, the
first station is reached, so named in honor of an eminent Argentine jurisconsult, of Irish Extraction. Now

again coursing though woods, with the shades of evening the air turns raw and cold. At General Cabrera
the station immediately before Rio Cuarto, the late
Mr. Slater, an Englishman, held an estancia of forty
square leagues of very prime land, which he kept
intact to his death, as he was determined to hand it
down entire to his children, in spite of the numerous
advantageous offers to the contrary. A few minutes
before 9 p. m. crossing the magnificent bridge over
the Rio Cuarto, the train, a little later, draws up in
the station of the same name, having thus traversed
82 miles since we started from Villa María. The Rio
Cuarto station, 1335 feet above sea level, is a very
fine building of two storeys and yet although the
sleeping accommodation for travellers belongs to it, such
has to be sought at another house across a small plaza
behind the station, rather an inconvenient arrangement especially in bad weather. Here, from the busy
scence around him, the English visitor may, without
much stress upon the imagination, fancy himself in the
Old Country again : the crossing of the trains, the
rush of passengers into the refreshment room, the hive
of workshops, the English stationmaster, the good
dinner and lastly the famous Mendoza wine which
henceforth is exclusively drunk all the way to the city
of vineyards, contribute in their turn to enliven the
scene and create interest. Having business in the
town, three quarters of a mile away, I started off in a
carriage to visit the snug little place with its 6000
inhabitants, two churches and convent, and pretty little
plaza, the whole encircled by charming quintas : no

matter how small or poor a town is in this country, it always possesses one or more plazas.

This southwest-district of the province of Cordova, known as the Rio Cuarto, is well-watered by numerous streams and acequias (artificial canals) and considering that its sandy, weedless soil consists entirely of pulverized debris from the Andine spurs, is wonderfully fertile, although subject to drought, the ravages of locusts, and hail. Here luxuriant pastures of strong permanent grass with lowing herds and a few scraggy sheep, alfalfares for artificial fattening, crops of maize, wheat and rye, meet the eye. The region, which is but a sample of the chief part of the western and upper provinces, has been reclaimed from the dominion of the desert, and rendered fertile by the industry of man; but as it only exists by sufferance, directly the care, that has converted it from absolute sterility to fecundity, is withdrawn, back its lapses to its pristine condition. Irrigation is the touchstone by means of which so magic a transformation is effected; remove a spadeful or two of earth from the acequia-walls and flood the land, no Egypt could yield finer crops; and what has been performed here by its agency, will produce like results throughout all the waste lands of the Republic. Up to 1878, Rio Cuarto was a frontier town and Indian invasions were frequent and very destructive to estancieros, now however the district is undisturbed and as its capital forms the military headquarters of the North-Western Division, the territory is well-fitted for the investment of capital in cattle farming with a certainty of large profits.

At 6-30 next morning the journey was resumed across undulatory Pampas, and from the first station Sampacho, around which lies a very flourishing colony, we obtain a glimpse of detached hills rising abruptly from the plain; and the only remarkable circumstance in this neighboorhood is the excessive cultivation of Sandias (water melons) which are such a drug as to command only a penny a piece. As we proceed, troops of wild horses cross our path, and to those accustomed only to see this noble animal spirit-broken; to witness the ears erect, the expanded nostrils sniffing the air, the head thrown back over an arched neck, the muscles quivering, the prancing and curvetting, the wild gallop and the sudden start, with manes and tails streaming in the wind, is a picture never to be forgotten and fit for a painter to gloat over.

I had a lot of officers for companions, amongst whom was Comandante Roca, a brother of the President of the Republic, bound for Villa Mercedes to join the expedition to the Rio Negro against the Indians, and most delightful travelling companions they were. We now descry the tail end of the sierras of Cordova and the gradient is steep all the way to Villa Mercedes. At Chajan, the last station but one on the line, a strong wind blows ceaselessly in one direction, and as it lies on an open exposed undulating prairie, it puzzled me to conceive what set of meteorological conditions should make it thus differ from all other places similarly situated.

Soon after leaving Chajan, a river of the same name is crossed by means of a temporary wooden bridge, the former structure having been washed away by a freshet, but a fine iron viaduct then in course of construction has been finished since, and proceeding onward to our destination, we reach Villa Mercedes 1578 feet above sea-level at 10-30 a. m.

Our term of railway travelling was thus completed, as this is the furthest point to which the State Railways have as yet been pushed: although at the present time the Government is making strenuous efforts to extend the Andine line to San Luis, an undertaking which will most probably be completed during the ensuing year. We thought the rain bad enough at Villa Maria, but here it was accompanied by a strong cutting wind as cold as ice. Another English station-master here greets me and a good breakfast having been despatched in the station refreshment-rooms, I sent my luggage forward in a cart and followed myself in a carriage to the Diligence-office situated in the town about a mile and a half distant: the only thing to complain of in connection with the public carriages here as elsewhere in the country parts of the Republic is the "ad valorem" style of the fares: and to me it always appears unaccountable why railway-stations should not be pitched in the immediate vicinity of towns to the comfort and convenience of passengers, rather than at the distance of two or three miles as is so usually the case. Rows of fine poplars and willows line, on both sides, the whole distance to this dreary town, which consists merely of scattered houses built of adobes (sun-dried bricks), interspersed with mud walls and trees: there is absolutely nothing to relieve the eye or ear, save the soldiers' uniforms, for being a frontier-town, a large garrison is quartered here, and the hum of the school-children conning their primers.

Between Villa Mercedes and Mendoza diligences run twice a week each way, and on one of these I embarked, not without apprehension, at 2 p. m. of the same day. The paralytic vehicle is not beautiful, nor were it ever so, would it retain that beauty long, considering the very heavy work it has to perform; in fact, at the tearing speed at which it is urged along, it is a miracle to me it does not suffer analysis; as to the motion, it is the Bay of Biscay in a nutshell; such a rolling, pitching and jolting, up to the roof and down again, such a churning of the contents of the stomach, as to produce violent indigestion, which usually lasts some days after the completion of the journey: but withal, it is seldom overturned, on account of its broad guage, and the pace which elsewhere kills but here saves. Well then behold the driver perched in front elevated a little above the passengers and having control over three shaft horses or mules ; ten feet ahead another triplet under the control of an outrider, at an equal distance a third with its postillion and sometimes, if the roads are bad, a fourth in like manner ; the whole forming a cortege that extends ninety feet and which is completely at the mercy of the extreme postillion, a matter by no means insigni-

ficant on roads where deep channels and pantanos
(holes filled with slush) abound. The diligence holds
ten persons at a pinch and the luggage is strapped on
the top or behind.

Passing at a rapid gallop through the streets and
leaving behind the *chacras* (farms), we debouch upon
the open country, all Indian territory, covered with
trees here and there in scattered groups and to the
right and far away behind, stretch the Sierras of Córdova in the hazy distance. Arrived at the Rio Quinto,
here from 50 to 100 yards broad, and the neighbourhood of which is well-wooded with Calden, we cross
it by a ford, for although in a flooded state,it is not
deep; on the farther bank a change of cattle awaits
us. This change occurs every two, four or five
leagues at corrales (cattle pens) tenanted by a solitary
man or boy without shelter, whose sole companions
are a mangy, cadaverous looking troop of dogs, which
seem to get their disreputable living by licking the
grease from the hubs of the diligence wheels. To
gain the first post-house, ten leagues from Villa Mercedes consumed five hours, but the roads were extremely heavy, as it had been and was still pouring with
rain Two other passengers besides myself were
all that occupied the diligence, and they, two
officers en route to join the Rio Negro expedition,
which they very much pressed me to accompany: and
and as we were so few, our first endeavour was to
make everything as comfortable as possible by fitting
up the centre of the coach between the seats with the
mail bags and then spreading the cushions on the top,

preparatory to a lengthened siesta on this luxurious couch — but it was ordained otherwise. As if the tremendous jerking, rolling and dipping of the lumbering vehicle were not enough, the rattle-trap windows came down with a run and a thud that plainly declared their determination never more to serve : one was bodily absent and not a bit of rag or newspaper even was to be obtained throughout the first day's journey wherewith to stop the gap, so as a general inundation threatened, a council of war was held and the result was that whilst two endevoured to sleep, the third had to keep the windows to their duty ; in my watch, I had the supreme gratification of putting up the set at least one hundred times. Just at dusk we came across an express diligence from Mendoza bound to Villa Mercedes with the new Chilian Minister, Balmaceda, whose destination was Buenos Aires, and after pulling up and exchanging a few words relative to the state of the roads, each drove off in a contrary direction. Another league brings us to the spot where a murderous battle was fought on the 1st. of April 1867, in which some seven hundred men fell : I asked the conductor, whether any relics still remained on the battle field, "Not a bone," said he, "for you know, Sir, old bones fetch ten Bolivianos the ton." The next posta called Fraga boasts of a frontier fort, containing one officer and twenty men and on a late occasion when they were attacked by the Indians, the men were found to possess only five rounds af ammunition each, having sold the rest to purchase tobacco and other luxuries. An old spiked cannon does duty as a bum-bailiff, the soldiers declaring they did not require artillery for use, as the mere sight of a piece of ordnance is sufficient for the sable warriors who, bold enough in the saddle and on the plain, have no stomach for earthworks. Here the accommodation was tolerable and immediately after dinner we tumbled in and slept until 2-30 a. m. when the conductor summoned us to renew our toilsome journey. A cold and cloudy morning saluted us, and as daylight broke the Sierra Morro displayed its lofty head, but about 7 a. m. down it began to pour again and everything was hid from view. In this inhospitable and bleak Indian region, the corrales where they change mules are only formed of branches of trees, and here live a man and a boy winter and summer without shelter, almost without clothing, and literally without food: the pack of fierce dogs, their sole companions, hunt the armadillos, which are found around in great abundance and form the only sustenance for both: the taste of the Dasypus is by no means to be despised even in civilized life, when it is properly cooked and served up in its shell with lemon, as in delicacy and flavour it rivals roast sucking-pig.

We now reach the "Tierra alta" (high ground), disclosing a very extensive view of the swelling plain, with the road melting afar into the horizon, and from this point, on a very clear day, may be traced the Andine peaks, at a distance of eighty leagues. About an hour more brings us to a small clump of trees called the "Chañares de la Matanza," where in 1870 some twenty five soldiers, armed with flint muskets, were attacked by a body of Indians during a rainstorm, and as their arms were rendered useless, were lanced to a man. On the left rises the Cerro Linse with its peak delving the clouds, and right ahead loom the Sierras which flank the city of San Luis at an altitude of 5000 feet. The country now becomes well-wooded, but the roads, to the last degree execrable, lead us to the bed of a river, which we cross, with scarce water enough to reach the axles, the result of a fine piece of engineering work, constructed about two leagues off to divert the stream for irrigation purposes; and then ascending a short steep incline, we wind round the foot of the Sierras, which present a fine bold outline, and worthily support their title as giant vanguards of the still more gigantic Cordilleras. A good turnpike road, along which stretch the Transandine Telegraph wires, invites us to bowl along its level course, and entering between long tapias (compressed-earth walls) a foot thick and six feet high, lined on both sides by poplars, and dotted here and there with adobe huts, at 10 a. m. after scudding over fourteen leagues since early morn, we reach the picturesquely situated city of San Luis which, in South latitude 33° 17' and at a height of 2500 feet above sea level, not only surveys from its eyry all the corners of its own province, but casts its wondrous vision over the seventy two intervening leagues to fix its gaze on the Andine summits.

In spite however of the beauty of its site, of all

the dreary miserable places for man to spend his existence in, this veritable city of San Luis beats them
all : two or three mud huts on each square, lying in
themidst of orange-groves, vineyards and willow-
copses of great luxuriance; narrow streets for the most
part unpaved and windowless dwellings, characterise a
town where dwell 4000 inhabitants, and these, according to report, in *comfortable* circumstances. We drive
into the patio of the " Grand Hotel Français, " presided
over by a fat French dame, and enter the dining-
room, a horrible window-less hole, where ricketty
chairs, a foul table-cloth and dirty food await us: the
billiard-room, surely the first of its series, is in possession of three crippled cues and a few chipped balls,
whilst the rat-devoured floor threatens a dislocated
ankle at every step. This hostelry detains us but one
hour and glad to escape from the reeking air, we
sally forth sight seeing, but there is literally nothing
to interest, save the evidences of the excessive natural
fertility of its well-watered soil, but none whatever of
any corresponding exertion on the part of its inhabitants; no civic monuments, nor buildings attest public spirit, no business activity ; in fact, the people of
San Luis appear externally at least to have anticipated
the rest of the grave. The male inhabitants of the
city are nicknamed Puntanos and of course the ladies
Puntanas, as the site of their city was formerly called
" Punta de los venados " (Deer point); and one redeeming feature of the Puntanas is that they are in
possession of lustrous eyes and know to what purpose
to apply them, and as they outnumber the rougher sex

in the proportion of four to three, it is really dangerous for a susceptible stranger to sojourn amongst them.

Thirty leagues have to be accomplished this day, so we leave San Luis, after little more than an hour's delay, and betake ourselves to the high road to Mendoza, pushing on at a tremendous pace. The telegraph-wires still accompany us and the roadway is fine, save here and there deep scarped gullies of sufficient capacity to engulf man and horse; these man-traps are scooped by the rain in the soft and friable arenaceous earth and necessitate many a long detour through the adjacent woods to avoid. On this side of San Luis, the country becomes more populated, and every mile or so we pass a hut with its enclosure, having a represa (reservoir) made by digging to the depth of three yards, throwing up the earth to form a sloping embankment, protecting the sides by stakes driven in, and puddling the bottom; this gives a total depth of twelve feet, and forms a capacious cistern for the purpose of receiving the rain-water from the higher ground in the immediate neighbourhood, to serve for a year's consumption; but as for the delectable liquid, faugh! we could not even wash in it. Within four leagues of our destination for the night, crops up a hamlet of seven or eight dwellings called Chósmes, boasting of an almacen, (store) and a government free school with forty pupils: and after a slight repast of cheese and native wine, on we push at a killing pace, accomplishing the remainder of our day's journey in one hour and a half. The reason of

our haste to reach the posta called Cabra may be ex-
plained in a few words: the diligence from Mendoza
was expected in, and the accommodation being limited,
there is usually a scramble for the beds: luckily we
were just in time to laugh at the nine passengers from
the opposite direction, who had to adjourn to the
open corridor to sleep. On unloading our things from
the diligence for the night, one of my fellow-passen-
gers, Comandante Aguilar, found himself minus a
fine revolver: it is very rare indeed to lose anything
en route by the diligence, as wherever a halt is made,
trustworthy peons (servantmen) are always in attendance. During supper the disconsolate *nine* entered and reported the roads very bad further up:
and so having thirty five leagues to accomplish on
the following day, we retired early and at six a. m.
the next morning, in the midst of a soaking rain, are
summoned to reenter the ark. Such continuous rain
as we have had throughout this journey is an exceedingly rare occurrence, as the fall is very slight in
these parts. The horses are put to but turn restive
and at last one falls and breaks a foreleg, a substitute
has to be found and harnessed, so that after half an
hour's delay, a start is made; the roads quickly veri-
fying the report of the strangers.   In the course
of an hour or so the Desaguadero is crossed by a wooden
bridge, and on landing on the other bank, we find
ourselves in the Province of Mendoza: for this river,
running due North and South, forms at once the
draining basin of the adjoining watersheds of San
Luis and Mendoza, and the boundary line of those

provinces: yet the rainfall is so scanty, that Artesian wells have been attempted for irrigation purposes, but with no great success hitherto.

The weather now clears and about a league before reaching the Posta, La Paz, a small town where breakfast awaits us, we come upon the rows of poplars which continue most of the way to the city of Mendoza : the road which has been straight as an arrow from SanLuis, deviates a little, but soon regaining a straight course, we reach La Paz at midday, scoring already fifteen of the thirty-five leagues. From this point, the eye spanning a distance of no less than forty-five leagues, or ten beyond Mendoza, descries the Andes as a blue line on the horizon, the mighty dome of Tupungato (21000 feet) standing sentinel over the lesser giants. It it usual for travellers to break forth into rapturous song on their first view of the towering Cordilleras, and indeed I was tempted to imitate their example, but the cruel torments of the road effectually repressed all sentimental gush: perhaps on a nearer acquaintance with these heaven-born masses, I may inflict on my readers a description of the feelings inspired by their presence.

The Posta at La Paz supplied a good breakfast which we sat lazily enjoying beneath the patio corridor, at the same time amusing ourselves with the gambols of two Matajos or Armadillos (*Dasypus tricinctus*) which, tied together by a string a yard long to prevent their burrowing and getting lost, could not agree on a common direction, so the matter ended in a continuous tussle. You may handle and fondle these animals with perfect impunity, but if by design or accident you happen to place a hand or finger beneath them, they roll themselves up into a ball in a twinkling and nip you very sharply between the scissor-like strong edges of their horny shield: no creature expresses timidity more clearly than the Armadillo: when handled, they always tremble violently. The habitat of that curious and beautiful creature the *Chlamydophorus truncatus* is in this neighbourhood, but it is exceedingly rare, and when obtained cannot be kept alive in captivity. At half past two p. m. we resumed our journey, passing through the town, which boasts of one or two stores, a Post-office, Telegraph-station, Church and Government Free-school of fifty pupils presided over by the worthy catholic priest, whose acquaintance I made on a subsequent visit. The camp here, as all the way from San Luis, is covered with low scanty brushwood and dwarfed crooked trees, the Retama (*Bulnesia retama*), a sad-looking stem, whose foliage is miserably developed or sometimes entirely wanting. The road becoming tortuous and rugged, continually leads through passes of nasty loose sand (*guadales*) in which the wheels suddenly sink to the axles, a *tierra infirma* such that to save our necks and make any progress, we are obliged to descend and walk for a time; then catching a glimpse of the river Tunuyan, which, further up, sends forth an artificial canal forty miles long and supplies La Paz and neighbourhood with water for irrigation, on we haste over abominable ground, till night overtakes our cortege and then a halt of an hour is called to allow the heated axles to cool; however by dint of hard driving, at half past ten p. m. we reach the Posta of Santa Rosa, the haven for the night and have the satisfaction of completing our projected thirty-five leagues.

In this neighbourhood, during the revolution of 1874, was fought the sanguinary battle of Santa Rosa, so called from an estancia in the immediate neighbourhood: it ended in the defeat of General Arredondo by General Roca and cost the lives of several hundred men, and the trenches are still visible by the road side.

From this point we begin to notice the excessive roominess and light construction of the buildings: the former due to the extreme cheapness of material, wood, lime and bricks; the latter, indicating approach to a volcanic region: so that the Posta of Santa Rosa surprised us with its large fine house, fronted with a magnificent corridor; nor were we less delighted with the grateful shade of a splendid vinery sixty yards long by twenty broad, bounded by *alfalfares* (lucerne fields) of vivid green, and hedgerows of towering poplars and willows, with acequias bubbling at their feet. Poplars and willows in Mendoza much exceed the European growth, rising to a height of a hundred feet and presenting masses of very thick foliage: all the verdure indeed of this province is entirely artificial; from a barren sandy waste, irrigation has evoked a blooming Eden and the

Mendocinos deserve great praise both for the magnitude and skilful execution of their water-vascular system. So exhausted were we on arrival at Santa Rosa, that even tempting refreshment failed to entice us and we hastened to repose our weary limbs, not on the usually inevitable *catre* (settle-bed), but on a structure which then, to my exhausted frame, seemed superior to anything Europe has yet invented for the solace of tired nature. It consists of a light wooden framework, across which thongs of hide are stretched, forming a soft, elastic cushion, almost equal to any spring mattress: indeed from this station, we begin to observe a civilization entirely native, to the exclusion of everything European; furniture, domestic utensils, baskets, dyes, bedding, upholstery, crockery, carpets &c., all the result of native fingers, and from which as regards design, form, colour, and substance, even the old world might condescend to take a lesson. At 5-30 on the following morning, which broke dull, cloudy, and cold, threatening more rain, the inexorable Jehu demands our reembarkation, but this time to the strains of a bugle, a serenade than which I thought I had heard nothing more sweet. For a league or more the road traverses an avenue of beautiful trees, dotted with residences, until we emerge on to the open camp, clothed as before with somewhat of a scanty arboreal vegetation, but without a blade of grass: a course of four leagues over this uninteresting tract brings us to the entrance of a fine, broad Boulevard, which continues more or less the whole of the fifteen leagues which now separate us from Mendoza. Nothing could

be more delightful than this *Via Appia*, straight as an
arrow, and wanting little but the master-pieces of
antiquity to give it quite a classic air: lined on either
side with Carolina and other poplars, Tamarinds and
flowing streams, a firm, sparkling sand beneath the
feet, and the long, long vista closed by the purple
mountain-chain with snow-capped peaks glistening in
the sun-light, a sward of intensely vivid green alfalfa
as far as the eye can reach, and vineyards jostling
the very roadway and thrusting their purple racemes
close to the actual touch of the thirsty traveller; my
gaze never tired of gloating over the grand, harmo-
niously coloured, and peaceful scene, which spoke so
forcibly of fecundity, industry and happiness. Habitations and gardens, trim, neat and clean, succeed
one another and give their aid in accentuating an
oasis, which contrasts so forcibly with the sterile tracts
through which our path has hitherto lain. The hedges
strike me as novel, but very effective, consisting of
strong, thick and dried brushwood, disposed horizontally between upright posts. Our route now lay
through the district of San Martin, so called from the
family-mansion and property of the illustrious general
whose fame the ocean even could not bound, and a
spot held in reverence by Argentines as the birthplace
of their Washington.

After another change of cattle, the road becomes
quite lively with cavaliers, troops of mules bearing
luscious burdens, carriages, and gaily decorated carts,
especially those of the *Panaderos* (bakers) which with

bells and bright paint invite to the hot morning roll so
common throughout America and which contrasts so
strongly with the stale stuff purveyed in London.
Suddenly however our satisfaction is clouded and our
olfactory nerves shocked by a most overpowering
nauseating stench, which not an ocean of Köln-water
would drown: this arises from the mode of repairing
the roads: the yawning chasms of the pantanos or
black Stygian pools of fœtid mud and slush, are filled
with green brushwood and dwarf trees, and the
churning under a hot sun and the natural decay, load
the air with sulphuretted hydrogenic miasma, which
in wet weather like the present, is positively sickening. We now pass two local diligences filled with
passengers and then 'cross the river Mendoza by a
very good wooden bridge, to the left of which rises
a splendid mill worked by a Mr. Brachmann. In
this neighbourhood are found salitres which, by the
inexperienced, are mistaken for snow; they consist of
Chloride of Sodium and Sulphates of Magnesia and
Lime, forming in dry weather a good hard, solid road;
but in wet, a slimy, viscous, argillaceous, saline mass
which, under an appearance of firmness, clogs the wheels
and into which they plunge irremediably: in fact
the soil of the whole Argentine Republic is more or
less impregnated with sulphates and chlorides, which
crop up especially in the north-western provinces,
forming salitres or salitrales, from which exhale mephitic vapours strong enough to asphyxiate travellers
even in the diligences: so that to cross them in summer is quite impossible in vehicles and almost equally

so on horseback. Stopping for breakfast at an hotel five leagues from Mendoza at a place called Rodeo del Medio, our surprise was great at the luxury displayed, but the mystery was soon cleared up when mine host stepped forward, a namesake of mine and a descendant of one of the prisoners taken from Beresford's expeditionary invading force, who, although not speaking a word of English, retained in figure, jovial manner, and love of good feeding, the traditionary John Ball type: a considerable number of such are scattered throughout the Upper Provinces, whither their ancestors were forwarded that they might not escape.

Hitherto we have travelled without style, but now that the last stage is reached, a team of pure albinos stand ready, wherewith our state-coach may make a triumphal entry into Mendoza. The horses are pulled together, whipped up and off we go at a tearing speed: the fact is, throughout the journey, the pace could not be complained of, wherever the roads permitted. As the floating branches indicated to Columbus his approach to land, so everything now betokens to us the vicinity of a populous, wealthy and civilized city; each second or two we pass roomy edifices standing in beautifully cultivated grounds, the road being alive with carts, horsemen and diligences. The vineyards increase in number and on all sides are presented to the view luscious purples clusters even interlacing with the poplar boughs and hanging their heavy heads within reach of the wayfarer: at times a double vineyard, one above the other, offers the

strange appearance of veritable hanging gardens. In
front lie in their mighty strength, blocks of mountain
masses 9000 feet high and peeping over their summits the everlasting snow-capped peaks of the Andes
proper.

To the loud cracking of the postillions' whips
and at full speed, passing through the Plaza of San
José, a suburb of Mendoza, we soon sight and then
enter the city itself and finally, at 2 p. m., draw up in
front of the coach-office, thus bringing to a close that
long and painful diligence-excursion which, although
my first, had well nigh proved my last : for, two days
subsequently, came a telegram detailing how nearly
our journey had ended disastrously. Not many hours
after we had passed the Post-house at Fraga in San
Luis, the Indians pounced upon a troop of twenty
mule carts heavily laden with merchandise, bound
from Villa Mercedes to Mendoza, killing eleven and
mortally wounding nine others of the conductors, and
carrying off the capataz prisoner with all the spoils.
They were no doubt lying in ambush as we passed
the spot, for the succeeding diligence was stopped
there and would have been instantly sacrificed, had
not the near approach of the mule train diverted the
attention of the Sables and given the passengers
time to take refuge with their luggage in the
Post-House and Fort which they hastily barricaded,
until the arrival of the troops from Mercedes. A council of Indians was held and they decided to abandon the
lesser for the greater prize and hurried off to surround

the rich but doomed convoy. Calling upon the guards to surrender with a guarantee of their lives, the peons were for fighting, although possessed of no other arms than their knives, but the capataz with his solitary Remington, ruled otherwise; and the fate of the whole party was sealed! The savages, triumphantly shouting their war pæan, rushed upon their victims, lashed their hands behind their backs and forthwith lanced them all, with the exception of the capataz and one of the men who palmed off the spider trick upon the unwary braves and thus escaped to give notice. The troops were soon upon their trail and inflicted heavy punishment upon the marauders, killing seventeen, rescuing the capataz and recovering the spoil.

These Indian raids are feared not alone by civilized man: even the beasts, the cattle, horses, deer, mules, ostriches &. all equally exhibit signs of terror on the approach of the dusky skins, whose proximity they herald unmistakably, when the duller human senses, are unaware of danger. The following curious mode of Indian attack. called a *Ronda*, strikes consternation into man and animal. Twisting together many lassos to form a very long, strong and heavy hide cable, at each end they fasten ten or fiften horses, which are driven at full gallop against their enemy, maintaining equal distance throughout. This cable, which no opposition can arrest, goes tearing, rushing and sweeping along the surface, breaking legs or casting violently to the ground every mortal obstacle; and the Indians follow its wave close and in a compact body, ready to lance the prostrate foe. One wily trick however begets another; so the soldiers taught by experience, stick their bayonets firmly in the ground obliquely towards themselves and when they see the death-dealing cord advancing, throw themselves down behind them, which although swept down by the violent impact, give sufficient deflection to the hawser to carry it over their prostrate bodies: then rising suddenly and pouring in a deadly volley the conflict begins.

CHAPTER XIX.

TRIP TO MENDOZA

The dweller on the vast plain of the Pampas, on being introduced for the first time into the region of the Cordilleras is amazed and humbled by the lofty masses which confront him, and although from the rising site on which stands the city of Mendoza, but little is seen of the true Andine chain, yet on the road to Ramblon and thence to San Martin or on that to Borbollon, or in fact any of the roads leading out of the city, they burst on the astonished view, whilst the gaze is instantly arrested and fascinated by the dome of Tupungato

" Whose sunbright summit mingles with the sky "

at the astonishing elevation of 21000 feet. From thence, north and south, the eye wanders over a continued serried line of snow-clad peaks, until they melt into the filmy grey gauze of almost infinite distance. On a nearer approach the scene becomes bolder, and the roar of cataracts, the howling of the winds, the bold and savage peaks, the fearful raviness and the overpowering, eternal masses inspire a thrilling awe and render man mute and helpless: yet in the midst of all this striking grandeur, glimpses are here and there obtaine 1 of nature in her more peaceful aspect ; valleys of fertile calm almost semi-tropical, boulders and fantastic rocks, brooks, rivulets and meadows, which brighten and elevate the soul to contemplate, in the midst of all this evidence of the throes of uncontrollable forces, that beneficent arrangement which produces even on the very crust of a volcano " the bread which strengtheneth man's heart and the oil which makes his face to shine. "

Nothwithstanding all the sublimity amounting almost to terror, with which the gigantic grouping of the Andes affects the contemplative mind: the picture that will ever remain freshest upon my retina was that obtained by rising before the orb of day and beholding his advance heralded by the successive delicate tinging of peak after peak, until at last the whole cadenic summit burst into one mass of golden blaze, whilst the valleys beneath lay still slumbering in blackness of darkness.

Of the numerous passes over the Andes into Chili, in the province of Mendoza, only three are now used : the *Planchon*, the highest point of which is 8225 feet ; the *Uspallata*, which ascends to 12370 feet and forms the projected route of the TransAndine Railway ; and the *Portillo*, reaching an altitude of 13240 feet. The Uspallata-pass presents the fewest natural difficulties and it is accordingly selected for the Post-office route, the service of which is maintained intact even through the severest winters, with occasional loss of life.

Tempted by the high monthly pay, men are found hardy and bold enough to risk their lives, at all seasons, in carrying the mails across, and considering the nature of the dangers and hardships undergone, richly deserve a far higher recompense: any attempt to employ mules on this service would only endanger both rider and steed and facilitate the already easy descent to Avernus; so, shod in snow-sandals, floundering, clmbing, sliding down the mountain sides, blown hither and thither by icy gales which are al-most always at hurricane point, at times sinking breast-deep, at others disappearing altogether, the poor letter-carrier toils on for from twelve to fifteen days in winter and would undoubtedly perish, were it not for the friendly shelter of those occasional "*casuchas*" (stone huts), which the government has erected as a refuge for travellers.

CHAPTER XX

The city of Mendoza, situated 2900 feet above sea level, and perhaps the most elegant of all the Argentine capitals, subject as it is to frequent earthquakes and still suffering from the disastrous catastrophe of March the 20ᵗʰ 1861, when 12000 out of its 15000 souls were engulfed, including amongst the number of the victims the geologist Bravard who had predicted it, has been rebuilt partially on the old site and in such a manner as to cover a great extent of ground, and thus presents a straggling appearance. So great was the affection of the survivors for the spot, that that motive combined with the abundance of building material ready to hand, led many of them to tempt Providence by again erecting their homes on what is now well ascertained to be the extinct crater of a volcano. A somewhat ancient poet enquires,

> Who in a steeple near the bell
> Would wish to make his bed?
> Who in a powder-mill would dwell?
> Who elsewhere had a shed.

but the Mendocinos, in far greater danger than either, boldly scoff at the apprehensions of the rhymester and

sleep soundly on beds for ever rocking by Titanic
restlessness. The houses which are constructed entirely
of *adobes* (sun-dried bricks), consist of ground-floor
only ; these adobes, the greater part of which is straw,
are found superior to any other kind of building material, as being more elastic and yielding to earthquake
shocks, than the rigid and brittle oven-baked bricks.
The present population of the city is about 14000, the
third part of which consists of Chilians, and the
remainder the descendants of a mixture of Spanish and
Guarpe Indian blood : and a more industrious, intelligent and peaceable people it would be difficult to find :
its streets are broad and wellpaved and in the new
town bordered with straight silverstemmed Carolina
poplars,which throw a dense shade and form a delightful retreat from the scorching summer sun : at the foot
of these, courses a swift stream of cool water, about two
yards broad in the principal thoroughfare.   The finest
of these Boulevards is calle San Nicolas, whose picturesqueness is increased by tastefully arranged tables
which, at every corner, beneath the shade of the
patriarchal trees, invite the lounger to partake of
sweetmeats, fruits and iced-drinks ; not the least
agreeable figure of the picture being the dark-hued but
regular-featured Provinciano who presides and whose
countenance, very prone to smile, adds a relish to the
refreshment; or, if more solid fare be sought, a stroll
of a few yards brings us where, as in the Vicar of
Wakefield, "a neat hearth and pleasant fire are prepared for our reception," for here and there sit women,
accompanied by their household gods, ready to dispense

hot maté and fresh-baked *empanadas* (meat pies):
during the summer evenings all these hostleries are
illuminated and form graphic groups in the midst of
the upright and stately poplar stems. But the liveliest
scene of all is the road, along which passes a never
ending train of carts, carriages, diligences of which
there are eight or ten, troops of mules with jingling
bells, and the stately, sedate Provinciano mounted on
a beast seemingly too small for him, his handsome
vicuña poncho flowing behind, with silver mounted
trappings and massive clanking spurs glittering in the
sunlight. At every cross road, looking westwards a
glimpse of the blue Cordilleras is obtained, with here
and there a snow-clad peak, just visible over the inside
lower Sierras. In the city of Mendoza, nothing strikes
the visitor more than the abundance of water, to the
attainment of which, the skill and means of the inhabitants ever have been and always will be exhaustively
directed: the rainfall being so slender, if it were not
procurable by artificial means, absolute sterility would
result, in fact such is the normal condition of the whole
province. Besides the double streams down every
street, whose sluices are opened at certain times of the
day for irrigation and cleansing purposes, street fountains of pure sparkling mountain-dew abound and
afford excellent water for drinking purposes, and
these are fed by an underground aqueduct conveying
the liquid five or six miles from a reservoir situated on
the hills at Challao. The water for general irrigation
however is obtained from the Zanjon canal connecting
the river Mendoza with the city, the Indian name of

which is *Guaymellen* after a cacique (chief) who ruled here at the time of the Spanish conquest and who constructed it with Indian labour.

There are at present six churches but of no architectural pretensions and with only low wooden towers to act as belfries : after the experience of the great earthquake, in which the falling massive churches committed the greatest havoc, the inhabitants have fought shy of erecting stately structures ; and so it is in fact with their private dwellings which, with the exception of four or five, exhibit so little solidity that they are set in vibration by a passing coach or cart : this lightness of construction extends especially to the roof from which, in case of a serious shock, the greatest danger is to be apprehended. Some architects indeed strengthen the houses with wooden or latterly wrought iron framework, the compartments of which are filled with bricks; in my opinion, a perilous innovation, as in case of a violent earthquake, the bricks would certainly be shaken out and each become a cannon ball, although it is possible that the framework might remain intact : the most secure form of dwelling for the inhabitants of an extinct crater, is indeed as yet far from determined.

The dread earthquake of 1861, in which Mendoza seems to have been the very focus of the undulatory movement, was ushered in by a continued rumbling, succeeded by the usual direct wave, and almost immediately followed by the return shock, which in all cases is the severe one. The notice given

to the Mendocinos was short indeed and as it was the
season of Lent and the people were at their devotions
in the churches, they could not take advantage even
of that short respite. Terrible confusion ensued which
was heightened to a panic when, as the survivors aver,
smoke and fire on the Andes and a fiery cross surmounting their summits, announced doomsday to the
affrighted city. The return wave was clearly exhibited
in the well-known case of one gentleman who, on experiencing the first shock, rushed out into the patio
just in time to escape the fall of one wall, by scaling
whose ruins at his utmost speed he avoided but by a
hair's breadth the inward tumble of the opposite one.
The stories of miraculous deliverances would fill a
volume. A rubicund-visaged Frenchman, sojourning
in Mendoza at the time, a man who boasted of cheat-
ing the scissors on seven or eight different occasions
in adventures of the utmost jeopardy in different parts
of the world, jested that he was immortal and on the
night of the earthquake imbibed his usual quantity of
Lethean. He slept in the open air on that sultry night
under his own vine and figtree, and arose another Rip
van Winkle; "not a sound was heard, not a funeral
note" by him during that fatal night. In the morning
he awoke bewildered amongst ruins, and sought his
house in vain : silence, death, destruction, ruin all
around ! relieved only by faint wails which struck his
guilty conscience : "c'est le purgatoire" said he, but
overpowered by thirst, he haply espied the wherewithal to gratify it in the shape of a bunch of grapes,
which had escaped the general fate. "Il y a donc des

raisins dans le purgatoire !" and knowing well the flavour of Mendoza grapes, was astonished to find them in the region of the shades. He soon became sensible however of the reality of his position, when a distracted mother seized hold of him to aid her in rescuing her only child from the fearful debris. To this frightful visitation succeeded a fire, which raged for eight days and to their eternal disgrace, a motley crowd crossed the Andes and aided robber gauchos in adding pillage to the other miseries of the survivors.

For two years afterwards the shocks continued and effectually prevented, by apprehended revisitation, any serious attempt to rebuild the city: even now, though diminished in force, they recur not less frequently than monthly and if the usual period elapses without the customary scourge, great is the terror of the inhabitants, lest they should again be made the unhappy victims of a cumulative force; an apprehension which is not unfrequently verified, and in the daily expectation of which they take great care to have the doors left open. During my residence of six months in the city, I had the gratification (for such it was to me) of experiencing seven or eight shocks, one of which was sufficient to set the billiard-balls in motion and the glasses jingling, whilst another aroused me from my bed in the middle of the night; and it is a curious fact that the more violent waves invariably occur during the hours of darkness.

Of the ruins little else remain, save mounds of earth, into which the adobe-built houses have col-

lapsed, and from which human bones still protrude,
interspersed with masses of solid masonry weighing
tons upon tons, revealing church-walls of the extraordinary thickness of fifteen feet, evidently erected in
these Cyclopic proportions to withstand the earth-
throes — vain hope ! — One remarkable pile of rugged
masonry there is which, towering to the height of
sixty feet, tapering to its base and surmounted by a
vast mass of brick arch-work, forms a terrific rocking
stone, wabbling with each successive shock, but
which for twenty years has remained in this state of
stable equilibrium, a fitting monument which for ever
sings

       " Requiem aeternam dona iis, Domine !"

I visited the weird-like scene on a moonlight
night ; it reminded me of Byron at the ruins of the
Coliseum and would be unique in its desolation, were
it not that the *Mataderos* or general killing grounds
for the modern city are located on these very ruins.

As many as seven plazas adorn Mendoza, of
which the Independencia is the principal, forming a
most charming square of sixteen acres, containing
on one side the Government House and Policia, on
another the Public Prison, the two remaining being
occupied by private residences. What with the pretty
walks amid the choicest flowering shrubs and creepers,
rustic arbours and bridges, kiosks, a cascade, artificial
mounds and labyrinthic paths, a central lake raised
eight feet on an embankment, reached by marble steps
and encircled by a fine broad promenade well-supplied

with seats, a splendid fountain spouting its cooling
showers to ripple the lacustrine bosom, and the magnificent *coup d'œil* closed by a background of dense
mountain scenery; I confess that, whilst lazily sipping a syllabub, not flavoured with an artificial watery
congelation, as on the littoral, but cooled by real
Wenham Lake ice cut in solid transparent blocks from
the neighbouring mountains, I was no less delighted
with the fairy-like, etherial, natural beauty of the
scene, than with the seductive but adventitious charms,
with which the Mendocinos have invested their principal plaza.

The native inhabitants of Mendoza are a peaceful,
orderly and industrious race, amongst whom few
robberies occur; whilst from the absence of the knife,
a constant companion in all other parts of the republic,
crimes of a deeper dye are still more infrequent : but
if a Mendocino, urged by anger or jealousy, does
happen to attack, a dark night is usually selected and
simplicity itself dictates the plan, which consists of
nothing more serious than throwing a stone from
behind a tree. The orderly conduct of the city at
night is further assured by the following police law
which obtains here : No servant or person of the
lower orders is permitted to range the streets late at
night without a papeleta or certificate issued monthly
by his master, containing a description of the bearer
and guaranteeing that he is bent on some lawful
business ; without this he is arrested and fined. Indeed
the absoluteness of police law in South America is

generally the subject of wonder to Englishmen, and
yet although these laws are stringent enough, and
executed in some respects with harshness and even
brutality, in others, the ministers of justice are very
lax in their administration.   Thus notwihstanding a
fine of five dollars is levied on all who use firearms in
the city or environs, it is a practice not unheard of
for persons in the side streets to shoot blackbirds from
their street doors; nay the landlord of the hotel where
I sojourned used at times to provide his Sunday dinner
thus, although his premises are in the very centre of
the town and only one square from the principal street
San Nicolás.   The Mendocinos, cut off as they are
from the sea-board by immense distances, have escaped
as yet many of the vices of Europe: their pleasures are
simple, save in the case of cockfighting, to which they
are passionately attached; a decorous people both in
public and private and never boisterous like the gaucho; and if the high standard of eastern civilization
has not yet been attained, they have most certainly
developed from within a pure and wonderfully progressive economy, which rests solely on their own
strength of character and untiring industry, backed
up by their internal and exhaustless resources.

CHAPTER XXI.

TRIP TO MENDOZA.—RESOURCES

If we then cursorily pass in review the resources and development of the province of Mendoza, the stranger will scarcely be prepared to expect so extensive a list as will certainly fill the programme of next year's local agricultural exhibition to be held in that city. Its pastures, in which drought and locusts are unknown, and irrigation works render independent of rain, fatten countless herds of cattle, principally for the Chilian market; thirty thousand tons of cereals are annually raised, much of which is exported; wool, hides, tallow, silk, hemp, flax, all kinds of fresh and dried fruits, especially raisins equal to the Malaga, and vegetables, luscious wines, oils, olives, honey, wax, aniseed, coal, petroleum, lime, marble, pumice-stone, flint, quartz, kaolin, iron, lead, copper, antimony, silver, gold, manganese, sulphur, plaster of Paris, and lithographic stone, either are or can be produced in abundance; whilst various kinds of constructive woods are easily obtained from the neighbourhood. No wonder then, that with these and other elements at command the inhabitants are industrious, or that the lesson of self-reliance which necessity first taught them, has been slowly but completely conned. However as regards the Wines and Petroleum of this favoured province, it behoves us to speak a little more at large. Whilst travelling towards the city my attention had been directed to the excellence both of its red and white wines, as supplied every where on the road after leaving Rio Cuarto; and on approaching Mendoza more closely, the visitor cannot fail to remark the number of cases, in which a fine of five shillings would be inflicted by a London magistrate; an excess not to be wondered at, considering the exuberance of the sinning element, which permits the lower orders to purchase a bottle of extremely good table wine for the paltry sum of 1½ d.; and yet the vice is all the more noticeable, as it is very rarely exhibited publicly in any other part of the country. At the present time the vineyards of Mendoza occupy an area of about 4280 acres, besides multitudes of private grounds. Each acre contains 625 plants, or a total of 2672500 vines, and yields on an average 38 *arrobas* (25 lbs. each) of fruit, giving a total of 162640 arrobas, equal to 25656 pipes annually, nearly the whole of which is consumed in the province; the number of pipes, the product of home industry, is likewise considerable, so that at least one hundred quarts per an. of the pure juice of the grape must be at the disposal of every man, woman and child of its population of eighty thousand. Here however, the grape is as yet cultivated only to supply home consumption, but when facility of transport raises a foreign demand, there need be no limit to the production.

Red wine is produced in greater quantity than white, as the white grapes are more delicate and more subject to *Oidium* (blight) than the red, a curse which, after a short respite, returned in renewed force in 1879, owing most probably to an excessive rainfall : the question of the presence of the Phylloxera has given rise to much discussion both here and in Buenos Aires and has not yet been satisfactorily determined. Spirits and liqueurs are manufactured in endless variety; one, Chicha, deserves notice as it not only forms a common drink of the people in Mendoza, but is the almost universal tipple of all classes in Chili. It is prepared by reducing fresh "must" by boiling in the proportion of 5 to 4, the liquor is then casked and drunk during fermentation, forming a sweet, slightly spirituous but very pleasant acid drink.

In Mendoza, the soil and meteorological conditions are abundantly favourable for the cultivation of the vine to an unlimited extent ; yet the industry is at present in its infancy and although claiming increased attention, awaits deliverance from its swaddling clothes by the wand of the locomotive, a boon which will be granted by the executive in less than two years from the present time. The difficulty, expense and risk of the present mode of transit imperatively limit its consumption to the province : a journey of 98 leagues on mule-back to Villa Mercedes, the nearest railway station, over very rough roads and principally in summer time, when the wine is exposed to fierce heat after quitting the cool cellars of its early days, is scarcely consistent with anything but utter deterioration in quality; and further deterioration both in quantity and quality results from the common practice of those jaunty Bacchantes, the peons, of boring holes in the casks *"in transitu"* and filling the place of the abstract with the concrete, water. It seems absurd that a great enterprise should be hampered by the scarcity of the meaner apparatus; yet so it is in this case, as bottles and barrels are almost worth their weight in gold, and the hotels put by all their earnings to invest in the former, whilst, as regards the latter, 15/. for a hoary Bordalesa (IIhd.) and 30/. for a veteran Pipe, are prices at which the demand is intensely eager. One would imagine that with sand up to the ears and soda-pants in rich profusion, the glass-factory would be coeval with the vineyard; one was, in fact, started in 1872, but mismanagement, the death of so many Argentine enterprises, cut short its career within twelve months. The difficulty with regard to barrels, arises from the absence of any wood suitable for coopers' work nearer than the neighbouring province of San Luis, where the Calden (a species of mimosa) is well adapted for the purpose, but the cost of transport at present precludes its use. This wood Calden, if cut in the winter months of June, July or August, when the sap is not in motion, becomes almost indestructible in the ground, and is much used for posts to wire-in estancias, as well as for barrels. Posts that have remained fixed in the earth for forty years have been found in a state of perfect preservation.

As regards the Petroleum, it is scarce credible

that a supply equal to the demands of the whole republic for many ages lies wasting its bituminous odour on the desert air and only awaiting a Mackay to transmute its fœtid ooze into bullion exceeding the Bank of England reserve: yet so it is, as the following facts will prove. The springs in the Argentine Republic stretch from Jujuy 25° S. L. to San Rafael 34°30' S. L. a distance of about 650 miles and are, besides being so extensive, extraordinarily rich in yield.

Curious to relate, although scarcely anything but kerosene is used for illumination throughout the length and breadth of this vast country, the supply is all imported from North America, only very feeble attempts having as yet been made to explore and utilize the exhaustless stores within easy reach. With respect to the springs in the neighbourhood of Mendoza, one exists eight leagues from the city, at the foot of the sierras of Cachuet, and hardly three from the Village of Lujan, vomiting forth is viscous meerschaum so as to form great lakes of the oily liquid, in which cattle are sometimes irremediably engulfed. A natural cart road leads to the very springs by a gentle ascent, with absolutely no difficulties in the transit. Here nature, displaying her treasures from an overflowing cup, has disrupted from the mountain side a rock, whose western face forms a perpendicular wall and from whose eastern flows a continuous stream of the unctuous liquor, out of a bed of shale. From this source, by simple digging alone, a ton per day of the crude mineral could easily be extracted; subsequently by means of increased

capital, and the sinking of an Artesian well, the result
would exceed expectation a thousandfold, judging from
the quantity of exuding waste that pours unaided from
this shaly deposit. Some enterprising native, seduced
by the prize of £ 10,000 offered to any one discovering coal within the limits of the Republic, wasted his
time and money by tunnelling horizontally into the
shale, but absolutely no attempt has as yet been made
to utilize the petroleum by depriving it of explosive
agents and refining it into kerosene, save one which,
with a small whiskey still, succeeded in producing
such oil as gave a light superior to that from North
America. A quarter of a mile to the north of this
spring lies another close to a house occupied by some
miners who, so intent upon the pursuit of the precious
metals, have overlooked a product whose value exceeds
that of either silver or gold: at San Rafael likewise,
30 leagues South of Mendoza, occurs another fine
spring, the natural overflow from which is so great as
to form a vast bituminous lake of such a pitchy consis-
tency, that animals up to the size of a lion have been
known to become imprisoned in the viscous fluid, beyond the power of extrication. In traversing these rich
districts, their resources actually make one's mouth
water, and we begin to wonder how it is that with
cheap labour, a prohibition tariff such as could be
easily procured from the National Government, a ceaseless demand for, and an inexhaustible and easily
worked mine of oil of superior quality, the benefits
are not seized by the present, but abandoned for future
generations.

Again, the progress of Mendoza is evidenced, not merely by material resources and its purely native manufactures which, without the aid of machinery, include as before mentioned all domestic articles, skilfully wrought woollen goods, such as ponchos, carpets, blankets &c., leather and woodwork, and silver ornamentation; but above all, by its aptitude for and appreciation of, education. Out of a provincial population of 80,000, upwards of 1,000 pupils attend the city schools, of which number about 200 are entered in the National College and 500 in the fine Sarmiento Preparatory academy, the latter of which, imports from the United States not only its teachers, but the apparatus down to the very lamps and hinges. A magnificent building has lately been erected for a Girls' Normal School, wherein to train mistresses; and much surprise was excited to find, so far from Cirencester, a Quinta agronomica (Agricultural school) in full working order, containing 20 students from various provinces, who undergo a thorough training in scientific and practical farming; a branch of industry which, although heavily handicapped in England, is here a sure source of profit: the model farm attached to the college lies about a mile and a half from the city, and is well worth a visit.

Shops are numerous and very similar to those of the country towns in England; of no external pretension, no bazaar-like appearance, indicating import but little productive industry, these disclose to view the worker inside at his trade, no Eastern-like lounger: and every almacen (store) hangs up on the outside a black board on which are chalked all the novelties for sale.

The Hotels are three in number, two Italian and one German, and throughout the Republic it is pretty much the same, almost all of them are kept by foreigners: in these the food, although abundant, good and cheap, is rendered not altogether agreeable to English palates by the excessive use of oil in the cooking.

Undoubtedly the food of a people indicates in general terms the degree of their civilization and so it is necessary to say a few words upon this subject. Sucking pig is a very favourite dish amongst all classes, in fact pork in all its multifarious forms drenches the population: the beef is really superior, and fattened up quite in the English style, mutton very scarce, pigs abundant, and game and fish are brought into town weekly by the Laguneros (Lake-men). Of vegetables the supply is very ample, including watercress, and such succulent asparagus as I have never tasted elsewhere; this asparagus grows wild in the viñas (vineyards), requiring no attention, coming in about September and lasting two or three months, and although small is exceedingly tender and full of flavour, and every particle of which may be eaten ; the excellence of this favourite vegetable is no doubt due to the nature of the soil, which is impregnated with salts: raised beds and earthing up, the "fortes" of English gardeners, are unknown here. Of making of sweets, as of making of books there is no end, as says quaint Fuller; the land o' cakes is no longer Caledonia, Turkey no more the

paradise of sweets, Mendoza surpasses both in its exquisite fruity, sugary compounds. As the diligence
stopped at the Hotel Europa, I was in some manner
forced to make that my headquarters during my six
months' residence in Mendoza, and for 45 Bolivian dollars (£ 6,10) per month, was provided with board
and lodging; but I afterwards discovered that the Hotel Nacional, in front of the Post Office, is superior
both in locale and internal economy; although in all
three there is great room for improvement.

In order to develope commerce and instigate
exploration, there is but little monetary facility in
Mendoza, and capital is very scarce. The Bank, that
was established by the Provincial government, with
an unlimited paper issue, after inundating the city and
province with its worthless shinplasters, to such a de
gree that they fell in value almost to zero, and people
at last refused to receive them, suddenly closed its
doors: a branch of the National Bank however has
been opened there and was in treaty to purchase the
business of the defunct institution, but its operations
generally are too stringent and its charges too high
to be of much service to the community : the inhabitants of Mendoza as well as of other capitals in the
republic sigh for the introduction of English banks,
and in my opinion they would do a very lucrative and
safe business.

In spite of Goître, which affects three per cent. of
the population, and that peculiar form of idiotcy, the
result of the continued intermarriage of close relations,

the people here live to a green old age : during my
residence amongst them, there were six macrobiots
who had reached 100 years, and one 120, and it is a
common custom of the lower orders, in their ignorance
of chronology, to reply to the question "How old are
you ?", " I was born after such or such a battle " or
" when General so and so passed through the city" : and
the same custom is universal in San Juan.

Foreigners abound in Mendoza, but chiefly Chi-
lenos, who do not command much sympathy from the
natives for personal and political reasons : the Catalans
however are quite at home and render themselves both
agreeable and useful, they say the general appearance
of the country reminds them so forcibly of their own
native land : the remaining exotic quota comprises
about a dozen Germans, many French with their
consul and two or three English, including Dr. Day
the skilful physician and Mr. Gibbs one of the largest
estancieros in those parts.

Within the city precincts, locomotion is both agreeable and cheap; a drive to any part costs no more than
two reales (6 d.) and then there is some satisfaction in
engaging a clean and respectable coach, eighty of
which ply for hire within the city : moving mountains
of alfalfa too, traverse the streets, and without a close
inspection, the motive power is not easily discernible ;
a poor horse or mule is so laden with the towering fodder that scarce a glimpse of nose, tail or hoof is to be
had, and aloft in his "houdah" sits a small urchin
retailing the vivid green for 6d, a load.

In the environs of Mendoza are no forests but a virgin growth of scrubby prickly shrubs, chiefly Mimoseæ; whilst, travelling upwards towards the mountains, a wonderful cactus region is entered, whose grotesque and varied forms, giants these, pigmies those, clothed with gorgeous rainbow-coloured flowers give a characteristic physiognomy to this strange landscape: the plains likewise are furnished with Opuntiæ but not in such profusion, growth nor variety. These cacti are nature's provision, in a droughty climate, for thirsty animals: the cattle in order to save themselves a long journey for water, tread under foot these zig-zag stems and slake their thirst with the exuding juice: nor is man himself too proud to resort to the same artifice. The Patay cakes prepared by the Laguneros from the seedpods of the *Algarroba negra* (Prosopis nigra) are much esteemed as a remedy for indigestion; as well as the leaves of the Coca (Erythroxylon coca), a Bolivian plant, which, mixed with cenizas (wood ashes) or any alkali, and slowly masticated but not swallowed, give immunity from fatigue equally with relief from dyspepsia; in the Upper Provinces, in fact, it forms the universal *"quid"* amongst those who have labour to perform or distances to traverse. In the absence of other materials, on a long and hot journey, I have even partaken of a salad compounded of young Acacia flowers, but our Æsculapius, who was the suggester and concocter of it, paid the penalty in a deep slumber from which we could not rouse him for many hours; the flavour resembled that of green peas and produced a slight nausea, quickly followed by brain disturbance.

CHAPTER XXII.

TRIP TO MENDOZA — PUBLIC REJOICINGS

May the 25th., a day ever memorable in the annals of the Argentine Republic, as the one on which burst forth the revolution destined to free it for ever from the yoke of Spain, is honoured here as elsewhere throughout the country with noisy demonstrations of joy, to celebrate the anniversary of its political redemption: but on the principle of " gathering your rosebuds while you may " the festive season always commences on the morning of the 23rd. and terminates on the evening of the 25th.

In Mendoza every householder was obliged to whitewash his premises, and a general preparatory cleansing took place, so that the town presented a bran-new appearance on its natal day. At daylight of the 25th., the booming salute of artillery drove me from my couch to enjoy during the remainder of the day, the rattle of musketry, the crash of trumpets, the clangour of church-bells, the salvos of rockets and maroons, and all the other noisy demonstrations that ingenious powder and brass could devise. Sallying out after breakfast, there, in one of the exterior Plazas, is a veritable Old World Fair (ramada) for the lower orders, consisting of a number of booths constructed of planks and matting, and roofed with branches of trees, leaving streets between with a footpath on each side protected by very strong wooden barriers on the outside, the purpose of which will be evident from the sequel. In the roadways assemble the *ginetes* (horsemen) to the number of several hundreds to carry on the rough game of *"pechando"*, which consists of an equine tussle, forcing, by whip and spur, one horse against another, to see which can stand the firmest on its legs without giving way: I noticed as many as twenty-five couples at one time thus lashing their steeds against each other in the midst of deafening shouts, many riders holding a bottle of wine in the bridle hand, from which they partook freely during the contest: at times the struggle merged into wrestling and a considerable number of saddles were emptied. Satiated with this rough tournament, I take a peep within the booths and behold a counter for the sale of wines and spirits, benches arranged around the sides for the women, and at one end a raised platform, on which the musicians, with two or three guitars and sometimes a stray harp, discourse their monotonous and melancholy music: in every tent the same famous Chilian, very sedate and decorous dance of the "Cueca" is proceeding. This consists of very slow but elegant movements of three or four independent couples, alternately advancing and retiring, making all the while graceful passes with the pocket-handkerchief: the "Samba", a variety of the Cueca, is another dance much in favour, in which the castañettas are employed instead of the pocket-handkerchief: the musicians meanwhile both playing and singing low plaintive airs.

In the centre of the Plaza, rows of shanties are erected, with fires perpetually burning, where hot maté, *asado* (roast meat) *tortas* (unleavened cakes) &c. are vended, and close adjoining, twenty or thirty roulette tables, at which the pockets of the yokels are soon emptied of spare *medios* (sixteenths of a dollar) and *reales* (eighths of a dollar). Dancing, singing, gambling and drinking are kept up day and night, but although instances of inebriety are not rare, they are unaccompanied by fights or rows such as disgrace like scenes in Europe; even in his cups the Mendocino is decorous. The tertulias or dancing parties in Mendoza last sometimes two or three days; the guests, fluttering like *heterocera* to the lamp light, but overpowered by couch gravitation as long as the sun is above the horizon, are alternately the victims of kinematic energy or static inertia: never was there a people so addicted to Terpsichore as the Argentines; and if there be not, as Lawrence Sterne says, Religion mixed with the dance, there is at any rate grace.

The city boasts of a pretty little theatre capable of holding five hundred persons, but the Mendocinos have but little opportunity of witnessing or listening to the Drama or Operatic music; as it is only on occasions when companies on their route to or from Chili open the doors for a solitary night, that they have the advantage and pleasure of supporting either.

In company with other passengers by diligence,

I was once passing en route through La Paz, a distance of 40 leagues from Mendoza, when tired, hot and thirsty, an unexpected invitation to a festive scene was extended to the whole party by the buxom widow who keeps the *"posta"* there: no introduction was necessary, a delightful freedom from etiquette reigned : so after a hasty toilet, we were at once ushered to the banquet, where we saw a welcome in every eye. The lady of the house stood at the head of a long table carving and serving each person and when all were helped sat down to discuss her own plate. The first course consisted of thickened soup, and that finished, the toasts began, the young ladies pledging the gentlemen in bumpers. *"Te obligo"* from bewitching lips and sparkling eyes behind the amber nectar, is enough to drive the sheepishness out of any man in a moment, and although there was no shyness, which is unknown on Argentine soil, the principal duty of the hostess, after provisioning her guests, seemed to be to urge the girls to " bring out " the gentlemen and certainly they succeeded ; beyond measure was I astonished at the freedom, boldness, playfulness and sprightly repartée of the " *señoritas* ", who made the very glasses jingle in admiration of their sallies, and yet withal perfect decorum reigned. *Puchero* (meat boiled in the soup) followed ; then five or six other courses, succeeded by *asado* (roast) and finally *cal lo* (broth), an odd dish wherewith to close a feast and one peculiar to native society in Mendoza : then *postres* (dessert) with its various fruits and sweets wound up the entertainment.

The tables were now removed, chairs arranged round the walls, guitars introduced, and the main event of the evening commenced. Most of the dances, the Cielito, the Media-caña, the Gato and the Zamba-Cueca, were accompanied by songs, some of which were impromptu, describing or paying compliments to each person present, an accomplishment in which the campesinos throughout the Republic are exceedingly proficient. The tertulia terminated at midnight, many of the guests having to travel on horseback or in tilburies seven or eight leagues to their homes; and at four o'clock the following morning we, the diligence passengers, were peremptorily summoned to renew our journey.

CHAPTER XXIII.

Having heard much of Borbollon, one fine afternoon two friends and myself hired a carriage drawn
by three horses and set out to visit the thermal springs
in that neighbourhood, distant only three leagues from
Mendoza. Emerging from the northern extremity of
the town and skirting the fine Alameda before mentioned, we course along the fine broad road leading to
San Juan, passing a monastery which excites surprise
by its vast size, and thence through two miles of real
Devonshire lanes, lined with poplars and willows,
which form delightful avenues, interspersed with
dwellings, alfalfares, vineyards and gardens. As we
roll along the hard roads, our attention is frequently
attracted to the glorious *vista* (scene) at our back,
terminated by blue mountain chains, differing in tint
and revealing tier upon tier, culminated by the hoary
peaks of the distant Cordilleras, amongst which, far
away to the south, stands forth prominently the lofty
bold dome of Tupungato, robed like the rest in its
wintry mantle : further on summit succeeds summit in
never ending succession, dwindling at last into a grey
hazy mass. Debouching upon the open country, which is

here dotted with low shrubs, we cross several extensive patches of ground covered with salitre, presenting the appearance of snow; the lease moisture
converts these deliquescenet salts into almost impassable,
sticky, oozy morasses. About half a league from our
destination, the *medanos* (sand-hillocks) are met with,
which, extending northward, form further on very
rough and broken ground. Up to this point, the plain
has been rising, but I suspect more in appearance than
reality owing to the deceptiveness of the mountain-
ranges in the rear, and hence the road commands
a clear and uninterrupted view of such bold, rugged,
serrated yet picturesque masses, as are not to be surpassed in the world : and now we descend into the
valley of Borbollon, a mere village containing an hotel
and about half a dozen scattered dwellings, let out in
the season to persons frequenting the baths. Having
brought my gun, I took a stroll amongst the dunes,
but saw nothing save a Jote (*Cathartes fœtens*), a
species of vulture, sailing high, and a few Chimangos
(*Milvago Chimango*) : and upon my return was surprised to find my companions had already bathed and
were preparing for the homeward journey ; so I determined to remain the night and go back next day
on foot. All the houses were empty, as the cold season
(June) for taking the baths, had only just commenced ;
but at the inn, a steward and two female servants left in
charge, were ready to provide me with accommodation.
In this lonely spot then I was driven to the billiard-
table for amusement and was not sorry to be summoned in an hour or two to my solitary dinner. In a

lengthy post-prandial chat with the capataz, I discovered to my delight, that he was wonderfully intelligent on the subject of Natural History; indeed, in
all my experience, I have ever found the uneducated
dweller in country-districts, a more intelligent ob-
server than the most scientific of savans.

The intensely cold evening made me turn in
sooner than customary: but it was useless, as the
hardness of the bed, the freshness of the air and the
ceaseless strange cries around, made me attentive
and sleepless. About a square (150 yards) away,
commences an extensive *ciénaga* (swamp), whence
issued through the dismal hours the most unearthly
sounds, as from a pandemonium; the "*brekkokax korax
korax*" or frog chorus I could have stood, but the
moanings, screechings and howlings of the various
species of waterhens, in all varieties of the animal
gamut, effectually banished rest. On emerging at
daybreak from my room, what was my surprise to find
my well-informed companion of the previous night
deep in the most enviable of sleeps, beneath the corridor, on an open *catre*, with the temperature below
freezing point. I awoke him and he remarked that it
was his custom, winter and summer, wet or fine, thus
to sleep out in all seasons, and I believe, in spite of
physicians and their babble about noxious night air,
such a habit to be highly salutary even for invalids;
at any rate the practice is universal in the country-
districts throughout the Republic. I now proceeded
to take my bath before sunrise. The water, clear but

slightly greenish, flows from a basin which in the
centre is unfathomable and about thirty yards wide.
Sulphur, potassa and lime form the chief ingredients,
acting mainly as a Rheumatismafuge, but being besides a certain remedy for all sorts of sores and ulcers,
a veritable pool of Bethesda, whose cures are almost
miraculous. From the surface is given off much va-
porous exhalation, accompanied by a slight sulphurous
odour, but this is the result of the low morning temperature; when the sun gains power, no steam is observable, neither is the high temperature (77° Fahr.)
of the water then noticed, but in my matutinal tub, the
warmth was very pleasant. The liquid comes away in
a stream about a yard broad, and convenient bathing
sheds are erected at intervals along its course. On
emerging from my bath into the cold air, a run was
necessary to sustain the circulation and then a couple
of glasses of goats' milk soon restored my equanimity.

In the course of conversation with mine host, he
was telling me of some curious rodents called "*Tun-
duquis*" found in this neighbourhood, and as from his
description I was in doubt in the matter, we determined
to trot off a few squares to their burrows and unravel
the mystery. Spade in hand we reached their habitat
and began digging up a burrow where fresh footprints
evidently of the " *Ctenomys magellanicus*" were discovered; but after exposing the horizontal and superficial tunnel for sixteen yards, to our chagrin, the animal was not at home. Subsequently I remarked these
burrows undermining the whole surface in some dis-

tricts of the province of Mendoza, so that to walk
without sinking in, but not to any great depth, was
absolutely impossible. This *Clenomys magellanicus*
is a gregarious rodent, found from the neighbourhood
of Mendoza completely down to the Straits of Magellan, always inhabiting the high ground skirting
the Cordilleras, but never the plains; it is exceedingly
difficult to capture, but is often heard emitting peculiar
cries from the burrow, although very seldom seen.
There seems to be an allied species, *C. brasiliensis*,
whose habitat is the Atlantic coast.

Judge of my surprise, when in this secluded spot
I chanced, in one of my rambles, to stumble upon the
disreputable spectacle of the socketless eyes of real
STOCKS! which, in my innocence, I took to be one of
the supports of the British crown alone. Yes! there
stood in all their nakedness and severity those silent
bracelets which adorn the persons of evildoers in this
remote nook of South America. What travelled ge-
nius introduced them? Two tough wooden beams,
with a dozen holes for the wrists and ankles, and
necklaces corresponding but of superior dimensions,
the whole fastened with iron bolts and padlocks, testify
to such a severe local treatment of crime, that the
desperados of the neighbourhood must abandon all
hope of immunity and patiently await their transfer to
Mendoza to receive the due reward of their misdeeds:
and yet I was assured on good authority that prisoners
have been known to escape this degrading punishment
by actually *cutting off their heels*. This reminds me

of a harrowing tale I heard in Yorkshire of a forester who, as his custom was, sallied forth one morning from Sheffield into Wharncliffe wood to cut broom, wherewith to manufacture besoms. After securing a load, on his way home, as he was passing through a desolate part, one of his legs unfortunately slipped into a deep hole at the foot of a tree and although he succeeded in disentangling himself quickly of his burden, and then endeavoured with all his might to extricate the limb which was jammed amongst the thick roots, his efforts were fruitless, it was a case of Aunt Jemima's plaster; at length, on the approach of darkness, exhausted with his ceaseless efforts and despairing of aid, as a brave man he came to the fearless determination to cut off his leg rather than die of starvation. Out flashed his sharp blade and by dint of hacking, slashing and sawing he severed the imprisoned member, and then like the hero in Chevy-chase crept home upon his stumps — *one of which was wooden.*

In the vicinity of Borbollon, I noticed a beautiful red, ferruginous clay, which is much used for coarse pottery ware and can be had in any quantity for a shilling a cartload. I now prepared, gun in hand, for the return journey of three leagues on foot, and after considerable wandering through flooded and muddy roads, the result of broken acequias, managed to reach my comfortable hostelry just about dusk and in time for a hearty dinner, although with an empty bag.

CHAPTER XXIV

TRIP TO MENDOZA — VISIT TO PALMIRA

Although introductory letters are of little service in this country, on account of the universal freedom of intercourse and manners, nevertheless amongst others taken from the capital, Dr. Burmeister had kindly provided me with one to a Mr. Brachmann living in the neighbourhood of Mendoza, and I soon had an opportunity of presenting it to that gentleman on an accidental visit of his to the hotel wherein I had taken up my quarters. A very short time was suf-ficient to establish a good understanding between us and the consequence was that on the morning of the 27ᵗʰ of April, I mounted a fine horse sent round to the hotel by that gentleman and being soon after joined by him, off we started together on a visit to his mill at Palmira.

It was a cloudy day, just sufficiently so to ward off the scorching rays of the sun, whose beams even in winter are fiery, and make it anything but pleasant to ride far when exposed to them ; at that period of the year however the nights and mornings are bitterly cold. The steeds were all that could be desired ; strongly built, with a dash of Barclay and Perkins,

sprightly, sure-footed and gifted with a very easy
pace: the difference between a roadster here and one
in Buenos Aires astonished me accustomed to the
uneasy step of the slight and small Pampa mustang
of the littoral. As we emerge from the city and reach
an eminence in its environs, it is scarce credible that
a town of 14000 inhabitants lies enveloped amongst
that dense mass of vivid foliage; for on looking back
nothing else but one vast arboretum is visible. The
whole of our way, with the exception of one or two
open tracts of scrubby, bushy and stony ground, lay
between cultivated farms, enclosed with thick *tapias*
(earth-walls pressed in frames) and lofty trees, or
across occasional small mountain streams. Every now
and again a house is passed and many little modest
shops present their sign-boards in the shape of a long
cane carrying a white flag, on peeping within one of
which, nothing is discerned save a small counter, a
back-shelf or two with perhaps a dozen bottles, a
demijohn surrounded by a few tumblers and may be a
basket of fresh *tortas*; the wants of the neighbourhood
must indeed be few and simple: and yet these insignificant stores thrive by making no show on principle. They rely chiefly upon the custom of the ready-
money purchasers of the lower order, who, they say,
would be ashamed to enter premises more pretentious;
as to the upper classes, they demand, here as elsewhere, too long credit to induce the shopkeepers
to seek their patronage. When we had accomplished
half of our journey of 7½ leagues(*) a halt is called

(*) By leagues, when travelling on the main postal roads, such as

for rest and refreshment. The amount of business and pleasure movement on this high road is surprising; carts, carriages, horsemen and mules pass in quick succession, followed every now and then by whole convoys of heavily-laden beasts diligently tracking the steps of their *madrina*, who leads the way with jingling bell: then approaches the tall, finely-formed, sedate *paisano* on tiny mule in silver trappings, but in vain we look for the *facon*, without which no Gaucho on the plains of Buenos Aires is dressed; it appears not; and if a native be questioned as to the reason, "Sir", says he, "I am no *bravo* or cutthroat; no honest man who has employment needs such, which is the mark of roving vagabonds alone". Travellers however, who are passing from one province to another, invariably go armed in this and other respects. Indeed I found the whole province of Mendoza quiet in the extreme, so much that no one dreams of going to sleep with closed doors; and so different is the whole scene from its coordinate in Buenos Aires, so picturesque and interesting the landscape, so simple and Arcadian the manners, that it is difficult to realize the fact they are both members of the same Republic.

We now remount to continue the journey and soon have to cross *salinas* and then the road leads through extensive swamps, presenting a nasty black, boggy appearance which, when wet and stirred by traffic, emit a most offensively fœtid smell. These

---

this, is universally meant postal leagues, which are somewhat shorter than geographical.

swamps are traversed by very narrow tolerably firm
bridle-paths, the slightest deviation from which, an
event likely to occur in the excitement of hunting or
shooting, would ensure, as it has not unfrequently,
instant engulfment of horse and rider in the deep filthy
slush. The river Mendoza, which here consists only
of two or three shallow channels, is soon reached and
we cross it by a ford, prefering that method to the
path over the fine wooden bridge, that lies somewhat
out of our way to the left. In front on the opposite
bank is espied our destination, the *Molino de Palmira*
(Palmyra Mill); and lest my readers should picture a
solitary mill, devoted to nothing but grinding corn, as
the water-mills in England, I may as well at once say,
that this is an establishment, a miniature Saltaire,
with its village and store, farm and outbuildings,
artisans and labourers, comprehending more than one
hundred souls, and of which the mill is only an adjunct.
After breakfast I set to work to become familiar with
the topography of the place, its inhabitants and their
various industries.

Directly in front lies the peak of La Plata, and
on the left the lofty Tupungato, which although at the
distance of 180 miles, appears not 50; in fact there is
no method of realizing the remoteness of such lofty
masses, as peak succeeds peak in interminable array.
From the summits of the other mountains indeed, on
a clear day, may be discerned serrate points lying far
away to the South at the astonishing interval of 300
miles, and if any mathematical student be inclined to

dispute this, he must remember that in such a case
the altitude would be increased 25 per cent by re-
fraction. The dwelling-house is built on a slight eminence commanding a fine view of the Andine chain,
and is one of those large rambling buildings, with
broad corridors, so common in Mendoza, where the
materials are so cheap and I may say so suitable for
a region subject to earthquake. The adobe-built walls
form an extremely tough and tenacious structure, not
brittle yet hard; the roof, made by placing canes very
close together, supported by rafters, and over this a
layer of mud mixed with straw, produces a light cheap
and elastic covering which, on account of the very slight
rainfall, is not liable to be washed away nor even indented by such showers as do occasionally occur. The
woodwork throughout, including the furniture, is constructed of poplar which is so abundant and easily worked; indeed in every part of the province, poplar takes
the place of pine. As with the wood, so with everything
else, the Mendocinos, shut out from European markets,
are obliged to rely upon themselves alone, and it is
really astonishing to notice the degree of civilization
they have attained, and the amount of ingenuity displayed in adapting materials to their exigencies: so
different this to the artificial and extraneous glitter of
the metropolis, where every article is imported from
Europe and native intelligence and ingenuity but little
exercised. On one side about fifty yards from the house
stands the mill, supplied with excellent machinery, the
wheel measuring 24 feet in diameter and which plying
its ceaseless revolutions day and night is able to grind

150 *fanegas* (eleven tons) of corn within the twenty four hours. The water that feeds the mill is brought from the river Tunuyan, by means of an artificial dyke twenty-one miles long, and is used all along the route for the purpose of irrigation. Adjoining the mill rises a large granary 115 yards by 20, and capable of holding 40000 fanegas (37746 quarters) of wheat, al-though at present there are only about 10000 in deposit. Upwards of a hundred hands here find employment, for besides the mill-business, cattle farming is carried on; the estate consisting of 700 squares (3000 *acres*), most of which is under cultivation, including the "*sine quá non*," of a small vineyard which yields four to five pipes annually, sufficient to serve the family.

Four hundred cattle and about three hundred pigs of good breed are here fattened for the markets, and in addition poultry innumerable of all classes strut the large English-looking farmyard, in which under sheds repose thirteen carts that, with their complement of one hundred mules, feeding in the alfalfares outside, suffice for the traffic of the establishment, which necessitates constant journeys, to and fro, to San Luis and Villa Mercedes; and the whole property is guarded by a pack of fifteen wary watchdogs, not the usual class of curs kept on the estancias of Buenos Aires, but animals of nobler and fiercer lineage. The great abundance of running water in this province offers great inducements for the erection of mills, and in consequence no less than forty-seven such may be counted.

On the evening of my arrival, whilst closing the

bedroom window for the night and having no light,
some insect stung me inflicting intolerable pain, accompanied with great swelling of the finger and although
I cauterised the wound almost immediately, obtained
no relief until ammonia was applied, but the next day
both pain and swelling subsided ; this is a very rare
circumstance indeed, as Mendoza is singularly free from
pests verminic or bestial, except the black ant which,
here as throughout the republic is a veritable curse especially to vegetation.

The water used for drinking purposes is brought
from the same river Tunuyan and is considered medicinal and very serviceable in cases of indigestion. I am
not inclined to dispute the general verdict of its thera-
peutic properties, but not being a subject for dyspepsia,
my first day's draught of this medicative produced
violent diarrhœa, which I ascribed to the stream passing
over, in some places, a muddy, although generally a
sandy, bottom, whereby the natural properties of the
water become contaminated in some degree.   My host
however was equal to the occasion and administered a
warm decoction of pomegranate rind in milk which was
found a very effectual as well as agreeable remedy,
which cannot be said of all medicines; and many are
the Widow Trubys amongst this simple folk, whose
normal herbal prescriptions, although unknown to Phar-
macopœias, vie in efficaciousness and exceed in palata-
bility the resources of the faculty.   Every house here
possesses, although it does not always use, a very serviceable method of rendering water potable.   In the

neighbouring valley of Tunuyan, is to be obtained an
unlimited supply of exceedingly porous pumicestone
which, cut into the shape of a truncated cone of about
eighteen inches in depth and upper greater basal diameter six inches, is let into a framework standing
sufficiently high to allow an earthenware pitcher to be
placed beneath, and thus forms a very simple and
perfect filter, yielding a continuous stream of sparkling,
limpid and cool water.

Two spe·ies of Coleopterous plagues (*Calandra*)
infest the mill and commit dreadful havoc amongst the
wheat: and no method I could devise was of any avail
to get rid of them. The plan pursued in Europe with
these weevils is, I believe, to throw the grain into water,
when the sound sinks and the unsound floats: but such
a procedure is impossible with a large quantity and
would be attended moreover with deterioration to the
sound corn.

The perishable fruits are kept for a long period,
on account of the extreme dryness of the climate and
the comparative mildness of the modern winters; even
in midwinter it is customary to find on the dinner table,
ripe melons and grapes with all the freshness and luscious juiciness of those just plucked; these are hung
up under shelter but exposed to the atmosphere and
remain good for months: the air however that blows
over the Salinas bodes no good to man or beast and
like the east wind in England, chaps the hands and
lips to a painful degree.

The necessaries and many of the luxuries of life

are very cheap and abundant: the bread is certainly the best I ever tasted; beef about a penny a pound and very much resembling the English in flavour, which cannot be said of that on the littoral: but mutton is scarcely procurable, as sheep are difficult and expensive to rear throughout the whole province, on account of the absence of suitable indigenous grasses. Sometimes however the residents at the mill indulge in certain dishes which might cause nausea in a European; for instance the Armadillo *(Dasypus villosus)* which has been mentioned before as a supremely nice dish, and the wild Guinea-pig *(Cavia leucopyga)* which is common throughout the country and styled "*Quiso*" by the Bonaerenses, but *Conejo* (Rabbit) by the Mendocinos: one morning I went out and shot a few of the latter and they appeared at the table as a *guiso* (stew), to my taste resembling rabbit in the delicacy and insipidity of the flesh, but much tougher and very bony: a peculiarity about these Cavias is that on being handled their hair comes off.

The lowest orders here as in all the Upper Provinces being of Indian descent, it is necessary to treat them with a stern air of command, to which they have always been accustomed, otherwise it is impossible to get them to work properly; let anything approaching familiarity be displayed, there is no end to their encroachments and the floodgates are let loose to an irrigation of deceit and fraud: in fact, I found the whole population sharp and fully alive to their own interests, and that great caution was necessary in busi-

ness dealings with them. The soil both in the neighbourhood of Mendoza and in all parts of the province
is completely arenaceous, but prodigiously fertile when
irrigated, so as to excel all other territories as yet in
agriculture and the magnificence of its fruits, especially
the grape, which here arrives at perfect maturity; in
some districts, above all on approaching the Cordilleras,
it becomes stony, owing to uncomminuted mountain
debris, so that the province with its sand is the direct
antithesis of Buenos Aires with its rich humus and
tosca; and as its minerals are as yet unexplored, it is
properly styled an agricultural region. Rural operations indeed might almost be performed with the hand
alone, and although machines have been imported, the
sale is extremely limited, inasmuch as they are neither
needed nor do the inhabitants possess the requisite experience to use them.

As the vicinity of the Palmira mill lies outside the
earthquake focus and possesses many advantages in the
fertility of the soil, cheapness of land and labour, abundance of water for irrigation, a superb climate, a delicious landscape, profusion of the means of living and
easy and cheap communication with Mendoza, it presents itself to my mind, as a locality every way suitable
for the man of limited resources, where by means of
the culture of the vine, silk, flax, cochineal, castor oil,
or any of the grosser forms of agricultural pursuit, he
might pass an enviable and peaceful life, with the certainty of enriching himself into the bargain. As to the
price of land, it varies very much according to level

and facility for irrigation; but depends not so much
upon distance from the high road; compared with the
cost in Buenos Aires, it is of course cheap; unenclosed
plots ranging from 2*l.* to 8*l.* the acre, but those already
sown with alfalfa and enclosed fetch as much as £ 14
for a like area. With respect to communication with
the capital, it is frequent and reasonable in charge;
besides the two local diligences plying each way daily,
two others pass the mill weekly on their journies to or
from Mendoza and Villa Mercedes, and the fare is
about 2*l.* for the 23 miles intervening between the mill
and the chief city of the province.

Happening to be on the spot when a purchase was
made of fresh mules, I was invited to the corral (*cattle
pen*) to witness the operation of marking. The enclosure
consists of about 1500 square yards, or 50 by 30: the
whole is surrounded by a thick *tapia* about five feet
high; in the centre is a small pond of water, and at
each end an entrance guarded by a strong well-made
wooden gate. When I arrived, the capataz, mounted
on a beautiful black spirited mare, was awaiting within,
the commencement of operations. In one corner was
observed a fire in which lay the heavy marking irons.
and close by two peons on foot who were on the alert
poising their lassos. About twenty mules, with the
madrina, had been driven into the cruel den and their
egress securely barred, and nine of these had to undergo the ordeal by fire. The capataz now disengaged
his lasso from the saddle, and holding it ready coiled
in his left hand, made the loop of the slip knot about

eight to ten feet long which, by means of his right, he
kept in continued circular movement above his head,
when suddenly digging his spurs into the mare, he
made a dash at the cowed and huddled drove of victims, driving them before him at full speed round
the corral. In a moment, one of the scared herd is
selected, and the lasso descends with a graceful curve
and unerring aim around his neck. The touch of that
dreaded instrument of torture serves only to increase
the speed and fright of the mule and amid a cloud of
dust, letting the coils slip out of his hand, with a light
touch of the bridle, the mare springs into position,
with fore-feet extended, her body inclined sideways
and rigid and with muscles quivering, to receive the
shock; it came and firm as a rock stood the obedient
and well trained animal, whilst the mule went spin-
ning round and round, its fastened fore-feet acting as
a pivot. For a second the victim seemed stunned and
then attempted to dash off as before ; but quick as
lightning one of the peons despatched his thonged
messenger encircling the hind feet, when, with a
spring, giving his lasso two or three quick turns
round a stump that stood handy, at the same time that
the capataz drew his taut, the unfortunate animal
came sprawling to the ground with heavy thud but
hidden from sight in a dense whirlpool of ascending
dust. Up hastened the third man drawing a poncho
over the mule's eyes and tying it under his neck.
Without loss of time, the capataz dismounted, leaving
the mare standing with the strain still on, and immediately looped three of the animal's legs together,

which now lay perfectly quiet. Running up to the fire
and bearing away one of the heated irons, he first
scraped clean with a knife that part of the buttock
destined to receive the mark and then quickly pressed
the red-hot instrument on the bare skin, whereupon
arose a cloud of smoke filling the air with a villau-
ous nitrogenous smell of burning hair and flesh. After
a second or two the dormant mule awoke to the fact
and made vigorous efforts to plunge and kick out, but
was too securely lashed: once again was the cruel marking iron applied and with the same results, when as
one of the attendants carefully unloosed the fetters, the
other stood ready to remove the poncho. As soon as its
legs were free and the covering removed from its eyes,
the mule started to its feet and dashed away seemingly
free, but henceforth bearing the indelible badge of
slavery. The whole nine were treated in a similar manner, with a celerity and dexterity both of man and horse
very surprising. Some were unusually restive and
unmanageable and it was as much as the three men
and mare could do to take their feet from under them:
once the lasso, while at full tension, slipped off one of
the animals and recoiled directly upon the capataz with
tremendous force: the blow struck him full on the head
but luckily his felt hat, which was pressed tight, in
some measure broke its severity; as it was however
the hat went flying and he himself remained for a few
seconds completely stunned.

In the same way are marked all cattle and horses
throughout the republic; but it seems to me that some

method less cruel, less savouring of rough babarism, less injurious to the hides and at the same time less hazardous and laborious to the peones, whilst equally efficacious, might, in these days of inventive skill, be discovered.

It was now time to think of returning to Mendoza: for a whole month had I enjoyed hospitality such as smacked of the olden time; so with a reluctant farewell I bade good-bye to the Mill at Palmira and its worthy master Señor Don Federico Brachmann.

CHAPTER XXV.

I had heard many stories of guanaco (Llama huana-co) hunting which had inflamed my desire to engage in this perilous and toilsome sport, and so on receiving an invitation from Dr. Anzorena to join him in a three days' expedition into the Cordilleras for this purpose, nimbly packed up my traps and in the very depth of winter started with him in a carriage from Mendoza, taking with us plenty of wrapping, food, guns and ammunition. Our destination was the baths of Papa-gallos, a quinta or summer residence belonging to that gentleman, situated on the high lands abutting on the sierras, which we reached about dark after a laborious climb.

This quinta lies in a romantic spot, about 1300 feet above and two leagues from Mendoza, snugly ensconced in a ravine, a hundred yards below the sloping plateau which ascends towards the mountains, a fit habitat for that exquisitely formed and coloured fire-tailed Hum-ming-bird (*Sparganura sappho*), of which, to my delight, I saw two specimens on a subsequent summer visit. Down this gully, as usual, flows a mountain stream and by the house side is a fine spring whose waters are diverted into an expensively constructed stone bathhouse measuring fifteen feet by eight and over six feet deep. We found here a delightful little oasis, cultivated at great expense, and used as a summer bathing station. The coach could not reach the house but was obliged to remain on the high land above and on dismounting at dusk, the cold was so terribly severe that we were extravagantly delighted to gain the shelter of this warm, elegant and hospitable habitation. The vaqueano (guide) was at hand to counsel us for the morrow and so after settling all arrangements and dismissing black care, we proceeded to discuss a good hot dinner and very soon afterwards retired to bed. At 5 a. m. on the following morning, the moon the while shining gloriously, the old and faithful attendant summoned us to a warm fire, maté and then to the saddle. Our troop consisted of three horses and two mules; one of the latter carried Dr. Anzorena, the other bore the weight of provisions for two days and was also destined to bring back our game; the guide took one horse, I another, and the third formed our reserve in case of accident. Our principal arms consisted of a sporting needle-rifle and a Remington, but the former I soon found of comparatively little use for the long and deceptive ranges of those precipitous heights.

Our plan was to remain two whole days on the mountains shooting and sleep the intermediate night at a hut which the guide assured us existed, but which, alas! turned out the baseless fabric of a vision. Day broke at six and then we started, but on reaching the plateau above the house, so intense was the cold, that though muffled up to the very eyes, we could hardly hold the bridle, even with the hands enveloped in a thick woollen poncho. A league further brought us to two or three low huts with a corral, the last human habitations; and here we dis-mounted at sunrise to partake of several glasses of goats' milk dashed with aguardiente (spirit). After half an hours' adjustment of saddles and baggage we resume our journey, passing several species of giant cactus which, in these elevated and bleak regions, grow in extraordinary luxuriance, beauty and variety. A ride of a couple of miles brings us to the sierras and now the guide, a practised guanaco-hunter, takes the lead and we begin to thread in and out amongst the valleys, but always ascending, our goal being the very summits in the interior. Suddenly the vaqueano espies two guanacos! and I may here remark upon the extraordinary quick-sightedness of these men, who will instantaneously distinguish the game upwards of a mile off, which it would take a novice a long time to make out, even with the aid of a good telescope such as I had : the fact is the guanaco skin is of exactly the same shade, as well of the coarse dry herbage, as of the rocks; and moreover the eye, accustomed to objects on a plain, cannot readily adjust itself to the ever varying distances of precipitously escarped regions. A naturally quick eye trained by mountain experience is the " sine qua non " of the successful guanaco stalker.

It takes us two hours more to arrive at the first

patches of snow, then succeed the snow-fields and frozen mountain rivulets, the slipping and sliding of the animals on which, make it lively for their riders. Five long weary hours are consumed ere we attain the summit of the first chain, an altitude of 8300 feet above sea level, and here, amongst the crevices of the rocks I was surprised to see two specimens of the mountain biscacha (*Lagidium Cuvieri*), which belongs to the family of the *Chinchillidæ*. The hunters of the Chinchilla, who are usually Indians, make use of the same method to obtain their prey as the ratters in England: only instead of the ferret they employ one of the species of the Pole cat (*Mustela putorius*) to drive them from their burrows and then they are bagged in a sack placed at the mouth of the exit: but the animal is becoming rare on Cis-Andine territory and at the present rate of destruction must soon share the fate of the *Dodo*.

The eye, from this point, is bewildered with the multiplicity of hoary peaks which assail it, stretching away north, south and west, studded here and there with undulating plateaux covered with long coarse grass and styled, as if in derision, Pampas. This is the very home of the guanaco, and dotted here and there on contiguous eminences they stand, like sentinels. The tactics employed by guanaco and chamois hunters are somewhat similar, but on the whole, the pursuit of the former is perhaps not quite so hazardous as of the latter. Proceeding noiselessly on horseback along the summits, until they arrive at a precipice, they then dismount, cock the rifle and crawl carefully to the edge to survey the crags beneath; and if the head of a guanaco be visible projecting over some ledge, they set to work to stalk it by creeping or sliding down the steep side and jumping over chasms, being extremely careful to avoid giving notice of their approach until within range, as of all animals known the guanaco is perhaps the most wary. In nervous creatures such as this, all muscle, sinew and tendon, restlessly alive to motion, even the shadow of a shade of a sentiment of impending danger is sufficient to set them off in that elegant canter which, degenerating into a graceful trot interspersed with springs and leaps of daring magnitude, render it at once hopeless to seek a nearer acquaintance. When uncertain of the range, and it is sheer impossibility for those unaccustomed to mountainous regions to be otherwise, the usual plan is to fire, for in case of a miss, the animal seems bewildered, jumps a yard or two, wheels round and remains stock still listening with ears erect and gazing intently with its beautiful gazelle-like eyes, offering another chance for the hunter's bullet to find its billet.

The sentinel males linny from peak to peak, warning the herds below of approaching foes, and echoed in the tranquil dells of the mountainous enclosures, I have never listened to a more delicate or more musical note from any animal; but in captivity they lose, or more strictly speaking, no longer require it.

Pushing on further into the interior, we saw many solitary males, but wild in the extreme by reason of the bitter cold and deep snow, and having chanced on a small and secluded valley, wherein lay some patches of herbage free from snow, and intersected by a mountain rill one mass of solid ice, we thought both the spot and the hour, 1-30 p. m., suitable for our morning meal; for, in the Argentine Republic it is not usual to breakfast until after some work has been performed

All hands set at once to work to disentangle from their hoary mantle and collect dry herbage and twigs and soon, as fire-making is an Argentine specialty, a blazing fire curled up; for cooking purposes ice was melted to yield water, and as for the poor horses, we did not know what to do, they tried a mouthful of snow or an ice-crystal, but it did not agree with them, so, laboriously breaking up some of the thick ice in the bed of the solid stream, just a mouthful of the precious liquid was found beneath, which sufficed merely to wet their lips. So with a roasting sun above, a mantle around of the coldest nitrogenic-oxygen I ever felt and solid ice-boulders beneath, and well-nigh exhausted and famished, we breakfasted.

After an hour's rest, we saddle up again to renew the chase over bluff and brow; but although many guanacos were seen at a distance, they were beyond range and we did not get a shot.

As the sun was now declining fast, all haste was made to seek the shelter promised by the *vaqueano*, but what was our dismay on reaching the spot at dusk, to find it levelled to the 'ground; no signs of any roof nor walls, the charred remains of some beams strewn about were the only evidences of a former habitation. Unprepared for such a contingency, we surveyed the scene with blank dismay! here we were at an elevation of 6000 feet above Mendoza in midwinter, swathed in ice and snow, the sport of rude blasts, and darkness threatening. By extremities man is reduced to action, so we immediately set off in pursuit of some spot where, *sub Jove*, to spend the weird and bitter hours of that dreadful night. Half an hour luckily brought us to such, in the shape of a dry gulley, about three feet deep and six wide; great was our rejoicing as though we had discovered a feather bed. Dismounting, unsaddling and unpacking was the work of a moment, and then Dr. Anzorena and myself proceeded to scoop out from the bank with our knives, a level couch and a recess for the heads. With such implements, and in frozen ground, the labour, as may be imagined, was very severe; but the puna, or exhaustion consequent upon the rarified air of such an elevation, it was that consumed our force; five or six vigorous digs with the knife produced utter prostration; even Samson himself, under the same circumstances, would soon succumb to an influence which not only robs the muscles of their strength, but at the same time, the mind of all determination to exercise them.

This accomplished, our next anxiety was to rig up some sort of a shanty with blankets and other wraps.

The rifles propped by boulders formed the uprights
and the peon now returning with dry branches of
shrubs, these were lashed to the rifles to form the
framework of the roof on which were piled three
empty sacks and a poncho surmounted by my water-
proof coat; on one side a sheet, on the other a working
apron, at the back a towel to ward off the damp from
the gully side, and our dwelling was complete. The
bed consisted of saddle cloths and one blanket beneath,
a rug and two blankets on the top, a knapsack and a
log of wood for pillows: such was our accommodation
for as bleak a night as ever man endured.

The peon having again returned with another
load of dry brush-wood, a fire was soon blazing and
around it we squatted swaddled to the nose, whilst the
hissing, spluttering and savoury odour of a glorious
asado assailed our ears and nostrils. Talk of roast
meat! nothing is comparable to the asado as prepared
by the natives: a long, pointed, flat iron bar (*asador*)
is threaded through short ribs of beef or half a breast
of mutton, the bar is then stuck into the ground over
wood-ash glowing embers and turned and returned
until done to a tee; the English sometimes try it at
picnics, but it is by no means the same thing. Once
or twice in the midst of our wizard-like meal, we were
startled by what we considered *pumas*, roused by the
air-laden scent, to visit our encampment, but which,
on seizing our arms and reconnoitring resolved themselves into blackened boulders staring from the snow
and dancing threateningly in the lurid glare of the

embers. The mantle and curtain of darkness had now fallen upon and surrounded us — they might perhaps have been a trifle warmer—so piling high the fuel, in we turned, not however to sleep, for in spite of the closest contact of our bodies and the muffling of our persons even to the very nose and ears, grim cramp soon clutched our limbs in his iron grasp and effectually banished rest, by rendering one position impossible; and yet it is my opinion, from some personal experience, that dry, cold air however severe, never yet injured the health of either man or beast; nay more, that it is positively serviceable in pulmonary troubles especially at considerable altitudes; although certainly it is no uncommon circumstance to meet with mule drivers and peons, whose business it is to cross the Andes, deprived of fingers, toes and even limbs from frost-bite. The principal occupation during the hours of darkness was to consult the time-keeper every five minutes and long for day, the severity of the early part of which drove us from our couch an hour before dawn; when the dying pile was replenished and food became the dearest wish of our hearts. In the providence and forethought of the previous evening, some horns had been filled with water to serve for the morning meal, a useless precaution, as they were found so hard frozen, that it was impossible even to break their contents: the wine was so solid a lump of ice, that chopping had to be resorted to, to provide us with alcoholic lozenges, and the cold chicken, usually so tender, was transmuted into hard wood, and as a wind up to the slight repast, day began to dawn. Our

minds were still upon the chase, so dismantling our
cabin with infinite gusto and saddling our beasts,
which had too much sense to stray during darkness, we
commenced travelling upwards to other summits called
Cuchillas (knife-edges) 9500 feet above sea level, the
highest point of the first range. The footprints of
two lions were observed but did not divert us from
our object; but the guanacos, of which we saw many,
were as wild as the day previous. A fine view of
the Cordilleras was the reward of the ascent; in front
rose majestically the peak of the Cerro de la Plata
to an altitude of 14000 feet and covered with snow
from its base in the valley to its summit, whilst massive Tupungato is our constant companion on the left;
thus traversing one mountain-top after another and
occasionally making long shots, we succeeded in
wounding only three guanacos which, tumbling head-
long down precipices, were irretrievably lost; so that
although not a very profitable, it certainly was an
exciting hunt. About midday, with appetites as keen
as the very air, we called a halt for breakfast, and
at 2 p. m. turned our steps homewards, our extreme
disappointment being as nothing to the supreme wrath
and disgust of the vaqueano, who declared we had
spoiled the sport by the noise we made, by our hurried
arrangements and by having too many horses. A
lively picture of a true hunter was this hoary-headed
guide, who, when alone, never fails to bag one or more
guanacos: clothed in garments furnished by his own
rifle and manufactured by his own hands, he started
up before my imagination as one of Britain's skin-clad

warriors in the time of Cæsar; quick of eye, stealy, thoughtful and full of resource, and endurance stamped upon his whole physique; for half a league with rifle in hand would he run, jump and climb, and then lie down behind some projecting ledge to recover breath before he fired; whereas a few yards' spin was more than enough for us tiros.

The experience of one night in such an inhospitable region, suffices to quicken our homeward pace and as we descend by a completely different route through a deep tortuous ravine (*cajon*) filled with ice, to keep one's seat is no easy matter; and then, leaning back in the saddle, down we slide over snow and ice, in a zigzag course, a hundred feet at a time. Perpendicular walls towering a thousand feet above us at times enclose our path: then bursts upon our astonished gaze a frozen waterfall of over fifty feet, a cascade actually arrested in its fall and converted into solid ice, forming one vast icicle of an infinite number of tapering, refracting digits: certainly one of the most beautiful objects upon which my eyes ever rested. Gliding, sliding yet, and stumbling down this steep ravine, we come upon another cataract still grander than the first and frozen in the same manner: how did I regret the absence of a camera!

Just at dusk we arrive at the sloping plateau beyond the mountains, which is still much rent by gullies 200 feet deep, scooped out by the mountain torrents, and skirting which in the gloom is a most perilous undertaking. An hour and a half more brings us, in the midst of complete darkness, into the vicinity of the house at Papagallos, but although close to it, the road to reach it was full of danger; the narrow paths over the deep ravines, which a single false step would have rendered fatal, are however safely traversed thanks to our reliable leader, and then all our griefs and fears soon vanish in the vestibule of a warm and comfortable dwelling, and in anticipation of a good, hot and substantial repast. One dish had been specially prepared to gratify our appetites, Guanaco *charqui* (dried like venison), but although not at all particular, I cannot say I relished its coarse and sickly flavour which it required strong seasoning to drown. The dinner ended, with our feet upon the brazier(*) and clouds of perfumed smoke issuing from our lips, we sat discussing the events of the last two days, deeply chagrined that none of the 150 noble guanaco-heads, which we saw in our expedition, then lay in the hall to reward our toils and sufferings.

After a night's revel in clean sheets from which we rose without a trace of yesterday's fatigue, we early bent our steps Mendozawards, with the hope of having better luck next time.

(*) Mendoza houses possess no chimneys and consequently no grates nor open fires, but *braseros* filled with glowing wood-embers are placed in the rooms, surrounded with a footboard, on which each person puts his feet, and thus a cozy family circle is formed.

CHAPTER XXVI.

In a purely agricultural province such as Mendoza, comparatively few artisans can find employment, nevertheless for such, the wages are from 6/. to 7/. a day, whilst the expense of living is very insignificant from the profusion and cheapness of all kinds of food, even to luxuries ; for tillers of the soil however there is always abundant opening, and very many foreigners who arrived here penniless are now, after the lapse of a few years, wealthy, some very wealthy, although the natives say that Mendoza is a fine place to live in, but a bad one in which to make money. The lower orders of Mendocinos have not as yet the opportunities, nor the requisite cunning to prosecute some of the methods of gaining a livelihood, such as the like order of Cordovese practise. Bone gathering with the latter is a regular occupation and they have a playful but rather dangerous method of supplying themselves at the expense of their neighbours. As the cargo trains on the railways carry immense quantities of bones down to the littoral for shipment, and they are piled high on open trucks, the ossiquestants place small obstacles on the

rai's sufficient to jolt some of the contents off the waggons and then fill their bags at leisure from the fallen
spoil.

From the extent of its unoccupied lands, Mendoza
can offer to the immigrant vast and fertile regions
beyond all other provinces : but as the whole of the
lands of this province have been reclaimed from the
desert by means of irrigation, and as water is generally
abundant, suitable but simple works are alone necessary
to render every part of it prolific. An "*acequia madre*"
or main ditch is first cut on the highest level from
which water can be obtained, and from different points
of this and at right angles to it, lead others of less
capacity, following the lay of the land. Temporary
sluices are opened in the sides of the latter at any point
required, by merely removing a spadeful or two of
earth, and are closed again by its restoration. This
simple and efficacious process need not be repeated
more than once a month for agricultural purposes and
is not so laborious but that one man can water a square
league in a week. Immigrants, who do not desire to
commence on their own account, are usually accepted
by estancieros on halves; the proprietor advancing land,
seed, oxen and agricultural implements, and the stranger
supplying the labour ; in which case the profits are
equally divided ; a friendly union of capital and labour.

In the new city, building plots of 20 yards by 50
can be purchased from £50 to £300 ; on the site of the
old ruined town however, the same extent of ground
costs only from £16 to £50 ; but although in Rome one

walks over stones that have been Cæsar's and Pompey's gods, to the dwellers in Mendoza it can scarcely be a pleasing contemplation that they are erecting their domiciles with the very ashes of their fathers. In the neighbourhood of populous centres, cultivated and enclosed farms can be had at the rate of £7 to £20 an acre ; whilst distant, uncultivated and therefore unenclosed tracts, suitable for estancia purposes, may be bought for £250 the square league.

Until lately, a large proportion of the business of Mendoza, perhaps to the amount of £200,000 annually, consisted in fattening cattle on its vast alfalfares and exporting them to Chili, into which, through the Andes, there are three principal passes Uspallata, Portillo and Planchon, necessitating a journey of about 85 leagues from Mendoza to Santiago and occupying the drovers from ten to fourteen days.

The prices of domestic animals in Mendoza at present are : Oxen £6 to £8 ; Cows £3 to £4 ; Carthorses 30/ to 60/ ; Saddle horses £4 and upwards ; Mares 6/ ; Mules £5 to £6 ; Sheep which are very scarce 3/ to 8/ ; Fat Hogs, fed on cereal refuse and fruits, and whose number is enormous, 16/ to 20/.

The climate of Mendoza which is dry* and healthy and very beneficial especially to such as suffer from Consumption or Asthma, has undergone a remarkable change of late years, due principally to the extensive cultivation of trees. As before remarked, from the

---

* In fact the air is so dry between the Cordilleras that domestic vermin can scarcely exist.

heights adjacent to the city, nothing can be discerned
of its dwellings; nothing is presented to the eye but a
dense mass of arboreal foliage, consisting principally of
white, black, Carolina and Dutch Poplars, various
species of Willow, Acacia, Oak, Paradise, Laurel,
Chestnut, Cypress, Pine, Elm, etc.; which forest is com-
plemented by innumerable species of fruit trees: by
this means the rainfall has been increased and the
severity of its chimenal temperature reduced. Not many
years ago, the thermometer was usually so low in June
that it was enough to empty a pail of water on the
ground, to ensure the freezing of the liquid almost
as soon as it touched the earth.

The treatment of consumption, which is very common indeed and increasing on the low shores of the
Eastern littoral, has lately become more rational than
formerly, at any rate in the Argentine Republic, to the
manifest advantage of the patient; and this is due in
a great measure to the persistent preaching of that
apostle of the Sierras, Dr. Scrivener, who himself arriving in this country young, with all the seeds of
consumption already sown in his frame, after living
amongst and constantly travelling over the Sierras for
a number of years, succeeded in entirely eradicating all
tendency thereto, and has already reached a ripe old
age in the full enjoyment of health. It is now well-
understood and received here as an axiom that cold air,
especially when allied to moderate elevation, such as
that of Mendoza, far from being dangerous to the
phthisical, permanently invigorates the sufferer; the

system of treatment antipodean to this is irrational and cannot be sustained much longer. Shutting up a patient in one uniform artificially-heated atmosphere may just possibly maintain for a time the physical condition *"in statu quo"*, but cannot act as a curative, every vigour-giving element is wanting, and the natural relaxing airs are in the same category. Mentone, Nice, Cannes, San Remo, Pau, Hastings, Devon, Madeira, *"et hoc genus omne"* are all worn out themselves as they have worn out their votaries : here, in this veritable Utopia, rather than in Brompton, should be located the Hospital for Consumptives ; transfer its death-stricken inmates to the Cordilleras and then will cease that daily apprehensive weighing, that intensely timid hourly inspection of the rapidly curving nails, those two exterior barometric readings that herald the advance of the scourge, and which are so frightful to witness ; and in their stead the joyous consciousness of rapidly returning health and strength.

But in addition to a benignant climate, Mendoza possesses in her bosom other remedial means in the form of a numerous array of medicinal springs both cold and thermal, whose united efficacy surpasses far what Europe has hitherto placed at the disposal of the afflicted : and yet we import Apollinaris, Vichy, Friedericksall &c. by the shipload. There are at least ten Spas in Mendoza the analyses of whose waters differ from any other in the known world, and five or more others which offer but little novelty in their composition ; but the authenticated cures of various diseases

of the skin and stomach, of intestinal and uterine ob-
structions, calculus, rheumatism, gout, venereal disease
and especially scrofulous ulcers, confirm the universal
belief in the potency of these beneficent founts. Many
are still unknown, and of the rest the majority are too
far distant or inaccessible from the centres of her sparse
population to be much utilized : nevertheless during the
season, it is not uncommon to witness four or five
hundred people of both sexes camping out together for
months under canvas in the most ultra-democratic manner, and availing themselves of the advantages which
these various pools of Bethesda undoubtedly afford.

What is here said of Mendoza is likewise true of
the other Andine provinces, only as yet they have been
less explored.

Amongst the best reputed and most easily accessible of these Spas is first the Boca del Rio, 4000 feet
above sea level, and 50 miles S.W. from Mendoza, a
thermal water, the temperature of which varies from
77° to 113° Fahr. and whose constitution may be
gathered from the following analysis, per litre :

Carbonate of Soda	,2750
Carbonate of Lime	2,2050
Sulphate of Lime	2,2800
Sulphate of Magnesia	,0158
Sulphate of Soda	,1850
Chloride of Sodium	1,1600
Silicic Acid	,6140
Carbonic acid in excess	6,1348 grammes

Next may be mentioned the noted baths of the *Puente del Inca* (Inca's bridge), whose fame has been sung
by so many modern writers. These baths are situated

in the Uspallata pass at an elevation of 9078 feet
above sea-level, 200 miles from Mendoza and 24 on
this side of the mountain ridge, which forms the
boundary between Chili and the Argentine Republic.
The Chilians are so well aware of the virtues of these
springs, that they have repeatedly offered to build and
maintain an hotel and extensive bathing establishments
there, but the Argentines are very jealous of the encroachments of their Trans-Andine neighbours. The
Puente del Inca is familiar to Europeans from pictures
and is certainly a most marvellous master-piece of
nature excavated by her workman water over the bed
of the river Mendoza. Its span is about 120 feet and
breadth 27, at an elevation above the river level of
about 65 feet. The immense stalactites of capricious
and elegant forms which depend from the arch, impregnated with metallic salts, clothe the whole in
varied hues. The water of these baths,for there are many,
has a temperature ranging from 51° to 97° Fahr. and
rises frothing and hisses like soda-water, which it
resembles likewise in taste; its composition may be
understood from the following analysis, per litre:

Silicic Acid	,0330
Alumina	,1190
Sulphate of Potash...	,5086
Sulphate of Lime	2,1281
Bicarbonate of Lime	1,8993
Bicarbonate of Iron	,0532
Chloride of Magnesium	,1386
Chloride of Sodium...	11,4644
Carbonic Acid free	,0549

16,3994 grammes

Of the chief remaining Spas and each possessing its special healing qualities may be mentioned : Villavicencio, in the Uspallata Pass, distant from Mendoza 70 miles : Capia, situated 100 miles South : Challao, 7 miles North-West : Borbollon, 9 miles North-East : Lagunita, 5 miles East : Arroyo de Leyes, 25 miles East : Papagallos, 6 miles West ; and Lulunta, a mile and a half from the town of Lujan on the river Mendoza.

CHAPTER XXVII

I had long had a desire to investigate the habits, structure and home of that beautiful little plantigrade aberrant member of the Armadillo family, the *Chlamydophorus truncatus* or *Pichiciego*, (little blind animal). Its range, I discovered to be, in latitude, from 31° S. to 34° S., that is, from the valley of Zonda in the province of San Juan, down to San Rafael 70 leagues south of Mendoza; and in longitude, from the city of San Luis which lies on exactly the same parallel as Mendoza, to the Andes. A remarkably characteristic feature of the landscape of this region, and the one that mainly determines the habitat of our silky little friend, is the *Médanos* (sand-dunes) which, from ten to thirty feet high, and studded with stunted vegetation, extend in nearly a meridional chain; they are not unfrequently met with in other parts of the republic, but only occur in cadenic array in Mendoza and San Juan. I therefore determined to cut into the centre of this zone, in which are likewise found three species

---

(*) For a fuller account of the Pichiciego vide the author's paper in the London Zoological Society's Proceedings of January the sixth 1880.

of true *Dasypodidæ*; but to accomplish this a ride of forty leagues was necessary from Mendoza to the neighbourhood of La Paz; and this I undertook in month of August. La Paz, the theatre of a festive scene detailed in a former chapter, was once very prosperous when kissed into fertility by the river Tunuyan, but now affords a melancholy instance of a territory gradually lapsing to the desert. As the waters of that river, by virtue of the increased occupation of land, yield an insufficient supply, and are thus absorbed on their journey of forty miles, ere they reach La Paz, nothing can save that district from becoming a vast irremediable waste; and yet forsooth, due to private influence, the projected route for the extension of the Trans-Andine railway actually makes a long detour to reach this doomed spot, passing through what before long will become a wilderness, deprived of a drop of water either for engines or passengers, instead of taking a direct line to Mendoza, whereby a saving of at least one hundred miles might be effected.

For six days then, accompanied by a large number of men, a diligent search was prosecuted for this tiny *Chlamydophorus truncatus* (truncated cloak-bearer), which bears the appearance of an animal cut in two, so that its posterior is flattened, from which at the bottom springs a rigid tail, for all the world like a pump-handle, and the head, back and truncated end, as its name indicates, are covered by a beautiful pinkish horny shield. I was fortunate enough to secure one living specimen which, in spite of the utmost attention and care, survived capture only three days : in fact, like the lovely humming birds, the Pichiciego droops rapidly in captivity and has never been known to live longer than eight days in that state. That both these delicate creatures succumb under the tenderest hand of man, the same causes may be assigned ; the absence of any certain knowledge as to their food, or the temperature suitable. An inspection of the dental system of the *Chlamydophorus* clearly indicates the *Coleoptera* as its prey, a conclusion which is rendered all the more probable by their abundance in the neighbourhood of its burrow. My solitary specimen was fed on milk, which it lapped like a cat and on introducing by artifice some tiny pieces of chopped meat into its mouth, these it did not reject. So extremely sensitive however is this little mail-clad burrower to cold that, after passing the night in a box of earth covered with flannels, it was found the following morning in a very exhausted state, but wrapped in warm envelopes and placed near a fire, quickly recovered. On taking it into my hand under a warm Mendoza sun, it shivered violently, but whether through chill or fear, it is impossible to say. Its normal paradise appears to be, when the temperature of its sandy dwelling is such as almost to scorch the hand.

With regard to the fiery-tempered humming-birds, whatever the nature of their food, whether the nectar of flowers, or insects, or both, man has not

yet discovered the secret of preserving them alive in
captivity: but, in my opinion, in this case, the failure
is due rather to the high spirit of these winged jewels,
than to the want of suitable nourishment or even proper
temperature. View them in their natural state ! at one
time darting like an arrow from flower to flower; at another poising themselves erect and stationary at the open
corolla, with alatory movement resembling the vibra-
tions of a musical cord, accompanied by a shoot of the
long attenuated tongue as quick as lightning; at another, pursuing with a fury, that the very air re-
sounds, birds twenty times their size; at another,
satiating their rage on innocent but sterile blossoms ,
the very type of restlessness! why, impatience, caprice
and rage are stamped so manifestly on their every
motion and are reflected so powerfully from their
gaudy suit of topaz, emerald and ruby, that to think
of taming such creatures is as chimerical as to attempt
to chain the thunder-storm. A young lady of my
acquaintance in Buenos Aires took a fully-fledged
young one from the nest and, day and night even,
nursed and fed it with the utmost care. Syrup was
its diet, which it imbibed eagerly, almost every five
minutes, from the end of a feather dipped therein and
presented to it: at night she retired with it into her
bedroom and placed a warm lamp by the side of its
cage to maintain the temperature during the darkness,
and yet with all this attention, it survived only 21
days, which however is a period unusually long for
the life of a captive Trochilus.

But to return to the Pichiciego: when walking

the *Chlamydophorus* plants both the fore and hind feet flat on the soles and not on the contracted claws, as is the case with the anteater, and carries its inflexible tail, which it has no power to raise, trailing along the ground. Sluggish in all its movements, except as a fodient, in which capacity it perhaps excels all other burrowing animals, the *Chlamydophorus* performs the operation of excavation with such celerity, that a man has scarcely time to dismount from his horse before the creature has buried itself to the depth of its own body. As it commences to excavate, the forefeet are first employed, and immediately afterwards supporting its body on the firm tripod afforded by these and the extremity of the tail, both hind feet are brought into play simultaneously, discharging columns of sand with incredible swiftness. My solitary living representative I placed first on brick and then on wooden flooring, but knowing it could not burrow in these, it merely walked round and round in irregular circles, an evidence of the very great or total deprivation of the power of vision, at any rate during daylight : but far different was its behaviour on being transported to the exposed soil where, after a preliminary and very audible dog-like sniffle or two, indicating keen scent, it set to work immediately to delve at a very rapid rate.

The light fine sand in which the Pichiciego burrows proclaims unmistakably its presence as well as that of even the minutest animals by the tracks left : the fox, the cat, the beetle and the spider &c., are thus equally betrayed. The natives are apt observers and even from the saddle will decipher and distinguish at a glance the various footprints and unerringly detail the animals that have passed any assigned spot during the night. With regard to our elegant little subject, there is no mistake : besides the impressions of the four feet, the inclined stiff tail leaves its central deep fosse ; of course, after rain, which falls but seldom, the indentations are accentuated, and the only sure way of effecting a capture is to follow them, as they lead directly to a small hillock of sand, by removing which, the entrance to the tunnel is exposed to view and the host usually found at home ; and if the tracks were numerous, the animal would no longer be rare ; but it is a fact that years sometimes elapse without any trace of its existence.

And now the time for my departure from Mendoza drew nigh. I had spent in her precincts many months both pleasantly and with benefit to my health and shall ever remember her hospitable people with affection and her climate with gratitude, and when I hear of insurmountable difficulties oppressing the husbandman, shall never cease to point to the example of her who, from a desert, has evoked an Eden, planted in the midst of an army of barren dunes a Damascus, and rendered her borders worthy, in the estimation of every traveller, the title of the hitherto undiscovered "Gard.n of the Hesperides".

CHAPTER XXVIII

TRIP TO SAN JUAN

Having a penchant for a dry climate, and the province of San Juan, from its geographical position and topography, offering such; one morning I booked a place in the tiny diligence for its capital, distant 53 postal leagues from Mendoza.

Now, as a fourth part of this region is occupied by mountains and sandy wastes, and the whole is subject to hardly any rainfall, besides being bounded on the west by the Andes, on the north and east by sierras, the dry plains of Rioja and the salinas of San Luis, and on the south by the parched province of Mendoza, we have here a combination of desiccating conditions sufficient to satisfy the most fastidious of mummies.

The general aridity and consequent sterility of this province is however relieved by numerous valleys of exquisite fertility which are self-fecundated, that is they need no manure, as the streams bring down from the mountains the necessary fructifying detritus.

I was awakened at 5 a. m. to take my seat in the *Silla de Posta* or Post-chaise, a kind of razeed diligence under weigh for the city of San Juan: the vehicle, to my surprise, was not of the lumbering class with which I was so familiar, but partook more of the character of a mail-cart, accommodating but three travellers, on account of the paucity of passenger traffic between Mendoza and that city ; and accompanied by a driver and a postillion with five horses, formed a very respectable convoy for three fares.

After leaving the cultivated lands of Mendoza, deserts covered with salitre and dotted here and there with hard, stunted, spiny brushwood which the eye loathes, characterize the road, and in summer it is very difficult, nay even dangerous to attempt to pass over these *travesias* by day ; so during the hot season the diligence runs by night, whilst in rainy periods, which are exceedingly rare, these districts cannot be crossed at all even on horseback. The deep sand becomes super-heated and the wind drives its scorched particles in penetrating, blinding, suffocating clouds, producing intense thirst, to allay which not a drop of water is to be had ; the blistering fiery air coupled with malarious exhalations add to the torments of the traveller, who sometimes falls a prey to the accumulated sufferings which oppress him. In these inhospitable regions especially it is that the *jaguar* exhibits the ferocity and bloodthirstiness of his nature.

As there is no grass or water and but few habitations on the route, we had to take a troop of horses with us and change them every two or three leagues as occasion required : nor were we less provident in the matters of food and drink.

Fifteen leagues from Mendoza wood-cutters were observed busy loading their carts with Algarrobo trunks for the use of the city, as it is now difficult to find solid fuel nearer than that, although the Jarilla (*Larrea divaricata*), a shrub belonging to the *Zygophyllœ* family, the planes of whose flattened fan-like bunches of leaves face East and West, is still found in quantity in its vicinity. About half past three p. m. we arrive at the hostelry of Cañada Honda, where we had to pass the night: this Posta, with its adjoining school, forms the advanced guard of the village lying two leagues further up towards the mountains, and fine, large, commodious premises it offers, but absolutely nothing else; as bare as a regular Eastern caravansary it stood, but nevertheless its shelter was very welcome, after the burning deserts we had crossed. At 5 a. m. on the following morning, an early call for midwinter, we were summoned to renew our journey and by dint of hard driving arrived in San Juan at 10 a. m. just in time for breakfast and rejoiced to terminate one of the most uninteresting excursions I ever made: a few guanacos, three ostriches, a fox and a hare were the only living beings met with on the way.

On my arrival all the English in a body called upon me, but as they amounted only to two, I was not inconvenienced by their number.

The modern town of San Juan lies on a river of the same name, in Lat. 31° 4' S. at an elevation of 2100 feet above sea level, enveloped in the snug valley of Tulan, and is distant upwards of 1000 miles from Buenos Aires. Surrounded on three sides by sierras about two leagues distant, with the remaining side lying exposed to the deserts, the present city, thanks to extensive engineering works in the shape of a murallon or dyke 1000 feet long, is free from those periodic inundations, which used to devastate and in fact ultimately in 1833 destroyed the old one, the remains of which, in the shape of a church and plaza, lie on its northern outskirts. These solitary mementos attest the folly of allowing military men to found cities without adequate protection, in valleys subject to the sudden and irresistible overflow of streams rendered impetuous by the melting of the snows on the adjacent heights.

San Juan, with its 10,000 inhabitants, rests packed in the small compass of little more than a square mile, the compression all the more evident after the noble expansion of horticultural Mendoza: the contrast of its narrow streets, thirteen yards wide, with the broad and handsome Boulevards of the city I had just left; of its villanous road and causeway pavement, threatening a sprained ankle at every step, with the even pathways and hard sandy highroad to which I had been accustomed for so many months, made me quite out of love at first sight with this provincial capital: nor was the impression dissipated on an inspection of the dwellings, whose exterior, in general, rises but little above the hovel, roofed by means of bare poplar stems bearing transverse canes and covered with earth; some few however, perhaps a dozen, exhibit a little more ambition and are constructed of thick adobe walls, plastered and coloured. The portals of four churches and a cathedral neatly and substantially built, but without the slightest pretension to architectural beauty or even design, stand ever open to minister to the spiritual wants of the faithful : but withal, the dead, it seems, are better cared for than the living, as the small but elegant cemetery is the only dwelling place that reflects any taste; its fine broad gravelled walks, flower beds and trees, all kept scrupulously clean and trimmed, vie with its numerous magnificent marble monuments in investing with a charm a scene naturally so gloomy.

As the population is so closely packed, the overcrowded city needs lungs and for this purpose the Plaza 25 de Mayo affords a fine open space in the centre of the town, but I had no eyes to discern its beauties, if it had any, as I had been spoilt in the Plaza line by that of Mendoza; a fine market of large dimensions, but the majority of whose stalls are unoccupied; a National College, a Sarmiento Normal School and a School of Mines, pretty well complete the list of public establishments, omitting the wretched *Cabildo* (Townhall) as scarcely deserving notice. The National College, attended by at least 150 pupils is a fine building and well worth a visit : in its halls may be seen the nuclei of really good Museums, especially in the department of Mineralogy, but owing to the reign of " *Aploutos* ", their development is retarded.

In the "*Salon de Física*" I was surprised to find abundant modern apparatus for illustrating the domain of Natural Philosophy and in the Chemical department, a fine laboratory under the direction of an able professor, but the Zoological disappointed me, presenting, as it did, only an embryo, although the rector Señor Alvarez is evidently fond of live specimens, as on going to visit him, I was confronted in the patio of his residence by four condors, one puma. three eagles and a Patagonian hare. And here it was, in the house of a medical gentleman, that I was grieved to be the witness of a literary sacrilege, such as I never before beheld. The floor of his drawing-room was strewn with the wreck of Gould's magnificent work on the Toucans, and I trembled lest that on the Trochilidæ, which was at hand in a book-case should share the same fate: these splendid tomes, the gift of well-known English ornithologists from the West Indies on their visit to San Juan, leaving their natural use, had degenerated into nursery playthings.

The only hotel or rather café in San Juan is the Hotel Comercio, and hither resort, in the evening, the élite of the town to do little else but play at billiards and dominoes, and talk politics. What astonishes a foreigner however is, that all these visitors never drink anything but perhaps an occasional cup of coffee; such abstemiousness is remarkable especially after Mendoza, where indulgence is carried to excess : nay the Maine liquor law might be in full operation here, such difficulty is there to quench one's legitimate thirst, and that not from the absence of the wherewithal to gratify it, as it is the region of the wine vat, but from the paucity of bars. The San Juaninos are a population in no need of Father Matthew's philanthropic preaching as they only drink at meals; in fact, their nerves are so highly strung by the dry, rarified, electrically-tensioned air, that their very existence is determined by extreme moderation; the atmosphere itself is a perpetually stimulating draught, which the numerous sudden deaths sufficiently attest. Intense cold sometimes reigns in San Juan during the winter, although snow is almost unknown, falling but once or twice during the year.

The amusements of the inhabitants, apart from billiards and politics, seem centred in cock-fighting, as every Sunday and holiday the people, from the Governor downwards, ardently pursue this ancient sport, a practice no doubt derived from their ancestors, the Iberian Dons; and yet, their fondness for music is a redeeming point, counterbalancing in some measure the barbarity which leads them to enjoy the spectacle of feathered gladiatorship, and gives rise to numerous amateur concerts and dramatic representations.

One never ending source of merriment to me was to witness the usual way in which little San Juanino urchins mounted tall horses: many could not reach even the stirrups and yet by clutching hold of the flowing tail and planting their feet against the hind legs, hand over fist they were in the saddle in a giffy.

Fruit is abundant in San Juan, especially grapes, sweet limes, lemons and *toronjas* (enormous citrons); and as for oranges, the very finest cost no more than a shilling the hundred, although Rioja supplies perhaps the best, five of which are to be had for a halfpenny.

Until the present Governor assumed office, the city suburbs lay at the mercy of a gang of highwaymen, as lawless and daring, but not so merciful, as Dick Turpin: black-mail was levied and submitted to by all travellers, under pain of death, so that at last, locomotion beyond civic bounds became wellnigh impossible. The first step however of this active magistrate, was to seize some of their persons and try the *"suaviter"* by consigning them to the tender mercies of the law; the judges were required to sentence these outlaws to legal execution. Not a bit of it! Rhadamanthus having respect to his own safety, a not uncommon failing in the Argentine rural bench, is lenient, and so after a slight imprisonment, the banditti return to the scene of their former operations. Then came the *"fortiter"*, when the Governor issued the order to his soldiers, "Go out, capture and slay those ruffians without benefit of clergy!" and forthwith ten of them slept and San Juan became as peaceful as quakerdom.

From the neighbourhood of Mendoza to that of San Juan, forming in part the limit of the two provinces, exists a chain of intervening salt lakes, called *Guanacache*, the asylum of countless flocks of water-fowl and fish of various kinds, including a species of trout; whilst their banks afford excellent culinary salt. In this isolated district and unmoved by the onward march of civilization around, amidst the lofty rank grass, sedge and rushes, dwell the Laguneros, the pure descendants of the Guarpe Indians, whose customs and habits they preserve almost intact. Industrious and honest, as agriculturists, artisans, hunters and fishermen, these hardy lake-men supply the neighbouring towns weekly with fish, fowl, cheese, *patai* (cakes made from the ground algarroba pods), and *aloja* (fermented liquor from the algarroba seed); whilst baskets, cigar cases, portemonnaies and canoes (one of which was sent to the Paris exhibition) constructed entirely of grass or rushes, and of exquisite beauty in form and colour, denote at once their lithesome fingers and the accuracy of their natural taste.

The San Juaninos, sprung from a union of Spanish with Guarpe Indian blood, resemble Europeans, more than do any other people in this republic, not so much in physique, for they are characterized by high square cheek bones, massive heads, bony frames, dark complexions and jet-black hair and eyes, as in their industry and thrift, enlightened appreciation of correct taste, subdued tone and thirst for knowledge; and in spite of the inferiority of their dwellings, the execrableness of their pavement, and their penchant for cockfighting, much luxury and elegance exist in their midst, and as for the education it is really superior, and no less than five daily newspapers are issued. Ready at all times to seize every opportunity

of turning to account advantages of soil and climate
for the acquisition of products that minister to the necessities and comforts of man, they untiringly devote
their efforts to the cultivation of the soil, the rearing
of the cattle and the growth of wines. As for the
soldiers, although only National guards, I must say,
they present a remarkably fine appearance, splendidly
developed men and well-drilled, and if all the nine
thousand, of which this province boasts, be of the
same calibre and warlike mien, even a Frederick the
Second, commonly called the Great, might well be
proud of such an army of Anakims. The San Juani-
nas are noted all the world over for their lustrous eyes,
of which I saw enough one night in the theatre, to
convince me it was perilous for a susceptible stranger
to tarry long in their midst.

San Juan has at present about 7500 acres under
vine culture, which yield, on an average, from 750
to 2500 lb. of fruit to the acre; and as a natural consequence of the difference in latitude, even drier air
and higher temperature, the grapes of San Juan contain more saccharine matter than those of Mendoza.

Of the numerous vintners' establishments, one
especially claims notice, on account of the magnitude
and completeness of its operations. The Bodega (wine
stores) of Luis Bergallo & Co., into which I entered,
is a fine well-constructed building 60 yards by 20,
having vaults beneath of the same floor-area and of
a capacity sufficient to store 6000 bordalesas; and in
the year 1880 this firm produced 7000 bordalesas of

superior wine. Eleven jolly oak tuns, purchased in France at an expense of about £200, and each containing 500 arrobas (25lb) of fruit, immense coils of elastic hose worth £400, and powerful pumping machinery, besides a whole host of less aspiring but not less perspiring vats made of native poplar, greet the visitor: and during the harvest, at least 200 men work night and day in this busy hive. The wine produced is mostly of the sherry type, very little red wine is made as yet in San Juan; and a distillery, fitted up on the Dutch model, is attached and yields a pipe of alcohol daily. The great drawback, here as in Mendoza, is the want of suitable wood for barrels, as the poplar vats, by their excessive porosity, entail in the aggregate the very serious daily waste of at least half a bordalesa.

CHAPTER XXIX

During my residence in San Juan, I experienced that most terrible of all winds the Zonda; all the Solanos, Siroccos and Simooms in one would not equal this death-dealing blast in malignancy which, blowing from the N. W. or sometimes due West, launches, usually for three successive days, and from 9 a.m. to 5 p. m. each day, its fatal and impetuous halitus over the land. Fortunately it is not frequent, otherwise the Cuyo Provinces would soon be desolated: August is the month most subject to it and altogether at the most two weeks in the year may be thus black-lettered. This dry, scorching wind, which mounts at times to a hurricane sufficient to uproot trees, comes laden with finely comminuted dust and sand to such an extent as to threaten suffocation and blindness; the sun despoiled of his rays appears like a red hot millstone; the heat increases every instant; the skin becomes feverish and parched, the countenance red, the nostrils and mouth are filled with heated particles, the respiration is seriously impeded; and to be exposed to its full fury without shelter is not only very dangerous but often suddenly fatal: and what makes this oven-blast still more trying is, that it is always and immediately succeeded by a strong cold South wind.

As I had not my registered thermometer with me in San Juan, I can only state generally that on this Sunday afternoon at 4-30 p. m. my attention was aroused by seeing people hurrying in every direction to shut their doors and windows; and as this was in midwinter, the thermometer indicated the vicinity of freezing point, but suddenly obeying the fiend without jumped to 96°, Fahr: whilst the next day, snow having again fallen, the temperature was a second time reduced to 34° Fahr. On this occasion three people fell dead in the streets. Although the focus of the Zonda seems to be in San Juan, the tail end reaches Mendoza and even Buenos Aires, though happily with much diminished force, and it produces in those cities like but tempered results, in the latter rendering people cross and irritable even to derangement of the faculties. During its prevalence the lower orders may be seen with the temporal fossæ adorned with talismanic split beans, as a counter-irritant to relieve the oppression in the head, the flat-surfaces of the lobes being applied to the skin by gentle pressure, where they remain without adhesives.

At Mendoza I had an opportunity of noting its thermometric effects more accurately with a registered instrument. On rising one morning and looking at the thermometer in my bedroom, it marked 56° Fahr., whilst in the patio at 9 a. m. it fell to 44° in the shade: at 11 a. m. I went to breakfast and just as I was leav-

ing the table at ten minutes to twelve, was informed
that the Zonda was blowing; upon which, making an
attempt to go outside, I was completely driven back
by the hot blast and retreated to my bedroom which
struck me as icy-cold, but the temperature again recorded there was 56°: a bold advance now into the patio
enabled me to register, in five minutes by the watch,
the incredibly sudden rise from 56° to 81° Fahr. in
the shade.

With this exception, the climate of San Juan is
most delightful and equable, the air being continually
renewed by the vivifying breezes from the neighbouring heights; in fact, throughout the republic, anemo-
logical conditions have a greater influence in deter-
mining the climate than any other factor: the chemical
constitution of its atmosphere, in my opinion, differs
from that assumed as a general law, and although from
an increased amount of oxygen either allotropic or
otherwise, the people live a faster life, longevity is by
no means rare, notwithstanding the prevalence of some
diseases such as pneumonia, dysentery, and liver and
heart affections.

San Juan, like the other Andean provinces, being
situated in volcanic territory, possesses various thermal sulphurous Spas, which are much resorted to for
the cure of Rheumatism and venereal and skin diseases.
I visited one called "Los baños de la Laja", distant
about five leagues from the city and lying in a valley
of ochrous clays between the two ranges of Villicum
and Pié-palo, in the department of Albardon, whither

a good carriage road runs. the whole distance. The entire valley is composed of contemporaneous limestone rock, in which the footprints of guanacos are visible everywhere ; and it is remarkable tha the Sanjuani-nos, usually so alive to improvement, allowed their city to remain ill-paved so long, when at this insigni-ficant distance, they possess an unlimited supply of material suitable for flag-stones and of which they have now begun to make use. The surrounding country presents physical features very similar to, but bolder than, those of Borbollon in Mendoza ; the rocks of the one being the correlatives of the sand dunes of the other.

The baths consist of three pools, each of about six feet diameter ; the two former, very nearly contig-uous, lying by the side of the road and contained in natural limestone basins : the third, offering many points of interest, is found sixty yards away, and fifty feet above the others, bursting from the base of a solitary conical mound seventy-five feet high. On climbing the steep sides of this eminence, its similar-ity to an extinct crater was palpable, the interior being partially filled with sand and gravel, and on striking the bottom with a geological hammer, a hol-low sound was emitted. About twenty years ago, the water overflowed this summit, but the pressure of the superincumbent column of 75 feet seems to have been too much for its base, and so now the healing stream rushes from a rent at the bottom. The conical shape, the horizontal, stratical, calcareous formation of the sides of this remarkable structure, as well as the analysis of the waters issuing from it, all pointedly declare its artificial origin, which is further manifest on inspecting the concurrent elevating action of the liquid on the edges of the lower aperture. These are being gradually raised by the deposition of fresh lime from the overflowing stream, and in this way undoubtedly arose that massive truncated cone, which would assuredly have been completed, had the strength of the walls been sufficient to resist the ever increasing pressure of its liquid contents. It is not uncommon to pick up relics encrusted with this calcareous precipitate or to find objects undergoing the process of incrustation. The chemical constitution of the waters of these three springs is identical, but not so their temperature; that of the highest is 76° Fahr., of one of the lower 77° and of the other 79°. The Spa water though of a milky green hue, is very clear and emits a slight odour of sulphur, and flows away in bubbling streams of not more than six inches in breadth. The accommodation for visitors is but slight and consists merely of one or two little bare stone huts erected in the year 1843.

The following is the analysis, of these waters, per litre :

Sulphate of Potash...	...	0,6162
Sulphate of Lime ...	...	1,4338
Bicarbonate of Lime	... ...	0,2901
Sulphuret of Calcium	... ...	0,1890

Chloride of Magnesium   0,5568
Chloride of Sodium...   4,6443

                                    7,7292 grammes

Free Carbonic Acid   1,1276

CHAPTER XXX.

About five leagues due West from San Juan lies
the picturesque and fruitful valley of Zonda, the virtues
of whose waters the San Juaninos highly extol, and
so on the morning of the 25th of July, I started in a
coach to reach it. Traversing the rising plateau leading to the mountains, the entire distance to the very
base of the Sierras presents nothing but a cultivated
plain, on passing over which we have to cross a deep
acequia, and soon after enter the *quebrada* (ravine) of
Zonda, which winding away southward, then takes a
turn to the west, leading into the valley of the same
name, a peaceful scene which reposes at an altitude
of 3300 feet above sea level.

On threading our way through this ravine, which
is flanked by bold mountain scenery on both sides
dotted here and there with lime kilns, we have to cross
four or five times a broad, swift, voluminous stream,
flowing from a spring in the valley to which we are
hastening ; and on approaching the end of the defile,
the current sweeps through a deep narrow gorge, across
which is erected a fine, massive and lofty stonework
embankment to dam the heavy floods that sometimes

pour this way from the river Zonda, lying about a league distant northwards up the valley : only a small body of water is thus allowed to escape, and at the same time, a noble reservoir is formed at the head of the pass.   As we traversed the quebrada, I was astonished at the immense number, fully 200, of condors circling in the air, which was quite alive with them, as also at their tameness in descending so close, but they seemed a smaller variety than what I was familiar with on the sierras of Cordoba; on our return the next morning, there they still were, asleep on every jutting rock, but no doubt watchful, as they flew up in succession at our approach: instead of Zonda, this spot might not inaptly be styled the " *Quebrada de los Cóndores* ".

We now arrive at the edge of the defile and emerge upon the verdant valley which, inclined towards the second range, stretches out north and south quite a league in breadth, constituting a well-cultivated and populous department.

In our progress, many well-built houses are passed, until arriving about the centre of the valley, we pull up at the hospitable residence of Señor Arévalo, which lies about 600 feet above San Juan, buried amongst orange groves ambered with their luscious spheres and surrounded with fruit and flowers.   To this gentleman I presented my letter of introduction and he welcomed me warmly.   Although I had often dwelt amongst orange groves before, yet I here learnt what I never could have suspected without ocular demonstration, namely, the existence of a race of fru-givorous rats. The rats in the valley of Zonda ascend the trees, bore a neat round hole in the apex of the orange, just sufficient to admit their heads, completely scoop out the fruit and leave the skin hanging to the footstalk and thus destroy a whole orchard; and being evidently equally good judges with man of the nature of fruit, proceed likewise to pay their respects to the vineyards to the utter ruin of the harvest.

After looking over the premises and partaking of refreshment, my host supplied me with a horse and told off his capataz as guide to lead the way to the *"Piedras pintadas"* (painted stones), which are no doubt the rude artistic remains of the Calingasta In-dians, that here as in other parts of the Andes are found in incredible numbers. These so-called paintings are situated on the western side of the valley, about a league from the house and are really sculptures, vary-ing in depth, graven in the hard limestone rock-faces, and which if cut with flint instruments must have necessitated a fine and well-tempered tool.

The side of a mountain has here become disinte-grated and formed huge masses of rock piled one upon another with inclined, plain, weather-blackened surfaces, and on these smooth faces occur the rude chisellings, which represent footprints, hands, guana-cos, tigers, ostriches, tortoises and innumerable other forms animate and inanimate: they have all been cut with the same kind of instrument and show white on a black ground, although in some cases they are very

much weather-worn and in others well nigh obliterated. In many cases, blocks presenting a surface of
about nine square yards were crowded with the figures
of men and animals arranged in perfectly straight
lines. On two slabs which I copied, several modern
inscriptions appear by the side of the ancient; that
with a date of 1837 looks quite recent by juxtaposition
with the Indian sculptures. There must be in all
several thousand figures, reaching more than fifty feet
up the hill side, the task of a very long period. Under
these massive blocks, many natural caves occur, which
have been filled up with debris from the mountains : I
succeeded however, with my geological pick, in partially excavating some and found that the entrance, in one
case, had been enlarged by chiselling the rock on either
side, and then I chanced upon a bed of charcoal. In
my estimation, these caves served either as habitations
or more probably tombs of the early Guarpe or Calingasta Indians. In this neighbourhood a few years
ago, a mummy was disinterred in a perfect state of
preservation, but unfortunately was lost to archæologists
by the ignorance of the surrounding population : since
then, pieces of crockery and various implements have at
times cropped up, so that with a little trouble in excavation, valuable historical and scientific remains
might be discovered.

I now rode across the valley about a league on
the opposite side to the sulphur mines, which lie not
far from the mouth of the quebrada opening into it,
the entrance into which is elevated about a hundred feet

above the general level : into the caverns I delved but
found all as solitary as the grave, the expenses of
transport having swallowed up all the profit of a previous desultory effort to work them ; there is no doubt
however about their richness.

And now whilst in this valley, the dreaded Zonda
began to blow, and being on the spot whence it is said
to arise and collect the fine sand on its northern extremity at the other side of the river San Juan, I was
in a position to judge whether the fair valley could be
justly accredited as the cradle of such a pestiferous
Æolic, and in my opinion, she must be, if not completely, very greatly exonerated ; she may indeed swell
the fatal breeze, but originate it, she certainly does
not. It is true, as her maligners assert, that the wind
blows down the valley from the north, but it is to the
vast Saharas, Atacama and Arica, of our neighbours
Peru and Bolivia, we must look for the source of this
azotic blast. Nor can any argument be maintained
from its name which, in Quichua, simply means "strong
wind", and is equally applied to other places in the
Republic; the Wind giving the name to the valley
and not vice versâ. This little, peaceful, elegant and
prolific valley, besides being debited with the Zonda
wind is, it appears, the habitat of a really formidable
insect, which the natives dread exceedingly and term
Cuyucho. Of the Cuyucho, apparently, there are two
varieties, but as I could not succeed in obtaining a
specimen of either, and the Provincianos are anything

but exact in zoological diagnosis, I imagine it to be perhaps a species of ant or tick, families but too well recognized amongst us. However there is no doubt it is highly venomous and that death frequently results from its bite; no inflammation is perceptible, scarcely is there visible even the mark of a wound and yet the nervous system becomes seriously affected producing muscular paralysis, accompanied by great swelling of the intestines and body generally. Dr. Alexander the resident American physician in San Juan, administers aperients and stimulants and thus has saved many patients from the bite of the terrible Cuyucho.

On the morrow I bade adieu to my kind host and returned to San Juan. And here I cannot terminate my remarks upon this province, without referring to the wonderful mineral wealth, which she, in common with all her Andine neighbours, treasures up in her bosom for future generations. At present more than a hundred mines are in operation, the majority in a very crude way 'tis true: those of silver alone cover an area larger than Wales, and in addition, gold, copper, iron, lead and crystalized marble, exist in abundance. In my opinion, the time is not far distant, dependent of course upon increased transport facility, when the hills and valleys of the Andine provinces will be black with diggers, to whom the yields of California and Ballarat will be but as bagatelles; why there is one spot in Catamarca, where the inhabitants have been accustomed for many years to pick up the gold-bearing quartz, crush it with a hammer and extract sufficient of the precious metal to defray their daily expenses.

END OF VOL. 1.

INDEX OF VOL. I.

www.ingramcontent.com/pod-product-compliance
Lightning Source LLC
Chambersburg PA
CBHW032026120726
47901CB00006BB/1668